Outside THE Gates OF Eden

BOOK THREE OF THE FIRST PEOPLE SAGA

To my sister Marg
Enjoy
RA Williams
1/6/23

RONALD A. WILLIAMS

AUTHOR OF THE FALL OF AUTUMN LEAVES

ARCHWAY PUBLISHING

This is a work of fiction. All of the characters, names, incidents, organizations, locations, and dialogue in this novel are either the products of the author's imagination or are used fictitiously.

Archway Publishing books may be ordered through booksellers or by contacting:

Archway Publishing
1663 Liberty Drive
Bloomington, IN 47403
www.archwaypublishing.com
844-669-3957

Scripture taken from the King James Version of the Bible.

ISBN: 978-1-6657-2935-2 (sc)
ISBN: 978-1-6657-2934-5 (hc)
ISBN: 978-1-6657-2936-9 (e)

Library of Congress Control Number: 2022916147

Print information available on the last page.

Archway Publishing rev. date: 11/07/2022

Prologue

*N*otah Bitsoi moved quickly through the moon-illuminated desert night, his steps sure. To the left, he could hear them, and his heartbeat quickened. They had moved faster than he anticipated. Notah made a slight adjustment, bearing to his right, away from the steps that he could hear as clearly as if the men were right next to him. They were clumsy, and every so often, one of them stumbled. A man cursed softly, and Notah smiled, moving noiselessly in the night. They would not find him. These were city men from Alberquerque, he believed, and they were not accustomed to the desert where his people had lived for half a millennium.

Still, I am the one running, he thought grimly.

His feet, as if having eyes of their own, avoided the loose shale in his path, seeking a less noisy way. Suddenly, he froze, his right foot poised. Something had moved, and Notah reached out, his every sense searching the air and ground. His breath was stilled. Then, he started as a hesitant rattle identified the cause of his alarm. Moving his foot back, he reversed course as the rattlesnake slid away.

Go, my brother, Notah thought, saluting the snake. *We are the same, and we have no home.*

For several minutes, he continued to drift to his right, the muted sounds of the men on his left a guide. They moved to the right as well. Maybe they were not so clumsy after all. He abruptly stopped. *They had moved with him.*

A tendril of worry slid into his mind. They should not have been able to hear him if they were as clumsy as he thought. Notah lay, his ear to the hard ground of the desert floor. It was flat, rubbed to an even consistency by the flash floods that had become more frequent. For a long time, he listened. Then, he sat cross-legged, breathing evenly. These were not clumsy men from the city. These were killers, and he was trapped. To his right, he heard them, four men who were so still he had not been aware of them. He saw nothing in this night of death, but they were there. The three to his left had purposely pushed him toward the waiting men on his right. Slowly letting the air out of his lungs, Notah thought. He could not die there. He had to get to Santa Fe to warn the Council. Stoltz's Raiders had come, and the delegates were dead. The Council needed to know that nothing, no one, was safe. Then, maybe they would make a decision.

To his right, he heard the low tones and began to get a picture of big men who spoke with deep voices. Sure of him now, they were no longer worried. Notah was angry, feeling a deep hatred of Eric Stoltz, the man whom his brethren called Ghost Death. He pulled the Ruger P345 from his buckskin coat pocket and slid the long knife from the sheath stitched to his elkskin boot. When he jacked the live round into the gun's chamber, its sound filled the night. It was unmistakable, and the other sounds were stilled.

Now they know, he thought with a grim smile. *I will not go quietly into the good night.*

The three men to his left moved closer, but still he sat, cross-legged, his breathing slowed, marking their positions. He would probably die there, but Notah's only regret was that he might die in vain, that he might not be able to persuade his people. Sooner or later, word would get out about the massacre, but those in Santa Fe would dither, using every excuse not to decide, not to act. His friends Anne Ernsky and Rene had given him this task: bring those among his peole who would come to the east, the starting point for the relocation to Africa. He had had little success. Notah sighed and immediately chastised himself. There were more immediate problems.

When the attack came, it was swift and professional, but he waited. Then, a shot buzzed by him, and he returned fire, hearing a curse in the darkness. He shot again and missed. The four on the right moved swiftly, silently forward, and their dark shapes were in his mind. Their movements were precise, and he shot but hit nothing.

These are experts, he thought. *They are drawing my fire on purpose.*

He was not aware of how many times he had fired until the sharp clack of the empty chamber told him he was in trouble. Not expecting an attack, he had brought only one clip. Dropping the warm gun, he grabbed the knife, every muscle in his body taut. They came slowly, approaching him the way a hunter approaches a wounded grizzly. He was still a threat, but they knew that he would die there. Shapes were in front of him. Six. At least, he had gotten one of them. They began to advance in a skirmish line.

Inconsequentially, he thought, *Definitely military.*

He held the knife low, hoping they would come close, but these men were too smart for that. Ten yards away, they stopped, looking like a firing squad. Notah turned the knife in his hand, grasping the tip. Maybe he could take someone out with a throw.

He was just tensing to fling the knife when his blood ran cold. Behind the six men, an animal of some kind reared up on its hind legs. It was short but big. God, it was big! It jumped into the air, its hind legs swiftly snapping in and out. Notah did not think to count the number of times it struck, but his stomach turned as he heard bones break. The creature landed, then leapt sideways as the men tried desperately to bring their guns to bear. They were moving so slowly. Way too slowly, and the creature was in the air again, those impossibly powerful hind legs flying. Two more men fell. Only two were left, and their heads snapped about as they tried to find the attacker, some instinct bringing the guns up. Notah, not sure why he did it, threw the knife. There was an abbreviated scream as the man closest to him died, a gurgle in his throat. The other man turned to see what had happened to his partner. It was the last thing he saw, for the creature launched itself, its feet rigidly pointed. When they made contact, Notah heard the cracking sound of the man's chest plate collapsing.

All was still. The creature walked quickly from one body to the next, making sure no threat remained. Slowly, it stood erect. Notah felt a chill in his bones as the creature moved toward him, covering the ground with short, powerful strides. He stood, accepting his death, a prayer to the Great Spirit on his lips. The creature chuckled.

"Hello, Dream Stalker."

Notah's knees weakened with relief, and he sat abruptly.

Chapter 1

*I*n another desert on the other side of the world, a figure stumbled and then leaned heavily on a staff. He was long-haired and bearded. Salt sat in flecks on his face. Lifting his head to the sky, which was cloudy, he gazed at the bright luminescence that gave evidence of a light source somewhere behind the mist. Then he looked at the four corners of his world. It was a frightening landscape of white sand that stretched in every direction. So flat that he could see for miles, the view only emphasized the nothingness of the southern Plain of Sotami. Somewhere to the north, near Ghalib's Land, the plain became a grassy veldt with winds that came down from the heights and, though sometimes cold, brought some relief. Where he now trudged, several hundred miles to the south, there was nothing. Not a blade of grass grew, and sand snatched at the footsteps of the unwary.

Andreas had learned to depend less on his eyes and more on his mind sense. This turned out to be a good thing. Some time ago, he approached a patch of sand that looked much like any other but which felt wrong. Grabbing two handfuls of sand, he had thrown it forcefully on the ground in front of him, watching in fascination as the ground moved, falling smoothly away from the surface, dragged down by the shifting sand below. Andreas had scrambled back to avoid being sucked in. This was a land of innocence and danger.

Now, he stood, allowing his mind sense to search the land, seeking the one thing he desperately needed—water. His water bladder was almost empty, and staring at the bone-dry, uniform whiteness around him, Andreas felt a flash of fear. Then, the archeologist in him wondered at the sand's whiteness.

"This must have been all below water at some time in the past."

His voice surprised him, and shaking his head he moved on. Water was out there somewhere. Malaia had said there were caches all over the desert. He had only to trust his mind sense, and he would be all right. Andreas did not worry about predators. Nothing lived there except death, which awaited those stupid enough to venture this far into the southern Plain of Sotami.

As Andreas trudged on, mind sense alert, he thought of the strange circumstances that had led him to this place that should not exist. Three seasons ago, he lost his wife and his son. Time had not dulled the sharp pain of that loss. Eurydice had been taken by Natas to Ghalib's Land as a prisoner, and Malaia had told him that his son, Lona, was no more. He had also watched his friends from the mountains die at Natas' hands. It was not pain that dominated his thoughts now, but anger and a pure, crystalized hatred of the man who was his brother-in-law. Natas would one day face him, and one of them would die.

Andreas stopped again, sniffing air that smelled clean, untouched. His visions had become clearer in the last three seasons. A war was coming, and he was the harbinger of that war, for he was Maatemnu, the Great Slayer, and through time he had come to end life or a way of life.

"I've been in this land too long. I'm beginning to sound like Malaia."

His irony was half-hearted because the visions were powerful. He had existed from time before time, striding through the history of the First People. Andreas thought of the order he gave to kill the last of the hairy men as they sought to return to the north, out of Africa. It was he who destroyed the nascent empires of the east. Above all, he had pursued the woman through time. The woman. So many places, so many times. So confusing because the woman had been present both in the Land of Tiamat and also in Africa. He could not explain the power of the love he felt for her in her many forms, but he accepted it. Yet, always she was Empheme. She who had become the beloved of the Goddess Tiamat. She was also his wife Eurydice.

Where is the damned water? he wondered, taking a sip from the water bladder.

The air was sucking moisture from him, and he sipped carefully again. He had changed in the last three seasons. The physical training had been brutal. Malaia was his guide, and Andreas learned much about survival. Mother Mutasii, the old woman who sat at the foot of the giant statue of Tiamat, would watch with emotionless eyes as he dragged himself into the hut in the evenings to fall in the darkened corner and seek sleep. Mornings came much too quickly, and Malaia, looking fresh as if he had rested for days, would shake Andreas awake. One morning, Malaia came, his lithe body moving like a wraith in the dusky light. Andreas stumbled up, reaching for the leggings that kept the cold at bay.

"Today, your test has come," Malaia said.

That day, he was not only denied leggings but the water bladder, and Malaia set a fast pace through the all but hidden pathways of the Ilegu Forest. Within minutes, they reached a brook. Malaia invited him to drink and then told him to take a mouthful of water. He could neither drink it nor spit it out. Andreas had no idea how far they ran on that occasion, but the day was almost over when they returned to the village in the forest. He defiantly spat the water out as his guide smiled.

"Sleep now," Malaia said.

He thought that day was his final test but should have known better. Now, here he was, in the middle of nowhere on a quest for a vision. He had wanted to go after Eurydice, but Mother Mutasii and Malaia held him back, guiding him toward something he did not know, strengthening him for some ordeal he would bear alone. In time, his impatience turned to a hard determination when he began to understand the woman he knew as Eurydice, and whom the First People called Empheme—the beloved of the Goddess.

Andreas moved resolutely forward, his mind sense leading him toward the cache of water. The desert floor looked the same, but he felt a change in the sand's density and hurried forward, falling to his knees and digging. After several scoops, there was water, and he bent forward, drinking thirstily. The water bladder refilled, he stood, staring into the deep desert. There would be no more caches until he reached the other side. That was more than fifty miles away. At the thought of this final test before his pursuit of Eurydice could begin, worry crept into his mind. The tall, lean man squared his shoulders and placing the staff in the sand before him, took a step into the heart of the desert.

Chapter 2

*R*ome had been miserable for four straight days. It was cold, too cold for this southern capital, but then, nothing made sense anymore. Rome was abuzz with the supposed secret meetings in the Vatican, and the old beggar woman who sat on the pedestal of the giant pillar in St. Peter's Square listened carefully to it all. She watched the big cars arrive, carrying powerful men from the other side of the Atlantic. Once, she had been part of that power. She had, in fact, directed it. Now, Anne Ernsky existed between worlds, belonging to no state. Not since the Expulsion thirteen years earlier. They, the African Americans not shipped to Antarctica, moved north into the Borderlands, the very northern end of the United States and southern Canada, where the rising waters had pushed out the Whites.

They survived and had, by some measures, thrived. They became strong, confident and, though the anger still burned, they watched as their erstwhile homeland became enmeshed in the struggle with China. The European Union said the right things but stood on the sidelines waiting, it seemed, for something definitive to occur. Not even Greater Russia's angry acceptance of the Chinese movement west was able to pull the Europeans out of their lethargy. China's quick victories in Kazakhstan, their takeover of Tajikistan and, aided by India's neutrality, their hard push south took the West by surprise. Everyone knew that the lull in which they now lived would not last. Even with its reduced population, the United States needed oil and space. China, even more urgently, needed those very things. China dominated Central Asia, while the United States controlled the Middle East. For three years, the war dragged on—a war of attrition with high casualties and not much gain—at least not for the United States.

Anne Ernsky knew that a conventional war favored China. They had four times as many men under arms as the United States. Yet the United States could not go nuclear. They had tried it once at the beginning of the war when President Highland wanted to frighten the Chinese, hoping for a swift negotiated settlement. The missiles aimed at China exploded harmlessly in the south Atlantic, far away from anything, except for the fish which floated around for a while.

Now disguised as a beggar woman, Anne Ernsky wondered how her friend Etienne Ochukwu, known to the world as Pope Celestine VI, was faring with the powerful men who came to do battle with him. Three years earlier, Etienne had warned her about the American attack, giving her people time to move north on an eight-day forced march that took them out of the killing zone. When the war against China later started, that aborted nuclear attack changed everyone's thinking. Branniff Corporation built pretty much all of the armaments in the world and had an intimate knowledge of their electronic innards. Signals to these bombs were intercepted by Branniff, and the corporation had redirected the missiles south. Word went out to the world's capitals. No nuclear weapons. No one had pressed a button since.

Anne Ernsky leaned forward, shaking her head. The war for Central Asia was being fought with a quiet ferocity born of hatred, need and desperation. Oil. China had to have it, and while Central Asia would quench China's thirst for the moment, they needed the Middle East and Africa. Africa offered oil, the rich, new pools under Sudan having been discovered only a couple of decades earlier. More important, Africa offered space. Sitting high above the ocean, the continent was less affected by the dramatic rise in sea levels and so became what many were calling the new Eden. Branniff stepped in there, too. Africa was off-limits, the corporation said, and while America and China pondered, the lull in the war continued.

Anne Ernsky stood slowly, her feeble movements a perfect disguise for the vibrancy of her body. She smiled at the conversations going on in the building in front of her. Etienne had straddled the fence for too long. Now, the men who came in black limousines would force him to choose. Branniff had called her from Santa Fe the night before, indicating that things were ready. Soon, they would come from the shadows. "Africa is ready to re-enter history" was Branniff's quaint way of putting it. She smiled, thinking that after more than four hundred years in the Americas, her people still felt pride in the old continent. Anne Ernsky hoped the Americans would push Etienne too far and a break with the American Church would result.

Shuffling along Via Della Porta Angelica, she saw at the corner of the Via di Conciliazione, in front of the Vatican souvenir shop, a newspaper the headlines of which blazed ASSASSINATO! She bought the paper and shuffled around the corner, stepping into a waiting car. Immediately, it moved south. She had a meeting with the Holy Father later that evening. Then, she would know how the conversation with the American cardinals had gone.

Chapter 3

*I*t was close to midnight when Anne Ernsky pulled up to Vatican City and was quietly escorted into the bowels of that quaint survival of the Roman Empire. Inside, she hurried down a broad corridor, the walls of which showed the age and the glory of the institution. No fewer than ten Renaissance masterpieces caught her eye on that short walk. The ceremonial guard opened a door that must have been at least fifteen feet high, and she was ushered into a large room. Etienne Ochukwu came forward, a smile on his face as he reached out with both hands.

"Dear, dear Anne. You always seem to come to Rome in troubling times."

"These days, Your Holiness, are there any other times?"

"True. It is good to see you. I notice you are still the beggar woman."

Anne Ernsky laughed, and he joined her, directing her to a deep crimson chair and pouring two glasses of wine. It was from his vineyards to the south of Rome. Anne Ernsky sipped as he waited for her response. Her palate sprang to life under the influence of the grape, and Etienne beamed.

"I am afraid, Anne, I shall have to beg our Savior's forgiveness. As you can see, I have not yet conquered the sin of vanity."

"I'm sure God will forgive you, Your Holiness. You certainly deserve to be proud of your vineyards."

Etienne Ochukwu, the first African pope, bowed, accepting the compliment. For a while, they sat in silence, both savoring the wine.

Then, Etienne said, "You did not risk coming to Rome simply to enjoy my wine."

Anne Ernsky nodded, acknowledging that the pleasantries were over.

"No, Your Holiness. I came to discuss the Church and its future."

"Which Church, Anne? You are not a believer. At least, not a believer in the Holy Church."

"No. I'm not, but I respect your beliefs. The Church has been good to us."

"Us?" Etienne said.

"We of the old religion."

Etienne's face changed, and a certain tension entered the room.

"Ah, yes. The old religion. It would seem that our relationship is changing."

Anne Ernsky looked him straight in the eye and nodded.

"As the world changes, so must we, Etienne."

Her voice was soft, and he smiled. Three years earlier, she had come to him, asking in the same soft tones what a man he had met in Africa—if he was a man—asked more insistently. They had wanted the infrastructure of the Catholic Church to be used as the means by which the new Changoist religion—the old religion to which Anne Ernsky referred—would be transmitted across the globe. The bait—indeed, the bribe—was Africa, his life's work. He was promised that Africa would remain ostensibly Catholic, and the tithes would flow into the Vatican's coffers. He had also been assured that the violence being perpetrated against Catholics would end.

Branniff has kept his word, Etienne thought bitterly.

Africa was still nominally Catholic, the tithes flowed in, and Etienne was revered, but the religion that emerged in Africa, Latin America and much of western China bore little resemblance to what they practiced in Rome. This, among other things, had brought the American prelates to Italy.

"Change. It is precisely because Mother Church is eternal that she is a light to all men," Etienne responded.

Anne Ernsky smiled at the "all men" but said nothing, and the pope continued.

"The Church cannot bend on the issue of the vestments, Anne. I assume that is why you have come."

"It is not for all of the Church, Etienne. Africa alone demands the symbol. The old vestments carry too many of the wrong memories.

The African Church remembers the old oppression, slavery, and the brutality of racial domination. It resents these things still. The change to the traditional dress of the old religion would go a long way toward removing some of the complaints about the Church."

Etienne chuckled.

"Shall I say, 'Get thee behind me, Satan?'"

"Would that make you the Savior then?" she said and was immediately contrite when she saw his face.

"Sorry, Etienne. Poor joke. The matter, however, is critical."

Etienne did not immediately respond, but moving to a small, ornate table trimmed with gold, he picked up a book.

"I see you have published a liturgy," he said.

"Yes. It is a restatement of the Catholic liturgy."

"Have you read it?"

"I have not," she responded with an embarrassed laugh. "My forte is politics, not religion, although sometimes, I wonder if there is any difference."

Etienne did not laugh. He liked Anne, but he did not understand people like her who could not comprehend the majesty of God and the sacrifice of Jesus Christ for man's sins.

"There is a difference, Anne, but I doubt we have time for that discussion now. I will not argue theology with you, but this is not a restatement of our liturgy; it is downright blasphemous. When I agreed to use my influence to help the Changoists, it was out of respect for the old ways and to help Africa sooth its tortured soul. I did not agree to undermine the Catholic Church."

Etienne's voice, though quiet, was steely, and Anne Ernsky knew she had to tread lightly. From what Branniff said, they needed Etienne. The new religion's survival was not yet assured, and until it was, they would have to proceed carefully. Etienne must be placated for a little while longer.

For three years, they had used the Catholic churches on three continents, and the movement had grown. North America, Europe and Australia lived outside the Changoists' sway, but even in those regions, fairly sizeable pockets had taken to the religion that promised peace. Yet it was not a quiescent religion. Its attractiveness was ironically contained in its militancy and its insistence that peace was possible now. To her, most religions were simply mumbo jumbo, but they could be used, and she was not shy to do so.

"Your conversation today, what did the Americans want?"

For a moment, Etienne's face shifted and something ancient and angry seemed to look out. It was, however, almost immediately gone.

"I despair of the American church. So modern, yet so lost," he answered with a sigh.

"So proud, you mean."

Anne Ernsky sounded angry. Etienne observed her, a great sadness on his face.

"Anne, you must learn to forgive. In forgiveness, we find our divinity."

"I'm sorry, Etienne, but forgiveness is your business. I cannot forgive. The Expulsion destroyed any chance of that."

Etienne did not argue, though he felt that barbaric act of the Americans continued to hurt them. In the world's eyes it certainly had, but more important, the pain remained in the American psyche. They were still powerful, still swaggered, but their certainty had been shaken.

Ironic that their own foolish actions have done what no foreign enemy was able to do, he thought.

With the Expulsion, that massive removal of the African Americans from their body politic, America had turned on itself, and now that great country seemed wounded. Branniff, the power that this woman before him represented, was everywhere, seemingly blocking the Americans at every turn. Though not the only nation frustrated by Branniff, as the world's erstwhile superpower, accustomed to acting independently, the United States felt the most constrained. Branniff was building something the scale of which was beyond belief. Yet no one seemed to know exactly what it was.

To me, Branniff has promised the salvation of Africa, but what has he promised to others? Why do the Chinese do his bidding?

Deep in thought, he started when the woman gently touched his hand. Etienne looked up, noting her face. It had aged since he first met her. Then the American secretary of state, her face had been unlined, her voice sure. She spoke with great purpose and poise, and he, then a cardinal, had felt unreasonably proud of her. Unreasonably because, though he disagreed with her on almost every point, their common blackness had somehow overridden their policy differences.

The Expulsion has taken so much from you, dear Anne.

Something of his thinking must have shown on his face.

"You look so sad, Etienne, as if the weight of the world sat on your shoulders."

"I am no Atlas, Anne."

She smiled. Etienne was big, over six and a half feet tall.

"The Americans have threatened to break with Rome, ostensibly over the vestments issue, but it is deeper than that. They think Rome is now alienated from American interests. So, you see, Anne, you and the Americans want contradictory things."

"You will lose Africa over this issue, Etienne. Maybe much of Latin America as well."

"The Americans said I would lose the United States and most of Europe over it. I could say, does it profit a man to gain the whole world if he loses his soul, but this is not a choice between the spiritual and the worldly. We are discussing power, aren't we, Anne?"

"It is not a dirty word, Etienne. Only its use determines whether it is good or evil."

She pulled a newspaper from inside her loose clothing.

"Have you seen this?"

Etienne glanced at the newspaper and, face sad, nodded.

"I wondered if you were involved. So much anger. So much violence. So much despair," he said.

"It's Stoltz. His raids on our people have become bolder. We have almost daily battles in the Borderlands now."

"But this was in the southwest. Far away from the Borderlands. Two groups of people dead. Thirteen American Indians in one group and a few miles away, seven of Stoltz's Raiders."

"The papers did not say they were Stoltz's Raiders," Anne Ernsky noted.

Etienne smiled.

"We have survived for two thousand years, Anne."

She should have known. Behind the beatific smile lurked one of the shrewdest minds in Europe. A financial genius, Etienne Ochukwu had rebuilt the Catholic Church after the scandals of the early part of the century. Trusted by two popes, he was in an unassailable position when it came time to select a new occupant for the Throne of St. Peter. Or rather, his position became unassailable after Branniff guaranteed that Africa would remain Catholic. The wealth coming to Rome as a result of that guarantee had not hurt. A man of enormous integrity, Etienne had, with Branniff's help, placed the Roman Church once more in an ascendant position in the world.

There had, however, been a compromise. The new religion was allowed to spring up within the very breast of the Catholic Church, using its churches, and as important, its financial institutions. This caused a rift in the church, but it was controllable since so many poor Catholics found something consoling in the new religion. Tithing increased dramatically, and church attendance, declining during the early part of the century, rebounded. In many respects, the church was more influential and more powerful than it had been at any time in the last few centuries.

At least, it appeared to be. Its increased influence now came from the power of the new religion and the enormous wealth of Branniff Enterprises. Anne Ernsky knew that when Etienne said the Church had survived for two thousand years, it was of these things he thought. The Church always adapted to circumstances, finding the eternal within the transitory. Deep down, Etienne believed this was a crisis to be managed. She, on the other hand, saw it as the end of an era. The recently published liturgy and the changed vestments were the symbols of that end. Etienne would soon have to be shown that, but it was not yet time.

One hour later, Anne Ernsky was on a private Lear jet, flying north. Natas Branniff had called while she was with Etienne Ochukwu. He was in Salzburg. Though never having visited the famous Schloss Branniff, she had heard about its beauty. Leaning back, she closed her eyes, hoping to get some rest during the short flight.

Chapter 4

*A*ndreas stumbled and went to his knees, the staff holding him up. For a long time, his head hung. Brain on fire, it was hard to breathe. The dryness in the air sucked the moisture from him, and he was having a hard time blinking, his eyeballs having started to dry out.

Shaking the water bladder, he thought, *Still a few drops.*

He had to preserve them. The desert was all around. Nothing stirred. Even the wind had died. Andreas rested his head against the staff.

"Get up. Keep moving."

Stopping was death because it became so easy not to move. Already, there was numbness in his right leg as dehydration began to take effect. He pushed himself upright and took one step, then another. Soon, he achieved a rhythm of sorts, halting but constant. His tongue felt swollen, filling up his mouth, and his hand went to the water bladder.

"Not yet, Tama."

He used the name given to him by the First People. Two steps later, he fell, the hot sand burning his face.

"Get up."

His voice was slurred. Standing painfully, Andreas stared ahead. Something was different about the horizon. A thin slice of darkness appeared. Not sure if this was real or if he was hallucinating, he squinted. The darkened edge disappeared, and he trudged laboriously forward.

"Desert devil," he croaked.

The sound created the illusion of company, but the voice was unrecognizable. His heavy tongue and dry mouth changed his accent.

"Stupid quest. Should have ... stayed in the ... Ilegu Forest. There is nothing ... here except ... sand and desert devils."

Staring at the horizon again, he saw that the thin strip of darkness was back. Something in the deepest recesses of his mind thought it looked familiar, but his brain had slowed. He trudged on, aware that his mind sense was weaker.

Then, a voice said, *"Turn toward Ghalib's Land, Tama."*

Andreas looked around but saw no one. Had he imagined the voice? Ghalib's Land was to the north, but there was considerably more desert to cross if he went in that direction. He had little water left. Andreas continued in the direction of the growing darkness on the western horizon.

Those must be the mountains of the west, he thought.

He had barely taken a step before the voice in his head said,"Go toward Ghalib's Land."

This time, it was insistent. The air was now brittle, and, if possible, the stillness of the empty desert intensified. A warning went off deep in his brain, and, desperate now, he stumbled to the right. That dark strip was no desert devil, the hallucinations that those who die in the desert see, but Harton, the desert god, striding across his domain. At least, that is how Malaia had described it to him. He needed shelter. Those sandstorms had the force of hurricanes, and the sand could tear skin from a body. Andreas did as the voice instructed. It was difficult to run. Already, the sand was shifting, loose grains moving toward the approaching storm. Soon, they would reverse course, flying in the direction from which they had come. It was difficult to breathe, and Andreas, needing the strength, sucked the last drop of water from the water bladder.

Suddenly, the desert floor was not there. He fell, tumbling help-lessly down a slope and coming to rest with a violent bump against a sand dune. His staff was gone, as was the water bladder. Andreas felt panic. Without water, he would die. Looking frantically up the slope from which he had fallen, he saw only sand. The wind picked up, and hurrying to the western end of the dune wall, Andreas sought some protection from the blasting sand that was beginning to fill the air. The desert was no longer quiet. It roared. He pulled the loose folds of the robe over his head.

The day turned black, and he burrowed as blasts assaulted his ears and body. He tentatively extended his mind sense, but it was as if it touched something possessed of great fury. The noise went on for a long time. When it finally ended, he dug himself out of his hole. The world had changed. The eastern side of the slope was tightly packed with windblown sand, forming a steep but manageable pathway out of the depression. That was the good news. The bad news was that his staff and water bladder were nowhere to be seen.

Filled with a sense of foreboding, Andreas surveyed his surroundings. The western wall of the depression was not much changed since the sand had blown over it, but there was a good deal of slippage. Andreas noticed what looked like white stone. Approaching it, he saw that it was a giant pedestal from which a column pushed up through the sand. He scrambled up the slope out of the depression. Looking back, he frowned. Before him was a building with huge columns. It was uniformly white.

Must be why I didn't see it.

It fit into the whiteness of the desert perfectly and was constructed in such a way that even now he could see no shadows. Without having noticed the pedestal, he could have passed by within a hundred yards and not seen it. Andreas walked around the rim of the depression until he came to one of the pillars. Its coolness told him it was constructed from the famous white marble of Ghalib's Land. Andreas stared at the dark entrance. He was thirsty and needed food. Maybe there was water inside. He slowly climbed the steps and, after crossing a wide portico, entered. A low hum was the first thing he noticed.

Electricity. The building may be ancient, but its technology is modern.

Inside, it was quite expansive, and except for the hum, silent. There was a broad hall, with alcoves off to the side. Andreas moved cautiously forward. He could not see the ceiling, as marble pillars disappeared into the gloom. Feeling dwarfed by the size of the hall, he turned toward one of the alcoves that was covered by a heavy, purple cloth. Pulling this aside, he walked in.

A figure was contained in a glass case, muted light outlining the body. No more than five and a half feet tall, its musculature was exceptional, the proportions perfect. The face was remarkable in that it seemed familiar. Andreas stared as it dawned on him that he was seeing something that very nearly resembled the mummy he had found so long ago. It was not the same. This looked younger. Yet, the same serenity was there. The eyes were closed, but the face gave the impression of having existed for all time. Andreas' tiredness and thirst disappeared, and he sat for a long time staring at the mummy, feeling oddly connected to it. He now knew what was in each of the alcoves, and excitement coursed through him. This was the Hall of the Onyes.

Andreas strolled back to the great hall. Later, he would explore the other alcoves, but now he needed water and food. Several hundred paces from the alcoves, he reached an altar, at the back of which were three entrances. He stepped through one and found himself in an apartment. There was food, and he wolfed down the dried figs and *motas'u,* a fruit that tasted like a pear. Water was in a marble basin, and he drank deeply. Then, he slept.

Chapter 5

*A*ndreas was puzzled. In each of the alcoves, he found several mummies showing the same perfection, the same serenity. As an archaeologist, he found the excitement of his discovery almost too much to bear, but caution lay at the back of his mind. This place was well kept. It was clean and bore no signs of neglect or great age. Furthermore, what he knew of the Hall of the Onyes suggested that it was much farther to the north, somewhere near, or maybe even within, Ghalib's Land. At least, that is what he had been told by Mother Mutasii, the ancient who had instructed his wife Eurydice in the ways of the First People.

His mind was consumed with his wife's face as he ascended the steps at the end of the long hall. The broad platform was of the ubiquitous marble, and Andreas marveled at the perfection of the construction. The whole building seemed seamless, a beautiful unity, powerful in its simplicity. Even the huge pillars that disappeared in the gloom above seemed less to separate the space than to bind it together in some mystical way. Standing there, Andreas thought of the mysteries inherent in the mathematics of building, and of the ancient masons who found in the shaping of space not simply function but the form of the divine. So, when he said, "My God! It's beautiful," it was as if he was actually addressing some deity.

Now over his initial excitement, he went back to the platform and cautiously entered another room. It was a modern apartment, luxuriously furnished. A refrigerator sat in an adjoining room, and Andreas found water and juices of many varieties in it. He drank slowly, allowing his parched throat to accustom itself to the water. There was an assortment of cheeses and dried fruit, and these he ate sparingly.

His immediate needs fulfilled, Andreas sat on the small bed, evaluating his situation. If this was the Hall of the Onyes, he asked himself, why was it here on the southern Plain of Sotami? Why had Natas moved the mummies away from Ghalib's Land, his ancestral home? Three seasons earlier, after Eurydice was taken and his son lost, he and Malaia crossed the northern Plain of Sotami to the Marble Mountains in the west of Ghalib's Land searching for the Hall of the Onyes. They found a deserted temple.

Andreas, furious, had wanted to return to Natas' new city to hurt and destroy. Malaia prevented him but not before they fought in those mountains for what seemed like days. He had assumed that, with his more refined mind sense, he would overpower Malaia, but the Ulumatuan was a master of the martial art of *tusiata*. In the temple of Tiamat, Malaia had seemed effete, but in the wild remoteness of this land, he was a tiger, a warrior whose skill was known. Yet, Andreas fought him to a standstill. Each thrust was countered, and even when Malaia moved to the higher levels of the art of *tusiata,* executing the perfect *sa vili,* the seven revolutions of the body, with feet systematically slicing the air, Andreas matched him. They had landed simultaneously, a look of surprise on both their faces. Malaia had said, "Enough, Tama. Your skill is now as great as mine. To go forward is to court death." The voice penetrated Andreas' madness, and his anger had been pushed into some part of his mind sense, a coiling, living thing that was controlled, though not extinguished.

"Thank you, Malaia," he now said. "You have taught me much."

In the three seasons since, Malaia had been his guide, and what Andreas did by instinct in that fight on the northern Plain of Sotami, he now did intentionally. As if to prove it to himself, he exploded from his sitting position, flying upwards, legs moving at blinding speed with powerful, deadly kicks. He floated back to the bed in the lotus position. He had done eight revolutions without exerting himself, one more than Malaia's maximum.

Andreas knew that he should rest but was too excited to sleep again. One question tortured him. Where was Eurydice? His mind sense could not find her. She was in Ghalib's Land, in a castle at the top of a hill, but something blocked his mind sense in that area. He could not control the blinding anger at Natas, his brother-in-law. Immediately, he heard Malaia's voice in his head.

"The Son of Ghalib does as he must, Tama, as do you. You are both in the path of the gods."

Andreas did not know what path that was and could not see himself and Natas, whom the First People called the Son of Ghalib, having a common purpose. Their opposition was primal. Once unsure about the coming conflict, he now felt certain of his skill. The time was approaching when he would leave this land. That had been in his visions for some time now, and though he did not know what role he would play, the visions pointed to something important. Something would die and something would live, but, as yet, it was not clear what. He only knew that he and Natas played roles in this ending and beginning.

He ate more fruit, the tension easing out of him. His visions spoke of destruction in the world above. He sometimes heard the death cry, though he was not certain whose it was. Natas held the lance that caused that cry, but Andreas would be the one to remove it.

"I am Maatemnu, the Great Slayer. I end the beginning and am midwife to a new age."

He heard the words clearly and looked around, surprised to find that he was alone.

"Am I losing my mind?"

The voice was the same that had earlier warned him to move toward Ghalib's Land. It had saved his life. Could a voice of madness save him? And if he had been guided to the building, why? The mummies were a wonderful find, and twenty years earlier, then a practicing archaeologist, he would have been ecstatic. Now, he felt excitement, but it was different. Malaia said that Natas' power had grown now that he possessed the mummies of the first and the last Onyes. Andreas frowned, thinking that dealing with the improbable civilization in which he now lived was enough to drive a person mad.

"No wonder I'm hearing voices."

He walked from the apartment, going back to the room he had first entered. Discovering nothing new, he soon left. The third room was bigger and had no furniture. On the far side were three tubes, back lit with fluorescent lights. In each was a mummy. Intuitively, Andreas knew that two of them, the adult-sized ones, were the mummies that Malaia referred to as the first and the last. Andreas had found the one on the left in Egypt. In the stories of the First People, this was the Great Onye who led the people from their ancestral lands, across the barren land, to the south and west of Africa. He was the first being to be preserved in this way, at least twenty-five thousand years before the Egyptian mummies. The features displayed full lips, a broad, flat, powerful nose and bulging eyes. Those features had led Andreas to expouse the theory that these original people were an advanced Negroid civilization from northeastern Africa. That assertion destroyed his career.

He moved to the next adult mummy. The technique was more refined; at least, the clothing in the accompanying drawing was. This man, though physiologically similar, was bigger, almost six feet, but his eyes possessed a sadness entirely missing from the first.

The last Onye. He lost the land dominated by the god Chango to the women followers of the goddess Tiamat.

And yet, it was not as simple as that. In the First People's myths, their supreme god, to whom the people gave no name, had told them to worship all of the gods—Chango, Tiamat and Baal. The victory of any one god did not destroy the others but simply affirmed their dependence. This thought brought to mind a conversation he had with Malaia.

"But if this is the time of Tiamat as you insist, how come her temples have been destroyed? Why is Empheme, her priestess, imprisoned and the goddess herself now hidden in the Ilegu Forest?"

"Are these the things that have happened, Tama?"

"Are not these the things you see?"

Malaia became more serene.

"The goddess' time has come, and she has freed herself of our cares, Tama. The god listens now."

"But you still have the statue of Tiamat in the forest. Why go to all that trouble if you can now pray to Chango?"

"We are the *Ulumatua*. We are guardians of the goddess. Some day, we will speak to her again."

"When? A hundred years? A thousand?"

"Do you seek the time of your death, Tama? No one knows the minds of the gods."

Andreas gave up, exasperated. As far as he was concerned, these people's religion made no sense.

"I prefer when religions fight it out, and somebody wins and somebody loses," he said.

"The gods cannot win or lose, Tama. They simply build *fata aigu*."

Fata aigu, their obligations, was the network of relationships on which this strange society was built.

Now, staring at the mummy, Andreas sighed.

"Was it as confusing for you, too?"

According to Mother Mutasii, the last Onye died of a broken heart, having lost his mind when his consort Empheme, the high priestess of the goddess Tiamat, saved Ghalib, taking him away after the Onye's armies defeated him.

Looking at the careworn eyes, Andreas said, "Don't tell me that gods don't lose. You knew you had lost."

Andreas felt sadness claw at his mind. The Onye had lost not only his life and his wife but his world. In the moment of his defeat, the goddess ascended to rule the land that still bore her name.

Moving to the third mummy, Andreas thought, *He also lost his child.*

According to the stories, this child, the offspring of Empheme and the Onye, died on the ice above during Empheme's and Ghalib's escape. Empheme appeared to the heart-sick Onye, asking him to recover the body, but in his anger, the Onye refused. Andreas wondered if this act, more than the loss of Empheme, drove the man to madness.

The child looked to be about ten or eleven years old. The ice had preserved him perfectly. Something in the child's face, open yet displaying the arrogance of youth, reminded him of his own son, and, for a moment, his eyes swam. Lona. Lona, who for so long he could not acknowledge because, according to custom, Empheme could have no consort. Lona who had, for a short while, shown some affection for him. Lona whose arrogance was so evident but whose grace on the *tusiata* mat had thrilled Andreas' soul. Lona of whom Malaia had said, "Do not seek him, Tama. Lona is no more."

Andreas stared at the child Onye, grieving silently. That was something else for which Natas would pay. He wiped his eyes, and, in turning, noticed a space behind the mummies. Curious, he stepped forward. A door, almost hidden in the marble, opened as he approached.

Motion sensors.

Inside, it was dimly lit, and the humming was louder. Running his hand along the wall, Andreas found a switch. The lights flickered for a moment, and then, the place was ablaze with light. It came from everywhere and cast no shadows, so he could not tell how large the room was. It was, however, larger than the hall and sloped downwards.

The whole complex is under the desert.

He descended the steel stairway. At the bottom of the steps, he looked around. The room stretched in shadowless whiteness in every direction. Everywhere machinery hummed.

"A power plant of some sort, but what do you power?"

A large computer displayed numbers. He leaned on the computer, trying to interpret the numbers. After a while, he concluded that they were geothermal readings.

"Why would anyone need to know the temperature of the continent at this level of calibration?"

The numbers changed fractionally every second or so. A light flashed, but he was so engrossed in the rapidly-changing numbers that, at first, he did not notice the rising pitch of the hum. Then, suddenly, the lights began to go out, starting at the far extremities of the room and blinking off one by one, moving toward the center. Andreas ran to the stairway and charged up, two steps at a time. When he grasped the door handle, it did not turn. He tugged desperately as the room began to darken, but to no avail. Within moments, it was pitch black. Andreas stood frozen, his every sense alert. In the darkness, all awareness of spacial relationships disappeared. He once again tugged at the door. It did not budge. He was trapped.

Chapter 6

*F*or a moment, Andreas panicked, the darkness evoking some primal fear. Keeping hold of the door knob, he slid to the floor.

Sit still.

Slowly, the fear subsided, and he ran his fingers along the side of the door knob, seeking a break in the wall. There was none. He moved his hand back to the knob, reassured by the contact. There had to be a way out. The place was stocked with food, but that was in the other rooms. This room was as antiseptic as a surgeon's theater. The other apartments suggested that someone was there from time to time, and if this was Natas' property, then whoever came would be unfriendly. Three seasons ago, during his escape from Ghalib's Land, two of Natas' soldiers were killed. Natas would not forget that.

That was not the immediate problem. He wondered what had happened to the light from the banks of computers. It, too, disappeared when the ceiling lights went out. Andreas extended his mind sense. The computers were still working, though the powerful hum had receded to a whisper. He followed the wall with his mind sense, "feeling" the unnatural, inhuman evenness in the surface. There was no other door. Then, his body tensed. His mind sense. Maybe ....

Andreas turned to the door, "seeing" the knob. Concentrating fiercely, he "looked" into the door. This was new. He had still not fully explored his mind sense, but he thought of those times in the temple of Tiamat when Mother Mutasii had asked him, "What do you see?" Using what she had taught him, he guided his mind sense along the electronic circuitry of the door. Soon, he "saw" the circuit breaker that had shut the place down.

"Now comes the real test."

He had often seen Eurydice control objects with her mind sense, and in the stories of the First People, the ancient Onyes were said to be able to change shape using their mind sense. He had never achieved that kind of proficiency, though he could communicate with another adept. While able to see beyond solid shapes to the physical and, indeed the chemical structure beneath, he had never attempted to manipulate physical shapes.

"I can shape men's thoughts. Those are electrical impulses, too," he said, reassuring himself.

His mind sense moved like a thin, extraordinarily sensitive finger, touching the electricity in the circuit breaker. His eyes were closed, and his concentration fierce, but nothing happened. Andreas sat, his back against the door, allowing his energy to return. He had never focused his mind sense like that before, and though it had not reversed the effect of the circuit breaker, he now felt more confident. Moreover, the room no longer felt dark since his mind sense created the illusion of luminescence. Standing carefully, eyes closed, Andreas stepped away from the door. Out of touch with the door knob, he felt a momentary flash of anxiety, but, hand against the smooth, cool marble, he took another step along the steel catwalk.

With each step, his confidence grew, and soon, he was moving comfortably along, his mind sense acting like a line of sight in the darkness. At one point, he had to descend to the floor of the room as there was a break in the catwalk, but he soon ascended by another stairway. Because of the room's size and the care with which he moved, it took a while to reach the power room. Inside, he sensed the lines of electricity emanating from all over and carefully picked out the strand that he had earlier "seen" leading from the door to the circuit breaker. He pushed a round button, and immediately the lights began to blink back on, starting at the far ends of the room.

Andreas smiled with satisfaction. Then, since the hum had become loud enough to be irritating, he glanced at the bank of control panels around him. Everything seemed to be in order. There were no flashing lights suggesting a problem, but the hum was louder. Fighting off the distracting sound, Andreas searched the panel until he saw a knob under which was the word DE-ACT.

"De-act? What does that mean?"

He guided his mind sense behind the panel, tracing the power line until, with a sinking feeling, Andreas punched the knob. Immediately, the hum subsided. He rushed across the room toward the stairs, aware of what he had done wrong. When the electricity shut off, the security system was activated. This, it seemed, needed to be de-activated before the system was brought back on line. He had missed something else. The circuit breaker was not simply for the local system that had taken the lights offline and locked the door. His mind sense was indicating that the circuit breaker de-activated a larger source, really an integrated system of power sources. There could be only one consumer of that much power. As he ran up the stairway toward the door, Andreas thought of the profligate use of electricity in Ghalib's Land, the burning lights of that long valley beneath the hills on which the castles stood. The city had to be the recipient of that power, and if that was the case, then it was certain that someone would have noticed the changes in the output of energy. If he was right, someone would be coming to investigate.

Andreas yanked the door open, his heart pounding from exertion and concern, and ran to the closest apartment. Looking anxiously around the room, he saw what he needed—a water bladder. Grabbing this and filling a small bag with dried fruit, he hurried out into the large hall. He stopped, his mind sense stretched to its maximum. It took only a moment to recognize the sound—the peculiar whup-whup of helicopter blades slicing thin air. He sprinted for the entrance of the temple. On arriving at the broad marble portico, he turned right, plunging into the desert. His mind sense told him that there were three aircraft. He was not worried about being seen. Malaia had taught him how to fade into any landscape, and his white robe would be invisible from the air if he kept still. His footprints were another matter. Andreas stopped abruptly, a thought at the edge of his mind. He had not been able to manipulate the circuit breaker with his mind sense, but the sand was light. Maybe ....

He put his bags and water bladder down and turned in the direction from which he had come. Extending his mind sense and immediately feeling the contact, he concentrated. At first, nothing happened, but then, a few grains of sand moved. Had the wind moved them? He blocked out the image of the approaching helicopters and tried again. This time, the sand did move. Having found the right degree of effort—he thought of it as a frequency—the footprints were quickly obliterated as the sand shifted to fill in the indentations.

Three dots appeared on the horizon, and he dropped to the hot sand, covering himself with his robe. The helicopters approached with a rush, two landing immediately and one circling the building. After a while, it, too, landed. Six men emerged from each chopper and ran, guns held low, toward the portico. Four peeled off to guard the entrance, and the others ran inside. After a few minutes, the men emerged, immediately fanning out on the far side of the building. They were examining the sand. A low groan escaped Andreas.

Fool, he thought.

He had forgotten the prints left from his approach to the building. His eyes followed the soldiers who were making their way toward the depression in front of the building. They split up and now formed three groups, two moving left and right respectively around the rim, the third heading directly for the depression. Then, the group on the right yelled, and a soldier held up Andreas' water bladder and staff. Their circuit around the depression continued, but when the three groups met on the far side, they had found nothing else of note.

The leader of the group was oddly dressed. He wore traditional military fatigues, but over those was a scarlet cape. Andreas thought he looked familiar but was not sure. The man said something and pointed in Andreas' direction. The soldiers were confused. There were footprints leading into the building, but none led away from it. The group split into three again, this time doing a walking circuit. Clearly, the commander felt that whoever had entered the building was still in the vicinity. Andreas drew further into himself. If they were going to walk in ever-expanding circles, then it could be a long wait. Meanwhile, one helicopter went airborne again to widen the search radius.

The sand was hot, but Andreas ignored it. Time slowed. The heat was constant. In front of him, the soldiers carefully scoured the ground. The commander stood rigidly on the broad portico, taking a report after each circuit. Then, he yelled something, and four soldiers began to walk in Andreas' direction, their snub-nosed, semi-automatic weapons held at the ready.

Now what?

The distance between him and the soldiers quickly diminished, and then, Andreas heard it. Rather, he felt it. His robe was moving in the slight breeze. This had caught the commander's eye. The four soldiers fanned out. Andreas, feeling tension in his stomach, forced himself to relax. He could do nothing about the robe without moving, and that would attract more attention. He ignored it. Three of the soldiers stopped, guns trained on the spot where they had seen movement. The fourth moved forward cautiously. This close, they would see the hump in the ground, and if the soldier lifted the robe, the game was over. The man was now fewer than ten yards away.

Andreas extended his mind sense, projecting an image of flatness and calm into the soldier's mind. For a second, the man's face went blank. The soldier shook his head and came forward. Reaching down, he lifted the robe. The soldier saw nothing except what Andreas placed in his mind. He quickly dropped the robe and turned away.

"Nothing. Old piece of cloth," he yelled to his comrades.

The man spoke with the singsong lilt of the African American, and instantly, Andreas knew who the commander was. It was the young man, Marcus, who grew up in Ghalib's Land but who was born in Philadelphia.

Another victim of the Expulsion.

Andreas observed Marcus. It was evident from the way the man carried himself that his confidence had grown in the past three seasons. When he first met Marcus, Natas had just appointed him a provincial governor. It looked like he had been promoted since then.

Another enemy, Andreas thought, wondering how he had gone from being a simple academic to being hunted.

When the three helicopters took off, Andreas followed them with his mind sense long after they disappeared. Then, he once again moved west across the terrifying southern Plain of Sotami. Slinging the water bladder and the bag with the dried fruit over his shoulder, he trudged across the blindingly white sand. The thought of the African American expulsion brought heaviness to his spirit, but behind that lay the even heavier presence of his disappeared wife. He was moving away from where she was being held, but Malaia had said that his final test was somewhere in this godforsaken desert. After that, he would be ready. If he survived. Andreas glared at the frightening wilderness and wondered what survival meant.

Chapter 7

*R*oute 193 was wet and slippery. Because of the snow, Sidoti had spent the night in his office at the National Security Agency (NSA). Now, he was hurrying to Washington to change clothes. A surge of satisfaction rushed through him as he thought of the patience it had taken to ascertain what he suspected for thirteen years. Branniff was building something in Antarctica. A heat signature had sparked his curiosity almost a decade and a half ago, and through three presidential administrations, he tried to have it investigated. Branniff was too powerful, too much in control of the technology on which the United States and the rest of the world depended, and no one wanted to act. In addition, Branniff's ninety-nine-year lease of Antarctica kept everyone off the continent.

The heat had spiked again, and this time, there was no mistake. It had lasted long enough to be measured, and it was powerful. Something at the western end of the continent, where the giant iceberg broke off thirteen years earlier, was generating enough energy to power a fair-sized city. There were no cities on Antarctica except the make-shift one built for the African Americans transported there during the Expulsion. That was farther to the northeast, and its heat signal was much weaker. Something big was at the western end, and now he had proof.

Sidoti tapped his briefcase contentedly as the Chrysler slid through the darkness of Prince George's County. He always felt uncomfortable in the county. Before the Expulsion, the area was hailed as "the wealthiest African American jurisdiction in the country," but that success disappeared along with the people who had occupied the large homes. Strangely, no one moved into those houses, and they stood, hulking stalks uncared for and falling apart, mute testimony to a policy of fear and desperation. Most of the African Americans had not gone to Antarctica but had fought their way north into the so-called Borderlands. Even today, the conflict continued, pushed to almost outright war by Eric Stoltz and his Raiders.

Sidoti grimaced at the thought of Stoltz. The man, consumed by his hatred of anyone not white, was also the leader of the New Nationalists, the political party that more and more of the country seemed incline to accept. Ten years earlier, the party was a mere splinter group, but in the last three, they had become more organized. Stoltz was campaigning for the presidency. Sidoti made a sound. Stoltz as president of the United States was scary.

Lots of things are scary these days, he thought, braking for a red light at Route 450. *Strange that they have kept these lights. Almost nothing passes through the county now.*

As if people wanted not to be reminded of what happened there, most of the stoplights on Route 450, through Prince George's County from Washington to Anne Arundel County, were removed. Sidoti started as his phone rang.

"Sidoti," he said.

"Where are you?" a gruff voice asked.

"The intersection of 193 and 450, sir. Something wrong?"

It was General Blount, the new head of the NSA.

"Get back here. We have a situation."

Sidoti's heart rate accelerated. He spun the car around the divider in the road and drove back north. It took him twenty minutes to reach the campus of the NSA, the United States' sprawling spy center. Even at five in the morning, General Blount appeared dressed for the parade ground, the four stars gleaming at his collar. Sidoti resisted the urge to salute.

America is definitely at war, he thought.

"Well, Sidoti, it took you long enough," the general said by way of a greeting.

"Sorry, sir. I was on my way home to change."

"Sit. There was an explosion in Kansas."

The president was at an event in Kansas, and Sidoti asked, "Was it the president, sir?"

The general glared at him. He did not much like his civilian number two. Sidoti had bent over backwards to please since Blount's appointment two years earlier, so he could only assume that he lacked the necessary spit and polish to satisfy the general. It did not much matter. Directors did not last long as a rule, and in any case, Sidoti was career civil service. He was also acknowledged as the best analyst in all of America's spy establishment.

"It was not the president. Somebody blew the hell out of Eric Stoltz's home."

"Was he there? What about his family?"

"Not clear yet. We just got word. You know what this means, don't you?"

Sidoti thought for a moment.

"This is not good, sir."

"No shit, Sherlock."

Sidoti ignored the comment, adding, "If Stoltz was in that house, the New Nationalists are going to be as mad as hornets. They will blame the government for not protecting him, although he has no official capacity. Still, he's head of the party. If he wasn't in the house, then this could give him a halo effect. His numbers are already very strong. Either way, the New Nationalists will come out of this a winner."

The general looked at him as if he had seen an amoeba do its math sums right, and Sidoti, conscious of the look, added, "Sir."

The hostility decreased. A notch.

"Exactly. Stoltz is an asshole, but we could be calling him Mr. President in two years if he didn't go up with his bricks and mortar. I want you out in Kansas. Find out what the hell is going on. We can't fight the goddamned Chinese and have this country torn apart by this bullshit. You get me, son?"

Sidoti did not but knew better than to say so.

Instead, he tentatively asked, "Isn't this work for the Kansas State police or the FBI, sir?"

"Police couldn't find their turd while they're still sitting on the latrine, boy. You have the reputation for being a smart cookie. Find out what the hell is going on out there. Clear?"

"Very, sir," Sidoti, a sinking feeling in his stomach, replied crisply.

He was an analyst. He took information in, processed it, and gave the analysis to the policymakers. He did not work in the field. Now, General Blount was asking him to do just that.

"There's an aircraft waiting for you at Andrews. Call me when you have something."

He had been dismissed, but he did not immediately move.

"Sir, we've found a power source in western Antarctica. I think we should investigate."

The general looked up from under bushy eyebrows.

"Is that why you were going to Washington, Sidoti?" His voice possessed a brutal edge. "I know about your little extra-curricular activities with Ambassador Hargrove a few years ago. I am not Kerrigan."

Kerrigan had been the Director of the NSA three years ago when Sidoti, unable to get a hearing, went around his boss to notify Ambassador Hargrove of the disguised Chinese military movement west. That piece of deductive work had earned him a handshake from the president and his boss' enmity.

"Leave what you have with Del Pietro and get to Kansas pronto."

Sidoti nodded and hurried from the room. Forty-five minutes later, he was in the rear seat of an F-2B aircraft rocketing west. In the darkness, Sidoti looked at where he thought the Blue Ridge Mountains were, imagining the beauty of the land he loved. Another part of his mind was terrified at what he was going to investigate.

Chapter 8

*E*tienne Ochukwu, known to the world as Pope Celestine VI, ran his hand along a gold crucifix, his fingers lovingly touching the relief of the Christ figure. It was late, and the Vatican was silent. It had been a long day. He was weary, but the day was not yet done. He turned to a young man who stood silently, hands clasped before him.

"Ah, Kwaku. Soon, you will sleep," he said with a tired smile.

The young man was small and completely bald. When Etienne brought him to the Vatican as a personal assistant two years earlier, the usual noises about nepotism were made. Kwaku was the son of a Ghanaian friend who wanted the boy to enter the church. Etienne agreed to look after him. As he observed the lean face with the dark, soulful eyes, he wondered, as he often did, if he had done the right thing. Kwaku was not Catholic, was not even Christian, he felt certain. Some other passion burned in him, and Etienne knew it was Africa. This passion they shared. Yet, something else moved Kwaku, and Etienne feared it was the new religion emerging from the dark mists of ancient Africa. He felt a burst of pride that was tinged with guilt.

Lord, have I lost my way? Has my love of Africa blinded me to the needs of Mother Church?

When he made the deal with the Changoists, his intention had been to strengthen the Church. In some ways, this happened, but the compromise now threatened to split the Church. The Americans were on the verge of breaking away, and the archbishops of the European Synod, though more respectful, were just as vigorously expressing their displeasure. Etienne had few allies among the group and no friends. He was elected to the Throne of St. Peter because of the conclave's fear that Latin America and Africa would break away from the Church if he were overlooked. There had been a good chance of that happening since Branniff controlled both continents. The cardinals were told in no uncertain terms that the Vatican would be weakened, maybe mortally, if Etienne were not elected. With their votes coerced, the cardinals' resentment burned. Branniff's gift to Etienne was Africa, which had remained within the fold of the Catholic Church.

Three years on, the cardinals were no longer as afraid, and the Changoists had become more aggressive. The recently published Changoist liturgy all but denied the centrality of Christ to the church. The prologue to the liturgy referred to what the Changoists called The Descent. It started with Jesus, but went back in time, showing not, as the Bible suggested, His descent from the House of David but rather indicating His life as a continuity from the pagan gods of the Middle East. The Descent particularly emphasized the lineal descent from the ancient gods Tiamat, Baal and Chango, arguing that the original people, whom the Changoists called the First People, worshiped those gods and had disseminated them in various forms throughout the world. That was why the Chinese had returned to their ancient god Shang Di and why the North and South American Indians found it so easy to organize their Changoist Church around Yocahu or Shang-Deo, the ancient god of thunder and lightning.

Etienne shook his head, wondering why the world suddenly felt like shifting sand. He was supposed to be the Rock on which the universal Church stood, but that was becoming more difficult. Torn between his love of Mother Church and some other not fully understood impulse, he occasionally felt as if another being lived inside him. This was frightening because it conjured up a memory of his father, many years earlier, dancing on stilts in a clearing in the Nigerian forest. When lightning struck his father, Etienne, then a mere boy, felt the pain, but he did not scream, understanding that his father had been touched by the god Chango. Almost immediately after that, Etienne was shipped off to the Vatican. He learned to love the church and to prostrate himself before Christ. Lately, however, he was beginning to feel as if his loyalty was split, as if some other self of his knew who these Changoists were. More important, he felt Branniff was not only familiar but that he and Branniff shared something of which he was not fully aware but which seemed to be coming alive within him. Etienne shook his head.

"You must be tired, Kwaku. You may go to bed."

The young man hesitated, and as he took the surplice from the pope, asked, "Father, what will you do?"

"First pray, my son, and ask for God's guidance."

Kwaku nodded.

"Are the archbishops right, father? Is Mother Church in danger? Would there be a church if the Americans left?"

The boy's voice was earnest, and Etienne dared to hope that Kwaku was beginning to feel some attachment to the Church. If that were so, then the crisis might be worth it.

Our work is always to serve one soul at a time.

"The situation is complicated. The Americans are very important to the Church, but for many years, their social instincts have outpaced the dogma of this office. We have had to bend to keep them with us. They are a secular people in spite of their religiosity, and I fear dogmatism does not sit easily with their materialism and pragmatism."

"But will they really leave the Church?"

"Not if I can help it. The issues the Americans have placed on the table are not the issues of central concern. They are an acceptable smokescreen. Not that the change in vestments and the blasphemy of the new liturgy are not important, but the true American concerns are political."

"Yes, father. The Americans are always political. Didn't Cardinal Dibenidetto say that politics is their true religion?"

Etienne smiled without answering. They would have to be more careful what they said around the boy.

"In this case, they do have very pressing concerns," he replied.

"Like China, father?"

He glanced at Kwaku, surprised by the sudden interest.

"Yes. China is very much on their minds. Three years of war, and the two armies are at a stalemate, but with America having lost the Central Asian bases. Greater Russia and China are allies, and India is waiting to see which way to go. Yes. China is very much their concern."

"And the Church, father. Is it also on their minds? Do they think we are opposed to them?"

Etienne stared admiringly at a painting of the battle between the angels of the Lord and Lucifer's hosts. It was a curious painting, showing darkness in heaven and in the regions below, but with a single strand of sunlight illuminating the faces of Jesus and Satan. It had irritated him when, a gift from the sardonic Natas Branniff, it first arrived, but, in time, the ambiguity grew on him.

Turning, he asked, "Do you think we have taken sides, Kwaku?"

The boy hesitated and then, voice surprisingly firm, said, "We must, Your Holiness. Africa needs allies now."

Etienne noted the controlled fire within Kwaku and felt fear for the world. Anger was so common now. Long ago, preaching in Africa, he despaired of the continent's lethargy. Beset by AIDS, malaria, civil and tribal wars and, probably worst of all, a succession of leaders who made raping the continent into a profession, Africa seemed old. He remembered one western journalist writing that Africa was living out mankind's senility. There were protests, and the journalist was fired, but Etienne was not sure the man was wrong. Now, observing Kwaku's tense face, he wondered about the replacement to that lethargy. Did he, with his ministry of faith and pride in Africa's origins, unwittingly liberate something once dormant in the soul of the continent?

God forgive me, he thought, wondering about Kwaku's eyes that spoke not of faith but vengeance.

"The Church will always be Africa's ally, Kwaku."

"Is that why they attack you, father? Because you have made Holy Mother Church Africa's ally?"

The pope sensed tension in the boy.

"These questions. Why do you ask them? You never seemed very interested before."

The boy hesitated and, in an apparent non-sequitur, said, "Tonight, Mr. Branniff comes to see you."

Etienne could not control his surprise, and he frowned. Even the papal guards did not know who was coming. That Kwaku knew the identity of the visitor was worrying because Natas insisted on the utmost secrecy.

Funny how Natas, who only a few years ago was on the cover of practically every magazine, has disappeared from view.

Occasionally, there were stories of Natas' work in Africa, but the frivolous playboy was gone. Branniff Corporation's power had always been threatening, but now, Etienne heard fear in the voices of those who should have no fear. He heard it in men who, only a few years before, strode the earth with unconscious arrogance. Sensing it in the meetings of the last few days, he knew that the archbishops who came did not bite their tongues because of him.

The pope has always been more fallible inside the Vatican than outside.

Fear of what the giant corporation might do held these men in check. At the head of this corporate behemoth was Natas Branniff, the erstwhile playboy turned world leader. Kwaku watched Etienne closely.

"Yes. That, however, is not common knowledge," he finally said.

"I apologize, father. I was guessing. The secrecy."

"Kwaku, men come to the Vatican in secret all the time."

"That is true, father, but it is only for Mr. Branniff that even your personal guards are removed from the corridor."

The pope felt discomfited for a moment. If Kwaku noticed the pattern, then it was certain others had as well. Just then, there was a discreet knock on the tall oak door. The boy left, and for a moment, Etienne sat, composing himself, feeling the slight flutter of nervousness that Natas Branniff's presence always brought. Then, he pressed a button, and the door opened.

The man who walked in did not seem someone to be feared. He was tall and broad-shouldered, with a face that seemed conjured from a young girl's fantasy.

Natas breezed into the room, his smile displaying even teeth.

It is as if he is the host and I the visitor, Etienne thought, extending his arms in greeting.

"Well, Etienne, I come as a courier, bearing gifts, so to speak."

Etienne smiled as he hugged the man who, though not quite as tall, still gave the impression of dominance.

"Welcome, Natas. Are you a Greek, then?"

The man laughed, his blue eyes twinkling in the light.

Chapter 9

*S*idoti stood inside the yellow tape that clearly demarcated the crime scene, watching the Kansas state police and the FBI search the area. He was still not sure why he was there. This was not his bailiwick, and he did not collect information that way. For him, an investigation meant sitting in his office watching millions of data bits stream by and searching for patterns that could threaten the United States. This business of tramping around a crime scene was new to him, and Sidoti swore under his breath as he huddled in the cold. It had snowed heavily earlier, and he now shifted from one foot to the other, trying to keep warm.

The agent in charge (AIC) was not happy to see him, but the NSA tag allowed him entry to the crime scene, if a very large hole in the ground could be called that. Whoever had done the work made sure that nothing would survive. It was still not clear if Stoltz was inside, but so far, they had found no human remains. That was not a surprise. The AIC had sniffed and said "C-4." This was a military explosive that delivered a highly intense charge.

Although, Sidoti thought, *calling C-4 military is not exactly accurate anymore. If you know how, you can get it as easily as soda these days.*

Feeling useless, he walked toward the crowd of curious onlookers that any disaster draws, his eyes taking everything in. Then, he saw them. The two men would have been hard to miss at any time, but in that place, at that time, they just immediately grabbed Sidoti's attention. One looked like a full-blooded Indian who towered over the crowd.

He must be close to seven feet tall.

Even in the uncertain light, he looked powerful, dangerous. The man next to him was even more remarkable. He was short, broad and deep-chested. Sidoti could not see his face because the light seemed to disappear into his skin so that he was indistinct. This was not what arrested Sidoti's gaze. This man was black, and it was over a decade since Sidoti had last seen a black person in the United States. It was the man's attitude that caused Sidoti's eyes to narrow. He stood with his large feet solidly planted, hands behind his back, the power of his stare holding Sidoti.

Sidoti did not know what the man was doing in Kansas, but he had seen him before. Three years earlier, his face appeared in a satellite photo taken of the Chinese as they moved west and also among a group of Changoists in South America who were pushing Catholics out of their churches. This man was also close to Natas Branniff. Now, here was the same man at the site of what appeared to be an assassination attempt on a presidential hopeful. Quickly organizing those bits of data, he turned, seeking out the AIC, who was directing two men toward a corner of the hole in the ground. Other bits of information came together in his mind. The Indian. Stoltz's Raiders had killed a group of Indian leaders a few days before. Now, here was an Indian looking on calmly at this scene of destruction.

When Sidoti reached the AIC, the man looked angry and harried, and his answer was short. This attitude changed as Sidoti related what he had seen. The AIC called two blue-jacketed agents over, but when Sidoti turned to point out the men in the crowd, they were gone. The AIC barked an order, and the two agents disappeared into the crowd. They searched for a long time but found nothing. Several people remembered the big Indian, but no one could recall a short, black man. The AIC looked at Sidoti skeptically, but at least part of his story had been confirmed. Sidoti moved away as the police and the FBI talked about how to proceed. He felt certain they would find nothing and no one. Right now, if Sidoti had to guess, he would say that this was a revenge killing, Stoltz's family's lives in return for the murdered Indian leaders. But if that was so, then why was the black man there? Who was he, anyway? Three years earlier, when his photo showed up in those unusual places, those at the NSA had assumed he was a member of the Changoist priesthood. Now, standing in the frigid Kansan night,

Sidoti was no longer sure. It was almost two hours later when the AIC came over to him.

"Well, there may be some good news. Stoltz has surfaced. He's in Chicago. His wife is with her sister in Wichita, and his daughter's at school. They all have security assigned to them."

"Thank God for that. Has anyone spoken to Stolz?"

The AIC chuckled.

"Yes. My boss had the honor. He's not a happy camper."

The grin quickly disappeared, and he asked, "Why are you guys interested in this? I thought you boys were concerned with terrorism stuff."

Sidoti, thinking of the disappeared black man, said, "What makes you think this isn't?"

The AIC shrugged, making a face.

"Looks fairly simple to me. Stoltz has irritated one person too many, and they struck back."

"I wouldn't assume that the simple answer is the right one," Sidoti replied.

The AIC frowned.

"Is there something you know that you're not telling me, Mr. Sidoti?"

"No. I just wonder who Stoltz's natural enemies are. Half the country's in love with him. His message of racial purity seems to have struck a chord. Every time there's a report of one of Stoltz's raids, his popularity jumps in the polls. So who in America would want to kill him?"

The AIC looked at him speculatively.

"Lots of people don't agree with his message. Don't you think that your disappeared Indian, for example, would like to get rid of Stoltz?"

"Just keep all your options open."

"We always do, Mr. Sidoti."

The AIC turned, striding back to the brightly-lit bomb site. Sidoti strode to the black Lincoln that would return him to McConnell Air Force Base. He noted with some irritation that the driver had not gotten out to open the door. Then, he smiled, thinking how quickly one can become accustomed to privileges. He pulled open the rear door, and as he sat, immediately saw that something was wrong. There were three men in the car. Sidoti gave a startled cry and started to clamber out, but someone yanked him back in. The short, black man had him by the arm. His other hand went to Sidoti's neck, and pain exploded deep in his head. Then, mercifully, everything went dark.

Chapter 10

*L*iu rose from his prostrate position. He squeezed the tips of the incense sticks, putting out the ember that called to Shang Di, ending his nightly prayer. He was in a large tent that accommodated ten men, but the others had all gone to the town six kilometers to the west. There, the noise would be loud and the laughter brittle. The war was only thirty kilometers away. They had become accustomed to the sounds of big guns and bombings. For the most part, American artillery did not come this far back, so a kind of normality existed.

Stacking his incense sticks in an ornate jade box, Liu stared at three photos leaning against two cups pushed close together. Ling, Wui and Zhan. His eyes hardened as he thought of his three older brothers, killed by the Americans in Tajikistan. The battle for that country had been hard. They lost many but gave as good as they got, and China now controlled that land.

Liu lit a cigarette and inhaled deeply. Summoned by the generals earlier, he missed out on going to town. Something was not quite right, and he had heard words that he never expected to hear. The war against the West was honorable, and he and his brothers, with nothing left of their family, had quickly enlisted. It was a rewarding five years, with quick promotions, and when General Xu, the hero of the Battle of Taiwan and the architect of this glorious march to the west, selected Liu to be adjutant, he could not have felt more honored. The war had gone well. When they surprised the Americans, pushing them off their newly-won lands in central Asia, there had been time for celebration.

Then, for eight months, the war stalled. They sat on their side of an invisible line, and the Americans did the same, conducting an insane war of attrition. No territory was gained by either side in all that time, and the discipline of the soldiers began to suffer. That is why the general allowed them to enter the nearby town. It would temporarily boost morale, but the sharpness that fighters need was being dulled by a war that took lives but gave no glory.

Tonight, the generals had talked of shortages, and for the first time, Lui heard doubt. One general officer cursed someone named Branniff, but General Xu had harshly cut him off. Apparently, Branniff's factories supplied their munitions. Liu wondered why they did not control their destiny but depended on outsiders.

Laowai, he thought angrily.

This foreigner seemed to be very powerful, and even the generals spoke his name in whispers. When one general wondered aloud whether Branniff had betrayed them to the Americans, General Xu answered coldly that the Americans seemed no better off than they.

As Lui was leaving, another man had come to the general's tent. He wore a western business suit made of what seemed, to Liu, very rich cloth. His face was covered by a hood that did not quite conceal dark, piercing eyes and a face that seemed to smile as a snake does. The Persian. The generals often spoke of him. Apparently, he was the key to the next move. The upcoming year of the campaign would be the most dangerous. It was not only the Americans they now threatened but the Indians, the Pakistanis, the Iranians and the Israelis. Each country possessed nuclear weapons and the will to use them. The only thing that held them back was the warning from this same Branniff. He said "No nuclear weapons," and the world obeyed, aware of what had happened to the American attempt three years earlier. Everyone understood that the same intelligence which guided that missile harmlessly into the south Atlantic could send it anywhere.

The generals did not entirely trust Branniff's protection, particularly now that their interests may be at cross-purposes. Branniff had warned the world off Africa, and acquiring this continent was the whole purpose of General Xu's foreign policy. Africa was defenseless, fertile and rich, and the general wanted it. Sooner or later, there was going to be a break with Branniff, and though the generals tried to disguise it, they were clearly nervous.

Liu's watch read 8:40. The Persian would have left by now. Crossing the compound quickly through an underground tunnel, he went to General Xu's current headquarters. The general moved constantly. American murder from the skies was not unheard of. The guard, who knew him, asked for his pass, and Liu made a note to mention this to the general. He prized order.

Inside, six general officers sat in comfortable chairs. There were fifteen bunkers in the rotation, all connected by a network of underground tunnels so that it was never clear where exactly the general was.

"Ah, Liu. Sit. We could use a young brain," General Xu said.

Liu smiled shyly, nodding to the other men. Three of them, General Wu, General Chen and General Zhou had made the ten-year western trek with General Xu, and these he counted as friends. The other two, General Wang and General Li, won battlefield promotions during the war. These latter two ignored Liu as he sat. General Li was speaking.

"I do not think he can be trusted."

General Xu, obviously to irritate Li, asked, "Well, Liu, do you think the Iranians can be trusted?"

Liu thought for a moment and then said, "I have not met their envoy, so I cannot trust."

Li frowned, though Liu had agreed with him. Xu nodded, smiling. He was very fond of his adjutant.

"Well spoken. They would betray us in a minute, but not yet. They, too, worry about the Americans, and at the moment, we stand between the two. The Iranians would use us as a buffer and take their chances later, hoping that we will exhaust ourselves. It is a foolish hope."

The three older generals smiled, but Li said, "I think we should go now when they are not expecting it."

Again, Xu looked at Liu, the playful tone of his voice at odds with the granitic face.

"Should we, Liu? Go now, I mean."

"To attack the Iranians now gives the United States an ally, if not a friend, sir. We would have to fight in the south and in the west. Also, the Indians are not yet decided. Their neutrality is to our benefit, but if we further upset that region, there's no telling where the Indians will go. The mullahs are holding General Khan in check in Pakistan, so his support for the Americans is lukewarm at best. The stalemate is frustrating, and it has undermined discipline, but the Americans have the same conditions. A stalemate favors us."

"How in Shang Di's name does sitting on our backsides favor us? We are rusting, I tell you. I—"

General Xu raised his hand, and at once, Li was silent.

"Sometimes, I wonder if you do not have too much of the West in you, Li. You have all their impatience and rashness. Sometimes that is an aid to wisdom, as it was at the Battle of Tashkent when you smashed through the American lines, but it can frequently be destructive. Boldness and rashness are cousins, General, but very distant ones. Liu is right. The stalemate favors us. We will have to make certain that discipline is maintained, but that cannot blind us to the broader strategic objective. Unlike the Americans, we are past the point of no return. We have several hundred million people searching for a home. That makes us the greater threat. Those in front of us will worry until we are past them. It is a time for reassurances not attacks."

He stood, a man of medium height who was built like a rock. In the last few years, there were rumors that he, tired of the timidity of the old men in Beijing, had killed the chairman and forced the march to the west. Liu did not believe the story about him killing the chairman.

This is China's greatest living hero, and men only follow a man who is pure, Liu thought.

They stood, and each stiffened as the faint sounds of the big guns came from the west. The bloody stalemate was continuing.

Chapter 11

The television was transmitting images of a funeral, conducted earlier that day, across the world. The politicians prattled about Hargrove's bravery in that long-ago war, his brilliance as an archaeologist, his Medal of Honor and his career as a shaper of young minds at the University of Pennsylvania. Yet, after all the words, Anne Ernsky could not help feeling they missed the most important thing. They talked about his patriotism but not his ambiguity, his bravery but not his old-fashioned sense of honor. The Expulsion trampled on that honor, but she could not hate him. He had acquiesced, and for that, she despised him, but three years of seeing Hargrove on a bed took away the anger. He had died only a few weeks earlier, the disease having robbed him of his dignity long before taking his life. She muted the television so that only the images came to her, in this way making the death ritual more personal. Hargrove would be buried in Arlington as befitted a war hero.

"It is your due," she said, raising her glass in a salute.

He never recovered from the cancer that struck him down while he was on a diplomatic mission to try and make an accommodation between her people and the United States. When he died, and she indicated that he would be returned to the United States, her people had thought her mad, seeing it as an unnecessary risk, but she insisted. Hargrove would not be tossed in some hidden creek to rot in anonymity. He would have his honors. The camera cut to the president who had a look of deep solemnity on his face.

He may even mean it.

In two years, he would be gone from office. Until recently, she would have taken a good deal of satisfaction in that, but the man who could replace him worried her.

Too bad the Indians didn't get him.

Her jaw tightened. Notah Bitsoi had acted in anger and outside the chain of command, but she could not be upset with anyone who tried to eliminate Stoltz. Anne Ernsky crossed the floor and looked out on the darkness. There were no stars, and as she opened the window, a biting cold penetrated the room. The day before, it had been thirty-seven below zero, the warming trend that allowed the Canadians to live farther north within the arctic regions, suddenly reversed. The cold came like a scythe, and many, caught unawares, died. There was no longer any predictability to the weather. The tear in the ozone layer let in an evil that stalked the globe, claiming lives as food. She closed the window, noting the absolute lack of defining shapes, so dark was the place. In the Borderlands, they lived simply and without waste. The long, desperate fight north had taken many of them, but it also prepared them for a life of simplicity and communality.

We have survived.

Now, Branniff was indicating that it was time to relocate. Africa. She, unlike the others in the Borderlands, had known about it for some time. They had listened in silence when she told them. For thirteen years, they had made a life in the watery wasteland between the Canadians and the Americans, always fearful, always fighting. At first, the battles were with the remnants of the American Whites. Lately, they were on the defensive, fighting off the constant attacks of Stoltz's Raiders.

Her eyes flicked back to the television. The camera shifted to the left pews of the cathedral, and she saw Stoltz, his red face showing little sympathy for the dead man. The expulsion policy had not been Stoltz's creation, but, in spite of this, the hatred boiled up in her. Hearing footsteps, she turned.

"Rene, that you?"

"Yeah," came the laconic reply, and she walked downstairs.

"I brought you something to eat. Figured you would be watching the funeral."

"Thanks."

The young man was tall and angular and, unlike her, very light-skinned. The room was sparsely furnished, with only a sofa and two overstuffed chairs that looked as if they were taken from a flea market. Anne Ernsky scrutinized the room, thinking of the house she had left in Woodmore, in Prince George's County, Maryland.

Probably occupied by some White now.

"Hey. You there?"

Rene's voice was playful, and she leaned over, resting her head on his shoulder.

"What are they saying out there?" she asked, voice low.

"They're surprised, uncertain and maybe a little bit afraid."

"Afraid? Why?"

"Well, it's the unknown, Anne. Africa for most of them is still the dark place. Voodoo, headhunters."

He laughed, opening his eyes wide and blinking rapidly. She joined him, her laughter deep.

"Come on. Nobody believes that anymore."

"Well, maybe not headhunters, but it's been a place of coups, wars and chicanery for so long that I'm not sure the image has changed much since the days of voodoo and shrunken heads."

"But so much has happened since Branniff took an interest. They've completed the north-south highway from Cape Town to Tripoli."

"Yeah. It's impressive what's happened. How much longer before the east-west highway is completed?"

"Not sure, but it'll be soon. The cathedral in Bumba is also nearing completion. You should go see it. That little town has grown so much in the last fifteen years. It now has three international airports, and the Changoist pilgrims are always in and out."

The pride in her voice was evident, and he hugged her, not convinced. He, like so many others, had not given up hope of a return to the United States. The discussion after she left had been contentious. Many wanted their old life back. Only members of the governing council had been present, but they represented the opinions of millions. And they were split.

"They'll need to be persuaded," he said.

"Then you'll have to persuade them."

"Me? I have no weight in the council. They tolerate me because of you. You are the spiritus mentis. Nobody cares what someone from the south side of Chicago thinks."

She smiled, knowing Rene was deliberately understating his influence. His forays into the United States to the south to gather information were legendary.

"We'll have to prepare them then," she said.

"How soon will the relocation take place?"

"Not sure, but Branniff says we need to begin the preparations now."

Rene hesitated and then asked, "Are we putting too much faith in Branniff, Anne? I mean, they've been helpful and all, but we don't have a clue why they're doing these things."

Anne Ernsky turned to the young man.

"Have they failed us yet, Rene?"

"No. They've always been there when we needed them. And yes, we would've been destroyed without their help during the Expulsion, but what do they want? And this religion. It's taken over so quickly that no one seems sure how it happened. That, too, is sponsored by Branniff. It's almost as if with their interlocking corporations they controlled people's lives, and now, with this Changoism, they're controlling people's minds."

"Is that all you see, Rene?" She ran her hand over his curly hair. "I see something different. You're right. We have no idea what Branniff's motives are, but for the first time in my life, I feel purposeful. I know you think I held power once, but when I was secretary of state, I always felt like a mouthpiece, within sight of the true power, being able to taste it, smell it, but never in possession of it. Now, I feel different."

"How different?"

She did not answer immediately, sifting through her feelings.

"More in control, perhaps."

They both looked around the scantily furnished room and burst out laughing. Hysteria lurked within the laughter, for they were fugitives. Trapped between two countries, living in fear of the United States and on the largesse of the Canadians, the control of which Anne Ernsky spoke was not much in evidence. Yet, something was different, and it was this she addressed.

"In the decades before I was born, there was a revolution in the United States. We, the African Americans, fought the establishment and forced concessions from it. Africa was not an insignificant part of that resistance. Her ancient glory had been the bedrock of the struggle for rights. In some sense, we liberated her from the darkness as she gave us the strength to fight."

"But Africa didn't live up to its promise. At least, that's what the history books say."

"No. Africa didn't live up to its promise, but some Africans did. Etienne Ochukwu, for one."

"Who's he?"

She laughed, as always, amazed at how little he seemed to know, but she was not too hard on him.

"He's now the pope."

"Oh. That's right. What did he do?"

"Too much to tell now, but he saved Africa from itself. As a young priest, he took Africa on his back and carried her while she was weak. Etienne did not allow Africa to destroy herself even when she seemed bent on her own suicide."

Anne Ernsky's voice possessed a musical tone, and he felt a flash of jealousy until he remembered the vow of celibacy that Catholic priests took.

Then, steel in her voice, she added, "Now, Africa is ready."

"Ready for what?"

"I'll take you with me to Bumba soon. You'll see the Africa that's emerging."

He nodded uncertainly and not sure how to respond, changed the subject.

"Why was it so important to send Hargrove back to the United States?"

"He deserved it. Every man should be buried in the land he loves."

She seemed not to be aware of the irony, and Rene did not point it out.

"Just before the Expulsion," she continued, "I sat in a room with men who were discussing the destruction of our people. I was the "honorary White" in the room, I guess, but in all that talk, all that rationalization of the evil they were going to commit, Hargrove was the only one who raised a moral argument. The only one."

Her voice was wistful. Rene often wondered about her role during that time of horror. It must have been extraordinarily difficult to sit in those rooms day after day, pretending to go along with the planning while secretly organizing the cells that would resist the Expulsion. They had not won. Over one-fifth of their number was now in Antarctica, and it was Branniff who organized that transfer of human cargo. Though Rene did not say it, that was on his mind. It was also on the minds of several members of the council. They revered Anne Ernsky, but Branniff gave them pause. In spite of the giant corporation's aid, its role in creating their condition was, at best, ambiguous.

Anne Ernsky was also thinking of Branniff, but her thoughts were different. It was too early to tell Rene and the council what the move to Africa meant, but her heart beat rapidly at the thought of what Branniff said was being created in Antarctica. She had known nothing of this plan until some years after the Expulsion, and she still occasionally felt a flash of anger at how her people had been used. The greater good, Branniff said. She sighed, and Rene held her.

Soon, Africa would no longer be helpless, nor would they. In Antarctica, Natas Branniff was building a force, specially bred and trained, that would change the face of international politics. As she leaned into the hard body of the young man, Anne Ernsky could not help but think that she was lucky to be alive at that moment.

Chapter 12

*T*ime ceased to make sense. Andreas was not sure if he had been in the deep desert for days or weeks. The perpetual sunlight of the Antarctic summer was disorienting, and dehydration added to his confusion. His body felt desiccated, and staring at his hand, he saw the skeleton beneath.

I'm dying.

He felt no hunger, though not having eaten for some time. The water bladder was half full. Andreas wondered how that could be since he had been wandering for so long. Around him, the white desert stretched in every direction.

"Why am I here?"

He blinked with some effort, his eyes gritty from dehydration. Opening the water bladder, he took a sip. His palate thirsted for more, but he turned his mind sense inward, blocking his desire. It was now easy to do that, almost as if the gradual dying activated some part of his mind sense he could not access when fully conscious.

Images frequently floated in the air, and these he accepted as hallucinations. Many were reminiscent of his earlier visions but now included flashes about Maatemnu, the Great Slayer, he who carried death through time. He came in many shapes, at many times, but always death followed in his wake.

"Am I going mad? Who am I?"

There had been no hallucinations for what seemed like hours now as he moved, one ponderous step after the next, farther and farther west. He tried to determine exactly where he must be in the Land of Tiamat. From the Ilegu Forest, he had traveled due west. No one seemed to know, or was much concerned with, the size of the southern

Plain of Sotami. Far to the northeast of where he trod was the capital city of Tiastan. He had lived there for a decade. To the north of Tiastan was the Land of Malaia, where the dead went and where the white crocodiles, sacred to the Goddess Tiamat, lived. To the southwest was the secret land of the *Ulumatua*. Three seasons earlier, during the ceremony of *taimi'una ananafi*, he had asked about the *Ulumatua* and was warned not to investigate any more. The people of Tiastan pretended not to see these small people whose beauty had drawn his eye. They were old and remote.

"Who are these people? More important, how far away are they?"

Seeing the top of a single tree, Andreas dismissed it as another trick of his fevered mind. Still, he turned toward it and, to his astonishment, reached a wadi in seconds. He stopped. The tree's shade covered the whole wadi, in the center of which was a pool. This would have made him happy, except that lying next to the pool was a white crocodile. Under the tree, a woman with smiling eyes gazed at him. Next to her lay a boy who appeared almost dead. He still breathed. His body was discolored, white in some places and black in others, as if he was dying in parts. The woman observed Andreas. Her smile seemed not of this world, not of the present, but the result of some cosmic joke heard millennia before and which had only now come back to her. Her resplendent robe, a shimmering garment of gold, purple, ochre and burgundy, had sleeves fringed with white lace. Andreas could see no evidence of a body beneath the robe.

Then, he heard, "Come. Drink, Tama/Andreas/Maatemnu, the Great Slayer. Your journey must have tired you."

The voice sounded familiar, but Andreas had no time to think because he was instantly beside her. The crocodile's red, saurian eyes watched, unblinking.

How fast do these things move?

He had heard somewhere that they were fast but not very agile. One could evade them by constantly changing direction. Andreas was not reassured. He leaned forward and drank deeply from the pool. The heat of the desert receded. The tree gave off a kind of luminescence.

"What are you doing here? Is he your son? What's the matter with him?" he asked.

The woman's smile broadened.

"I live here. I am always here. Always where I am. Yes. He is my son, as you are my son. As to what is wrong with him, you will have to determine that."

"Me? I'm not a doctor."

She laughed, and Andreas thought, *She does not care about her dying son.*

"You are many things, Great Slayer. Many things you have not discovered."

Andreas squinted at her as she added, "You look so young again."

He saw his reflection in the pool. He did not look young. His hair fell in unkempt locks around a face that showed white lines of dried sweat. His cheekbones were so prominent that his eyes sank into pools of fire. His forehead bulged, and his jawline was sharp. Most of his flesh was gone, and yet, he did not feel weak. In fact, he felt refreshed. Andreas turned. The dying boy had moved. His head now lay in the woman's lap. She stroked his hair. The scene looked familiar, but Andreas could not quite place it. The tree, too, was odd, not the palm that one would expect in a desert, but a pine.

A tree you would expect in northern climes.

"Am I having another vision, or is this real?" Andreas said.

"Real?"

She seemed to handle the word like a precious stone, turning it in her mind, training a jeweler's glass on it, before replying.

"Yes. It is real. The question is, is it real for you?"

"What do you mean? Either it's real, or it's not."

"Hmm. Are your dreams real, Great Slayer?"

Andreas thought, but before he could answer, she playfully asked, "What do you see, Andreas?"

He started. She sounded exactly like Mother Mutasii who had repeatedly asked him that question in the temple in Tiastan. He instantly knew she was real and yet not real.

"Reality is the limit you place upon yourself, Great Slayer. It is the margin of the universe you see and because you have seen, you call it real. What was it before you had seen it? Unreal? Not real? You must shed the borders you imagine. It is only these you call reality. Those limits destroy you."

Andreas had not noticed when the crocodile slid close to him. Its great jaws opened and snapped shut with a harsh, clacking sound. The eyes were impartial, seeming to see him, everything and nothing. Andreas tried to control himself, but a long, slow shudder went through his body. The boy twisted his neck so that, as he lay on his back, the almost lifeless body was bent at what must have been an uncomfortable angle. His head turned, and the sad eyes, death contained within them, fell on Andreas. What was in those eyes? Pain, to be sure, but also something else. Andreas discovered, with surprise, that it was pity. The dying child pitied him. Why?

"What do you see, Great Slayer?" the woman asked again.

Andreas, unable to stop himself, answered. Words gushed from him. The pain, the suffering, the hunger and the thirst came first. He spoke of the visions, and the confusion they brought, of Eurydice his wife, priestess to the goddess Tiamat and his love for her, and of the death of Endele, his friend from the mountains. He also spoke of his son, Lona, who died in Lusani at Natas' hands. Finally, he told of the images of himself as the Great Slayer, he who ended an age, and of his sorrow and guilt at those acts committed from what seemed to be the beginning of human existence. The boy's eyes gleamed as if he recognized something, but as Andreas ended, the dead look, tinged with disappointment, returned. Laboriously, he turned to his mother.

"Yes. His blindness is disappointing. What do you see, Tama?" she said.

Andreas looked and saw. He recognized a world the features of which were familiar but whose spirit was changed. There was peacefulness and contentment. It was his old world, but from that vantage point, he recognized landmarks that should not have been visible from a single perspective. There was the Mississippi, and next to it, the Andes; the slicing, serpentine movement of the Yangtze River and, bridging it, the Rockies; the Congo sliced through the landscape of his mind, and he recognized the Tower of London beside it.

Most amazing of all, there were islands being reborn, and on one was a tall, black man whose nudity seemed like clothing and who stood on one leg, his eyes fixed on a distant horizon to the east. He chanted, a low, powerful sound that seemed to be carried on the winds and the waves, traveling fast and sure until it joined other sounds coming from separate directions. Africa. It was distinctive but over-grown with lush vegetation. It looked like a garden. Andreas understood that there was Africa's past and its future. In the midst of the land was a long, white streak from north to south and another from east to west. Where they crossed was a light. It was this light that Andreas sought, but it was too bright, and he squinted. The word "Bumba" came to his mind, and he knew that there was the place of the beginning. There, a human had stood up and sought the sky.

The image faded, and this time, the dying boy looked excited, his sickly, pale face, with the black spots, giving the illusion of life. Again, his head laboriously turned to the mother. She smiled sadly.

"What have I seen?" Andreas asked.

"Reality," the woman answered, her ironic smile back. "You still see borders, Great Slayer. The gods see all at once."

"But I am no god."

"You seem to think that you are not many things. What are you?"

A man.

His mind sense rebelled against the thought. He knew not what he was. The dying boy reached across, his spindly hand a claw, and touched Andreas. At first, there was fear in Andreas' mind, but that soon passed, and a hint of something—a shadow, a death, a great emptiness—was at the edge of his consciousness. Still, he could not quite comprehend it. The boy, a look of frustration on his pain-wracked face, sighed and withdrew his hand. For a moment, the mother seemed sad. Andreas watched the white crocodile as it crawled from the wadi, its broad, powerful body leaving a trail in the white sand. It reached the top of the sandy ridge and was gone. When Andreas turned back, so were the mother and son. The pool was rapidly drying. He filled the water bladder. Then, the pool and the tree were gone.

A great loneliness descended upon him, and his spirit was assaulted with memories. Had he imagined them, the mother and son? The white crocodile was directly from his memory of what he had been told by the priestesses; that is, the white crocodiles were sacred to the goddess Tiamat. In fact, he had seen the crocodiles when saving Natas' wife and child.

"Am I going mad?"

Around him, the great desert was silent, and the echoes in his head mocked him.

"Did I just fail a test?"

The visions had to mean something. The boy's sadness was for Andreas and much more. And the disappointment. Why that? Had Andreas' failure hurt him in some way? He extended his mind sense, hoping to find a trace of the boy and his mother, but the desert gave back only heat and dryness. Finally, he moved again, stumbling west.

Some time later, he fell, and at first thought it was from weakness. When he looked up, the world had changed. Sand, coming in waves from four directions, was suspended above the quiet of the desert bed. Confused by this, Andreas stood and was immediately knocked down. Stinging sand raked his skin. He blew hard, driving the grains out of his nose. Whipping the robe's hood over his head, he covered his mouth. The wind slammed him to the ground. When he gasped, his mouth and nostrils filled again. Andreas coughed, ridding himself of the invading sand, but it came right back. The four sandstorms converged, dropping their weight upon him. The desert floor and the sky disappeared.

I am being buried alive.

Sand crawled like live snakes around him, tightening its coils, so that if he did not drown, he would certainly be crushed. Hands trapped, he kicked as best he could. His eyes closed, and the darkness, the pressure and the sand's movement gave wings to his imagination. In each sand cloud, a face appeared. He knew them. They had his face, and their names were a fire in his mind. In the lower right quadrant was Osiris, and on his left Orpheus. Tammuz, too, hovered, his face all anger and darkness, and next to him was Opollo, a son burning life from the land. Each mien showed the same disappointment as the dying boys had. They pressed on him, their will manifested in the sand, seeking his death. Andreas resisted feebly. When it seemed that he would die, for the breath had left him, his mind sense took over, forming a cocoon, keeping the weight and the snakes in the sand away from him.

Then, the faces were gone. Andreas pushed the sand away. The desert was as it had been, but his mind sense seemed alert to something. It searched the desert and detected an altar to the west. It was that he had to find. Heaving a sigh, Andreas set out again.

Chapter 13

*E*tienne Ochukwu felt a sharp pain in his knees as the uncovered wood cut into them. He had been praying for a long time in the small cell that was his place of communion. It was without decoration, but in the uncertain light of a single candle, a golden crucifix glowed. Etienne stared at it with a suppliant's eyes.

"What would you have me do? Am I being tempted, or is it your greater glory that is offered?"

His anguish was evident. The crucifix gazed down, the wretched figure, spear thrust visible, silent. Etienne continued to kneel. He had been praying since Natas' visit two nights ago. As seemed to be the case whenever a Branniff appeared, there was a promise and an implied threat. Life and death. Always a contradiction, always an opposite. Natas had offered the cathedral being finished in Bumba as a "gift", and Etienne wondered why Bumba was suddenly important. Natas spoke glowingly of the architecture—the breadth of the nave, the delicacy of the transept, the soaring height of the stained-glass windows—but never once of God. Etienne had listened, a chill around his heart.

"Not in a thousand years, Etienne, has the Church built like this."

"And what do you want of me, my son?"

He felt a little foolish referring to Natas in this way because, in spite of the man's youthful beauty, he gave the impression of being ancient.

"We would like you to dedicate it."

"Is that all?"

Natas laughed.

"Such suspicion, Your Holiness."

In Natas' mouth, the honorific sounded faintly mocking.

"You know what you ask, Natas. If I dedicate the cathedral, I implicitly agree with your vestments and your liturgy. I cannot do that."

Natas shrugged, his face the picture of affability.

"Theology is for priests, Your Holiness. I know little of that."

"But I am a priest, Natas, and it is my business to know."

He crossed the room to a large desk. Picking up the liturgy of the new religion, he read a line.

"'And the savior's ecstasy occurred once again.' What do you mean by that? And please, let's not pretend that this is beyond you, Natas."

Natas' face did not change, and Etienne wondered what the man really thought. The silence continued for a long time.

Then, the preternaturally beautiful man said, "As you wish, Etienne. What is really bothering you, my friend?"

Etienne lifted the book and shook it in front of Natas' face.

"This is my bother, Natas. This is not Catholic. What is it?"

Natas pursed his lips.

"Etienne, what does the old religion mean to you? There's something older than your god alive in the world, don't you think? Do you really believe that it has been replaced by this church?"

"I sometimes despair for you, my son. Evil has always existed. It is this that the Savior came to banish from the world."

"Not very successful, is he?" Natas said and immediately apologized, adding, "Why do you think the new religion has spread so rapidly? Why is it that hundreds of millions have responded so enthusiastically to this spirit that has come into the world? Even you would have to agree that we preach no evil. Our fundamental principle, like your own, is peace. Peace now and on Earth. Why has such a simple message been so powerful?"

"It is not the first time that heresies have found adherents among the multitudes. This is a heresy. You have replaced the Savior's Passion with a recurrent ecstasy."

"And how many, do you think, have noticed?" Natas replied irritably.

"I have seen a whole parade of bishops who noticed, Natas. It is tearing the Church apart."

"The new religion's energy is derived from the people's fundamental beliefs. It is their search for ecstasy, which they see reflected in nature, that inspires them. You should see our services. The energy pulses."

Natas was excited. For a moment, Etienne saw something other than the laughing playboy, and when he spoke, his voice was sad.

"Natas, you seek to return man to nature, but Christ's glory is his triumph over nature. It is his glorious resurrection that hails and memorializes that triumph. You're not giving men something new. You have simply allowed them to indulge their baser natures."

"No, Etienne, it is their true natures that I have liberated. It is this that your Church has always fought against. You have pushed men's true selves into the background, but did you think that they had therefore died? They have not. The triumph you claim of faith over instinct is destructive. Men have shown that. Look at your world after two thousand years of that faith. War after war, murder after murder, and an all-pervading hatred of both self and other. Your god could not be very proud of you and what you have accomplished."

Natas' tone had changed, becoming more resonant, powerful and guttural. Etienne found himself responding to a voice that had subtly become his father's.

Still, he said, "Do not allow your pride to put you beyond God's redemption."

Natas laughed, a sweet sound that Etienne, though distressed by the conversation, could not help but admire.

"Pride! Do you hear pride, Etienne? I speak to men of their secrets, to souls that need freedom. The other, this infernal restraint, is destructive. Men must find themselves, not be herded like sheep toward some safe haven."

"Is that what you think the Church does?"

Natas shrugged, not answering. They talked a little while longer, but there was no common place from which they could gain an understanding, and Natas left, his step, as ever, jaunty. With a heavy heart, Etienne watched him go.

Now, he kneeled in prayer before a silent god. He would not dedicate the cathedral, but he was curious. Word had come to him of its beauty but also of disturbing practices. He thought of the offensive line from the new liturgy: "And the savior's ecstasy occurred once again."

The Passion is permanent. Our Lord ended the recurring cycle of life and death by His resurrection and His ascension to sit on the right hand of God. In this, He has given the hope of eternal life, ending the transient discovery of self through the ecstasy of a Dionysus or Orpheus as in the pagan beliefs, Etienne thought.

"Why, Lord," he implored, gazing lovingly upon the crucifix, "does Natas want to confuse men now? Is there not enough confusion?"

Natas was introducing something older than the Greek mysteries, a belief that was dominant before Egypt was formed. Then, there was no mystery, for all men had participated in that great darkness at the center of existence. That belief was African, and try as he might, Etienne could not entirely divorce himself from it. Pride, the sin of which he had accused Natas, lay at the heart of his dilemma. This original idea that was sweeping millions along was African; it was his own, and that gave it an authenticity he could not, would never, entirely deny.

"Have I sinned, O Lord? Is my pride a betrayal like Judas'?"

His voice was sad and quiet in the confined space of the cell, but as he continued to pray, an idea formed. He would go to the dedication but not as Pope Celestine. To do that would push the American prelates over the edge, and maybe the Europeans as well. It was certain that neither group would be in Africa. Still, the rest of the world, those who saw the new cathedral not simply as the Catholic Church but something else that both subsumed and transcended their religions, would come. Many saw their god revealed in the new religion and so felt no betrayal. They would come, but America and Europe would be absent.

He stood slowly, painfully, waiting for the blood to flow into his cramped knees. Bowing deeply, he made the sign of the cross and limped from the cell. The door led to the extensive chambers of his apartment where Kwaku was asleep in a high-backed chair.

"Poor boy. Serving me must be a far cry from what you imagined."

He gently woke the young man and sent him to his room on the other side of the hall. Tomorrow, he would tell him of the trip to Africa, to the place called Bumba.

Chapter 14

The Raiders came at dawn, big men who rode quiet trucks, exhaust floating in the air like mist. Cold lay like a blanket on the New Mexico night, and most of the small band of Indians who had been running for days slept deeply. Some were old, the elders who weeks earlier gathered in Santa Fe when Notah called. Like the others, Tricks of the Fox was unsure. This was their land, and Notah was asking them to give it up and go with the black people to Africa. It was hard. Though starvation, disease and death stalked the reservations, the gods lived there; their ancestors' voices, faint though they were, still sang. How could they leave? These young ones did not understand, consumed as they were with the world of cars and televisions. They did not dream as the old ones had dreamed. They did not feel the breath of the land anymore.

Tricks of the Fox turned under the blanket, listening to the quiet hum of trucks in the valley below. He felt another consciousness awaken and knew that it was Notah. Tricks of the Fox breathed softly. The young man next to him was different. Though Notah had attended the white man's university, he had not left his people but continued to dance with power and grace. He was a blessing to the people, but now he had got hold of this idea of joining the black people and leaving the land. The elders were torn and could not decide. It was then that Notah called leaders from across the country together, strong men who, though not elders, had influence.

The young are so impatient. And yet, was it not the impetuosity of youth that created the heroes of the Indian? Tricks of the Fox thought.

He chuckled.

"Are you laughing at death, old man?" Notah whispered.

The voice was affectionate.

"Only a fool laughs at death, boy. That is the question of an un-blooded child."

Notah grinned.

"Have you heard them?"

"I would have to stop my ears not to hear them. Do you think they know we are here?"

"They know we are somewhere and that we are not traveling quickly."

Tricks of the Fox felt a pang of regret. Notah should not have to die because nine old men could not move fast enough. The Raiders wanted them dead. The murder of the thirteen band leaders several days earlier had sent a chill through the tribes, and fear stopped all discussion of the move to join the black people. Still, something marvelous had happened. The burials became a celebration. From as far away as Connecticut, tribes came. The Winnebago and the Lakota, the Ojibwe and Cree, Shoshone and Navajo, the Salish and the Kootenai. They came in a thousand, thousand feathers to praise the murdered thirteen. They danced. Oh, how they danced! Prayers ascended to the sky upon the winds and the fire. Even he had danced long into the night on his old legs.

"They have stopped," Notah said quietly.

He stood, checking the long gun and the two knives he carried and feeling for the dyke pliers stuck in his boot.

"Three trucks. Eight men each. Twenty-four to ten. Not bad odds," Tricks of the Fox said.

"You are too bloodthirsty, old man. I still hope to get out of this without trouble."

"As Trickster said, Notah, 'We are born into trouble.' The only way out is death."

Notah did not answer. He sniffed the air, which contained some combination of stale cologne and sweat. The Raiders had started their ascent.

"Well, old man, can you see well enough to hit anything with that old rifle, or should I make sure that I never get in front of you?" Notah asked, laughter in his voice.

"As you head to *ya'aashii, awe'e'*, know that if I shoot you, it would be no accident."

They both chuckled, and without further comment, Notah slipped into the darkness. The old man quietly woke the others. Each had a rifle, and in spite of the elders' advanced years, each could use it. Below, they heard the labored breathing, the dislodged pebbles, this giving them a picture of the Raiders' movements as clear as if it was daylight.

Notah moved obliquely away from the ascending men. The Raiders did not know where the elders were and had simply chosen the easiest ascent, so he figured he had some time. Notah stopped, ears pricked for sounds.

God, they are noisy!

Still, he remembered when they came after him in the desert. He was fooled then, thinking them clumsy. Now, he listened carefully. Eighteen were ascending the hill. Six were guarding the trucks. It was cold, so they would probably be inside, and that was good for what he had in mind. Notah resumed walking. At one point, he again stopped, listening for any sound from where he had left the old men.

They can still move quietly, he thought, smiling.

The elders would move uphill, following an almost invisible desert mule deer trail, using the noise of the ascending Raiders to cover their movement. His idea was very simple—disable two of the trucks and escape with the third.

All I have to do is get past six men.

The slope became less steep, and Notah angled back to where the trucks were parked. The lights were off, but the engines were running.

Keeping warm. At least, I don't have to go searching for them in the dark.

He followed the low purr of idling engines until the trucks' outlines were visible. He also smelled the cigarette that one man smoked, heard the whispered conversations and the occasional laughter. Notah dropped to his stomach and slid forward, thinking of his brother the rattlesnake. Within moments, he was under the last truck in line. Sliding forward, he reached up and, with the dyke pliers, cut the fuel line. He quietly slid out from under the truck as it continued to idle. The fuel line of the second truck was soon cut as well. By the time the first sputter came, he was on his way to the third truck. Someone cursed as Notah moved sinuously through the desert night. Doors were being opened and closed.

Hope they all go to investigate.

They did not. Five of the men clustered around the middle truck, closest to the one he wanted. One man, gun ready, stood next to the first truck in line. Notah breathed slowly and slid the knife from his boot. Then, without thought, he was moving as the wind moves. The man never stood a chance. The long blade slid up under his chin and into his brain as Notah covered his mouth. He eased the man to the ground, feeling his life blood gushing. Then, he was in the truck, engaging the clutch harshly. The truck was moving before the first shot came. He accelerated, lights still off, eyes closed, creating a mental picture of the land and hoping amidst all the bumping, he did not break an axle. There was automatic gunfire and the sharp ping of a bullet striking metal. He swerved furiously. For a short while, lights followed him, but as the gas lines emptied, the sound of gunfire fell behind. He raced south, searching for the road through the hills that intersected with the deer path. He hoped Tricks of the Fox and the other old men were all right.

When he flipped the lights on, illuminating the valley and slowing to give himself time to see any holes in the ground, Notah experienced a sense of satisfaction. Stoltz had let it be known that he would exact vengeance for the destruction of his house, and he had gone after the elders.

A pity he wasn't in the house, Notah thought as he negotiated a dry river bed.

The raids had increased, and he was on the run. Two days earlier, he returned to Santa Fe to get the elders out. Stoltz's Raiders were waiting for him, but he escaped north into Carson National Forest. Once out of the city, it was easy to evade the Raiders, until the old truck broke down, and he was left on foot with nine old men. They never complained, but he needed to get them out of the region. Otherwise, they would be killed. They were headed to the Borderlands. There they could argue about what the tribes should do. He had made the case for leaving and thought some of the people would back him, but he did not want to offend the elders. In the coming years, their voices and wisdom would be the authority of the old tradition. Around him stretched the southwestern desert. Feeling the presence of his ancestors, Notah wondered if following Anne Ernsky's advice to join the black people in Africa was the right thing to do.

Chapter 15

*A*ndreas screamed as pain exploded deep in his brain. He fell to his knees, hands clutching his throat where it felt as though someone had stuck a hot poker. For a moment, he was blinded and clawed at the air. Sight returned, and he stared at his hands, expecting to see blood. His hands were unchanged. The pain gradually diminished, and Andreas turned to the altar on which lay the dying boy, whose eyes, of indeterminate color, stared hopefully at the kneeling man. There were more black blotches on his body since the last appearance, and his face was, if anything, sadder. Andreas stood with considerable effort and stumbled toward the altar. The mother sat some distance away, the white crocodile next to her. Around her, four glowing luminescences, the spirits that had been within the sandstorms, hovered. Why had they tried to kill him? Why did they fail? The desert had now attacked him twice, and he had survived.

When Andreas touched the dying boy, the crocodile leapt forward, its huge body surprisingly agile. He stepped back. It stopped. The boy's eyes called to him, and Andreas again stepped forward.

"You have suffered much, haven't you?" he asked.

The boy swallowed and, voice hoarse, answered, "Yes."

"What's the matter with you?"

"I am tired. I carry a burden."

"What burden?"

Something like a smile appeared on the angelic face.

"You."

As if exhausted, the boy closed his eyes. Andreas waited. The eyes opened again.

Andreas asked, "Am I to relieve your burden?"

This time, there was a definite smile when the boy said, "Yes."

Andreas glanced at the mother and the four luminescences. Understanding came to him.

"You have carried their burdens, have you not?"

As he said this, the luminescences changed, and four beings dressed in gold appeared. They were the gods of the sandstorm—Osiris, Tammuz, Orpheus and Apollo.

"Life, death and rebirth. You each represent that cycle," Andreas said quietly.

Turning to the boy, he asked, "Who are you?"

Andreas immediately saw many things but most important was a volcano with a huge crater and a figure dancing upon it.

"Are you Baal?"

"I have been many things. And their opposites. I begin and I end, and I have many names."

"The dying god!"

Surprisingly, the boy laughed, a sound like music.

"I have been called that, too."

"But an age dies with you, though you cannot die."

"An age begins, too. I am so tired, Tama. Relieve me."

"Relieve you?" Andreas, not understanding, said. "But I am no—"

"God? Nor was I. But men need faiths, and she gives birth to us."

Andreas turned. The boy's mother was now covered with leaves of various species—hemlock, juniper, holly and oak, among others. Her face still had a slightly playful, coy look, and to Andreas' astonishment, she winked. The boy raised his right hand, its thumb and index finger vertical, pointing to the sky. The other three fingers curled downwards to the earth. The four golden beings stepped back, returning to their luminescenses, and again hovering around the mother. The dying boy raised his left hand, four fingers straight and thumb curled across the palm. His lips moved, but no sound came. It took a while before Andreas realized he was praying.

For a long time, the boy went on, until a single note dominated Andreas' mind. It was a note of such purity, such beauty, that the desert disappeared and lushness surrounded him. Andreas recognized the sound as that which the Tiamatians called the Voice of the Goddess.

He thought of it as Eurydice's song. The voice he had heard that time in Tiastan was but a crude imitation, however. This sound bound up the poles of the universe. It had given form to chaos, created light and darkness, reconciled good and evil. It had no rhythm, and yet its pure, inflectionless harmony gave meaning to the music. Andreas felt the sound in the depths of his soul and understood his immortality.

The dying boy slowly reached out and touched him. Andreas, unwilled, bent, placing his lips upon the boy's and, open-mouthed, waited expectantly. The boy exhaled. It was a breath so sweet that, at once, Andreas knew what ambrosia was. His head swam, and the universe flowed before his mind as the dying breath filled him. Finally, the breath stopped. Andreas did not move, not wanting the kiss to end, feeling the loss, the unutterable emptiness of the passing. He wept. Then, he felt hands on his shoulders and saw the smiling mother.

"Come. It is done," she said.

He turned with her, aware that the luminescences had disappeared. Time bent, turning on itself, and she touched him. For how long she held the contact, he could not say, but as she left him, he sensed movement to his left. Before he could move, the crocodile reared up and struck, its great claw ripping across his face, tearing his left eye. The pain felt remote, and even as he fell, the desert was fading. Andreas had the impression of time and space collapsing as his body flew away from the wadi.

After some time, he floated through the thick trees of a forest, coming to rest on soft grass. Aware of movement, he twisted around. Malaia stood in the shadow of a tree, smiling.

"Welcome back, Andreas. Now, we go to Ghalib's Land."

Then, darkness came.

Chapter 16

A world away, Etienne Ochukwu awoke with a scream, hands going to his head. All around, he sensed the stillness that he, on occasion, invoked. This was different, more powerful, more resonant, yet, paradoxically, emptier. His body felt as if it was on fire, the very skeleton seeming to be changing, pulling itself out from his flesh. He tried to stand but could not, the fiery pain in his bones silencing him even as he tried to call for help.

Is this my death?

He tried to shut his mind off, to escape the fearful tearing in his body. Aware of his contortions, he attempted to roll to the edge of the bed, to throw himself off in the hope that the noise would attract some attention. His body did not obey. A sweet sound penetrated deep into his soul, bringing not peace, but a question to which an answer offered itself. From an unimaginable distance came his father's voice.

"It is time, Etienne."

Immediately, the pain was gone. Etienne lay rigid for a moment, expecting it to return. In the bathroom, he examined his face carefully, searching for some deformation. Throughout the pain-filled moments, his bones had felt as if they were shifting, but his face appeared normal.

"Did I have a dream?"

Something told him that was not the explanation. Returning to the bedroom, he opened a drawer and took from it the photograph of a tall man whose intense eyes stared out at him. He ran his forefinger over the glass covering his father's image.

"Who were you?"

Eventually, he returned to bed. As his eyes closed, he saw his father dancing with power and savagery in the clearing of a dark forest. Etienne also heard the remnants of that unimaginably beautiful sound. He wondered about the connection between the two.

Chapter 17

Two men walked without haste down a narrow, dusty side street. The showpieces of Llehastan, the capital of Ghalib's Land, were now far away. They had passed the great boulevard earlier, marveling at the grand Arch of Lusani, constructed by the Son of Ghalib, as Natas was called, after his triumph at the city of that name. The wonders were everywhere, and the great capital gleamed, its white marble shining in the last rays of the artificial light created by the powerful generators located in Tiastan.

"Soon, the darkness of *pogosi* will come," the taller man said, his eyes, one of which was covered by a patch, going to the sky.

The other man, much shorter but beautifully muscled, glanced at the taller one whose face was hidden by a hood.

"Yes, but *pogosi* is not yet here. *Malamalama* still rules the sky."

The shorter man stopped as they came to another side street. As was common, this one carried no sign.

"Are you lost again, Malaia?" the taller man asked playfully.

"Indeed, I am, Andreas. I have been lost since the Son of Ghalib destroyed the open lands with all these buildings."

"But you must admit it is impressive. A major city built from scratch in ten years. Did you notice the size of the castle on the middle hill? It looks impregnable."

Malaia snorted. Although he had lived in the temple of the goddess in Tiastan, Malaia was a product of the Ilegu Forest and the eastern desert. For him, three buildings together were a village, ten a city. Once, when Andreas and he were sitting on the bank of a slow-moving river, after several hours, four men passed. Malaia had risen and, disgust evident in his voice, said, "Multitudes!" Andreas had laughed but was still not sure if Malaia had been joking.

They stood, Malaia staring down the side street and Andreas leaning on a golden staff. They were searching for a locksmith who had relocated from Tiastan. He had forged the locks of the great castle, and one of Malaia's contacts had arranged for the locksmith to meet with them, possibly to help them get inside. The castle was protected by a giant wall that encircled the mountain. It gleamed, bouncing light this way and that. Because of his weakened mind sense, Andreas had not yet found Eurydice. He stared back at the bridge over the river called the Crossway of Baalin.

"Do you know what the locksmith's shop looks like, Malaia?"

"No. I knew it in Tiastan but not here."

"Most men are creatures of habit. Tell me what his shop in Tiastan was like."

"Well, it was near the markets. His name is Alli'im, and he had the sign of a forge and a hammer on his lintel. I do not know if he has that now."

"He probably does. He'll want the people of Tiastan to patronize him here, so he probably advertises that it is the same shop. In any case, we don't have anything else. Come."

They slid into a corner of the side street that was in shadow and leaned in apparent nonchalance against the wall. They were, however, anything but nonchalant. Andreas formed the sign of the forge and hammer in his mind sense, and the sign appeared. Malaia smiled and nodded. Andreas closed the eye without the patch. The street appeared in his mind sense, and he raced along it. At the end of the street, he turned left and then left again into the next street. This, too, showed no sign of the forge and hammer, but he continued, swiftly exploring each street. He found it in the fourth street and nodded to Malaia.

"The goddess has truly blessed you, Andreas. You move with such swiftness."

Andreas smiled, thinking of his withered left arm and his lost left eye.

"Yes. I'm truly blessed."

Malaia heard the bitterness and said sympathetically, "Our bodies are gifts of the gods. They dispose as they wish. How do you measure a gift?"

Andreas grunted as they strode toward the shop. The rhythms of the regional accents were all around them. The sweet lyricism of the people of Tiastan, whose voices reminded him of birds in springtime, was countered by the deep, rumbling tones of the men from the Marble Mountains. Dominant, though, was the sound of those cluster of dialects from Ghalib's Land, with their rapid, complex, polysyllabic words. Andreas needed his mind sense to decipher what they were saying.

The accent that gave him pause was not from that land, and it brought back painful memories of a lost world. The African Americans were there in force, and though they spoke the language of Ghalib's Land, nothing could disguise the graceful cadence of their sound. The accent danced in the sunlight, bringing a sense of normality to Andreas' perceptions. Still, it was not with joy that he saw these people whose somber faces were so at odds with the music in their voices. He knew how they came to be there, and his mind recoiled from the pain and death inherent in the fact of their presence.

"One day, I will make this right," he whispered.

"What did you say, Andreas?" Malaia, feeling the disturbance around his companion, said.

"Nothing. I was thinking of a debt I owed."

Malaia looked at him inquiringly. The idea of debt meant nothing to him. The First People had obligations but never debts.

"Is this fellow to be trusted?"

"He worshiped the goddess but now lives in fear in Ghalib's Land worshiping the god."

Everything is religion in this land, Andreas thought.

Malaia was telling him that a man who changed divinities so easily should be handled with care. Andreas glanced from under his hood at the man who walked beside him, grateful for Malaia's friendship and guidance. When Andreas entered the temple in Tiastan so long ago now, Malaia was *si'ufofoga,* the voice of the high priestess of the goddess Tiamat. He had seemed a remote being, entirely without personality.

The discipline it must have taken to subordinate his ego in that way. Incredible. Even his name Malaia means death, or land of the dead.

"Thanks, Malaia. For everything," he said, touching the Ulumatuan's shoulder.

The smaller man did not turn but replied, "We all walk in the path of the gods, Andreas."

No need for thanks. We do what we must. Strange people.

They reached the fourth street, and Andreas saw the sign of the forge and hammer three stores in. He quickened his step. This man could help him find Eurydice. They stepped inside. Shadows were everywhere, and the place was silent. Andreas' mind sense instantly went on alert, but it was too late. He heard the ominous clacking of guns being cocked and instinctively went into a fighting crouch, raising his golden staff defensively. Then, he almost immediately straightened.

"Good choice, Tama. I would hate to kill you before the Onye has a chance to question you," a familiar voice said.

A man came from the shadows at the back of the shop. He walked with the confident jauntiness of the African American, but his eyes belied both the walk and the playful voice. They were hard bits of flint in a face that, even in repose, looked angry.

"Hello, Marcus," Andreas said.

Eight men formed an arc around the room, and the short-barrelled, black guns did not waver. Marcus made no reply but walked around Andreas, looking him up and down.

"There are two murders on your hands. I will take the staff," Marcus said.

At that moment, the curtain at the back opened, and a little man came out. The locksmith's eyes showed fear as he stared at the staff in Andreas' hand.

"*To'oto'o,*" he whispered.

Marcus glanced at him, asking irritably, "What are you babbling about, shopkeeper?"

The man kept moving slowly forward. Andreas knew the word meant "staff," but apart from being golden, nothing else distinguished his staff. Then, he thought of how it had come to him. Awaking after his ordeal in the desert, it had been in his hand. He could not explain how it came to be there.

"*To'oto'o le lagi,*" the locksmith, awe in his voice, said more clearly.

One of the soldiers shoved the small man aside, and he stood silent. Marcus held out his hand, and Andreas handed over the staff. The soldiers shepherded them outside as two military vehicles drove up. They were quickly, and not very gently, shoved inside. The truck soon began a steep ascent.

"Well," Andreas said, "it looks as if we're being invited in. No need for the keys, eh?"

"What is it you say, Andreas? God works mysteries?"

"'God moves in mysterious ways.' The rest of the sentence is, 'His wonders to perform.'"

He sensed Malaia's nod.

"Some day, we will talk of your god, Andreas."

Andreas tried to think of what that conversation would be like. Would Malaia understand his doubt about the very god to whom he so casually referred? Not likely. Religion was too integral to the Land of Tiamat's soul. It was probably best if they never had that conversation. He thought of the locksmith's comment. *"To'oto'o le lagi"* meant "staff of the goddess." Why had the shopkeeper called his staff that? He would ask Malaia later. Meanwhile, he followed the route with his mind sense, seeing the beauty of the buildings that had been erected. Once, they passed over a deep gorge with a powerful waterfall, and he thought how strange this all was. This society was older than historical time.

History, like writing, is only about five thousand years old. The carbon dating indicated that the mummy that got me into trouble was at least thirty thousand years old. That means these people had a civilization capable of scientific thought over twenty-five thousand years before we were supposed to be civilized, he mused.

Andreas shook his head as the truck came to a stop. He sensed giant gates opening. After a while, the truck moved off again. Now that he was inside the castle, his nervousness increased. A quick scan of the space through which the truck moved slowly moved indicated it was expansive, with a large collection of buildings. Once, he heard a squad of soldiers drilling. It took a long time to cross the castle's courtyard, but when the truck stopped, his heart raced.

"She's here, Malaia," he whispered.

The rear doors opened, and Marcus, flanked by several soldiers, ordered them out. Andreas jumped down, his eyes searching the high wall for any sign of his wife.

Chapter 18

*T*hey fed him well, but he was separated from Malaia and placed in a cell. It was small, like a monk's, but that did not matter. Somewhere near was Eurydice. Once more, he extended his mind sense, but it was to no avail. It seemed diffuse.

Natas must have rigged something up to block it.

The cell itself was dimly lit, with a single bench along one wall. It was probably ten feet by eight, with a flat, uninviting pallet. Extending his hands in a rapid, though apparently effortless, movement, he performed exercises for a long time. It was something that had come to him in the desert. The art of *tusiata* was beautiful, but its rules limited a fighter to using only his feet. The moves he was now practicing he had observed during a fight between two *lagope'a*, small, stick-like creatures that lived near the desert's edge. They reminded him of locusts. The *lagope'a* had fought much like the *tusiata* fighter, leaping and battering each other with their hind legs. When one suddenly clawed with his foreleg, the other fell back as if surprised. Eventually, it slunk off. Andreas, impressed with both the speed and the effect of that movement, began to use his hands more. With nothing to do for weeks in the desert, he had practiced and was now gratified at the speed and power of his hand movements. He punched. The motion felt slow, but feeling the air being pushed before his fist, he smiled.

Andreas was about to leap when the door opened. Marcus stood framed in the doorway, looking at him speculatively.

"Something's different about you. What is it?"

Andreas did not answer.

"Yes. Something is definitely different. The Onye is very anxious to see you."

"Why?"

Marcus shrugged.

"Maybe he wants to kill you himself. Who knows?"

"Where is the Onye now?"

"Cleaning up the Ilegu Forest."

Andreas felt a dark fear.

"What do you mean, cleaning up?"

"The *Ulumatua* are the last resistance. We've already taken their land in the southwest. All that's left is the rabble in the Ilegu Forest. They won't last long."

Natas had conquered the Ulumatuans! Clearly, Malaia did not know. For weeks, they had traveled together, working their way north, hiding in the desert in which they were so comfortable. His thoughts leapt to Mother Mutasii. Was she all right? If she were to be hurt .... Andreas felt the slow burn of his anger come, and for a moment, Marcus seemed to be swaying before him, the face of an enemy to be blotted out. He fought for control, and soon, the anger was trapped under the blanket of his mind sense. When he spoke, his voice was calm.

"What does the Onye want of me?"

"No one's ever sure what the Onye wants, and it's dangerous to ask. I think he wants to pick your brain. After this campaign, the Land of Ghalib will be fully pacified."

"You mean the Land of Tiamat."

Andreas was surprised by the resentment he felt at the renaming. Marcus' eyes narrowed.

"No. I mean the Land of Ghalib, he who is the vessel of the god Chango whose servant the Onye is. The goddess is no more."

"No more? The people of Tiamat ... of this land serve all the gods. What do you mean, the goddess is no more?"

"The Onye has declared that only the god lives and rules, and he is his servant. The goddess' name is not spoken. Ask the woman who was high priestess to the false goddess when you see her."

Andreas' anger flared again, and his voice brought a strange chill to the room.

"If she is hurt, Marcus, your death is certain."

"All men live with the certainty of death, white man, but I believe yours will come before mine."

Andreas was immediately contrite.

"I'm sorry, Marcus. I should not have threatened."

"It doesn't matter whether you threaten or not. We are enemies. My mother never recovered from the Expulsion, you know. She lost her mind during the transport to Antarctica. For the rest of her life, she talked as if she was still in Philadelphia. I grew up with that."

"I know. I cannot change that. I can only say how sorry I am that the whole thing happened."

"Then why did you recommend that we be sent out? Was it hatred? What drove you? What gave you the right?"

The young man was breathing hard. Andreas felt the weight of his questions, and his heart was anguished.

"It was not my recommendation."

"You are a liar," Marcus responded.

"What makes you so sure? You're too young to remember what happened?"

"The Son of Ghalib said it was so."

"Natas?"

Andreas' voice was hoarse as the drumbeat of blood pounded in his ears. He knew that only a fraction of the African American population was transported to Antarctica. Where were the others? What if, thirteen years earlier, Natas leaked the news, knowing that panic would ensue? He would not have been suspected of the leak because it would appear not to be in his interest. He, after all, would lose money since Branniff would be transporting fewer African Americans than planned. Andreas turned to the young man.

"Marcus, you once told me that this group of African Americans was chosen by the Son of Ghalib for a special purpose. Doesn't it then seem strange that my so-called recommendation brought you here?"

"The Son of Ghalib said you'd say that. We would eventually have been brought together but not in these circumstances. You forced the Son of Ghalib to bring us here before it was time. He had to protect us for the war that is coming. And for that, you will pay, Prescod."

Marcus started to leave, but Andreas asked, "Why does the Onye want to speak with me?"

"You can ask him yourself. He returns within the week."

The young man turned on his heel and strode out, anger evident in every line of his body. With his mind sense restricted, Andreas was out of touch with people for the first time in weeks. Thoughts rushed around his head. Why was the Onye so anxious to see him? Who was the Onye? Clearly not Natas because Marcus called him the Son of Ghalib. Maybe Natas had left one of his henchmen to run the place. This thought brought his mind back to Marcus and the African Americans.

They, too, will hate for a long time.

Once, Eurydice, hearing his denial, said they were all responsible for what happened to the African Americans, but he did not believe in collective guilt. Humans acted according to the dictates of their conscience, as individuals. If he believed anything else, he would have to accept that humans were a herd, not moral agents. Still, something nagged him. When he, in his report to the United States governmnent, recommended "rationalizing" the population, what had he meant? He was fairly certain he had not thought in racial terms. Or had he?

Did I know where the logic of my recommendation would lead?

Suddenly, it was very important to know. Had he implicitly directed the policy-makers to the only conclusion possible? And what if it had not been racial? What if they had taken only poor people? Would that have been different? Would the guilt be any less?

"Oh, my God!"

The horrible weight of his choice was upon him, and into his mind came the image of the dying boy he had seen in the desert. There was so much pain, so much suffering, in the boy's eyes, and yet he felt pity for Andreas. When the boy breathed into him, he had felt as if his body was immediately inhabited, his soul seeming to shake off an outer crust. Now, that presence was like a separate entity, a righteous power within him. It had strengthened him and made his physical needs disappear, but it was not fully him. That power could only be his if he found a way to end the separation between himself and that presence. Andreas sighed, his heart heavy. To avoid the oppression of his thoughts, he searched for Eurydice with his mind sense but could not pin down where she was. Nor could he sense Malaia. He wondered if the Ulumatuan was all right.

Andreas fell asleep, and when he awoke, they brought him food. He assumed a day had passed. He was fed twice a day, and in this way, he kept track of time. On the fifth day, Marcus came again. This time, he had an escort and wore ceremonial clothes. Tight breeches of soft wool covered his bulging thighs, and the gold tunic had been made to measure. His burgundy cape made him look very official.

"You have been summoned," he said.

"By whom?"

"The Onye. Come."

Andreas stood, aware of his unkempt beard and the pungent odor surrounding him. He had not changed clothes since coming to the castle. Outside, the light almost blinded him, and he squinted, his hand shading the eye without the patch. The courtyard was cobble-stoned, and it was busy. This was a working castle, intended to be self-sufficient. Along the wall was a number of shops that supported the life of the castle. A company of soldiers jogged by. The courtyard was quite extensive, so he could not see the full length of the wall toward which they were headed. In the corner was a turret from which soldiers surveyed both the courtyard and the valley below.

They're not secure on this hill. Conquest never breeds ease.

They went toward an ornate wooden door directly beneath the turret. Inside, cobblestones gave way to a shiny floor, the wood of which came from the Ilegu Forest. The walls were decorated with tapestries of the most wondrous colors. They soon entered a well-lit corridor where the tapestries were smaller but, if anything, more extravagantly colored. There were, as well, on the walls, several paintings of well-muscled men. Andreas recognized the likeness to the mummies he had seen in the Hall of the Onyes.

Passing through an open door, the first person he saw was someone he recognized. Marcus bowed low to the woman. She ignored him, her eyes on Andreas.

"Well, Tama, we meet again."

"It is good to see you, Aduame," Andreas responded cautiously.

"Is it?"

Aduame's face displayed the slyness of which he always suspected she was capable. He did not know where he stood with this woman whom Eurydice displaced as high priestess to the goddess Tiamat. The last time he saw her, she had come to Tiastan from Ghalib's Land as ambassador for Natas. Having defied Eurydice and the goddess, she was condemned to death. Breaking the taboos of the Land of Tiamat, he saved her and her daughter Lakshmi from being eaten by the white crocodiles.

"Are you the Onye?"

She chuckled.

"After so many years, you are still a fool. Still *tagatu fuimai.*"

Well, I guess saving her life doesn't count for much, he thought, as he said, "Yes, Aduame. I'm still a stranger. You did not answer my question."

Something in his tone caught her attention, and the smile left her face.

"It is not your place to ask questions but to answer them."

Andreas sighed.

"Why was I brought here?"

"Murder. Treason. Conspiracy. Take your pick," Marcus answered.

"What are you talking about?"

"Three years ago, you killed two of our soldiers during your escape. That warrant was never executed. You colluded with the mountain people to resist the Son of Ghalib's rule. You're responsible for undermining the judgment of the temple of Tiamat. And now, you were caught trying to subvert our laws by seeking illegal entry to this castle. Did these not register as crimes to you?"

"I saved Aduame and her child from certain death," Andreas replied.

Aduame's face was blank. Marcus snorted.

"Had it been left to me, you would be dead by now, but the Onye wants to talk to you."

As he finished, a door opened, and a young girl entered, followed by a tall young man. Andreas blinked, and his heart raced. His mouth fell open. He tried to speak but could not.

After several attempts, he blurted, "My God! Lona? You are sup-posed to be dead!"

The young man turned to him, his clear, blue eyes cold as a Nordic fjord. Marcus and Aduame kneeled. The young girl bowed her head.

"Kneel, fool, before the Onye," Marcus hissed.

Andreas continued to stare until Marcus rose and kicked him in the back of the knee, forcing him to kneel. The young man looked on in amusement, his face showing only a modicum of interest. Andreas did not resist Marcus, although he quickly noted four areas of weakness in the African American's stance. He would be easy to bring down.

"You have the appraising eye of a fighter, but if I remember cor-rectly, you have little skill, Tama."

"Lona!" Andreas croaked.

Marcus tightened his grip on Andreas' shoulder.

"That is the Onye, you idiot. Be silent."

The young man raised his hand, and Marcus subsided.

"Sorry, Tama. Marcus is, on occasion, overzealous, and I under-stand he has a special reason to hate you. I am the Onye. Lona is dead."

"But you are—"

"Lona is dead! He died at Lusani as the Onye was born."

The voice was harsh. It was taking a while, but Andreas was sort-ing it out. The image he had repressed for so long of Eurydice lying on an altar of marble, a sacrifice to Natas, came to him. His body tensed. The boy before him, the son he was forbidden to acknowledge, had been part of that ceremony. Malaia had told him that his son was dead, although his actual words were "Lona is no more." Now, here was the boy saying the same thing.

"How can you be the Onye? The Onye is the product of Empheme and Ghalib. They would have to join to invoke the god Chango. That could not—"

"But it did," Aduame said.

Around him, the faces were wreathed in smiles, but the ecstatic quality in Aduame's voice could not contain the underlying note of malice. Andreas turned to her, fractured images of a creature mount-ing the altar in his mind. Lona looked on with a wry smile that did not quite hide his curiosity. Andreas' body was taut as his brain slowly accepted what his every instinct rejected. Natas and Eurydice. Ghalib and Empheme. They had coupled and symbolically produced the offspring of the god Chango. His son, whom he could not acknowledge, was now, according to these people's beliefs, Ghalib's son.

Hatred boiled up in him, and before he knew it, his hands moved. Marcus never stood a chance. His body crumpled as Andreas' rage exploded. From the corner of his eye, he noted that the young girl and Aduame were hurrying from the room. He moved deliberately toward Marcus who, swearing, was picking himself up off the floor. Andreas could see nothing distinctly. He took one step and jumped, his body an arrow of death. Before the kick could land, he was knocked off target, so that his left foot caught Marcus on the shoulder, knocking him down again.

"Is today your day to die?" Lona playfully asked.

Andreas could not hear. The noise rushing through his ears was too loud. Lona recognized the madness and moved into a crouch, his right foot sliding outwards. He jumped, his body floating through the air like some improbable combination of feather and bullet. Andreas noted the move, *Fa vili,* and shifted into *Fa Metic,* the defense of a master. Lona went flying by, and Andreas turned like lightning, his foot arcing in a brutal kick to the shoulder. Lona flipped backwards, landing upright, gliding in a semicircle to the left as Andreas followed his movements.

"You have improved, Tama. Is that what you learned in the Ilegu Forest?"

Lona leapt without warning, his feet, piston-like, snapping the air, going directly for Andreas' face. Andreas jumped, his body performing revolution after revolution until he was high above Lona's still accelerating body. He slashed down with his left foot, the heel connecting solidly with Lona's ribs. The boy crashed to the floor. He immediately jumped up holding his left side, a look of perplexity on his face. Andreas' voice, when he spoke, sounded hollow, as if someone else was speaking through him.

"You cannot win, Lona. Stop now."

For a moment, it seemed as if Lona would ignore the statement, and he might have, if, at his first movement, he had not winced, favoring his side.

"It's badly bruised. Stop now."

The fury on Lona's face was thunderous, but he did not attack.

"You anticipated my *ona ta'amiloga*," he said.

There was surprise in his voice. Andreas' rage was swiftly replaced by a deep sorrow.

"I could have killed you," he said quietly.

The boy shrugged, the warrior in him refusing to accept that possibility.

"You surprised me. I did not believe you had learned so much. I will not be surprised again."

Lona's voice was flat now that he had gained control of his pain, and Andreas, with great sorrow, recognized that he had made an enemy. Marcus rushed to help Lona, but the young man angrily pushed him away and, holding his side, strode from the room. Andreas started after him, but four soldiers guarded the door. In their eyes was a new caution. The young girl returned, intently observing him.

"You should not be here, mistress," Marcus said.

"You give no orders. You are *i tala atu*."

Called an outsider, Marcus' eyes narrowed, but he did not respond. The girl approached Andreas, her gaze appraising.

"You are the one they call Tama. They say you are a wizard from the land beyond Malaia." Before he could answer, she added, "I said there is no land beyond Malaia, and there are no wizards."

"Don't you remember me?" he asked.

"No."

"Don't you remember the white crocodiles in the Land of Malaia?"

"They were in my nightmares. Mother says my imagination is too active."

Andreas smiled. Evidently, they had persuaded the girl that she imagined her encounter with the white crocodiles when she was much younger. Andreas nodded, remembering the struggle to save her and her mother after they were condemned to death by the temple in Tiastan.

"Who are you?" he asked, amused.

"I am Empheme," she said proudly, drawing herself up.

Andreas chuckled.

"Empheme, eh! I knew another Empheme once. Are you named after her?"

The girl frowned, and there was a hint of anger in her voice when she said, "There is only one Empheme, you who are *i tala atu*. She whom you knew was false, pretending to be what she was not. Her pretensions ended at Lusani."

"Madam," Marcus said more insistently. "You should not be here. Come with me. The Onye needs you."

She hesitated a moment, obviously calculating whether she should listen to Marcus.

Eventually, she said, "I shall speak with you soon. Now, I must attend my duty."

With that, she turned to Marcus and authoritatively said, "Come."

They both left, and Andreas stood, uncertain what to do. The four soldiers watched him closely. He crossed to the window and looked out.

Some time later, the Onye returned. He had changed out of the military tunic and now wore a white robe with a scarlet shoulder decoration. He seemed to have recovered from the earlier blow. Andreas was struck by his bearing. Gone was the petulant arrogance of the boy he remembered. The tall young man who now dominated the room exuded the assurance of tested power.

"Well, Tama, Marcus says you should be executed for the murder of his soldiers and for striking me. What do you think I should do?" he asked playfully.

"I rather think you will do as you wish."

The Onye laughed.

"Indeed. Well, let's think of how to be rid of you later. Come. You must be hungry."

Andreas was ravenous, but he ate sparingly. The Onye watched him closely.

"What happened to you, Lona?"

The boy's eyes narrowed.

"Lona is dead, Tama. It is best you remember that."

"And your mother?"

For the barest hint of a moment, the young man looked confused.

Then, he said, "The woman you knew no longer exists."

"What have they done to her?"

"No harm has come to her."

"Why not release her then?"

"There is still a revolt in the south being fought in her name. Until the *Ulumatua* are crushed, she cannot be released." He paused, adding quietly, "Maybe not even then."

"She's your mother, Lona."

"No, Tama. I will forgive that statement only once. It is known that the goddess cannot produce boy children. Only the god Chango can do that. And, as you can see, I am a boy child."

Andreas ground his teeth in frustration.

So much superstition.

"She's your mother, Lona."

The boy's face hardened as he snarled, "As you are my father?"

Andreas' body tightened at the vehemence in Lona's voice, and in that instant, he understood. Lona's position in the Land of Tiamat was threatened the moment, three years earlier, when Andreas revealed his paternity. Already frustrated with his tangential role as the only boy in the temple, Lona had turned, or been turned, to something more certain. In taking on the role of Onye, he exchanged potential death for being a demigod. Andreas felt sorrow as he stared at his son. Once more, fate seemed to have trapped him.

"You wanted to talk to me," he said after a while.

"Yes. When I was a boy in the temple, you sometimes spoke of your land above. I always found your stories fascinating. I wanted to hear more."

"What would you like to hear?"

"Anything. For example, how big is your land?"

"My land is the United States, and as far as I can tell, it is about three times the size of the Land of Tia ... this land."

"You say 'my land' as if there are others. Are there other lands?"

"Several."

"And are they all larger than the Land of Ghalib?"

"Some are. Not all. Why do you ask?"

The icy, blue eyes became opaque.

"Knowledge always enlightens, don't you think?"

The evasive answer set off an alarm in Andreas' mind. He immediately thought of a night in the temple when Lona had shouted that the people above and those below needed to be reunited. "One day, I will go to your land," he had said. There was anger on his face then. How did he feel now?

"Where's Natas?"

Suddenly, the affability was gone.

"Do not ask questions of me, you who are *i tala atu*. The Son of Ghalib's whereabouts are not your concern."

Taken aback by the sudden change, Andreas watched as the young man fought to regain his composure.

Something is wrong. Could he and Natas have had a falling out?

Curious, Andreas asked, "Is there a plan to go to the world above, Onye? I know of your interest."

"There is such a plan, Tama, but it seems as if time has been stuck in the mud. The Son of Ghalib takes his time, though we are ready."

"Ready, Onye? For what?"

When the young man spoke, his voice was hushed, as if he feared someone might be listening.

"The Reunion."

"The Reunion? What's that?"

"In the time before time, all men were one and walked in the path of the gods. Then, Maatemnu of the withered arm fought with the Onye in the barren land. Some took his side. In this way were the people separated, some departing to the north with Maatemnu and the rest continuing south with the Onye. But in the heart of the god to whom the people give no name, the people have always been one. It is the Onye who binds the people. The Reunion is the will of the Onye."

Andreas did not know this version of the Great Parting, the story which told of how the First People had split up. Mother Mutasii once told him there were many stories, often having slight variations. This seemed to be such a variation, but the last two sentences of the boy's speech were ominous. He wondered what Eurydice's explanation of this story would be.

Hoping to extract more information about the relationship

between Natas and Lona, Andreas asked, "How is the Reunion to be effected?"

"The vision speaks of fire, Tama. Glorious fire."

Andreas thought of the soldiers he had seen at Lusani. So powerful. So efficient. So committed. Something fearful crawled into his mind, and, observing the predator's face before him, he shivered.

"By glorious fire, Onye, do you mean war?"

"Only if they wish it. I hope they wish it, for war cleanses. Look at the Land of Ghalib. Strife is no more. All are one now."

"Your attack on the Ilegu Forest was successful then?"

"Very. They are scattered, though the resistance is not over."

Andreas, worried about Mother Mutasii whom he had last seen sitting at the feet of the giant statue, asked, "The statue of the goddess, did you destroy it?"

Lona studied Andreas' face. When he spoke his voice was low.

"The statue of the goddess? Is it in the Ilegu Forest?"

Andreas mentally kicked himself. He had assumed Lona knew about the statue.

"I believe so," he replied, trying to cover his mistake.

Lona's face hardened.

"You do know, Tama. Where is it?"

"I saw it once. I couldn't tell you where. I don't know the forest well enough."

"Maybe your friends do," a familiar voice said.

Natas. He had entered the room through a hidden side door. Andreas' eyes narrowed. The situation had immediately become more dangerous.

"Bring the woman to the Room of Shadows."

Lona's face momentarily showed shock, but he quickly left.

"Come," Natas ordered.

It took them quite a while to cross the courtyard, enter the castle keep and descend four levels. The room they entered was macabre. On the walls were weapons from the past. Clubs, swords, maces, spears, knives, round stones, one of which had a suspicious-looking brown stain. One wall was devoted to a variety of helmets made of materials ranging from leather to iron. The third wall was adorned with shields on which were heraldic designs of many kinds. The fourth wall was modern. In fact, it was a glass window with a view into another room that had only a table in the middle. Natas stopped and stood quietly gazing through the glass window. When she was brought in, Andreas gasped, and his knees weakened for a moment.

"Eurydice!" he cried.

Natas smiled.

"Yes. Are you quite certain you do not know the location of the statue?"

"Why is that important?" Andreas asked exasperatedly.

"Because the *Ulumatua* use it as a symbol. It is blasphemous. Worse, it is treasonous."

"Is it treasonous to have a statue? That's preposterous."

Andreas' eyes were on the woman whom the soldiers were strapping to the table. Two of them affixed odd-looking shoes to her feet. Natas looked on, his face emotionless. Lona had not returned. Understanding that Eurydice was to be tortured to get the information from him, he turned to the man next to him, horror on his face.

"You can't!"

"Of course, I can."

"No. You cannot do this."

Andreas never saw the leg move, but it crushed his chest, knocking the wind out of him. He instinctively spun away, thus avoiding the second blow.

"In my name, all is possible, *i tala atu*."

Natas' voice was piercing, and Andreas heard the threat underneath. He was about to respond when the scream came. He rushed to the glass window as soldiers entered the room, covering him with guns. He stared, helpless. Eurydice was naked, and her body was jerking spasmodically as the torturer turned a knob to the right.

"Stop it," Andreas shouted, his fist pounding the glass.

Natas signaled, and the torturer stopped.

"Do you remember where the statue is?"

"I don't know. I saw it only once."

There must have been some signal because a second scream cut through him. He stared in horror at the woman's thrashing body. It was too much.

"All right. All right. Stop it."

The torturer turned the knob to the left.

"Where?" Natas asked.

Thinking swiftly, Andreas said, "I can't describe it. I'd have to show you. Even then, I'm not sure. Malaia would know for sure."

Natas turned away abruptly, saying to Marcus as he went, "Get a squad together. You leave immediately. And take the Ulumatuan."

"Natas." Andreas' voice was quiet but authoritative, and Natas stopped. "I will take care of her."

For a moment, Natas hesitated. Then, he nodded, walking swiftly from the room. Andreas followed him, turning right and entering the adjoining room. Eurydice lay quietly as if unconscious, and he covered her with a robe. Her eyes opened, and the edges crinkled in a sad smile as he came into sight.

"Hello, Andreas."

Her eyes closed. They moved her to a more comfortable room. Andreas ushered the soldiers out, asking them to find a doctor. Her feet were red. The doctor soon came and looked her over. She groaned once, but he declared her all right. Andreas sat watching her, the conflicting feelings of love and fear like live creatures in his mind. He had no idea how much time passed, but he must have dozed off because, at first, he did not recognize her voice.

"Oh, Andreas. Your path has been hard."

Eurydice's smile was feeble. He leaned down and hugged her close, feeling the life in her and the joy in his soul.

"Eudy, you all right?"

She made a face.

"My feet hurt, but otherwise, I'm fine. How are you? What happened to your eye?"

He put a hand up to the black patch and, trying to lighten the mood, said, "I lost a battle with a crocodile."

Instantly, her attention sharpened.

"A crocodile? A white crocodile?" she asked, pushing out of his embrace and studying his face.

"Yes."

"You have seen her, haven't you? When? How? What happened?"

"Slow down. One question at a time," he replied, laughing. Then, turning serious again, he asked, "What's the matter with Lona? How could he allow this to happen to you?"

Her face closed, and she said, "Lona is no more, Andreas."

"That's what Malaia said. What does it mean?"

"Lona as you knew him is gone. At Lusani, Natas called the god down upon him, and he became the Onye. Do not confuse the body with the person. It could mean your death."

Andreas snorted.

"A long time ago, Branniff said to me that if I acknowledged Lona as my son, it could mean my death. Now, you say the same thing. Why must I always ignore who he is?"

Eurydice smiled sadly.

"Sit here and hold my hand."

He did and felt an instant peace. Their mind senses touched, and Andreas closed his eyes, lying in her embrace.

"Lona follows his own path as laid out by the gods, Andreas. You cannot change it."

"But you are his mother."

"To Lona, I am Empheme, the vessel through which the god Chango passed to give him life."

"And Ghalib?" Andreas asked tersely.

She held him in her mind sense for a while before she answered.

"Like Lona, Natas acts as the stories dictate, Andreas. I'm sorry, my sweet, but we cannot escape our fate."

Andreas pulled back from her mind sense, trying to find space for his anger, but she held him.

"We must think of your future, but first, tell me of your stay with the goddess," she said.

Reluctantly, he spoke of the desert, the Hall of the Onyes, the underground data center and his visions of the goddess. As he related the events, a weight seemed to lift from his mind.

When he stopped, she asked, "And your arm? How did it become withered?"

He told her of his stroke, his time with Mother Mutasii and Malaia, and of the removal of the statue of the goddess from Tiastan to the Ilegu Forest.

Noticing the tension in his voice, she asked, "What of the Ilegu Forest?"

"You were tortured because I stupidly mentioned that the goddess' statue was there."

His voice dripped with self-contempt, but she smiled.

"Do not blame yourself, Andreas. The goddess is directing your footsteps. You can only follow. Now, tell me the rest of your vision."

"What do you mean? I told you what happened."

"Yes. You have accepted the dying god within you, and the sacred crocodile has marked you in her name. Just as the god to whom the people give no name has marked you through the withered arm. You are many things, Andreas, and you're becoming more fully what the gods intend you to be. In your visions, and as the withered arm indicates, you have become Maatemnu, the Great Slayer. It was you, in truth, who lay with me, Empheme, and gave life to he who is now the Onye. In this, you have become Ghalib."

"Ghalib? I thought Natas had become Ghalib."

"Natas walks a path he does not understand, Andreas. And yet, the paths converge as the stories tell."

Her voice was excited.

"Which stories of the First People?"

"Those that speak of a time when Baal, Chango and Tiamat become one, and the world is bathed in light."

"I have never heard this story."

"That is not surprising. There are thousands."

"Yes, but that's a pretty important one. A story that talks about the elimination of the gods and ushers in a time of light? That's pretty powerful stuff."

"It is not well known. Now, tell me of your vision in the desert."

He looked uncomfortable for a moment and then said, "All right. Just before the crocodile struck me—"

Marcus walked in.

"How cosy. Time to go, white man," he said.

Andreas started to stand, but Eurydice held his arm.

"Time to go where?"

"The Ilegu Forest to find your goddess' statue," Marcus answered.

Eurydice sat up, her eyes on Marcus.

"Has the goddess' statue reached the Ilegu Forest?"

For a moment, Marcus looked as if his thoughts no longer belonged to him. Andreas smiled, recognizing the subtle manipulation. Marcus shook his head.

"Damn your tricks. Always trying to confuse people. What do you mean 'reached'?"

"Did I say reached? My mistake. But it is in the forest then?"

"So he says," Marcus replied, pointing at Andreas.

"Andreas will be along. Go," Eurydice said.

Before Marcus was aware of it, he had walked through the door.

"I don't know much, but I first saw the statue when I escaped from Lusani three years ago. Mother Mutasii seemed to be guarding it."

"Yes. The goddess did descend," Eurydice responded excitedly.

"No, Eudy. The Ulumatuans simply moved the statue to the Ilegu Forest. That's all."

"No. No. She moved herself. She went to the *Ulumatua*. Don't you understand? Now, Natas goes to seek her. In the stories, it was in this forest that the First People met the *Ulumatua* and where Ghalib was killed. The champion of the god Chango fell there, Andreas."

"But if Ghalib fell there, and you say that I am, at least in part, now Ghalib, am I in danger?"

"I don't know," she whispered as the door opened. "Trust in the goddess. She will protect you. She always has."

After the man she loved was ushered from the room, Eurydice's face froze. In the stories, Ghalib had died in the Ilegu Forest, but now, there was no Ghalib. Natas was the Son of Ghalib, and all the signs suggested that Andreas was becoming Maatemnu. Ghalib would not go to the Ilegu Forest this time. On the other hand, the Onye would. Lona would lead the expedition. Her heart was icy with fear as she bent, praying fervently to the goddess to protect her husband and her child.

Chapter 19

The trucks jolted south. Several hours earlier, they left the roads, moving into the desert. The barren unevenness of the rock-strewn plain slowed them, but there was no longer any evidence of the civilization Natas had constructed to the north. It was two cycles of darkness since Andreas saw even an animal. He thought of his desperate run from Lusani three years earlier. The wilderness would have killed him had it not been for the Ulumatuan who sat quietly beside him.

"Malaia, can we find the statue?"

"No one knows the goddess' will, Andreas. I shall take them to the forest."

Andreas hesitated before asking, "Have the *Ulumatua* been defeated?"

Malaia did not answer but allowed Andreas to enter his mind sense, and there, Andreas felt the unity of the *Ulumatua*. They were like a single mind linked by the power of their mind sense. He felt the joy of that unity but also the depth of their loss. Malaia knew what had transpired in the southwest.

"But you said nothing," Andreas whispered, anguished.

Malaia shrugged, a gesture he had learned from Andreas.

"It would have changed nothing, Andreas. The *Ulumatua* fulfill their destiny."

"And what is that destiny? I know it is to serve the goddess, but is there more? I sense something is happening, but it's not clear."

Malaia smiled.

"No one knows another's path, Andreas, so it is impossible to explain or describe another's fate. Yours is more intertwined with the will of the gods than any I have known. Yours is a purpose beyond the *Ulumatua,* beyond Empheme, beyond the Onye, but only you can discover it."

Andreas pondered that as the truck moved south.

After some time, he said, "Malaia, do you remember what the locksmith said when he saw my staff?"

"To'oto'o le lagi."

"Yes. The staff of the goddess. What did he mean?"

"There are stories older than those told in the Temple of Tiamat. They speak of a time when the world was unformed, and the gods thought of how to make the First People. Each of the divine spirits proposed a shape to the god to whom the people give no name. Chango made a figure with four legs and a noble head. That is how we got the *solofanua.*"

"Solofanua?"

"The animals we once used for tilling the fields."

Andreas had seen the zebra-like creatures that now lived in the wild.

"Baal presented a dark, insubstantial thing. Because of this, man sees himself without his spirit," Malaia continued.

"His shadow?"

"Yes. And his death. The goddess presented a long, golden staff. This pleased the god to whom the people give no name, and he broke it into three parts. One he planted in the earth, and this gave rise to the trees and flowers. The second, he breathed life into, and this became the First People."

"And the third?"

"The third he gave back to her. This became the staff of the goddess. It is said that he to whom she gives the staff is the destroyer of worlds."

"Maatemnu," Andreas said quietly.

Maatemnu. The Great Slayer. Twice now, the stories and his visions had pointed him in the direction of this man whom the First People blamed for the Great Parting. Yet, the stories spoke of a time when the First People would again be one. His son, the Onye, spoke of the Reunion. What would that be? Andreas thought of the world he had left, its bickering, constant wars and ancestral hatreds, and wondered if this oneness was possible. His country, the United States, and China had been on the verge of war when he left the world above thirteen years earlier, but they were simply the most recent combatants. His explorations as an archaeologist showed, time and again, that humans had no capacity for building oneness. All civilizations fell victim to war, hatred, envy and weakness. Men had learned the hard way that to be weak was to be vulnerable. Vulnerability meant destruction, so they sought strength, and that bred fear, animosity and vengeance. Thus, the cycle continued. When he first arrived, the Land of Tiamat seemed peaceful, but it, too, fell prey to conflict. Now, his son, the only person, besides his wife Eurydice, who gave meaning to his life, was the marauding spirit tearing the land apart. Or was he?

From one perspective, he's unifying the land. The splits have always been there.

Would the Reunion be yet another war? Lona could not imagine the size of the world above, its power and its capacity for violence. He was also unaware of the cultural conflict inherent in what he intended. This would be seen as a black invasion. Lona thought in mythic terms, seeing the world above as some approximate parallel of the one he ruled, but despite the widespread destruction caused by floods and famine, the population above was probably still close to five billion. Even with the addition of the African Americans, the Land of Tiamat contained no more than two hundred million people.

Andreas observed Malaia's serenity and wondered where such faith came from. He himself had deserted his Catholicism years ago, the horrors and beauties of his archaeological discoveries showing him so much about man's desperate search for meaning. Gods were fashioned in such abundance that eventually he saw them as interchangeable, irrational and, therefore, disputable. His god had died in his heart, but in this strange land, religion still lived in the hearts of the people. Andreas reached out, gently touching Malaia's mind sense, feeling the man's peace and comfort. Malaia turned to him and smiled. Andreas' mind sense was now stronger than Malaia's, and his visions followed paths that were inaccessible to the other man. Yet, Malaia possessed something he had not quite found—contentment.

"*It comes in the act of submission, Andreas.*"

"*Submission to whom, Malaia?*"

"*Now, only to yourself. I accept all that you are, Tama, but your mind sense has a dark spot in it. You must submit to that before you find the peace you seek, Maatemnu. Forgive yourself.*"

Andreas was perplexed. It was very unusual for Malaia to give unsolicited advice.

"*Forgive myself for what?*"

"*So many things, Andreas. Submit to Marcus.*"

"*To Marcus? Why do I need to submit to him? And what does submission mean?*"

"*The dying god within you seeks life. Let him live.*"

Andreas was instantly aware that whoever had spoken through Malaia was gone.

"Did you hear?" he asked.

"Yes. It was a distant voice."

"Was it the goddess?"

"Yes."

Andreas was quiet for a moment and then asked, "Who is the dying god?"

"I do not know, Andreas, but he is your fate."

"When I first awoke with the staff in my hand, did you know it was the goddess' staff?"

"Yes."

The truck stopped, and they heard soldiers jumping down, talking nervously and moving around. The door opened, and light poured in. Lona and Marcus stood outside.

"There," Lona said, pointing. "The Ilegu Forest."

Andreas stared at the dark line on the horizon. Above the tree line, a thundercloud pulsed. The sky appeared menacing.

"We will camp here tonight. Tomorrow, we reach the forest," Lona said.

Andreas observed the soldiers preparing for the night. They were setting up two separate perimeters. Hearing the accents, he realized that the outer perimeter had only African Americans.

That makes sense. They have no fear of the Ilegu Forest. It is not part of their mythology.

The people of the Land of Tiamat, on the other hand, had lived with fear of the forest for millennia. There, Ghalib was slain in the first meeting with the *Ulumatua.* Several men in the inner perimeter put down their short-barrelled guns and took up what looked like flame-throwers. A flat, black canister was strapped to each soldier's back, and on one side, a small generator hummed. On the other side, a flexible tube with a nozzle was attached. Andreas turned to Marcus who was overseeing the preparations.

"What is that?"

Marcus smiled.

"A gift from the god Chango."

Chapter 20

The night passed in uneasy stillness. Even Malaia could not sleep, and Andreas, during the short period of darkness, went outside the tent to look at the sky. As usual, no stars could be seen, but the luminescence of the day had not completely disappeared. The underbelly of the clouds was a faded burgundy, and Andreas surprised himself by uttering a prayer. He stopped when he heard a chuckle. Turning, he saw Lona watching him.

"To what do you pray, Tama? Is it to the goddess? Or maybe to some god you brought to the Land of Ghalib?"

The voice was mocking, and Andreas felt the conflicting urges of his heart.

"Truth is, Onye, I'm not sure."

The young man came out of the gloom. He carried Andreas' staff.

Staring into the night, voice pensive, he said, "They say the staff of the goddess is given to the destroyer of worlds, Tama. Is that you, I wonder. And whose world, do you think?"

Gone was Lona's aggressiveness from earlier, and Andreas felt drawn to him.

You are my son.

His heart ached, but in his mind was Branniff's voice. "Do not think to claim him as your son. It could mean your death." Still, he had claimed him, and in so doing destroyed the security of the Land of Tiamat. But could death be any worse than the denial of his father-hood? Andreas sighed.

"Who are you, Tama? My enemy? I could have killed you before. Yet, something stayed my hand. Is there a purpose to your life that I do not understand? Men whisper that you are Maatemnu, the Great Slayer, but you seem harmless, lost almost."

Lona spun the staff around his open hand. It became a blur, only the whirring sound of displaced air indicating its deadly speed.

"Perfectly balanced, Tama. I do not know if it is *To'oto' o le lagi*, but it is quite a weapon. Where did you get it?"

The voice was too casual, and Andreas knew this was why Lona had followed him into the darkness.

Instead of answering, he asked, "When does the Son of Ghalib come again?"

Natas had left for the world above before their departure.

"Who knows? Ghalib delays the time of the Reunion. Maybe the war leader has grown too fond of the world above."

"Maybe Natas has a better grasp of the strength of the world above than you do, Lo ... Onye."

The young man snorted.

"No strength can stand before my armies, Tama. You should have seen them in the land of the *Ulumatua*. Even the highly respected military strength of the Ulumatuans faded away before them. And those who, like you, are *i tala atu*, are fearless. Once this campaign is over, they will need a task. Marcus is hungry for vengeance." He paused and then, chuckling, said, "Here. Take your staff. I doubt it will be of much use against us."

Andreas took the staff. It nestled familiarly in his palm. The young man turned away.

Just before the darkness absorbed him, he said, "Last time we fought, you surprised me, Tama. I will not be surprised again."

Then, he was gone. Andreas stared into the dusk, heart heavy. Lona was lost to him again. For a brief moment, when Endele and the men from the mountains helped him rescue his son from Natas' prison, there had been a connection. The thought of Endele brought a deeper weight to his mind, and he grimaced, his fingers folding into a fist. Before him, Natas' grinning face mocked him, and he lashed out. His fist connected with only the insubstantial air.

Chapter 21

*S*idoti took the Greenbelt exit off Route 95 South, slowing the car to a crawl. The cold and the heavy snow had practically shut down the eastern half of the United States for days, and several accidents proved fatal. He was tense, a result of the seven-hour drive from Princeton.

"And I still didn't get what I wanted," he said angrily.

He turned on to Route 193, going south to the Goddard Space Flight Center. The trip to New Jersey was to meet with a Dr. Faison at the Advanced Physics Lab after finally getting permission to investigate the two heat signatures in Antarctica. Dr. Faison refused to discuss anything on the phone. Sidoti, nervous and tired, still knew little more than he did before the long drive north. The scientist had grilled him for some time about the location of the heat signatures, while Sidoti patiently explained that all he needed was an explanation as to a possible energy source. The man hedged, and it was only when Sidoti threatened to have the lab's funding, most of which was provided by the Federal government, held up that he got some reluctant cooperation.

Dr. Faison had asked a very interesting question. He wanted to know if the heat signature had been detected in space. Sidoti did not confirm that, and the scientist indicated that their calculations suggested something he referred to as dark energy. The little that was known about it largely resided in the oversized brain of one Dr. Karl Metzer who was at the Goddard Space Flight Center, twenty minutes from where Sidoti worked.

"A totally wasted drive."

He turned into Goddard. It took another twenty minutes to get to Dr. Metzer.

"Hi, Sidoti. You still spying on us?"

"Hello, Karl. How are you?"

"Well, I'm out of the asylum. Although sometimes I think the sane people are in there. There sure are a lot of nuts around here."

Sidoti smiled, shaking the outstretched hand. Metzer, clinically insane, was frequently moved from the lab that he ran like a third world dictator to a very special asylum in West Virginia. Occasionally, there were questions raised about trusting this mentally unstable man with the world's most advanced astroparticle physics lab, but as Metzer seemed to have an almost divine understanding of nature and an uncanny ability to extract her secrets, he was given pretty much anything he asked for. It was said that outside of the physicists who were the mainstay of Branniff Corporation's business success, Karl Metzer was the best in the world. He and Sidoti had attended MIT at the same time.

"Well, it looks like they're keeping you busy. Have enough enemies to justify your budget yet?"

"They're your enemies, too, Karl."

Metzer made a braying sound.

"Not my enemies, old pal. All of mine are hiding somewhere between neutrons. Man, at the macroscopic level, is amazingly boring. Now, his subatomic nature ... there's a mystery."

"If a bomb drops or a chemical or biological agent is let loose around here, you go along with the rest of us, old buddy."

"Won't happen. Every scientist and politician in the world know where I am. They won't kill me. I'm too valuable alive." He cackled, running his hand through untidy hair as he asked, "Now, why the hell did you go to see Faison about your heat signature? He couldn't find his ass if you drew him a map."

"He heads up the Advanced Physics Lab, Karl."

"My point exactly. Anyway, he sent me the data. We're still running calculations, but I have some suspicions. Did you pick this up from space?"

"That's what Faison asked. Why would you say that?"

"That answer pretty much means you didn't. Then, my boy, if I'm right, we're royally screwed. You know anything about dark matter or dark energy?"

"Only what's in popular science books. I know it's considered the original energy in the universe or something like that."

"What was it you studied again? Math, wasn't it?"

"Actuarial science, actually."

"God! That's worse than admitting you're an idiot. Come with me."

He walked briskly down a long corridor at the end of which was a white door with a security lock.

"The holy of holies," Metzer declared. "This is more secret than all the crap you guys have over there at NSA."

It was a large room. A number of scientists were busy performing various tasks. Everywhere, there were computers, and data were being produced constantly. There was no frenzy to the room, but Sidoti sensed urgency.

"This seems pretty calm for a place you're running."

"Oh, I yell and scream from time to time to let them know I'm still crazy. Follow me," he said airily.

The lab angled away to the left, and Metzer went in that direction. He used his key to enter a room and flicked the lights on. The first thing Sidoti noticed were the hand-drawn charts strewn around the room. One, in particular, on an easel caught his attention. A drawing of a piece of chalk had been chopped into a large number of slices. Under it was a note: THE SOLUTION TO UNWANTED PREGNANCY.

Sidoti stopped to look at it, and Metzer said, "Zeno's paradox."

"What's that?"

"Christ! Didn't they teach you anything in the math department?"

"Actuarial science," Sidoti said patiently.

He knew Metzer would not hear him.

"Zeno's paradox deals with the ultra small nature of space and time. It essentially says that if a moving body is in a specific location at every instant, then there is no instant when it is in transition from one point to another. Therefore, motion is impossible."

"But we see motion all the time," Sidoti responded.

"So, they did teach you something in the math department after all. Think about it differently. If you have to move from point A to point B, you've got to make it to the midpoint of the trip first. Once you've gotten that far, then you have to reach the next mid-point. This is true infinitely. You've always got to go half the remaining distance, so you never get to point B. And if you can never come—"

"You can never get anybody pregnant. I got it," Sidoti said, shaking his head.

Metzer, hating to appear obvious, snorted. Charging off to the other side of the room, he entered a smaller office and sat in front of a computer.

"Very interesting stuff you've got here, me boy."

Four images came up on the screen. The heat signature was depicted in the form that Sidoti recognized in one quadrant of the screen; two of the other quadrants were composed of bar graphs, and the fourth depicted a god-like figure waving a magic wand. The face hinted at insanity.

"More of your humor?" Sidoti asked.

"Let me tell you. He'd have to be nuts to do some of the things we find out when we look behind the universe's surface. Now, let's talk about your little photographs."

He hit the spacebar, and a spectacular explosion came up on the screen. It was bright white in the middle, with bits of matter streaking away from the center at what looked to be incredible speeds.

"The Big Bang," Sidoti said and was immediately sorry when Metzer looked at him as if a prize chimp had spoken.

"Not quite, but a good guess. It is the representation of a supernova observed in 1054 C.E."

He hit the spacebar again.

"I assume you picked these two heat signatures up on Earth. Though you have taken out the latitudinal and longitudinal data, I'm assuming somewhere in the southern hemisphere. Antarctica, maybe? Also, since you're coming to me, I assume you guys had nothing to do with it. Right?"

Sidoti hesitated for a moment but knew Metzer would refuse to help him if he started playing games.

"Pretty much."

"Pretty much is not good enough. Am I right?"

Sidoti nodded.

"Then, if this is not naturally occurring, and I'm pretty sure it's not, somebody's fiddling with the universe's balls, old buddy."

"Meaning?"

"We've been chasing dark energy for a long time. It's the fundamental stuff of the universe. Think about it. Whatever caused the original show-stopper, the Big Bang, had a shitload of energy. Most of it we can't account for today. Energy, as even a mathematician knows, is indestructible. So where is it, old buddy?"

He stopped, looking at Sidoti who, feeling like an idiot, said, "Lost in space?"

"Actually, that's not bad. Except it may not be 'in space' but space itself."

"You lost me."

"Of course, I have. Basically, what I'm saying is that space is not the emptiness between the pretty stuff like planets and stars but is itself the important stuff."

He hit the backspace button, and the four quadrants came up again. Metzer touched the god figure.

"His little frigging joke. Give us all the pretty stuff to look at and marvel, and he hides the really good stuff right under our noses. No wonder the bastard calls us children. We fell for it, too."

Sidoti was having a hard time keeping up. Also, he was uncomfortable with the casual references to God.

"Karl, are you saying that most of the energy in the universe is actually in the space between the stars?"

"Yup. One giant fart. You see the person bending over but not even a glimpse of the gas flying away at warp speed."

"But what's that got to do with the heat signatures?"

"Patience, dear boy. Patience. Now, most of that energy out there we can't find. Hence, 'dark' energy. We know it's there, though. Faison and I fundamentally disagree on its propagation. That idiot thinks that baryons couldn't be the constituent material of dark matter. He's proposing a weakly interacting massive particle which is non-baryonic —"

"Slow down, Karl. I don't know what the hell you're talking about."

"Well, of course you don't, chimp. I left math behind several sentences ago. Anyway, to finish my thought, I think that ultra-high-energy protons, which are baryons, could be the constituents of dark matter. You don't need to understand that, but it's important."

Metzer pulled open a drawer, took out a newspaper clipping and handed it to Sidoti. The headline was, "New Class of Gamma Ray Objects Discovered in the Milky Way." Sidoti looked a question at Metzer who smiled.

"Twenty years ago, we released the information that half the previously unidentified gamma-ray sources in the Milky Way—that's our own galaxy—were a new class of mysterious objects. Even more interesting was that, unlike normal gamma rays which shine in bursts, these were continuously shining."

"This happened twenty years ago, you say?"

"I said it was released then. Actually, we knew about it before that, but we didn't release the information to the government for a while."

Sidoti frowned.

"It says here that NASA discovered the new gamma rays."

Metzer chuckled.

"No. We gave the information to NASA a couple of years after we found the new gammas."

"Who were you working for then?" Sidoti asked, a suspicion forming in his mind.

"The Laser-Technics Center."

"That belongs to the university, right?"

"Now it does. Then, it was solely funded by Branniff Corporation. It was great working for them. Never a shortage of anything."

Branniff. Again Branniff. Sidoti was not hearing anymore. He would check but felt certain that, around that same time, Branniff Corporation had paid untold billions to lease Antarctica for ninety-nine years. The ozone layer deteriorated rapidly after that, resulting in unpredictable warming, freezes, tornadoes and flooding. The current political and military crisis around the globe was directly attributable to that breakdown in the ozone layer.

"Hey, chimp. Am I wasting all this brilliance on you, or is that vacuous look on your face actually indicative of thought?"

Sidoti looked up sheepishly.

"Sorry, Karl. I got distracted by something you said."

"Of course, you did. Which particular thing that you didn't understand shall I elucidate? Of course, I'm assuming you understood something."

"No. No. This dark energy. Did you find some in the heat signature?"

"They really are complete nitwits over in the math department, aren't they? I said it was dark matter. Completely invisible, old buddy."

"Oh. So, it's not a threat?"

Metzer grunted.

"Of course, it's a threat. Anything we don't understand is a threat, but that's why you have me. To protect you. As I was saying when you got that autistic look on your face, this is big. Pay attention now. I won't repeat for the dunces. We can't see the dark energy, but we can see the halo around it. The halo of our galaxy contains proton energies with a range between 10^{15} and 10^{17} electron volts, which are called EVs."

"Electron volts?"

"Never mind what they are. Concentrate on the magnitudes, old buddy. What's important is that immediately after the Big Bang, we estimate these energies to have been at about 10^{25} electron volts. Obviously, the decline in energy over the last 13.8 billion years has been pretty dramatic."

Sidoti nodded uncertainly.

"Anyway, old buddy, while we can't see the dark matter or energy, we have a proxy of it through the halo. And before you ask, it's not the shiny saucer behind the Christ child's head. It's pretty complicated stuff, involving the extra-galactic magnetic field and gravitational attraction."

"Karl, I'm getting a headache. Is there a point to all this?"

"Now you know what it's like for a superior mind, such as mine, to communicate with mere mortals like you. Anyway, yes. There is a point. Our first-run calculations suggest proton energies in the 10^{34} EV range."

"But you said—"

"I know what I said. The Big Bang generated energies in the 10^{25} EV range. It looks like whatever you've got down there in Antarctica potentially has energy in excess of that range."

Sidoti let his breath out slowly, but Metzer was continuing.

"But here's the good part. The two signatures are different. The earlier one is of nowhere near the magnitude of the second. Ipso facto, some little genius has figured out how to enhance the electron volts. Boy, would I love to have a drink with him."

Sidoti's throat was dry.

Metzer, pretending to be upset, asked, "No applause for my brilliant deductive work? Not even a small genuflection?"

When Sidoti did not answer, Metzer, concern in his voice, said, "Hey, man, you awright?"

"Yes. Yes."

Sidoti thought for a while.

"Karl, could this electron whatever be weaponized?"

"Weaponized! Jesus. You obviously didn't attend any English classes either. Of course, it can be weaponized. It is energy, so theoretically, it can be converted into matter and back to energy again."

"Theoretically?"

"Yes. Theoretically. Of course, we need to run some more calculations, but what we have is suggestive."

"Of what?"

"If our readings are correct, then we're way past theory. If somebody has found a way to create those magnitudes in the EV's, then they have the engineering capacity to create a weapon."

"Shit! The goddamn idiots," Sidoti growled.

"That pretty much describes all your friends, old buddy."

"How important is what you're doing here, Karl?"

"Yesterday, it was the most important exploration of the physical universe in the world. Now, if I'm right, it's kindergarten. You got to let me in on this. We could be looking at the biggest breakthrough in physics since Saint Albert had his orgasm about relativity. In fact, there are implications here that could make Einstein either look like a jackass or confirm his godliness. You got to give me piece of this."

"You got it," Sidoti said quickly. "How soon can you quit here?"

"I sent my resignation four hours ago. By the way, why did you take so long to get back from Princeton? You got lucky on the way down?"

"Karl," Sidoti said tiredly, "when was the last time you were outside this lab?"

"Well, let's see. I came out of the asylum on January twentieth. What's the date?"

"March seventh."

"Okay. Six weeks."

"You have been in here for six weeks?"

"Same inside as outside. What the hell has that got to do with anything?"

"There have been blizzards for the last few weeks. The east coast has practically been shut down."

"No shit," Metzer replied with a boyish grin.

Chapter 22

*L*iu observed the black woman closely, seeking some evidence of what he had heard about black people in the United States. She did not look like "a displaced orphan," as General Xu had said. She looked formidable. It was not, however, the woman who created the flutter of excitement in Liu's mind. The big man standing in the shadows seemed to draw in the light so that he was never clearly seen. Liu glanced at the partially hidden figure and felt a slight chill.

"So, Secretary Ernsky, is it possible?"

The woman smiled at the title.

"Hardly a secretary anymore. More of a 'displaced orphan', don't you think?"

Liu's face betrayed nothing, but his mind was racing. How in Shang Di's name could she know about a comment made in the general's bunker thousands of miles away? The African Americans must have an ear in their meetings. Involuntarily, his eyes slipped to the dark, silent figure.

"Your people are massing in southeastern Canada. My government assumes that you are readying for Africa. We are willing to place our fleet at your disposal." He stopped and then added, "For transportation and protection."

"Transportation and protection. That's pretty bold, Mr. Liu, since it puts your fleet in direct conflict with the United States navy."

Liu shrugged.

"An inevitability, Ms. Ernsky. The aggression of the west—"

Anne Ernsky chuckled.

"No need for ideology, Mr. Liu. I represent no interest here except my people, and they don't think of themselves as either the west or the east."

"Forgive me. My instincts lead me where I ought not to go. In any case, it seems we have a common interest."

"Indeed? And what is that?"

"We both need space, and Africa calls to us both."

"Perhaps, but I cannot dispose of Africa."

"We both bring value to that noble continent, Ms. Ernsky."

"And what value do we bring? We have needs, and Africa has space. My people have been invited. That's all. I cannot grant rights to Africa."

Liu did not immediately reply. He wished that the figure in the corner would say something.

To fill the silence, he said, "Can I pour you some water?"

"Yes, please."

He went to the small bar. The villa was on the outskirts of Bumba, a city that was now a hotbed of intrigue and danger since Branniff Corporation made it the center of its operations. Africa was again the prize, but unlike a century and a half earlier, because of Branniff, the continent was no longer weak. Though the corporation had no army, just the threat of Branniff's withdrawal of support held everyone hostage.

That, however, was changing. The last three years had seen the United States, the European Union and China gradually rebuilding their capacity for independent action. These nations had launched new satellites, so their information was no longer being filtered exclusively through Branniff's gargantuan data centers. China and the United States were again becoming self-sufficient in arms production, and that made it all the more important to get this relocation business settled.

Anne Ernsky inspected the face of the Chinese official. If the Chinese sent a fleet of ships to eastern Canada, it would change the nature of the war. The United States would not stand for it, and, in the world's eyes, China would be the aggressor. So far, neither country had won the world's sympathy. People recognized the war for what it was, a conflict not so much of ideas—there was little difference in what they believed—but as a contest over possessions and power. Anne Ernsky, therefore, wondered about China's intent.

"Mr. Liu, your offer is very kind, but I will have to discuss it with my council. If the answer were to be yes, when could you provide the ships?"

"We are prepared to act on your timetable."

"That's very generous. And cost?"

"We will, of course, discuss this later, but in lieu of money, certain arrangements could be made."

"Certain arrangements?"

"Yes. You see, we are hoping you will intercede with Branniff. Some access to the continent for our people would be appreciated."

Anne Ernsky thought for a while. Clearly, Liu did not know who the dark figure in the corner was. She knew that Branniff was willing to allow thirty million Chinese access to the continent. That would not solve China's problem, but every little bit helped.

More of Branniff's wheels within wheels.

"Again, you have given me a proposal I will have to discuss with others."

"Yes, of course. Time, however, is of the essence."

"Is it? Why?"

"This war cannot go on as it has. The pressure is building for more dry land. It is only a matter of time before the war escalates again. We could relieve some of that pressure by having access to Africa."

This much she knew to be true. The Chinese push to the west was driven by the change in climate which had resulted in sea levels rising, depriving them of much-needed land.

The pressure on the government must be enormous.

"We understand China's dilemma, but much of the world faces the same problem. Access for China places Africa on the path to war, Mr. Liu, and the continent has been free of major conflict since this crisis began. That cannot be sacrificed or compromised."

Lately, Anne Ernsky found herself meeting with the continent's leadership. Because of her former role as secretary of state of the United States and her current role as leader of the *expulsees*, African leaders accorded her a great deal of respect. It was not simply because something about the exile's condition appealed to them. Nor was it their identification with her cause that gave her the authority she was now using. It was because she was selected by Branniff. Africans understood that the umbrella of protection the corporation provided was all that stood between them and wave after wave of invasion. China's current offer was simply the most diplomatic, but sooner or later, that politeness would end. She glanced at the corner of the room, but the shadowy figure was gone. Liu's eyes followed hers.

"It looks as if our silent host has left us. Maybe we overstayed our welcome."

Anne Ernsky nodded and stood, extending her hand.

"We will talk soon, Mr. Liu."

He bowed, and she left.

Chapter 23

General Xu put the phone down, his face thoughtful. Liu's call was not a surprise. He expected the ex-secretary of state to be cautious. Old Peng, as Branniff had first introduced himself many years before, having suggested he talk with Anne Ernsky, had provided safe conduct for Liu.

Thanks to Shang Di, I was able to see the possibilities and to shape them.

His hand caressed the incense sticks and the crab's carapace that constituted part of his worship. China was powerful now only because he had forced the issue and pushed them west. Thirteen years of sweat, death and deprivation, but they were now on the threshold of victory. The alliances were growing. Greater Russia had declared its neutrality but was secretly supportive. India, its own population adrift and restless, agreed, in principle, to the right of relocation. The central Asian republics were largely neutralized through conquest or intimidation, and now Iran was weighing its options. He walked briskly to the outer office and spoke to his new adjutant. In minutes, the generals who formed his inner circle were assembled. He offered tea.

"Lui has called to say that Secretary Ernsky wants time to think of her answer."

General Li's face wore a perplexed frown.

"Why don't we just go down the east coast of Africa and take our people there? Why this elaborate subterfuge?"

Xu had discussed his strategy with no one, and when he responded, his voice was cool.

"What would you say is our greatest area of vulnerability, Li?"

"When we move into south-central Asia."

Xu waited, but no one else said anything.

"Gentlemen, the moment we move south will be a time of great danger it is true, but it is not our greatest vulnerability."

He walked to a large map and slammed his open palm against the Indian Ocean.

"That, gentlemen, is our greatest vulnerability. Those seven carrier groups blocking the Strait of Malacca are forcing us to take this walking route to Africa. We cannot transport our citizens by ship even if the Africans give us permission. And as long as we move by this land route, we are a threat to every nation—every nuclear nation—in our way."

"General, how do we help ourselves by transporting the American Blacks? Our fleets will still have to get past the Americans," Li said.

"Shang Di once again comes to our aid. Branniff will provide a distraction."

"A distraction, sir? Are they openly going to support us?"

"Hardly. Branniff is more inscrutable than our ancestors. No. They are playing a tune to which we must dance."

"Then what kind of distraction are we talking about, sir?"

"That is not clear, Yang, but it will draw at least half the American fleet away. Once the Americans have split their forces, we move south out of the China Sea. They will have three or four carrier groups left in the Indian Ocean. No match for our fleet."

Li looked uncertain.

"Well, out with it, Li."

"Sir, no disrespect intended, but are we not putting a lot of faith in Branniff's promise?"

"It is a risk, but the reward is worth it. If we destroy half of the American fleet in the east, we will win this war."

"Why does Branniff do this? They are an American corporation. Or they were at one point."

"All men pursue their own interests. The value of judgment is seeing when yours intersects with another's and to make use of that coincidence. Branniff pursues its self-interest and we ours. So far, the partnership has been mutually beneficial."

"It makes me nervous to have an ally this powerful whose purposes we don't know," Li said.

Xu nodded, thinking of when he had moved out of western China and was poised to thrust into central Asia. Tajikistan looked strong, with American bases all around, but the nation went underground the moment Xu attacked. The Americans found themselves isolated in a sea of Tajik resentment. Branniff had also promised that "betrayal," sending the Iranian with the fevered eyes to negotiate with the Tajiks. That they now controlled central Asia was largely due to that act of betrayal orchestrated by Branniff.

Now, Branniff has arranged for thirty million of our people to relo-cate to Africa. It is not enough, but we have a toehold.

The others did not know that, so they were suspicious of the giant corporation. Not that he was not, but Branniff had delivered on every-thing he promised. If Branniff said there would be a distraction that would pull part of the American fleet away, then he was willing to trust that. He was also thinking of Liu's warning that Branniff probably listened to their discussions.

"I'm leaving for Beijing in the morning. I will return in three days. Continue the preparations for us to move."

They left, and he was soon in bed. Xu fell asleep almost immediately.

Chapter 24

*I*t was an unusual morning, dawning dark, the clouds' undersides sultry and threatening.

"*Malamalama* must be upset," Andreas said.

Malaia, too, awoke with a darkness around him. Andreas was trying to lighten the Ulumatuan's mood, but Malaia was lost in his own world. Outside, the preparations for the final thrust to the Ilegu Forest were ongoing. Andreas understood Malaia's mood. His people were at the end of that journey. Andreas, too, felt the pressure, but he could not give in to it. Lona intended to destroy not just the statue of the goddess around which the Ulumatuans rallied but the *Ulumatua* themselves. Malaia sensed this, and it was clear that he was prepared to die in his people's defense.

"It is not yet time, Malaia."

The man's eyes searched Andreas' face with a question he did not dare ask.

"Yes," Andreas said softly. "It is she who speaks."

Malaia nodded, and Andreas thought how comfortable he now was with the voices inside him. The dying god still struggled to fill him, but the goddess inhabited him fully, and he wondered what would be the result of allowing the dying god to possess him as well. Andreas sensed enormous power as well as great pain, for the god was always dying. He had bequeathed his pain to Andreas who was, as yet, still shielded from it.

The power and the pain are one. Forgive yourself, a voice inside him said.

The truck moved off. Andreas smiled, and Malaia looked at him inquiringly. It was good to have Malaia with him. Andreas extended his mind sense, searching the rock-strewn desert. He entered the forest, sensing the life that teemed there—animals that charged and played between the trees, small rivulets that watered plants, and the sibilance of wind whispering among leaves. In the forest, too, were shadows, essences that he felt, but not the bodies he expected.

"They're gone," Andreas said to Malaia, who nodded.

"Where?"

"Within themselves. Into the heart of the goddess. To the Land of Malaia where they are changed to white crocodiles. The stories say many things, Andreas."

Andreas' mind sense reached into the forest again and found something else. Immediately, he understood Malaia's dark mood. The *Ulumatua* were not all gone. A guardian force remained to protect the statue of the goddess. Andreas sighed. They would not stand a chance against the Onye's forces. Outside were two hundred men, heavily armed and possessing those frightening new weapons that had devastated Eurydice's armies early in the war.

One of the trucks carried no soldiers, and cautiously, he tested the inside, finding a large container that hummed. Investigating further, he discovered that it was a converter. But what was it converting? There seemed to be no energy source on which it drew, but he sensed a writhing, insubstantial darkness there.

"Malaia, do you know what's in the truck without soldiers?"

"No. I have felt it, but it is not of the First People."

"How do you know that?"

Malaia smiled.

"Do they not say that the *Ulumatua* carry the past within them? We feel all that the First People are and have been."

Andreas had at first thought the *Ulumatua* to be the historians of the race, but they did not simply remember or record the past. They felt it. It was literally inside them.

"And this is not of the First People?" Andreas asked uneasily.

"It is not."

Suddenly, Andreas was afraid. He was about to reach out again when the truck stopped.

"You are a strong ally to meet on the path of the gods, Andreas. May your way be without obstacles."

The voice was emotionless, but Malaia was saying goodbye. A deep sorrow weighed on Andreas' soul, and he touched the black man on his shoulder, aware of the difference in the texture of their spirits. The door opened, and Marcus ordered them out.

The Ulumatuans were in battle formation. Behind them, the statue of the goddess stood high in the sky. Though made of white marble, the sculpture was so delicate it seemed a living thing. Andreas was sad, knowing that those delicate folds of the goddess' gown would soon be no more.

Lona ordered a soldier to take the mysterious truck to the head of the column. Next to it, his troops arranged themselves in two skirmish lines. Alert soldiers with the odd-looking canisters that reminded Andreas of flame-throwers were close by. The *Ulumatua* stood in that ghostly silence Andreas had first experienced in Tiastan. They wore no armor, seemed to carry no weapon and did not appear particularly aggressive. Yet the soldiers were nervous. Lona had spoken of the *Ulumatua's* "highly respected military strength", but Andreas could see nothing military about them. Malaia stepped forward.

"Where do you go, Ulumatuan?" Lona asked.

"I will speak to them, Onye. Maybe they will give the statue to you."

Andreas felt disappointment. Malaia could not be that naïve. This was only partly about the statue. The Ulumatuans, too, must be destroyed if the Onye's will was to be dominant in this newly-named Land of Ghalib.

He was, therefore, surprised when Lona said, "Indeed, it is fitting that you should speak with them, Ulumatuan. Go then."

Malaia walked away without a backward glance.

"Goodbye, old friend. May the goddess clear your path," Andreas whispered.

The small man strode to the other side and slid into the center of the line. As if this was a signal, Lona's line stepped forward, the soldiers who carried the canisters in front. The line stopped. The men with the canisters knelt. Tubes snaked from the canisters back to the truck. Lona moved to the center of the line, and for a moment it appeared as if Malaia and Lona had met halfway between the groups and were staring at each other. Andreas gripped his staff tightly.

Lona's arm went abruptly up and down. Men with canisters aimed nozzles. The air contracted as if someone had sucked its constituent components out. The hum rose in pitch. Above, clouds roiled, appearing illuminated. It felt as if a presence was there. As the clouds turned darker, the weight of the air itself increased. Then, the nozzles blazed. Something flashed across the distance between the soldiers and the *Ulumatua*. Several of the Ulumatuans crumpled. A sharp pain went through every inch of Andreas' body. He screamed, falling to his knees. His consciousness slipping away, he raised his head with some difficulty. Lona was smiling. Andreas fought the pain, capturing it even as he felt the second eruption of energy.

Furious, he stood, the staff balanced in his hand. He leapt, landing among the soldiers with the canisters. They turned only to see the fury of his face and the whirling, deadly staff that landed on one soldier's shoulder. There was a cracking sound, and the soldier fell, his body jerking spasmodically. The staff connected with body after body, but the soldiers were disciplined. Andreas was losing. He was disabling them, but they were killing the Ulumatuans more quickly. Men fell before the staff, and something must have protected him because none of their shots touched him. Then, Lona was before him, and he hesitated. In that instant, the staff was knocked aside, and Lona thrust viciously forward with his right foot. Andreas felt the contact but not the expected pain, and he spun away, aware that he fought his son. The angry young man came again, but Andreas parried his thrust easily, turning three revolutions but not returning Lona's kicks. The remaining soldiers with canisters continued to fire into the *Ulumatua*, who were falling before the statue of the goddess.

Lona attacked again, but it was as if the young man had slowed. The kick took a long time to reach Andreas, and he wondered if Lona was hurt. Then, he realized that not Lona's, but his, speed had changed. Andreas jumped, matching Lona's leap and, with his left foot, knocked aside the kick aimed at his head. He swiveled, flicking his hard heel against the neck of his opponent. The young man fell, and Andreas, briefly checking to see that the boy was not hurt, jumped through the air. Again, the deadly staff flashed, and soldiers fell.

A soldier turned the nozzle of his canister on Andreas, who felt that peculiar sucking out of the air and leapt high over the soldier's head. The soldier's blast struck the converter truck, and it exploded. Turmoil was in the air when Andreas landed, and what he saw was, for a moment, incomprehensible. The air turned dark. It seemed to be rushing outwards, crushing soldiers as it expanded. Then, he understood. *He was seeing the explosion!* Soldiers were falling before the shockwave. Lona was lying on the ground, not moving. Marcus was standing, horror on his face, not yet touched by the expanding shockwave. In the opposite direction, high in the air, was the statue of the goddess.

Without thought, Andreas reached out to the dark shockwave. Instantly, the section rushing toward Marcus stopped writhing, turning as if finding a new victim. It flew at Andreas, and something old, powerful and lethal entered him. The dark thing formed a column up to clouds that boiled as if the elements themselves had gone mad. As he watched, something like lightning snaked down, following the column back to the earth where the converter truck had been. The energy penetrated Andreas' body, and he fell to his knees, consciousness ripped. In an instant, it was gone.

He stood unsteadily. Around him was carnage. The converter truck was completely destroyed, a hole in the ground having replaced it. The dead were everywhere. Andreas rushed to the pale body of his son.

"Lonaaaa!" he screamed.

The boy lay still, not breathing. When Andreas tried to lift him, he saw that one side of Lona's body was gone. Lona, his son, was dead. There was a shuffling behind him, and he turned. The remaining soldiers' weapons were trained on him. He easily distinguished those of Ghalib's Land from the African Americans because where the former were hostile, the latter displayed only uncertainty. Ignoring them, Andreas turned to where several Ulumatuans lay in the wrenching postures of death. At first, he thought the statue had survived, but even as he watched, cracks in the marble were spreading. Half of the face fell. Slowly, in uneven pieces, the great sculpture broke and tumbled down.

For a long time, he stared at the pile of rubble. Then, he walked slowly over to the Ulumatuans. He found Malaia, his body crushed by the shockwave. Andreas lifted him easily, carrying his erstwhile companion and guide into the Ilegu Forest. There, at the edge of the dark woods, he buried his friend. Mother Mutasii was not among the bodies of the *Ulumatua*.

Later, he returned to the battlefield. Marcus had taken command. Several of the bodies were arranged in a pile and others in a long row. The African Americans intended to bury their dead. Andreas stood outside the circle of grief as the remaining soldiers of Ghalib's Land lit the pyre.

"Marcus, do the same for the *Ulumatua*," he said.

Glancing at the pile of bodies, Marcus seemed on the verge of argument, but he nodded. Soon, two fires blazed, and dark smoke, buoyed by the soldiers' chants, joined at the underbelly of the clouds. Andreas went to his son. He took a long time to bury him. Afterwards, he stood, a solitary figure in a land of sorrow, mourning his loss. He felt empty, and the pain in his body could not mask the weight in his soul. He thought of the young boy from the temple, lithe as a cougar, fast as a striking snake and with a beauty that should have graced many more seasons. He did not remember Lona's arrogance or the violence of his combat. He saw only his son.

"Why?" he screamed into the glare of the Tiamatian day.

Silence answered his cry. His fists were clenched, for, cruelly and perversely, the day was now bright. After a while, he turned. The soldiers cautiously watched him. When he took a step toward them, several stumbled backwards. He stopped, surprised.

A soldier whispered, "Maatemnu, the Great Slayer."

Chapter 25

*N*atas came awake, and for a second, his eyes gleamed ferally in the darkness of the bedroom. Then, he stood, body still, every sense alert.

"The young fool!" he said, face distorted with rage. "Did you feel it?"

The other figure in the room rose from the bed and stood watching. She did not answer.

"Did you feel it, Teme?"

"Yes."

Teme's voice was emotionless. She picked up a flowered gown embroidered with graceful dragons and covered her body.

"What was it, priestess?"

Teme turned away, going to the other side of the room. When she spoke, there was a harshness to her voice that did not go with the placidity of her face.

"Maybe your end."

Natas, eyes narrowed, snarled. His face shifted, the planes changing until he was no longer handsome. Something looked out that seemed hungry and on the verge of feeding. The young woman did not flinch but faced him, her eyes calm. Natas, face normal again, laughed.

"Do you wish for my end, Teme?"

"It is not my wish but what the goddess wills."

"Your goddess is defeated."

"Then what did you feel, son of the mountain fire?"

Natas turned, staring at the serene woman.

"What did you call me?"

"Son of the mountain fire. Look at you. You do not even know who you are. Did you think your abomination would please the god to whom the people give no name?"

Natas stalked across the room.

"What has happened, Teme?"

"The goddess has been joined by the god in whose name you create your abomination, Natas, and your lie begins to crumble. Maatemnu comes."

Expecting the move of a *tusiata* fighter, she watched his legs. The fist was a complete surprise, and even as she dodged, Teme knew she was too late. She slid down the wall, barely conscious.

"Mind your speech, priestess. You live at my sufferance. Now dress. I have to know what that idiot has done."

He left abruptly, and Teme rose, a throbbing in her head. Twenty minutes later, they were on the way to Branniff's private airport on the outskirts of Bumba. The African night seemed a surging stream as the plane rose over the ancient continent, streaking south. Teme cleared her mind, trying to hear, above the plane's engines, in the air itself, some voice that would tell her of the future. Deep down, she wondered if Natas was right. In all the time since he dragged her from the Land of Tiamat, she had felt the goddess' presence, had spoken to her and gained faith in the contact. Empheme's voice was absent, but she trusted in the high priestess as well. The last time she saw Empheme, on that fateful night at Lusani, Empheme made the sacrifice, giving herself to the Son of Ghalib. The ancient stories told of Ghalib and Empheme creating the Onye through that act of union, but the ceremony at Lusani was a perversion. Nothing would come of it.

Teme sighed, thinking of her failure with Lona. She had been his teacher in the ways of the First People and in the art of *tusiata*. A flash of anger poured through her at the thought that she, the second most powerful person in the hierarchy of the goddess' worship, secret leader of the *leo-leos*, those fierce warriors, and personally trained by Mother Mutasii, the ancient who was closest to the goddess, was now in this pitiable position—concubine to the son of the mountain fire. Natas had brought her to the world above to spite Empheme and to insult the goddess. It was hard being away from the temple and the sisterhood, but she hated most that which Natas had made her. She got no pleasure from his body and prayed to the goddess throughout the act. Her *moi moi*, the bud of a woman's pleasure, had been removed when she was thirteen, and before Natas, no man had touched her.

She thought of the other man who had come so abruptly into the life of the temple. Strange but exciting, he was something the stories did not address. He was new and confused about so many things that she quickly got over resenting the assignment Empheme gave her. As his guide in the Land of Tiamat, she had learned as much as she taught and quickly realized that, in spite of his fumbling, Andreas possessed a latent power she felt certain came from the goddess. Empheme loved him—some said in ways that were odd—and Teme, too, grew fond of him.

Until Natas took her, no man would have dared even to look at her. That would have meant his death. Teme knew that Natas was not the Son of Ghalib, but many still believed. The story of the ceremony at Lusani was spread throughout the Land of Tiamat, and many rejoiced at the return of the god Chango to their lives. Natas, however, was something that had lived a long time and did not love them. As if he heard her thoughts, Natas turned, amusement on his face.

"You think deeply, priestess. Are your thoughts upon me?"

"Indeed, they are. Our confusion will end soon."

"You're right. The world begins to make sense."

"Whose world? I do not see sense, but misery."

"You see too little to judge, priestess. For all their miserable history, those who followed Maatemnu north, away from the dead land of our stories, have attempted unity. I offer them that one world of which they dream."

"But what kind of world? A world without uniqueness, and, therefore, without beauty. If you understood the instructions of the god to whom the people give no name, you would know why the First People were instructed to serve all the gods. But that escapes you, does it not?"

Teme's anger was gone, and she was again the priestess, seeking to teach, to enlighten. Natas laughed at her.

"It is a philosophy of weakness, priestess, to be expected from a goddess. This civilization I create will endure for eternity."

His voice rose, and his eyes burned with a fire that appeared molten and viscous. When Teme replied, her voice was sad.

"Good cannot proceed from evil, nor can wisdom spring from ignorance. Maatemnu comes."

He glared at her for a moment and then leaned back, closing his eyes. She had been forgotten. The even hum of the Lear's engine continued, a soporific sound, and eventually, she fell asleep.

The sudden change in altitude woke her. The co-pilot came back, indicating that they were making the stop in Cape Town to change planes. They were on the ground for less than an hour and then were airborne again. The next hop would be across the Southern Ocean to Dunedin, New Zealand and then on to Antarctica. Natas went to the communications center at the rear of the plane and from there made several calls. In capitals the world over, powerful men awoke, their minds instantly alert. Branniff was calling.

Chapter 26

One man, whom Natas Branniff had not called, awoke as well to the insistent ringing of the telephone. Sidoti snapped a greeting, only to groan when he heard Karl Metzer's cheerful voice.

"You'd better get your butt over here, ole buddy."

"Why?" Sidoti asked, a long sigh escaping him.

"Because, pardner, a few hours ago, we had one hell of a heat signature from your favorite location. It makes the other one look like a Christmas tree compared to the sun. This is exciting."

Sidoti was fully awake. Though not sharing Metzer's joy, he rolled out of bed, knocking to the floor several books he had been perusing the night before. The titles were related, dealing with various aspects of astrophysics. Two in particular, *Dark Matter and the Origin of the Universe* and *Entropy*, were heavily underlined. Sidoti dressed quickly, throwing on a thick coat before rushing out the door. The cold hit him like a punch in the gut as he slid down the steps to the short driveway. When he arrived at the lab, Metzer was smoking and holding a cup of coffee, which Sidoti, unbidden, took from him. Metzer grumbled.

"You're becoming entirely too familiar."

"What's going on, Karl?"

"Fireworks, me boy. The satellite we now have dedicated to that area detected two types of heat signatures. One is consistent with a city the size of, say, Chicago. The second one is what we thought it was. Someone—and given where it's coming from, it's got to be Branniff—has figured out how to accelerate dark energy."

"You didn't drag me out in the cold for this, did you? You explained that the other day."

"Well, knowing how dense you are, I thought I'd go over it again. Anyway, that's not why I called."

Metzer moved to the wall and dimmed the lights. A computer was hooked up to a projector, and an enlarged picture appeared on the screen. Sidoti recognized Antarctica, three heat locations clearly identified in faded red. He looked at Metzer who was grinning much like the cat in the canary story.

"What?" Sidoti asked irritably.

"Don't you see it?"

"See what?"

"Look here," Metzer said, pointing. "Here's the low-level heat signature for the settlement in the north of the continent. By the way, there's not enough energy there to sustain much of a population, so you might want to check out what's going on. Anyway, here's the original heat signature you snagged thirteen years ago. I have plotted both of these for you. Notice anything?"

Sidoti moved closer, his eyes fixed on numbers on the charts.

"Sure," he said uncertainly. "The values at the settlement are different from those of the original heat signature I recorded."

"Very good. Now, look over here."

Metzer pointed to a spot farther south. Even without the graph, Sidoti could tell that it was different.

"It's redder. I assume that means hotter."

"Jesus! A few more sessions, and you might be able to figure out which stick to pull out to get a match box to collapse. Yes. It is hotter. It's also different. Notice that we have not plotted values across the whole heat signature."

Sidoti peered. In the first, there was a heat gradient plotted across the surface of the graph. In the other two, the plotted values were in a circle around the circumference of a red center.

"He gets it," Metzer said in a child-like, sing-song voice.

Sidoti pointed to the figures that were in a circle.

"Is this the halo you talked about?"

Metzer laughed and pounded him on the back.

"Bullseye. Surefire way to spot dark energy, old buddy. You can't really see it, but you can see what surrounds it. Sorta like your a-hole. You only know it's there because of your fat butt around it."

Metzer roared at his own humor and punched a button of the computer.

"There you are, my little beauty. What do you think?"

Sidoti shrugged, and Metzer made a rude sound.

"That's the reason I interrupted your beauty sleep, old buddy. That is the needle in the haystack. Actually, smoking gun would be better."

He paused, smiling.

"Okay. I'll bite. What is it?"

"Thought you'd never ask. Remember a couple days ago you asked me if dark energy can be weaponized. Well, there's your answer."

"What's my answer?" Sidoti said impatiently.

"You're looking at a series of controlled energy bursts with the same heat signature as the dark matter. Ergo, you've got a weapon. Too regular to be naturally occurring."

Sidoti stared for a long time before asking, "What are we looking at, Karl?"

"Pretty much the obsolescence of every weapons system we have. Boy, I'd like to meet the son of a bitch who beat me to this."

Sidoti was no longer listening.

"Get a coat, Karl. There are people we've got to talk to."

Something in Sidoti's tone must have gotten through to Metzer because he nodded and, turning the computer off, grabbed a coat.

Chapter 27

*A*n hour later, Sidoti pulled up to General Blount's home in Bethesda, Maryland. Inside, a dim light showed. As he and Metzer got out of the car, the porch light came on, and he breathed a sigh of relief. He would hate having to bang on the door. The general was framed in the doorway. Sidoti slid up the driveway and walked into the foyer. He looked around uncertainly at the order of the place, thinking of the snow on his boots.

General Blount said, "Never mind that. Come in."

They crossed the large living room, going toward the back of the house. In passing, Sidoti noticed several photographs of the general with a boy at various ages. They were engaged in a variety of activities. One showed the general teaching the boy how to swing a baseball bat. There was also a graduation photo. Sidoti could not tell whether it was high school or college. They entered a study, and General Blount motioned them to sit. Sidoti was not as uncomfortable as he normally felt around the general.

Maybe the house robe humanizes him, he thought.

When the general spoke, the world righted itself. His voice was as cold and unfriendly as ever.

"So what have you got?"

"I think we have a problem, sir."

"You think?"

Sidoti, nodding at Metzer, said, "This is Karl Metzer. He's a research scientist."

"I know who he is, Sidoti. Astrophysics. Working on the origin of the universe. Expert in dark matter."

Metzer laughed.

"What's funny, Metzer?"

"No experts in dark matter, boss. At least, I didn't think so until tonight."

"Explain."

Sidoti, not trusting Metzer to get the tone right, repeated what he had been told.

When he finished, General Blount said, "Are you sure that what we have is a weapon, Metzer?"

"I ain't sure about nothing. The science says that we have a background energy source giving evidence of controlled bursts. If it's not a weapon yet, then it can easily be made into one."

"And you think that makes nuclear weapons obsolete?"

"Well, not entirely. After all, we can still kill with a bow and arrow, but it ain't our weapon of choice."

"Let me get this straight. You're saying that compared to this weaponized dark energy, our weapons are equivalent to a bow and arrow?"

"Actually, more like a thrown stone, Blount."

The general frowned, but Sidoti could not tell whether from the knowledge that his army was being compared to that of the prehistoric nomad or because of Metzer's familiarity.

"How would a weapon of this type work, Metzer?" the general asked.

"We've been working on a way to understand this for a while, but though we have had lots of breakthroughs, we have not gotten very far."

"Are you saying you know nothing?"

"Not exactly nothing. We know a shitload—"

"Mind your language. This is a Christian home."

Metzer shrugged, continuing as if the general had not interrupted.

"... of stuff, but we're trying to solve a 13.8-billion-year mystery."

"Looks like someone else figured it out," the general replied sourly.

He went to a small teak table on which were photographs of the young man Sidoti had earlier seen.

Marine. Just like his old man.

"Yes, but they may have had a head start," Metzer said.

He sounded irritated, and Sidoti smiled. Metzer hated to be beaten.

"Explain," the general snapped.

"Well, Branniff—"

"Branniff? What in God's name has Branniff to do with this?"

"Branniff was studying dark matter several years ago when I worked for them. You guys were still treating it like science fiction. Maybe worse, like mythology. Branniff was serious."

The general's large frame towered over the other men.

"Are you saying that Branniff has a weapons system about which we know nothing but which could be turned against us, and you knew they were working on it and said nothing?"

The voice was low and vicious. Metzer squirmed.

"Blasted scientists," the general said angrily, evidently forgetting that it was a Christian home. "We're at war, you jackass."

Hoping to avoid a blowup between the general and the only man who seemed to understand what was going on in Antarctica, Sidoti chimed in.

"In fairness, General, none of us thought about dark energy in this way."

Blount turned baleful eyes on Sidoti.

"I'll remember that when your evaluation comes up, Sidoti. For now, I still have to depend on you, although God knows that gives me no comfort. Here's what we're going to do. I want you ready to move at a moment's notice."

"Move where, sir?"

"Antarctica. Where else?"

The general sounded as if he was speaking to a moron, and Sidoti thought that between the general and Metzer, he was certainly in rapid descent on the evolutionary scale.

"Antarctica! But that now belongs to Branniff. No one's been allowed on the continent in twenty years."

"I think, soldier, we're way past the point of 'allow', don't you? I will contact the president."

Sidoti heard the lie but said nothing. Blount might inform the president, but no permission would be given. He was being sent into territory that belonged to Branniff Enterprises without permission to be there. If he was caught, then he would be on his own.

"Metzer will go with you. He, at least, understands which end is up."

Metzer looked up at this, his face alight like a schoolboy's. Sidoti's heart sank, but it would be useless to argue. The general picked up a phone and hit a button.

After a while, he said, "Zin, sorry to wake you. I need a ferry for a couple of my boys. Antarctica. Not sure when yet. No. Everybody's on board. Coordinate with me directly. This is ears only. Yes. Goodnight."

The general put the phone down. Sidoti deciphered what he had just heard. "Zin" would be Colonel Theo "Zin" White, commanding officer of Joint Base Andrews in Prince George's County, Maryland. The "everybody" suggested to Colonel White that the White House was on board. "Ears only" meant there would be no record of the conversation. They stood, Metzer fidgeting like a little boy, excitement all over his face. Sidoti wondered what he was getting himself into. He was not a field agent and knew nothing about surviving outside his office. The last time General Blount sent him out, he was promptly kidnapped and taken to the Borderlands. Fortunately, the African Americans only wanted him to take Hargrove's body home to the United States.

As he climbed into the car, Sidoti thought of the activities in which he had engaged for so many years. He had saved the United States from harm many times with his careful analysis of the data that streamed to him in his office at the NSA. His mind worked like a machine, integrating bits of information, finding patterns where others saw just disjointed messages. He was good and was acknowledged as such, but even the brief excursion in the field, when Stoltz's house was blown up, felt different. For the first time, he had known what it was like to be on the front line, and though it scared him half to death, it was also exhilarating. Now, as he made his way south on Interstate 95, the very emptiness of the white landscape was like a call to him. America was in danger, and he would answer her call. Beside him, Metzer was quiet, lost in his own thoughts, and Sidoti wondered about him. Unstable, though brilliant, Metzer had worked for Branniff on the same stuff that was now threatening them. Sidoti was not sure if Metzer was an asset or a liability.

One other thing worried him. He possessed every bit of information that flew across the globe at light speed, but this development had taken place under his nose. If Metzer was right, then the deadliest device since the atomic bomb had been created in the last several years, and he had completely missed it. Sidoti felt personally responsible for that, and though General Blount intended no favor, he was glad to be doing something other than sitting at his desk, making sense of others' actions.

Chapter 28

*A*ndreas walked unhurriedly through the streets of Llehstan, his face covered by a hood. The city was nervous, and fear lay like a blanket on the people's minds. In those minds was a vague picture of what happened hundreds of miles to the south. The Onye's expedition had not returned, but there were whispers of a tragedy. The city was quiet and cautious.

Andreas touched his eye. Sight returned to it two days after the explosion, and his once-withered arm increased in strength one day later. The soldiers had called the lightning that he absorbed Chango's fire. Years before, Natas absorbed a similar energy when they were descending from the ice above. It weakened him for a while, but that same energy restored Andreas to his full strength. Even now, trodding the cobblestones of the city, it was as if he floated above them. Increasingly, he was thinking of himself in terms that Eurydice used to describe him. He was becoming a believer in what she believed.

I'm a scientist, but science explains nothing that is happening to me.

He turned down a side street and entered a hostelry. Many of these had sprung up in Llehstan to accommodate those who visited the new city. He could not remember seeing any in Tiastan. Few people had traveled then. Llehstan was more commercial and possessed of a frenzied bustle, unlike Tiastan. Inside the darkened hostelry, some of that commerce was taking place. The tables were widely spaced, allowing the occupants, who all seemed to be whispering, to conduct their business, legal or otherwise, without much fear of being overheard. Andreas went to a table at the very back of the room where there was almost no light. As he passed, suspicious eyes followed him.

He ordered an ale. It was sweet to the palate but also had a kick. Andreas no longer felt the urge to drink, but he needed a reason to stay in the bar until the short period of darkness came. Then, he would get Eurydice and leave Ghalib's land. The details were not worked out, but he trusted himself to find a way. He sipped and thought, a deep sadness weighing him down. His son was dead, and it was as if a part of Andreas was transported to the Land of Malaia where the dead went. He thought of Malaia and uttered a silent prayer for his friend's voyage to the land of the dead after which he had been named.

Actually, not named but called. I never knew his name.

His friend assumed the name Malaia, the land of the dead, when he became Empheme's *si'ufofoga*, that is, her human voice. He once said to Andreas that one must die to become the voice of the goddess. Andreas had not understood then but thought he did now.

"Did you know of your actual death, my friend?" Andreas said.

Others in the bar glanced at him. Andreas extended his mind sense, calming their suspicions, and each, thinking it was his idea, went back to his business.

Could I have helped Lona?

Arrogant and violent, Lona had shown respect for only his mother and Teme whom Andreas had not seen since she left Tiastan three years earlier. He hoped she was all right. It had been a hard three years. Lona and Malaia dead. Endele, his friend from the mountains, killed and his people defeated. He thought of Endele's sister Osongo who provided him refuge when he was on the run and wondered if she was all right. And Teme imprisoned or, perhaps, dead. Andreas placed his head on the table, closing off his mind sense, not wanting contact with others. He sat for a long time, taking drinks he did not want. Time passed slowly, and faceless customers came and went. Something gnawed at his gut, and he knew it was guilt over his son. Should he have ignored the advice and insisted on his fatherhood from the beginning? Would that have saved the boy? He sighed. No answer was possible. Images from the days after his son was killed rushed into his mind.

He destroyed most of the surviving trucks, leaving Marcus and his soldiers on foot at the edge of the Ilegu Forest. Seeing his wolfish eyes, they stood, awaiting their fate. Andreas wanted them to attack so he could expiate the feeling of guilt, anger and loss that permeated his very being, so he did not leave immediately, giving them an opportunity to plot secretly, to attack in silence. He turned one of the strange canisters containing the unknown energy on the trucks, watching them crumple as if some invisible, giant hand was squeezing them into scrap metal. One truck survived his rage, and the soldiers looked at it with a forlorn hope. Marcus came to him.

"We will need food, Prescod. Unless you intend to kill us all."

His voice was surprisingly gentle, and this stopped Andreas' cold madness.

Then, another voice said, *"Forgive yourself."*

Observing Marcus, Andreas felt an unfathomable sorrow, something so deep that the pain stemming from the loss of his son and his friend seemed distant.

"You saved me. I felt it turn away from me and go toward you. I don't know how you did it, but you took it into you. Thank you," Marcus said.

Andreas stared at the small mound just outside the shattered camp. Marcus' eyes followed his.

"He was your natural son, wasn't he? Empheme really is your woman. There were rumors."

Marcus sounded surprised. Slowly, his face changed, showing great confusion.

"Why did you save me and not him?"

His voice was hoarse. Andreas turned away, the answer like a snake in his mind. When he spoke, his voice was hollow, as if it came from far away.

"You once asked, Marcus, why I made the recommendation that led to your people being transported here. I said it was not my fault." He paused, staring at the grave of his son. Then, he added, "Eurydice said to me that we're all responsible for that act. It seems so clear now. I'm sorry, Marcus."

The young man stared, searching behind the words for something that would give the lie to the expressed sentiment.

Finally, glancing at the grave, he said, "Your price has been high, too, Prescod. I've heard it said that you walk in the path of the gods. If so, they have not been gentle with you."

Andreas smiled sadly. Thinking of the vision that showed he was Maatemnu of the withered arm and jet-black skin, he wondered at the vagaries of time and fate. Would Marcus understand the nature of his sacrifice, or the peace he had felt when the dying god smiled? Trained to see color and race, would he understand that the Expulsion, like slavery before it, was a betrayal of their common humanity? Marcus saw a white man making a sacrifice for a black man, but was it really that? Or was it all smoke and mirrors, a historical construction as false as so much else with which the gods deceive humans? Soon after, he left them. They had food from the disabled truck and their weapons but no means of communication.

Sitting in the dimness of the hostelry, he checked the chronometer behind the bar. It would soon be dark, but there was only about an hour of darkness before *pogosi* left and *malamalama* returned, heralding the brightness. During that hour, he had to get into the castle and out again. He would traverse the northern Plain of Sotami, passing to the north of Tiastan, cross the River Wilongo, and on to Malaia, the dead land where the white crocodiles lived. It was possible there to climb to the surface using the Stairway of Pain. What he would do about the brutal Antarctic cold, he did not know. Andreas ordered another ale, but it sat untouched on the dirty table. Soon, it would be time to move.

Chapter 29

The time of *pogosi* came like a shadow covering the ground. Andreas moved stealthily from under the overhang. He was still some distance from the castle's wall. The night was quiet, amplifying a musical instrument's rhythmic beat being carried on the light wind. His dark robe blended with the night, but in just over an hour, the brightness would return. Gripping his staff, he stepped out cautiously, his mind sense, as always in that place, less effective. He moved swiftly across the open space that separated the town from the wall of the castle. This part would not be too difficult because the land was relatively flat.

High above on the castle's walls, the guards' eyes searched for any movement. He was hurrying through the darkness when, suddenly, his foot landed on something soft and furry. A screech tore the night apart. Andreas fell flat, pressing himself into the ground. He was not a moment too soon because a blinding searchlight illuminated the night, its glare crawling across the ground toward him. If he lay there, they would discover him. Four voices atop the wall were in discussion. One of them thought they were wasting time. Andreas' mind sense searched for the one who was handling the searchlight. He made a suggestion, and the light wavered.

"Keep the light steady, Makalo. It is the only way we can be sure we cover every bit of ground," a voice said.

"All right, Zatun, but nothing's down there."

The light continued its slow progress toward Andreas. A film of sweat appeared on his upper lip. He had to get away from the light, but the eyes above were alert now. He mentally kicked himself for his carelessness. Then, he stiffened. The cat. Maybe ....

Andreas extended his mind sense toward where the cat had fled.

It was cowering near the corner of the castle wall. He pushed the image of a large descending foot into the cat's mind, and the befuddled creature screeched again. The light jumped to the right. Instantly, Andreas was up and running, the dark coat billowing behind him. He slammed up against the wall just as the light reversed course. It passed, and then, he moved. Precious minutes of his hour had elapsed. The wall towered above him. He was prepared for this and slipped an odd contraption over his hand. It was relatively flat in the palm, except for several small spikes. Strapping the staff to his back, he placed the spikes against the wall and started to climb. Moving quickly, feeling the pull on his shoulder muscles, he thanked Malaia for strengthening him. Like a shadow, he ascended the wall. Reaching the top, he slid over and lay flat.

Every guard on the catwalk was alert, the absence of the Onye having heightened their tension, but Andreas was one with the night. He descended by a ladder to the castle yard. Before him was the keep. All was dark. Sitting cross-legged in the shadows, his mind sense fully extended, he searched for Eurydice. She was not in the uppermost rooms, and Andreas systematically worked his way down the floors of the keep. On the third floor from the bottom, he sensed her. His mind sense touched hers, and he felt the instant alertness.

"I am here, Eudy."

"Yes. In the castle yard. I can sense you."

"We have to leave. There's much I will explain later."

Her concern was a pulse in his mind sense, but she said nothing. Andreas slipped across the courtyard, a ghost in the night, and soon came to a door. The tumblers not proving to be a problem, he quickly ascended the steep marble steps. Suddenly, he halted. At the head of the stairway, two guards stood. He pressed against the wall. He did not want to hurt these men but had to move quickly to beat the returning light. His internal clock told him that he had already used almost half the time. Andreas projected an image and strode up the stairs. The men stood rigidly at attention as the ghostly figure passed. Later, they would swear under oath that the Onye had walked among them on that night. Andreas did the same thing on the next level, and this time, the soldiers accompanied him to Eurydice's room. She walked out. His mind sense suggested to the guards that she was asleep, and he commanded them to guard her closely. The men locked the door. He and Eurydice departed, soon reaching the outer door. They stepped outside, hugging the darkness of the keep's wall.

"Be alert now. Use your mind sense to project images of safety. That will get us past the guards."

"My mind sense is weak, Andreas."

"I can feel it. Do the best you can."

They moved away from the wall, aware of the sound of an engine ascending the hill. Suddenly, there was a great commotion in the yard. Soldiers were running toward the gate and falling into formation. Lights came on, and the towering gate opened. Andreas and Eurydice shrank back against the wall, sliding along the rounded corner, trying to find some shadow in which to hide. All eyes were riveted on the gate through which they could now see the lights of a large vehicle. It pulled into the courtyard, and the engine died. Andreas' breath stopped as a tall figure stepped down from the truck and turned to the keep, the great head held back. The face outlined by the light was noble, handsome and frighteningly cruel.

Andreas involuntarily whispered, "Natas."

High above, darkness still clung to the sky, but they were running out of time. Natas went inside. The soldiers were more alert, and though the lights were turned off, danger was everywhere.

"No chance of using the gate now," Andreas said.

"No. Come. We'll have to do this another way."

Eurydice went in the direction of a door at the side of the keep, but when she turned the knob, it was locked. He gently removed her hand. His mind sense found the tumblers, and they hurried inside.

"You have a power I never had, Andreas. Sometime, you must tell me."

She led him along a corridor, and after he opened another door, they descended into the bowels of the keep. He followed her, trusting her knowledge but all the while aware that time was passing. Soon, light would return. After a long walk on a damp floor, Eurydice stopped.

"Here."

Andreas followed her hand in the darkness and found a small door. He turned the lock and pushed the door open. Immediately, the smell hit him, and he drew back.

"What is this place?"

"It is where they dump the castle's refuge. Below is a branch of the river."

Andreas took a quick peek outside, fighting the rush of nausea the smell induced.

"It is a sheer wall out there, Eudy. We cannot descend it."

"I know."

Andreas' body tightened as she projected the image of their falling bodies, ending with a plunge into a fast-flowing, dark river.

"Trust in the goddess, Andreas."

As Andreas stood in the passageway with his wife, preparing to plummet into the darkness, he did not have the heart to tell her that the goddess had been destroyed somewhere near the Ilegu Forest. He took her hand, breathed deeply and jumped.

Chapter 30

They fell for a long time. He sensed dark rock rushing past, and then, they hit water. Their bodies made a clean entry, but the impact knocked the breath from him, and he lost his grip on Eurydice's hand. He plunged down, fighting the urge to open his mouth. The current tugged at him, and his submerged body was yanked along by the rushing undertow. Clawing his way to the surface, Andreas sucked in a huge gulp of air before he was tumbled by a dip in the river bed. Again, he went under. This time, he accepted the power of the river's current, and it soon tossed him to the surface again. The water was now less rough. The castle's lights blazed in the distance, and he wondered if Natas had discovered that Eurydice was gone.

Where is she?

He looked around. The water's white caps made it difficult to see, and struggling against the current, it was a challenge to focus his mind sense. Then, he sensed her. Caught in a riptide in the middle of the river, her body was flying along. Andreas angled over into the swifter-flowing water, and soon he, too, was being dragged downriver. He could not catch her, but she did not seem to be in any immediate danger. The castle's lights disappeared between two high cliffs. In the sky was a glow, the light of *malamalama* returning.

The current slowed. Up ahead, Eurydice was drifting to the side of the gorge. Andreas did the same. Soon, they were in gentler water, although it still dragged them along at a good clip. She was investigating the cliffs, which went straight up. Except for broken rocks, bush and lichens, there seemed to be no break in the sheer granite walls.

"We have to get off the river, Eudy. We'll be easy to spot from the

air. Once they discover you're gone, they'll come looking as soon as the light returns."

"Can you use your mind sense to see what's ahead?"

For a long time, he searched. Even at the very extremity of his mind sense, Andreas could find no gap in the cliffs. He shook his head. Eurydice grabbed a bush that clung precariously to the cliff.

"What are you doing? We have to get off the river."

She did not answer. Instead, closing her eyes and inclining her head, she prayed to the goddess. Andreas waited patiently as the roar of the river died, and the wind seemed a distant thing. In the great silence that he had learned was another voice of the goddess, Andreas' anxiety drained away, and peace overcame him. He saw again Eurydice's beauty, noticing, in a remote way, the darkness that had always lain beneath her skin. He was glad, for he had seen her throughout time, had watched her many evolutions. She was original woman, and yet she was here and now.

He remembered her as a furious creature who walked away from his camp in the time before time, a haughty woman who rejected his, Maatemnu's, offer of a mate. Returning from the distant northern lands, she had bowed, reluctant and snarling, before him. Then, too, her skin color was different. No longer the lustrous black of the women of his nation, it was instead a paleness they had found profoundly disturbing and slightly frightening. Yet, even in her strangeness, he loved her. She, at that time, brought strange tales about the head of Tiamat being seen in the great northern wasteland. They laughed at her because it was known that Tiamat lived in the west beyond the house of the setting sun. There, the god to whom the people give no name had placed Tiamat, and there she would remain until he freed her.

The woman had insisted, and he sent scouts to the north with her to find this imposter who called herself Tiamat. His scouts returned with fear in their eyes. They confirmed that the northern lands belonged to Tiamat. They had seen the whiteness of her head and felt the coldness of her breath. They also said that Tiamat was moving south, toward his land. In that time, this woman stood, a sneer on her face and contempt in her eyes, until, in his anger, he took her. She had not fought him, though she did not give herself. Their union proved barren, as it had always been throughout time.

Until now, Andreas thought.

She still prayed. Daylight came, and he glanced anxiously to the sky, expecting any moment to see helicopters searching for them. He thought of the old dream in which he was trapped and a helicopter came to rescue him and a faceless woman.

In that dream, I let go of her hand, and she fell to her death. I will never let go of you, Eudy.

Andreas admired Eurydice. The apex of two streams of human development, she walked across time. She was not always with him, but he had pursued this extraordinary woman who carried the human impulse through the ages. Though she was not the product of Maatemnu's land, he had found her there with the Neanderthals after the Great Parting, that mythological split of the First People into two contending groups. She had been culturally more advanced than the Neanderthals, and he never found out why or how she became part of their band.

She was also Empheme, the goddess/priestess of Tiamat, she who had gone to the southwest of Africa, across the dead land toward the setting sun. Empheme, in the stories of the First People, went to the lands of the New World. There, she merged with the descendants of the First People, those who had become their oppressors. No story told of these two remarkable women meeting, but he felt certain they had met, and Eurydice was the result.

"Andreas."

The voice came from far away. He wanted to ignore it, but it was insistent, and, irritated, he swam back toward awareness. Seeing Eurydice's luminous face, for a moment, he thought he was still in his vision. Then, he saw, as close to him as Eurydice, the cold, red eyes of a white crocodile. Andreas barely held back a scream, but Eurydice laughed.

"Calm yourself. She will not harm you."

As if to prove it, she patted the creature. The unblinking eyes, showing just above the rushing water, stared dispassionately at Andreas. He was transfixed by the great jaws that the unruly water periodically exposed. Just about to speak, Andreas heard the unmistakable sound of helicopter rotors coming down the gorge. Eurydice said something, and the giant crocodile slid past him. She released the bush, following the crocodile downriver. Andreas glanced once more to the sky. The black dots looked like flies in the distance. Then, he, too, let go and followed Eurydice.

Chapter 31

*E*tienne Ochukwu wound his way along the crowded streets of Bumba with mixed feelings. He was glad to be back in Africa. Contact with the soil always enlivened him, as if the ancient land was giving its most revered son a special welcome. It was three years since he had last come, and then, as now, he came in secret. Then, it was at the invitation of the man who called himself Branniff, when Etienne made the bargain that allowed the new religion to assume the garb of the Catholic Church. The religion had grown, and it could no longer be controlled. What emerged was not even ostensibly Christian, but he recognized the power of an ancient idea and a rite that humans had forgotten.

And it is African.

Unable to stop the rush of pride, he immediately asked God's forgiveness. Worse than pride, though, was the sense of something inside him, deeper than cultural association, responding to the religion. Ever since he heard the sound that he knew as the Voice of God, there was a feeling that something was awakening in him. Etienne thought of that odd tearing of his bones, almost as if they had been trying to escape his flesh, and whispered a prayer. The confusion of images in his mind persisted.

Too much imagination.

Etienne wore the brown robe of a simple Benedictine monk, having secretly left the Vatican three days earlier. Few knew where he was, and the fake passport worked as expected. Having celebrated the mass on Sunday morning in Rome, he left late that night on a secret mission to Africa. Those who lived in the Vatican did not ask questions. These were unusual times, and the Holy Father was much pressed. A hired jet took him to Amsterdam, and there, he boarded a commercial flight to Accra. His great height could not be disguised, but the fake beard was effective enough. Men's eyes saw what they expected, and the pope on board a commercial airline, unaccompanied except for one young companion, was not within their expectation.

From Accra, he flew to Bumba which, fueled by Branniff's money and the need of every government in the world to send representatives, diplomatic and commercial, to the city, was now a major world capital. The two highways, one running from Cape Town to Tripoli and the other, almost finished, from Addis Ababa to Accra, intersected in Bumba, binding together the African continent.

What he saw in Bumba both shocked and delighted him. Branniff had built a thoroughly African city. It was there in the emphasis on slanted, peaked roofs, and the use of African materials. The shops contained merchandise from around the globe, and business seemed to be conducted in every conceivable language. The bridge on which he stood was made of the thinnest steel he had ever seen, and its base was of a black, lustrous marble.

"It is a marvel, is it not, Kwaku?" he asked the young man who strode quietly beside him.

"Indeed, father. Did you see the aqueduct? Is it not beautiful? Did you see the mechanism of the wheels that turns the pumps? It is incredible. There for all to see, and yet, it is said that the best scientists in the world cannot figure out the power source."

"Yes, Kwaku. It is ingenious. It is also a little worrying."

"Why, father?"

"Because what men do not understand, they fear. Natas Branniff, when he brought the world's leading scientists here to see his wonder and to test their knowledge, did not simply create a test. Rather, he issued a challenge. He was letting them know that he possessed something they did not."

"But why would they be afraid of an aqueduct?"

Hearing the irritation in Kwaku's voice brought Etienne's mind back to the issue of the Church's role vis-à-vis the new religion. The Americans had sent a strongly worded letter to him just before he left. Either he separate himself from the new faith that was "poisoning the Catholic Church," as they had written, or the Church in America would "press for reform." It was the plainest statement yet that they intended to break with the Roman Church. This was in his mind when he answered.

"Not the aqueduct, Kwaku, but the unknown."

Terror showed in the eyes of the American and European bishops. That same fear, disguised as resentment, was on display when, three years earlier, he ascended the Throne of St. Peter. In the bishops' faces was the nagging doubt, the worry that, maybe, after more than a millennium, history was passing them by. Etienne remembered a line from some long-forgotten musician who asked, "Is this the end?" Something was ending, but he did not know what.

Where will I be when the end comes? Will I have a role, or will these trappings of power fall away as easily as a snowflake on a summer's day?

Admiring the tall, gleaming steel, glass and marble buildings, he also wondered what would become of Africa. It, too, was quickly changing. There had not been a single civil struggle on the continent for some time. Two years earlier, some warlord made a grab for power in southwestern Africa, and Branniff shocked the world with the swiftness and brutality of the response. The rebellion was put down in fewer than three weeks and the ringleaders publicly hanged. There was no trial, only the declaration of their deaths. Even more important and frightening, the world now knew that Branniff possessed an army. No one had known about it, but at Branniff's call, a frightening force came out of central Africa. It proved to be disciplined, fierce and effective. Many rumors started, the most interesting of which was that the soldiers sounded like African Americans. Etienne dismissed this.

A meeting of the Nine—the secret group that had controlled the world since the time of the Roman emperor Constantine, and whose power was undiminished after almost two thousand years— was called immediately after that. Natas Branniff attended, and Etienne watched as power shifted from seven of the nine provinces to Branniff. At Natas' insistence, the deceased Ambassador Hargrove was not replaced, so no American was present. Natas ignored their demand for an explanation of his actions in Africa.

The men in that room commanded governments, but Natas dismissed them as meddlers. When one of the Nine threatened to interdict all African commercial activity, Natas laughed, replying ominously, "It is not Africa that should worry you." Lately, every nation in the world had turned its attention to Antarctica where word had filtered out of a new, incomprehensible energy source of frightening power.

Etienne gazed at the point where the river narrowed in a bend, not really seeing the gaily-colored boats that moved so effortlessly at play on the water.

"Branniff has done something good here, father," Kwaku said quietly.

The landscape of the city was alluring. He wanted to agree with the boy but simply nodded and moved along the bridge, going toward the cathedral, the very top of which could be seen in the distance. Every afternoon, the choir sang the Angelus in the nave of the church, and the faithful flocked there to hear the angelic voices. Kwaku scampered after him, striving to keep up with the big man's stride.

It took him twenty minutes to reach the cathedral which occupied an enormous space and was surrounded by a circular road called the Street of the Saints. Etienne's eyes feasted on the structure. It was like nothing he had ever seen. The giant girders that soared up to the heavens were of some transparent polymer reportedly stronger than steel. These were planted like broad feet on the ground and rose to an enormous height, not in a straight line but with a gentle curve to the top. They looked like glass bananas, each bent at exactly the same angle of curvature, the inward lean bringing them almost together at the top. There were sixteen of these girders. Within them was the magnificent cathedral, its golden steeple emerging from the space between the girders. Etienne admired the lustrous, black marble, filleted with white stone, that formed the walkways around the cathedral which was itself constructed of the same unearthly polymer as the girders. He had walked around the Street of the Saints on the day he arrived, and it took over an hour. The scale of the building was overpowering. Natas was wrong when he said that not since the Middle Ages had men built on that scale for the worship of God. Not even then had they built like that.

Still, the structure had heightened Etienne's awareness of the contradiction within Natas because the man did not build a Christian cathedral but had constructed a perfect mandala, a Hindu "magic circle." Etienne, recognizing it immediately, understood that it represented the four corners of the world, at the center of which was the Great Man, man's mythological uberself.

Is Natas referring to Christ in this way, as some sort of superman? Or is he looking to an entirely different tradition?

Etienne did not know, but once, on a visit to America, he was invited to chat with a Navajo shaman. There he saw the mandala used in Navajo sand paintings to heal the sick.

"What is it, father?"

"Nothing, my son. I was thinking of how incomprehensible God is, how far beyond our understanding."

Kwaku, studying the mandala-shaped building, said, "Come, father. We must hurry. The grounds of the cathedral are already filling up."

And, indeed, they were. The inhuman harmony of the building confronted Etienne. He should have felt joy at this statement of obeisance to the Lord, but as he crossed the Street of the Saints and stepped on to the cathedral grounds, he shivered as if someone had walked over his grave.

Chapter 32

*S*idoti was feeling very sick. Below him was a cross on the deck of the research ship to which he was headed. The deck looked tiny. Having left Dunedin in New Zealand several hours ago, they had earlier landed at an old research station on Ross Island. They were then ferried west by a Bell UH-1 Iroquois helicopter. The clattering was deafening, but now that he could see where they were to land, Sidoti discovered that he was perfectly happy to put up with the helicopter's noise. The wind had picked up in the last twenty minutes, and the helicopter was being pushed sideways like a car skidding on wet pavement. There were white tops on the waves below.

The change in weather shut Metzer up, and the scientist was a little green around the cheeks and neck. Sidoti smiled, feeling gratified that he was not as afraid as Metzer. Though the helicopter was descending much too abruptly for his liking, he chuckled when a mouse-like squeal escaped his flying companion.

"Take you out of the lab, you just become a wuss, don't you?"

Metzer gave him a look that would have curdled milk and mouthed an obscenity, then immediately grabbed a canvas stay as the helicopter pitched suddenly.

Sidoti, feeling little sympathy, said, "A few more of those, and we'll be down. Of course, whether it'll be in one piece or not ..."

Metzer turned pasty. He had a sweater pulled over a sweatshirt down to the thighs of soiled jeans. Not for the first time, Sidoti wondered how Metzer could keep his labs so clean and himself such a mess.

"Did you bring the coat the captain gave you?"

"No," Metzer said, his teeth rattling. "You said it was summer."

Sidoti shook his head in disbelief.

Man-child.

"Don't worry. I'm sure someone will have an extra coat on the ship," he responded.

The helicopter began to sway as it hovered. Close up, Sidoti could see that the ship was much larger than it at first appeared, but he breathed a sigh of relief when the helicopter finally touched down. Two men ran toward the chopper and quickly secured it. Another opened the door. The cold hit them like a fist, and Sidoti drew back.

The man outside said, "Hello. I am Johann Schmidt. Put these on."

He handed them two relatively thin-shelled jackets, but as soon as Sidoti put his on, he felt warmer. They jumped down, running across the deck to escape the wind.

Once inside, Sidoti, teeth chattering as he looked at the bright sky, asked, "How cold is it?"

"Sorry," the man who had introduced himself as Schmidt replied. "Temperature dropped suddenly. It's only about thirty-five below, though."

"Thirty-five below!" Metzer said, his lips blubbery as he added accusatorily, "You said it was summer."

Schmidt laughed, a deep, booming sound.

"Coming to the end of summer actually. The light is disappearing for a couple of hours a day now."

"Somebody told me that in the summer the temperature is twenty above zero," Metzer persisted.

"It can be, but I've seen days in the middle of the summer when it was fifty-five below."

"No shit," Metzer said, eyeing his surroundings. "So you're a research vessel? What do you research?"

"Oh, all sorts of things. Let me show you your quarters. Then, I suppose you'll want to see the lab. It's been set up as specified. We were told that you had priority. You guys must have a lot of pull."

Sidoti shrugged, but Metzer said, "I'd like to see the lab now. Can I get a sandwich?"

They descended into the bowels of the ship.

On reaching the third level, Schmidt said, "This is the research center. Here is the lab that we have set up for you."

Metzer entered, excitement on his face, and then abruptly stopped.

"What the hell is he doing here?" he asked, glaring at Sidoti.

On the other side of the lab stood Dr. Faison, director of the Advanced Physics Lab. He was immaculately dressed in white shirt, cream slacks and blue tie. The white lab coat almost seemed a redundancy.

"Good evening, Dr. Metzer, Mr. Sidoti."

Metzer made a gargling sound.

"Calm down, Karl. This isn't your private party. I'm going to need as many points of view as I can get," Sidoti said.

"You should've told me he'd be here."

"You wouldn't have come. Anyway, you're here now, so let's see if we can keep the country's interests ahead of our egos."

Neither man answered. Metzer went to the long table and began investigating the instruments.

After a while, he grudgingly said, "This is pretty well outfitted."

The lab was set up in complementary halves. That would force the two scientists to work together. Sidoti looked around. This was not his playground, but Metzer and Dr. Faison had separately provided specs for the lab. The concern generated by the discovery of the new energy ensured that anything he wanted almost magically appeared. It took two weeks to modify the ship and to get everything in place, including freeing up Dr. Faison. Sidoti started walking toward the small conference room. The captain followed him.

"Sorry, Johann. This is above your pay grade," Sidoti said.

"Thought I'd give it a try. If you need anything, press that button over there."

The captain smiled and closed the door.

"Okay, gentlemen. Let's go over what we know. If I understand it, you both agree that we have an energy signature where it has no right to be. Karl believes this energy has already been weaponized and that it has been used. You agree with that, Dr. Faison?"

"Fundamentally, yes, but I can't commit to the weaponized part. It's possible that we have a random occurrence that also seems—"

"Horseshit," Metzer interrupted heatedly. "Nature doesn't behave in so uniform a manner as we saw with those energy bursts. I—"

"Wait, wait. I can't get anywhere unless I can hear an idea out. You two understand this. I don't, so bear with me. For the sake of argument, let's say someone has weaponized what you call dark energy. What would be the process? What would be the effect?"

Metzer instantly replied, "Look. The universe started with a bang. That took untold amounts of energy. We can't find most of it. If someone could find and mine it, so to speak, we would have an inexhaustible store of energy. One good thing is that it would put the A-rabs out of business."

"Karl, are we talking only about an economic weapon, an energy source that, if controlled by one person or corporation, would be able to hold the world hostage? Or are we talking about a military weapon?"

"Well, both actually, Mr. Sidoti. There is much we don't understand about nature at the sub-microatomic level, but some pretty strange things are predicted by some of my equations," Dr. Faison answered.

"Mostly stolen from my work."

Dr. Faison ignored Metzer.

"At the simplest level, anyone capable of mining and controlling dark matter or dark energy would have to understand the building blocks of the universe. How familiar are you with Einstein's theory of general relativity, Mr. Sidoti?"

"I'm about as stupid as the next guy."

"Well, very simply, Einstein's theory suggested that mass and energy are interchangeable—the famous $E = Mc^2$—and in the popular mind that means any object can be converted into invisible energy. It is commonsensical once you get over the notion that "something" can become "nothing." People have a sense that when a bomb explodes, the mass that was blown up is still "somewhere" out there. It is less well understood that the energy has simply changed form and that the reverse process is also possible. That is, energy—vibration, light, etc.—can also be transformed into mass."

"Let's see if I've got this. I can blow something up, and then I can un-blow it up?"

"Not very elegantly put, but not entirely stupid. Basically, all I need is the right converter, and I can turn light into this table," Metzer said, slamming his open palm down on the unfortunate piece of furniture.

"And you think that Branniff has done this?" Sidoti said.

"Absolutely."

"It's not clear from the evidence we have that this is the case. We need to test Dr. Metzer's hypothesis. That's why we are here, isn't it?" Dr. Faison countered.

Sidoti nodded. The second heat signature created a distorting effect on the atmosphere over Antarctica, so satellites that could normally pick out a two-inch nail on the ground were unable to detect exactly where the heat signature came from. It was at the western end of Antarctica, but exactly where, they did not know. That was the first problem to be solved.

Observing the two men who sat at opposite ends of the table, and who were even then arguing with each other, Sidoti marveled at the contrast. Dr. Faison was the leading expert in experimental physics on the properties of sub-microatomic substances. He was neat, tidy and ever the gentleman. Karl Metzer, on the other hand, had not published a paper since graduate school, his contempt for other scientists evident in that refusal. He hated experiments, trusting his own intuition and arcane mathematics to lead him to the universe's secrets. His insights were legendary and were the only reason he was tolerated. Unexpectedly, Sidoti thought of something that Ambassador Hargrove had once said about Dr. Andreas Prescod—that he seemed to have the ability to smell out an archaeological site, sensing where to begin before the research was complete. Karl Metzer had that same intuition, that same boldness in confronting nature.

They have both ended up on this continent. I hope Metzer fares better than Dr. Prescod did, Sidoti thought.

"I'll get out of your hair. The first thing we need to do is pin down where that energy came from. Do you know where your quarters are?"

The two scientists nodded.

"Good luck. The future of our country could depend on your cooperation."

He had no idea that was to prove the understatement of all time.

Chapter 33

*A*ndreas stood at the mouth of a cave staring into the distance. Behind him, Eurydice was sobbing, and the sound tugged at him, causing a pain in his chest. They had been on the run for some time. He was not sure how long because time now made no sense, seeming to speed up and slow down in entirely random ways. On the river, the white crocodile had led them to a tributary that was covered with overhanging trees. This provided some protection from detection by the men in the helicopters. They made their way overland until the spit rejoined the river. To his surprise, the white crocodile had been at the edge of the land, its red eyes unblinkingly staring into the woods. Eurydice went into the water, and the crocodile led them across the width of the broad river, acting as support when they tired. On the other side, they fell to the mud, exhausted. After waiting a moment to catch their breaths, they hurried into the woods. When he turned, the river had been empty.

Time lost its meaning as they pushed inland, often over ground that sucked at their feet. This was not the Ilegu Forest. That was far to the south. They were moving in a northwesterly direction toward the Land of Malaia. At some point, they would pass Tiastan on their left, to the south, on the other side of the River Wilongo that they had crossed.

Andreas tried to calculate the distance they had traveled. The swiftly- rushing river would have carried them miles, but given the odd way in which he was now experiencing time, it was impossible to say how far they had gone. Not even his mind sense, which grew more acute as he traveled farther from the city of Llehstan, was of much help.

He looked down from the height they had earlier climbed in the darkness. Both were naked, having washed their robes in a small mountain stream and hung them to dry on the branch of a tree. The forest was alive with sound. Andreas admired the startling colors of the fearless birds that approached the cave curiously, strutting like officious hosts. They had passed large animals in the forest, had heard their sounds and movement. Once, Andreas had held his breath as a long shadow crossed their path. The snake was as black as the darkness of *pogosi*, but it did not appear again.

The one thing they did not lack was food. Fruit was everywhere, ranging in color from red to green. Not everything was edible. As Eurydice explained, many plants were poisonous, but her hands were unhesitating and unerring, and Andreas thought of the First People's stories that told of Empheme's magic with the land.

He turned, observing the woman who sat quietly, no longer sobbing, near a small fire in the cave, and he thought how comfortably she functioned in that environment. On the fire was a large tuber that she had dug from beneath a gnarled tree. It was yellow-skinned, and when heated, it first turned red, then black. She put her hand into the fire and took out the tuber, breaking it into two halves and holding one out. Andreas took it, absorbing the heat with his mind sense.

"I'm sorry, Eudy. Please forgive me."

He sounded miserable.

"There's nothing to forgive, Andreas. My grief is that of any mother, but it is not a condemnation of you. Lona walked in the path of the gods, as do we. He is your sacrifice, my love. And mine."

"Sacrifice? How could my son be my sacrifice?"

She did not directly answer his question.

"I miss him, though he resented the goddess' possession of me, as he resented my love for you. With me, he was always gentle and sensitive. I wonder how Teme will take this."

"Teme? Why do you speak of her now?"

Eurydice sighed.

"In some ways, she was more mother to him than I was. She trained him in the ways of the temple and the goddess. She also trained him in the way of the warrior."

"The *tusiata*."

"Teme is more than she seems, Andreas. Only I outranked her

in the order of the goddess Tiamat. None of the *leo-leos* could stand before her in battle. She was Lona's secret mentor."

His face clouded over as images of Lusani filled his mind. There, he had fought Natas and lost. Eurydice, as Empheme, submitted to Natas' embrace even as the soldiers dragged Andreas' half-dead body away. He had awakened in the rocky desert. Knowing what he thought, Eurydice touched his stricken face.

"Do not think of it as a burden but rather as your *fa'afetai*. Your obligation."

"Teme once told me that I could have no obligations among the First People since I was *i tala atu*."

"You are no longer an outsider, Andreas. You are Maatemnu, the Great Slayer, and in you is contained the impulse of the gods."

"What does that mean, Eudy? And don't tell me I am the destroyer of ages. I hear that in the visions, and it sometimes makes sense, but mostly it does not."

She walked into the cave, picked up his staff and returned.

"This is her gift to you, and it is given to only Maatemnu."

He took the staff. It fit into his palm as if it had been designed for him.

"Before he died, Lona gave it back to me though everyone said it was the Great Slayer's staff. Why would he do that?"

"Our son had no choice. It was the only thing he could do. No matter your love for him, you could not change his fate. All we can do is continue to pray for his protection. Now, tell me about your last meeting with the goddess in the desert. We were interrupted when last I asked."

A blush covered Andreas' face, and he did not speak for a long time. Then, he turned to her, his shame evident.

She came in a different guise after the boy breathed his breath into Andreas. He was not sure how long he was unconscious, but night had fallen when he awoke. The altar and the dying boy were gone. The light of the fire made a small circle around him and the woman. The rest of

the world disappeared. She was different of skin and spirit. Yet, her face was the same, only shaded and capriciously changed by the flickering light. The slyness in her eyes surprised him, and into his mind came an irreverent thought that she seemed to have placed there. He stood, feeling strong, aware of her ripeness. She was a courtesan, and he could not avoid the bulge of her breasts that rose with a suggestive power as her breath quickened. Then, he was next to her.

There were no preliminaries, and in a moment, clothes gone, she pulled him to her. He cried out at the heat of her body. When she kissed him, his head was full of stars, and he saw the truth of his visions, understanding the pain that was his lot. Andreas felt his body twisted, tied into a knot behind which lay his desire, an expectant, painful thing. He tore at her, fighting for his release. Then, she took her tongue from him, and the cold came. He burrowed, trying to find in her warmth some protection, and she pushed him on his back, her loins extended. It was the great silence of the time before time. He groaned, feeling himself spread throughout that silence until he was almost nothing, just a mote floating in an emptiness that was black yet visible. Andreas knew that he heard the voice of the goddess.

He did not have the heart to say this to Eurydice, so he had allowed her into his mind sense.

"I slept, it seemed, for an age, and when I awoke, I was at the edge of the Ilegu Forest. This staff was in my hand."

Eurydice's face was ecstatic.

"You forged the staff together," she said in an awed whisper. "The stories do not speak of this, Andreas. The goddess has favored you."

"You don't mind?" he asked cautiously.

"At what you remember as sex? No. It's probably the only way your brain could make sense of what happened."

"But she did change. She was different. She was black."

"Just your way of interpreting the events. The goddess is not corporeal, so she has no color."

"In my visions, she was always white."

"As I have said, Andreas, you're growing. Think of your action in defense of Marcus. There's a lesson there I don't think you understand."

She gave him her sight. Again, the dark energy flew forward from the exploded truck toward Marcus. On the other side, Lona stood. The blast approached Marcus, and Andreas drew the evil thing away, taking it into himself. In her mind sense, he saw Marcus standing, shock and relief on his face, but on the other side, Lona lay broken and dead.

"Why?" he cried, backing away.

She followed him slowly, her face gentle, her mind sense trying to soothe. He stopped at the cave's edge, his hands up as if holding her off. His pain was allied to that in her soul. When she spoke, it was with Empheme's voice.

"There is a balance always, Tama. Your son was the price of the goddess' love. In saving Marcus, you fulfilled your *fa'afetai* to the dark people of the land above whom you have wronged."

Andreas heard, understood and, for the first time, accepted responsibility. He had recommended rationalizing the population, and the African Americans were pushed out of the country. That he did not intend this mattered not at all. The gods always exacted their price. There had to be balance. Eurydice held him gently, and his body shook as he poured out his grief. Her body was filled with pain, too, and in this way, they touched for the first time in three seasons. Their love was fire upon a bed of lilies, and she kissed him throughout, feeling for the nuances of his power and his pain. They loved silently in the great forest that seemed to have stopped its business in hushed adoration of their act of expiation and thanksgiving. She gave a sharp cry that was controlled and felt him grow stronger as he sluiced her with his life. Falling forward, she sought a place in his neck to fit her head, and, in this way, they slept.

Chapter 34

*P*ogosi, the darkness, came and went. Each time, its visit was of somewhat greater length, and so it was in the painted dawn that Eurydice awoke, her senses alert. They had been traveling for many cycles of the darkness, and though not certain of her location, something told her their steps were true. It was days since they last heard helicopters, but Natas would not give her up. His need would be even more urgent now that her son was dead. At this thought, her heart convulsed as pain and loss overwhelmed her.

Rest, my son. May the goddess bind you to her.

With the symbol of the Onye gone, Natas' rule of the Land of Tiamat would be shaken. Empheme and Ghalib had joined, producing the Onye, who was now dead after three short years. Empheme was gone, and there was no replacement Onye. In the stories of the First People, the disappearance of the Onye signaled the return of the goddess, and Eurydice could guess at the uncertainty that must even now be running through the land.

They will become more unsure, a voice said in her mind sense.

She turned to see Andreas' eyes in the dawn, alert but gentle.

"Did you speak, my love?" she asked, stroking his hair.

"No, but I heard the voice."

In the morning light, she seemed insubstantial, her bald head outlined in shadow against the dawn.

"The forest seems to go on forever. Do you have any idea where we are?"

"This forest is not on any map, Andreas. It should not be here. We came west from Ghalib's Land. On one side of the river there should be the Plain of Sotami and on the other, the rocky waste of the Land of Dolon."

"Are we lost then?"

"No. It is where we are meant to be."

He frowned, not sure that he wanted metaphysical explanations.

"When we leave this forest, we will have to find a disguise. Our skin color will give us away. Also, the days begin to shorten, and soon the cold will come. We have to find warmer clothing."

Eurydice smiled, accepting his need for practicality. She closed her eyes, immediately seeing, in her mind sense, a small temple. This was the purpose of their visit to the forest. Andreas felt the change in her and followed her vision.

"What is it?" he asked.

"It is a temple of the goddess."

Within minutes, they were walking briskly along the edge of a small stream, its water mottled by the occasional light filtering through the trees. Andreas glanced at his reflection, almost not recognizing himself. He was taller and more muscular. His face had sharp angles that he did not remember, but his skin was the biggest surprise. It had become dark over the years. Before, even when he worked in the field on archaeological digs, his skin resisted the sun. Here, in this strange land, he had darkened. His was not the pristine blackness of the First People, but in the world above, he could pass for a light-skinned black man.

At the thought of the world above, he felt a sudden fear and stopped. Eurydice stood with him. Slowly, his face changed into a frozen rictus, and he was forced to his knees. Eurydice knelt next to him, her touch soothing.

"Can't breathe," he gasped. "Pain."

Entering his mind sense, her body jerked as she felt his agony. The pain flowed from his nerve endings, causing a deep throbbing. Her own vision darkened, but she accepted the torture, guiding him, helping him to capture the hurt. Then, he had hold of it, and with great difficulty pushed it back until it was trapped in his mind sense.

"What was that? Am I sick?"

He was breathless, and she continued to stroke his shoulder. Her brow was damp.

"No. It is the world's anguish you feel."

He remembered the face of the dying god whose body seemed permanently riddled with pain, and Eurydice's words made sense.

"Is that my fate? To live with this pain always?"

"It is your fate to relieve it, Andreas."

Suddenly, he was angry.

"Why? I didn't ask for this. I don't even understand what "this" is. You were bred for this, not I. Why me?"

She let him rant, understanding his anger, remembering a time long ago when she, too, asked that question. Why me? The goddess' answer had been clear. Why not? Soon, Andreas would find that to be on the path of the gods was not to be favored, simply to be chosen. He stomped away from her, and she smiled. He had instinctively taken the path toward the temple. The cloud of his anger lasted a long time, and *pogosi* was returning when they approached a clearing.

"It's too quiet here," he whispered, stopping.

She strode into the clearing. It was not large, maybe a hundred yards across and covered with very green grass.

"What do you see?" she asked.

He gasped, suddenly tense. Everywhere under the grass was water and in it, the slinking, shifting forms of white crocodiles.

"We're in the Land of Malaia where the sacred crocodiles live, Andreas. Stay close now. There's only one path across, and they don't know you."

She took his hand as he glanced anxiously at the water where shadows constantly moved. Once on the other side, the outline of a temple became visible in the dusk. It was larger than he anticipated. The front was a façade, with the building extending some way into the forest. Three priestesses awaited them. One came forward, her head bowed.

"Welcome, mother," she said, her eyes shifting to Andreas uncertainly.

"Blessings, daughter. This is Maatemnu."

The priestess' eyes widened for a moment, but she said nothing, only bowing to Andreas. They were ushered into the heart of the temple where a meal had been prepared. Andreas did not ask how the priestesses knew he and Eurydice were coming. He was beginning to think that the very air spoke to these women who served the goddess Tiamat. They ate ravenously and then were led to separate baths. He thought himself too excited to sleep, but the warmth of the bath was soothing. When he stood to dry himself, his limbs were heavy. He slept. The vision soon came. He lay quietly as the goddess hovered. Unbidden, the word came from him.

"Why?"

She took his sadness into her, changing it to anger, despair, curiosity and finally, acceptance. Then, she spoke.

"Your questions are many, Maatemnu, who is called Andreas, and it is time that your purpose be made clear."

Into his mind, she placed an image that he recognized. He was staring at the mountain of his vision, and on top, the figure had stopped dancing. Natas—yet not Natas—stood, calling to the sky, which ignored him.

"Has Natas lost the power to call down the lightning?" Andreas asked.

"This creature you know as Natas never had the right to call upon my brother Chango. It is a privilege he usurped."

He heard the affection with which she said "my brother Chango," and the story of her punishment for attempting to drown her brothers Chango and Baal came to mind. She smiled, and it was as if the stars had come to him, their light providing joy.

"Ah," she said, laughter in her voice. "The stories of the First People. There is truth in them, but always be careful who tells the stories. They speak of Time, and my brothers and I live outside of Time. How, then, can the stories speak of us?"

"What then is the truth? Did you not try to drown them?"

She made an odd face, a cross between a very young child's and an old woman's, and in that moment, she seemed familiar.

"I did," she said without emotion. "But only after they conspired to make of me the Pain-Carrier."

"The Pain-Carrier?"

"I was to give birth to Time. The future was to be my child. I did not wish it, and so, we fought. I defeated them, and they were in thrall to me. Our Father felt the absence of the divine balance, and he restored it by freeing them."

"And he punished you by trapping you in the ice?"

"Metaphorically, yes."

"But why, if you had simply defended yourself?"

"I had defied His will. It was my fate to be Mother of Time. I did not want it."

"You were the disobedient one?"

She shrugged.

"Can anyone truly defy Our Father's will? And if not, what then is disobedience?"

Andreas thought of that and then said, "The stories say that Chango had done no wrong, and the god to whom the people give no name rewarded him with possession of the earth."

"Who else wanted it?" she asked with a laugh that seemed to send the stars into little jitters. "To be restrained to Earth was as much a punishment as mine, though he was free to move about. Chango knew he would become the caretaker of my children."

Andreas involuntarily thought of the act of union between Eurydice and Natas at Lusani, and his insides churned.

"Is that the reason for the union of Chango and Empheme by way of Ghalib?"

She nodded.

"Your lives, in Time, are reflections of ours out of Time. It is the magic of Our Father who not even we understand and whose purpose is hidden behind the obvious."

"And Baal?"

Her face changed, becoming dark.

"Our Father's inexplicable disorder. Baal is elemental, without restraint and full of passion. He introduced these qualities to the world Our Father made."

Andreas watched the goddess, thinking that with the mention of Baal she seemed to have become more emotional. Then, in a flash, he saw her mind.

"Baal raped you."

"It was bad enough having to submit to Chango in order to give birth to Time. Baal's embrace was an abomination. His jealousy of Chango threatened to rip Our Father's creation apart, so we were separated. Punished, as the stories say."

"But you always seek to come back together," Andreas said slowly, comprehension dawning. "That is the sin. The original sin. Your father's paradox. He separated you as punishment but left within you the powerful instinct toward union."

She gazed upon him, and the sadness in her eyes caused the stars to dim.

"I cannot help but love my brothers, and they cannot help but love me. And yet, that love is repulsive."

"Like atoms that are attracted to each other up to a point, but beyond that point, push each other away," he said, awed.

She did not answer, waiting for him to figure it out.

"Tiamat is free," he finally said. "It is the time of Tiamat. They do not understand, do they?"

She shook her head.

"No. The people never did. Not even Empheme, my priestess, fully understands what it means to serve all the gods."

"I understand. You're last to be freed. The others were here a long time ago. Now that you're all here, the repulsion begins to take effect. Right?"

"Crude, but essentially correct."

"But you're tearing our world apart. Your father's paradox is loose, and it is destroying us." Andreas stopped, a thought occurring to him. "Natas is not Chango then? Not his representative, I mean."

She again shook her head.

"He is Baal," Andreas said quietly.

Thinking furiously, he tried to make sense of her story. His mind was immediately full of the world's violence, the hurricanes and the droughts, the drowning water and the ripped ozone layer that was letting in the cosmos' violence. He wondered what kind of god would not only allow, but ordain, that. Millions, maybe billions, had died since the waters rose so precipitously. His throat tightened.

"Are we so small? So insignificant?"

A hard core of anger was at the center of his being. She looked into his soul, trying to soothe him, but his anger was too cold, too furiously alive, to be quenched.

"We have always sent you, Maatemnu."

"Sent me? What can I do?"

"What you have always done, Great Slayer. Destroy an age. Bring in an age."

"How?"

"You have always known."

He saw himself giving the order to his spearmen, and the Neanderthal group falling, dying, the last of its kind, eyes closing on an age. He had followed his mind sense down thousands, millions of these timelines, and each had ended the same—some act of destruction that both ended and began.

"Why me?" he asked.

The goddess replied, "Why not?"

Chapter 35

*S*idoti heard the bell ringing and turned over on the narrow bed, dragging the blanket more tightly around him. *Go away*, he thought, as sleep fled.

The ringing continued, and, swearing, he climbed out of bed, keeping his body wrapped in the blanket. He punched a button on an intercom.

A tinny, disembodied voice said, "Mr. Sidoti, you had better come to the communications center. A message came for you."

Instantly, he was awake, and dressing quickly in the chill of the cabin hurried out the door. He reached the communications room in five minutes, and Captain Schmidt greeted him. Shadowy figures sat behind brightly-lit instruments, and it occurred to Sidoti that there had been very few interactions between him and the crew. He had on occasion seen a squad of soldiers exercising on the deck.

"Thanks, captain. Where is it?"

"Looks like some kind of code, Mr. Sidoti," the captain said hopefully.

Sidoti took the paper but did not respond. He had a satellite computer, but whatever was preventing Metzer and Dr. Faison from accurately calculating the location of the power source was apparently also affecting his computer. His daily reports to General Blount were being sent through the ship's communications center. This was the first time a coded message had come through. He hurried to his cabin.

After eleven days on the unpredictable sea, they seemed to be no further along. Metzer and Dr. Faison were truly incompatible, and five days earlier, Metzer had thrown the other scientist out of the lab. Dr. Faison was not reluctant to go, but his sulking only subsided when Captain Schmidt freed up another lab for him. They persuaded Metzer to give up the duplicate equipment, but after that, he locked the door. Sidoti had not spoken to him in four days. Metzer only cracked open the door for the sailor who brought him his meals. The captain was not pleased, particularly now he knew how unstable Metzer could be.

Sidoti sat at a small desk, flipping the light switch. It was a short message, but a shiver crawled up his back.

PLUTO ACTIVE. POSEIDON SWALLOWS EIGHT. MERCURY DOWN.

"Jesus!"

He quickly deciphered the message. The first two sentences were easy since he had created the code names. Pluto was the new weapon—the so-called dark energy; Poseidon was the sea, and the message indicated that they had lost eight ships. Sidoti checked his code book for Mercury and was suddenly very nervous. Mercury, their most advanced satellite, the one targeting the northwestern end of Antarctica, had gone off-line.

Probably the reason our computers are useless.

Sidoti quickly composed a message and rushed back to the communications room. Message sent, he waited. After several minutes, an answer came back. General Blount did not believe the Chinese had sunk the ships, though it seemed possible they were the spur to the attack. Not sure what that meant, Sidoti sent another message and waited. The answer caused another chill all over his body. The Chinese fleet had sailed out of the South China Sea, heading west. The Seventh Fleet was monitoring things, but there was a clear sense that America was on the back foot.

"Still can't use the computer?" he asked Captain Schmidt, frustration evident in his voice.

"No. This place is becoming a dead zone."

"Damn it. Keep working on it. I'm going to see Metzer."

The officer who commanded the soldiers materialized from the gloom. The captain picked up a ring of keys, and the three of them descended to the third deck. Sidoti banged on the door, shouting to Metzer to open up, but there was no response. After the fourth shout, he signaled to the captain who unlocked the door. The three men walked in just as Metzer wrote another number. The captain swore fluently for a long time. Formulae were written on every square inch of the lab's walls. Some of the equations stretched for the whole length of a wall. Metzer did not turn, apparently studying what he had written. When Sidoti touched the scientist's shoulder, the man jumped.

"Oh. It's you," he said, without much interest.

Sidoti was shocked at Metzer's appearance. He had lost weight, and his clothes hung on him. His eyes were dark and sunken, his skin pale. Food was piled in a corner, uneaten. The place smelled. Apparently, Metzer had only accepted the food to keep them off his back.

"Karl," Sidoti said quietly as if talking to a child. "Come. You've got to eat, and they have to clean the place."

Metzer looked around, and his eyes widened as if he was seeing the room for the first time.

"Oh, Jesus," he said contritely. "I'm sorry, but I—

"Later."

Sidoti steered him away from the wall. Metzer resisted for a moment, but when the soldier moved to assist, he acquiesced. Sidoti turned to the captain whose face was flushed with anger.

Without much of an apology, he said, "Please have the lab cleaned, Captain Schmidt."

Metzer shrugged, lifting his arms helplessly to the captain. Sidoti led him out. He made sure the scientist showered and shaved and then took him to the mess to eat. They were silent as Metzer wolfed down everything put before him. He asked for seconds, and, in the case of the icecream, thirds. Finally, he leaned back in the metal chair and belched, brittle laughter escaping him.

"Well, that was good. Felt like I hadn't eaten all day."

"At least four days from what we can tell," Sidoti responded, some irritation in his voice.

"Four days! No shit. That's not the record, though. I once worked on a problem for six days without eating, they told me. Well, you look a little green around the gills, ole buddy. You need a woman. Speaking of women—"

"Karl, do you know why you're here?"

"That's a stupid question."

"What have you found out?"

Metzer's eyes widened with excitement.

"I have to go back to the lab. I'm close."

"Close to what? The location?"

"Location? Oh, yeah. I figured that out four days ago. Well, sort of."

"Four days ago? Why the hell didn't you tell me?"

"Because you are here to destroy it, aren't you?"

Metzer was looking him straight in the eye, and Sidoti did not bother with denials.

"Karl, this is not an exercise in theoretical physics. I just got a message from the general. This energy has been used to destroy eight American ships. It is not a toy. It is a weapon, and it has been turned squarely at our country."

Metzer sat quietly, as if taking in the information.

"Come with me if you like, but I have to get back to the lab." He looked up and said cheerfully, "Hiya, Antonius. Where have you been?"

Dr. Faison had quietly come into the mess. He stood in a v-necked, light-blue sweater with a large C on it. Sidoti guessed the C stood for Cambridge, Dr. Faison's alma mater. Metzer walked to the door.

"You two coming?"

The lab was clean, but the odor of cleanser hung over it. Dr. Faison, distaste evident, took in the disorder. Sidoti stared at what was written on the walls. It looked like the onset of madness to him. On one wall was the name Theodore Kaluza, and next to it were two words in block letters—GRAVITY and ELECTROMAGNETISM. Below these, Metzer had written FOURTH DIMENSION. Next to this was a long series of what seemed to be nonsensical drawings, followed by several equations. The drawings looked like little white squares on a black background. Inside of each square was something that resembled a snowflake. Sidoti turned angrily to Metzer but hesitated when he saw Dr. Faison hurrying toward the wall of equations. Moving along the wall, he nodded, repeatedly making indistinct sounds.

"Calabi-Yau," he said almost to himself.

Continuing to study the equations, he took a writing pad and began scribbling more equations on it. Sidoti silently hoped that he did not have a second madman on his hands.

"What's Calabi-Yau?" he asked.

"Oh, sorry, Mr. Sidoti. It's a shape that is mathematically derived from the work of two mathematicians, Eugenio Calabi and Shing Tung Yau."

Sidoti shrugged, uncomprehending.

"The shapes represent additional dimensions in space. The mathematics of string theory—Dr. Metzer's preferred explanation for the origins of the universe—demand an additional six dimensions to the four we now know. This is an area of dispute between Dr. Metzer and me. He has argued that these additional dimensions exist, but he has neither the mathematics nor the experiments to lead to that conclusion inevitably."

"Experiments don't prove! They are like glasses. They simply improve our sight. If they prove anything, it's simply how ignorant we are."

Sensing the onset of another argument over something he didn't understand, Sidoti said, "Stop! We don't have time for this. Can we find the power source?"

Dr. Faison turned to Sidoti, his face serious. When he spoke, his voice was apologetic.

"That's the point of Dr. Metzer's mathematics. If his equations are right, what has been blocking both our ability to find the power source and to communicate is a distortion caused by the presence of a Calabi-Yau shape."

"In English, please."

"It's perfectly obvious, chimp," Metzer interjected, his voice light. "This proves what I've been saying all along. There are multiple dimensions lying on top, around and beneath each other. We could pass through them and not be aware of it. Something or someone is somehow affecting these dimensions. I think that is what your dark energy is being used for."

Sidoti sighed loudly. He was no wiser.

Before he could respond, Dr. Faison said, "In theory, Dr. Metzer is saying that the weapon you fear exists in Antarctica may not simply be converting mass to energy as in a bomb explosion. It is doing something much more sophisticated. If his equations are correct, it may be displacing the molecules of the objects in time."

"In time? Like time travel?" Sidoti said.

"Not in the way you mean it. Actually, it would be better to say that they are displaced in different dimensions."

"That sounds like—"

"Madness?" Metzer said, laughing. "Tell you what. You said you lost some ships. Ask them if they found any debris."

Sidoti stared at Metzer for a moment and then hurried to the communications center. Twenty minutes later, ashen-faced, he was back.

"They found nothing, I bet," Metzer said, a satisfied grin on his face.

"Nothing. Not a single thing. One second, according to the report, the ships were there, and the next, they were gone. The only thing reported was a sound like metal being pulled apart."

"The breaking of the molecular bonds could sound like that," Metzer said.

Sidoti sat heavily. All those years of protecting the United States, and it had come down to this, a weapon they did not understand, that killed almost noiselessly and with pristine efficiency, not even leaving evidence of its destructiveness. If these two men were right, the technology was not even within reach. Nothing being worked on in American labs, as General Blount had confirmed, was even remotely close to what Metzer and Faison were describing. Los Alamos, Sandia and Fort Detrick were hopelessly obsolete.

The one ray of hope was that the Chinese did not have the weapon, though it seemed to have been used on their behalf. The intelligence agencies had no proof, but everyone agreed that only Branniff Corporation had the capacity to develop something like that. *And Branniff had attacked!* They were now in the open. Sidoti could guess at the confusion in Washington. Branniff was not a state, though it perverted the policies of nations. Its base had shifted over the last decade from the United States to Africa, and African foreign policy now had a unified purpose.

Sidoti was torn. Here he was, thousands of miles from nowhere while his country was entering a new phase of war. He felt helpless and angry. Worse, he was afraid because, though far away, he was very much a part of the war. General Blount had ordered him to find the energy source and destroy it, but that was not the original intention. At first, the heat source was a curiosity, something that threatened but could possibly be used. Making use of the technology was still his first instinct, but now that the general had seen its power, destruction was the preferred policy option. Sidoti shook himself out of his reverie. The scientists would not like what he was going to say.

"Gentlemen, we have a problem. We have to control or destroy the power source."

Dr. Faison nodded, but Metzer's face flushed angrily.

"We are scientists. We don't destroy what we find."

"Spare me the noble sentiments, Karl. What we haven't yet found just killed thousands of Americans. Either we get control of it, or we destroy it. No ifs, ands or buts."

Metzer turned away. Dr. Faison's eyes followed him.

The dapper scientist said, "It may not be as simple as that, Mr. Sidoti. Look at what Dr. Metzer was working on."

He joined Metzer in front of a drawing that looked to Sidoti like a radio antenna with the usual pulsing lines dispersed at the top. Two other lines, much darker, were drawn on the right-hand side of the figure. They were diagonal and connected to the top of the radio antenna. Dr. Faison then pointed to the set of equations on the adjacent wall. Sidoti saw only gibberish.

"What's all that?"

"Dr. Metzer is suggesting that someone is attempting to shift a dimension, or dimensions. That part is nonsense, of course, but according to his mathematics, we are not dealing with a single source, such as we are searching for. Think of the tear in the ozone layer as the opening of a funnel. The broad end. Whatever is sucking the dark energy in would have to squeeze it into a narrow band as it comes down to the earth. However, and here Dr. Metzer's equations are highly speculative, it seems as if the mechanism needs to be triangulated in some way."

"Triangulated? What does that mean?" Sidoti said.

"It's pretty sophisticated, but he's assuming that whatever we are dealing with travels faster than the speed of light. That—"

"Wait a minute. I thought nothing traveled faster than light. Don't they call it the universal speed limit?"

"Very good, chimp. Think about gravity, though. It's instantaneously effective. That means it must travel faster than light."

"Only theoretically," Dr. Faison responded irritably.

Sidoti was beginning to get a headache.

"What does all this mean in practical terms?"

Metzer giggled.

"That, Antonius, means he's lost. Not a clue what we're talking about. Simplify it, please."

"It means, Mr. Sidoti, that we don't know what we're dealing with, and any attempt to set it off may cause repercussions we've not anticipated."

"Sort of like picking up nitroglycerin and shaking it next to your ear to see if it works. Boom!" Metzer shouted dramatically.

"According to Dr. Metzer's equations, there would have to be three sites in order to achieve a dimensional shift. Destroying one could set off a chain reaction affecting the other two, and we don't know where they are or what such a reaction would entail."

Sidoti breathed out loudly, a coldness that had nothing to do with the weather surrounding his body.

Chapter 36

Xu's muscles contracted as the bombers came screaming in. Moments later, the hillside, over two miles away, exploded. There was no respite. Within seconds, another wave of FC-44s, the American super bombers, rolled in, tearing the skin from the earth. Xu shifted his view, looking to the left where Li's forces were exposed.

Bravery is never a substitute for prudence.

"Will he hold, General?" Liu, standing beside him, said.

Xu shrugged.

"Shang Di said to Master Zun that the way of Tian is constant, neither prevailing nor perishing. If men respond to it with good order, good fortune will follow; with chaos, misfortune is inevitable."

Liu, still conscious of his recent promotion, thought of the general's words for a moment.

"Did General Li respond with good order or with chaos?"

Xu stared through the binoculars at the constant explosions of dust and dirt as the five-hundred-pound American bombs rained down. He felt, for a moment, a burning anger at Li. His action threatened the success of their battle. They had pushed south rapidly after Uzbekistan fell. The Americans, with their giant bases around Hyderabad in Pakistan, counter-attacked, and the region around Karshi became a killing field. His casualties were in the thousands, and the Americans suffered equally. In a stalemate, however, China was actually winning. Every day eroded the American myth of invincibility. When he answered Liu, this was in his mind.

"Only a perfect man can distinguish between that which is human and that which is natural, for volition is often the act of Tian, and Tian is the dwelling of Shang Di. General Li often acts in opposition to what is proper, but whether for happiness or calamity, only Shang Di knows."

Lui nodded, understanding the general to say that no man knows the future. General Li had acted precipitously. These battalions were the burnished tip of the spear, a tip that was solid for fifty miles across, flaring out to the millions of Chinese behind them who were now crossing the lands of Central Asia. Its long shaft was the continuing stream of refugees from the populous east. The future that looked so bleak when he was a boy now promised hope. It was all due to General Xu who, only a few weeks earlier, had been honored as Hero of the Homeland.

The general always responds with good order. Look at how he forced the Americans to commit their fleet which now lies broken somewhere in the southern Indian Ocean, Liu thought.

The fate of the American fleet caused Liu to frown. They still did not know what destroyed the American ships off the southeastern coast of Africa. Their sailors brought back tales of horror and madness, of ships simply disappearing after the scariest noise. No Chinese ships were attacked, and the transport fleet had crossed the Atlantic, making for eastern Canada. That was Liu's triumph. He smiled, thinking of the call he received from the black woman who was once secretary of state of the United States. It came on his third day in Bumba, that oddly beautiful, new city in the heart of Africa. Secretary Ernsky's agreeing to the Chinese request earned him his promotion to colonel, jumping him over two ranks. Thirty million Chinese would be going to Africa. Maybe more would be invited later. He touched the new bars on his shoulder, pretending to be smoothing his collar. Xu smiled, aware of the young man's pride.

"You have done well, Liu. The transportation of the black people goes well, and the American fleets are too busy in the Indian Ocean and the Pacific to prevent it."

"Do they wish to prevent it, sir?"

"No, but they wish to prevent us from performing it. The Americans are not stupid, Liu. They know what this means. Those thirty million give us a foothold in Africa. That is why they fight so desperately on three fronts. We must consume their energies here on the plains of central Asia because it is in the Indian Ocean and the Pacific that we must win."

Behind them was the furious chatter of communications officers. Xu smiled as he heard his friend, General Wang, call a field commander something that involved a yak's ass.

Still fiery, my old friend, but loyal.

When they were cadets together, Wang had been a perfect soldier. His favorite saying was, "Anyone found using his ability against The Way should be condemned to death summarily."

A harsh philosophy, but one with much wisdom.

Xu wondered what Wang would do with General Li. The roar of battle continued, but with the incredible flexibility of the human mind, the violent noise became normal. Xu thought of his visit to Beijing. The honor had been a surprise, and a little irritating since he was in the middle of a war. The Americans had not folded, and no one expected they would. Xu was a realist and paid no attention to the propaganda about the softness of the West. The West had not won and sustained a world empire, beating back all comers for almost six hundred years, by being soft. He understood them in ways his countrymen did not. Their liberalism, a two-hundred-and-fifty-year experiment in restraint, was a veil behind which the iron of their will was well disguised.

In the end, we will be fighting all of the West. The Europeans are foolish not to join the Americans now. They wait, hoping to exhaust us and then to pick up the pieces.

Xu knew that the Europeans lacked faith.

"Whatever happens, Liu, always hold firm to inner power."

"Why is this, sir?"

"Because he who holds firm to inner power is first master of himself, and being master of himself, he is able to order others. In his response to others, he becomes the complete man. As Master Zun says, 'Heaven manifests itself in its brightness; Earth manifests itself in its breath; the enlightened man values his completeness.'"

Liu's eyes were bright with adoration.

"We had better see how the battle goes, my boy," the general said.

Outside the bunker, the noise of the battle was deafening. There was a furious, frenzied quality to the sound of the war machines.

Xu could distinguish the high-pitched whine of the F-405s as they screamed overhead, pounding the entrenched position of his men. Less frequently, he heard the lower cry of his new Yue-class fighters, built with Branniff's technology. These were faster than the F-405s and were there to harass them, not to win the air battle. The true battlefields were the two oceans. If China prevailed there, they would have the world. The deaths in central Asia would not be in vain. America had to commit to winning there because if they lost, then the Middle East would be China's. The crashing sounds of war engines became enmeshed with the groans of men, and Xu slowed as he came to a field hospital.

"How many understand this side of war, Liu?"

His voice was low. Liu stared at the broken bodies that were everywhere visible. Men seemed to be simply piles of incompleteness. He expected death, but this carnage, this death without dying, unnerved him for a moment. He fought the feeling of lightness in his stomach, not daring to embarrass the general before the men. Xu squatted beside a young soldier whose eyes seemed fiery with the honor. He placed six incense sticks in the ground next to the soldier and lit them as he recited a prayer.

"Shang Di, guard my spirit, and let me know the way. It is good that a man should respect his elder brother. It is better that he should revere his parents. But above all, it is felicitous that a man should prostrate himself before you. All men are sightless and stumble upon the path. Even the sages have sight only when you touch their eyes."

Xu closed the soldier's eyes. For a long time, his hand stayed on the dead boy. Noticing Xu's sadness, Liu thought of a maxim. The master Mencius said, "To be sincere is the Way of Heaven, and to think of sincerity is to be human. A man who is sincere is always able to move those to whom he speaks." When Xu turned, he was smiling.

"Shang Di will guide him," he said.

The soldiers within earshot bowed, and he stood.

"Let us fortify Li's flank."

The order given, his will was enacted, and the battle began in earnest.

Chapter 37

Thousands of miles to the west, Xu's transport ships ploughed through the Atlantic. They braved the tempest, avoiding the American eastern shore, not wanting to give that nation greater cause for alarm. Anne Ernsky watched as the latest fleet disappeared into the heavy snows falling on the St. Lawrence River. The transportation process had been going on for weeks, and she was finally beginning to feel some relief. The logistics were horrendous, and moving in the middle of this bitter winter made an inhumanly difficult job almost impossible.

Still, it looked as if they might pull it off. The Americans had not attacked any of the transport ships since the mysterious destruction of their aircraft carrier and its seven destroyers. The reports said men heard a tearing sound and felt the air collapse on itself. Then, the ships were gone. The whole world was on edge. Even the Chinese, though they tried hard not to show it, were frightened. The mysterious weapon appeared to have been used in their defense when the American fleet moved to intercept the transport ships, but the will behind it was uncontrollable. Now, there was doubt in the voices of the Chinese. Branniff had shown its power, and, in doing so, had subtly shifted the relationship with its allies.

Though no public statement was made, the United States had changed its position on Branniff. Anne Ernsky's reports indicated that all of Branniff's assets in the United States had been seized. That hardly mattered anymore. It was too little, too late. Branniff's main assets were now on the African continent. When, three years earlier, the Americans made the abortive attempt to isolate the corporation, Branniff's control of the world's financial markets was made clear. Not a single country, including America's allies in Europe, was able, or willing, to prevent the flow of Branniff's capital.

Anne Ernsky was not given to emotional responses, but she, too, was shocked by the brutality of Branniff's actions when the transport ships were threatened. It had snuffed out the lives of almost seven thousand men and women, without warning and without subsequent explanation.

"The loss seems to have traumatized the United States," she said to herself.

Rene, her boyfriend, not understanding, said, "What did you say?"

"Oh, sorry. I was thinking about the destruction of the American ships."

"Serves them right."

Rene's voice was cold. She leaned into him, glad of his body's warmth. It had been consistently in the minus-fifteen-degree range for days, and with the need to conserve energy, no one was comfortable. In front of them, the long, snake-like body of the St. Lawrence River was a pathway to a fairyland of ice and snow. Visibility was low, but the whiteness around them, broken only by the dark silver of the waterway, was eerie, a ghost land that, to her surprise, they had learned to accept. Many of her people had become attached to that piece of land and were reluctant to move. That thought prompted a glance at the other man with her. Notah Bitsoi stood framed in the dim light like one of the giants from his people's legends. His face looked miserable.

"Thank you for trying," she said.

Notah made a harsh sound.

"Fewer than ten thousand came. The elders spoke against it at the pow-wow. Their words were strong."

She hooked her arm through his.

"You did what you could. It was not a command, simply an invitation. Ten thousand is a good number."

He knew she wanted to make him feel better. Many of those who made the journey were strong in their claims of African American ancestry. They were those who lived between the twin confusions of the black and the Indian worlds and who, during the Expulsion, hid on the reservations. Heeding the call, they came to the northeast.

"It's difficult, Notah, to abandon the land of your blood."

"That is what the elders said."

"You are pure Indian. Why are you coming?" Rene said.

"One hundred percent Dine, though I lived with the Salish as an adult. It is where I met Olahl. As to why I came, it was my dreams that led me."

"What dreams?"

"Dreams of a new land with a sky of silver and a huge sun behind which is darkness. The visions speak of life and friendship."

"I didn't know you were a shaman," Rene said, laughing.

"That's what's so odd. I'm not. Before all this, I was a mechanic. I repaired trucks."

"How did you get involved?"

Notah hesitated, weighing his words carefully.

"I dreamed of a powerful figure who was called the Father of the Ilegu."

"Odd name. Is that a Navajo god?"

"No, and as far as I can tell, it is not any Indian god at all. But that's not the weirdest thing. Somehow, I knew that this black figure was also Coyote, the spirit father who placed the Indian in this world but who continues to play tricks on us."

"Why would a black god create the Indian people?"

Notah shrugged. The cold began to bite, and they returned to the relative warmth of the buildings that stood like dark sentinels in the northern gloom.

Once inside, Notah said, "I didn't tell you the strangest thing of all."

"What's that?" Anne Ernsky asked, removing the heavy coat and placing it near the fire to dry out.

"A couple weeks after my vision, this Father of the Ilegu showed up when I was hiding in Carson National Forest."

He stopped. The other two stared at him.

"And?"

Notah said, "I think the one you call Branniff was the figure in my vision, this Father of the Ilegu, the one I thought was Coyote."

"Why do you think that?" Anne Ernsky asked.

"The way you describe Braniff. You said it's as if light never entirely shows who he is. The one who appeared to me was the same way."

"That's pretty creepy, man. Do you think you might have just imposed Branniff on a half-remembered dream?" Rene said.

"That's what I thought at first, but he did not ask who I was. He immediately called me Dream Stalker."

"So?"

"Rene, a dream stalker is one who has no training to dream dreams. He's suddenly called by the spirit world to speak to the Indian."

"Well, you sure did that over the last couple of years."

Rene slapped Notah on the back to take any sting out of the words. The big Indian did not laugh, and when he spoke, his voice was hollow with sadness.

"The dream stalker is the voice of doom, Rene. He foretells the destruction of things. He stalks the dream that would drive a shaman mad."

Rene and Anne Ernsky observed the haunted face of the man who had been such a source of strength and inspiration over the previous three years. Anne Ernsky turned away, thinking about Branniff. Who was he? What did he and Natas want? She had no answer. After a while, Notah Bitsoi left for his quarters. Anne Ernsky and Rene snuggled, both to relieve the cold and for the comfort.

Am I in love? she wondered.

Resting her head on the younger man's shoulder and noting the spare furnishings, she thought how much her life had changed. Her displaced people were not a nation, but she was, in fact, a head of state, the international voice of those in the Borderlands. The Americans' response was complicated and ultimately pointless because they were trying to deny any official status to those they had expelled. That had not worked. Her anger dulled over time because she accepted that it was wasted energy, but the horror of the injustice was still very much on her mind. The man next to her carried his hatred like a pure, living thing, and nothing could turn him from it. He felt satisfaction at the destruction of the American ships, but her sadness at the deaths could not be denied.

What has changed? Where has my anger gone? Am I simply too tired now?

Natas Branniff intruded on her thoughts. Months earlier, arriving at Branniff's schloss outside Salzburg, she was immediately struck by the structure of the place, with its geometrical gardens and the perfect circle of the man-made lake. The house was not overly large, but its proportions impressed themselves on the consciousness, seeming somehow flawless. She had gazed admiringly at the symmetry of the arched marble stairway and the banister that was decorated in gold leaf. Her overwhelming impression had been that the building was designed to impress order on the space. This was not about ostentatious wealth. Odd as it seemed, she thought of it as understated.

Then, Natas had walked in with a black woman whose skin shone in the subdued light. Anne Ernsky could not take her eyes away from her. The woman was not beautiful in the classic sense, but she gave the impression of unity. The word "unblemished" had jumped to Anne Ernsky's mind. Not tall, she seemed to float, holding herself so straight that Natas' height did not dwarf her. "I am Teme," she had said in an accent that sounded African.

Anne Ernsky sighed in the darkness, and Rene hugged her tightly. She returned the squeeze, glad for his solidity.

"Do you ever wonder about the object Notah and I found in Montana? I've been thinking about it lately."

A few years earlier, the Salish told them of the mysterious object. Notah and Rene investigated, finding a preternaturally smooth, cylindrical obelisk in the forest near Flathead Lake. They never figured out what it was, but it seemed an energy source of some kind. Even more perplexing, the Salish had said that black people erected the obelisk in the weeks prior to its examination by Rene and Notah.

"So have I," Anne Ernsky responded. "That was ... what, three years ago? Strange. The scientists we sent out couldn't make head or tail of it. Their instruments couldn't even take readings. I asked Branniff about it, but he never answered."

"Weird." They were silent for a while, and then Rene said, "What do you make of Pope Celestine's actions?"

"He is acting curiously, but he's under a lot of pressure. Worse, Etienne is torn between two faiths, though he does not accept that."

"I always wondered why he helped the Changoists."

"The choices were hard. If he had not, the new religion of Chango threatened violence. Etienne thought he could control its energies and save the Catholic Church since so many Catholics outside the

United States and Europe had turned to the new religion. He did the pragmatic thing."

"But why is he going back and forth between Bumba and Rome? And why the secrecy?"

"Think about it, Rene. How would it look to conservative Catholics if their spiritual leader went to the Bumba cathedral? He's having a hard enough time holding the Church together as it is."

"Do you think he's lost his faith?"

Anne Ernsky did not immediately respond. The question was more complicated than Rene knew. She continued to keep an eye on Etienne Ochukwu, Branniff's plans being still dependent on the illusion that the new religion and Catholicism were the same. Given the arguments over vestments and the new liturgy, she had waited nervously for the European and American response. The threats of secession from Rome came. There had been no immediate action, but she knew that it would not be long in coming. The new religion was losing patience with the subterfuge. Behind all this stood Natas Branniff, architect of the new religion's growth and now the instigator of a measured break. At the schloss, she had seen how serious he was. Natas was a believer.

"No, Rene. Etienne has not lost his faith, but, like so many people, he has dual loyalties. It is this we exploited to bring him on board several years ago."

"But these trips between Africa and Europe. He's bound to be discovered, don't you think? He's not exactly an invisible figure."

"I wonder about that. Etienne is one of the smartest people I know. He must understand the risk. Still, while Europe is his power, Africa is his heart."

"I wish I could meet him. I think he's a great man."

"Someday, I'll introduce you. You'd like him."

Rene's face held a worried look as he said, "If he survives this. If the Church fractures, he will be at risk."

"No one will hurt Etienne."

Her tone was that of a woman who had once directed the power of the United States, and though not threatened, Rene felt the hairs rise at the back of his neck. He turned to her in the darkness and feeling her open to him, he loved her.

Chapter 38

O n the other side of the Atlantic, Etienne Ochukwu was preparing to celebrate The Easter Vigil Mass in St. Peter's Basilica. Kwaku handed him the pallium, but his mind was far away, in a land to the south where the Catholic Church was being simultaneously glorified and undermined. Etienne could not quite put his finger on why he was fearful. The new religion had changed the vestments and the liturgy, but after three visits, it was not doctrinal differences that worried him. Rather, it was his feeling that the act was not the substance. This sense of something ominous and threatening drew him back to search for whatever it was that made him uneasy. He was impressed with the devotion of the millions of adherents who came to Bumba. St. Peter's Square, too, was now swollen with the faithful. There was no question that a spirit of religiosity was alive in the world. In spite of the official clash between the Vatican and the Catholic churches of Europe and the United States, ordinary Catholics seemed more devout, more submissive to the will of God.

If this is true, why do I feel fear?

Kwaku reached for the papal mitre. The antiphon was being sung as Etienne proceeded slowly into the chapel. The papal ferula moved in flowing symmetry with his steps, and the sound of young voices flowed over him.

As he walked, he softly intoned, "We gather together to pray and ask forgiveness. In this, we prepare to meet Christ. This congregation celebrates our brotherhood in Christ and expresses our unity with him and with each other."

The antiphon ended as he approached the altar, and when he looked up, his eyes met the ironical gaze of Natas Branniff. Fortunately, his surprise came during a natural pause. Etienne quickly adjusted, smiling beatifically at the congregation and making the sign of the cross as he continued.

"In the name of the Father and the Son and the Holy Spirit."

The reassuring sound of the congregation's "Amen" came on cue. Natas' smile broadened.

"The grace of our Lord Jesus Christ and the love of God and the fellowship of the Holy Spirit be with you all."

The congregation responded, "And also with you." Etienne was surprised at the emotion that flowed through him. As if he had sensed the connection, Natas' smile disappeared. The service continued, Etienne's powerful voice filling the chapel. Natas became fidgety.

"Lord God Almighty, creator of all life, of body and soul, we ask you to bless this water; as we use it in faith, forgive our sins, and save us from all illness and the power of evil. Lord, in your mercy, give us living water, always springing up as a fountain of salvation. Free us, body and soul, from every danger, and admit us to your presence in purity of heart. Grant this through Christ, our Lord."

When the congregation responded, "Amen," he felt the first pain.

In his head, a voice asked, *Who protects you, Etienne?*

He grabbed at his chest, aware of the alarm in the chapel. It was all in slow motion. Natas was standing, gesticulating, and several cardinals were rushing to him. Kwaku, face stricken, gaped helplessly. Something seemed to explode against his ribs, and he fell into the arms of three cardinals who quickly took him from the chapel.

Etienne did not lose consciousness, and when they laid him on his bed, the physicians were there. He was already feeling better, but the doctors insisted on examining him. With the pain gone, Etienne's thoughts turned to Natas. Why had he come? Natas had not been in touch since the meeting of the Nine some time ago, and then, he had been inaccessible, overbearing and arrogant. Natas had treated the other members of the Nine as he would his servants. Remembering the anger in that room, Etienne wondered why Natas, as charming a person as he knew, chose to alienate these men whose power could be so useful to him. It occurred to him that Natas no longer needed aid. Branniff controlled everything, even the Nine. The world finally got a glimpse of

Branniff's power when the American ships were destroyed, but Etienne had seen it before that, in the secret room deep beneath the Vatican.

Around him, physicians rushed to and fro, running this test and that, but he knew they would find nothing. Had he simply been overly anxious because Natas was present? Was it the stress of the last few months, the worry over the American Church, and possibly Europe, splitting off from Rome? Or had Natas induced the feeling in him that he was having a heart attack?

Nonsense.

A long-faced Italian doctor attached electrodes to his chest. When he said, "Relax, Your Holiness," the voice was respectful but impartial. Etienne wondered if the man had any feelings about a black pope. Or possibly worse, a non-Italian pope. Kwaku stepped forward hesitantly. The doctors looked disapprovingly at him.

"Let him stay. Kwaku ministers to me. His presence will be an aid to your medicines."

The fussing over him seemed to go on interminably, but finally, they were done, and enjoining him to rest, they filed out. As the last one left, the cardinals came pouring in, and he sighed, preparing for the onslaught of worry that they brought. More important than his health, it seemed, was the need to reassure the world, and considerable time was spent finding the exact language for the release to the press. He finally agreed to something innocuous but reassuring, and they left after he insisted that he needed to rest. Only Kwaku remained, and he hurried to the pontiff's side, his eyes showing deep affection and concern.

"Are you all right, father?"

Etienne smiled, trying to reassure the young man.

"Yes. I am sure it is something simple, like not eating breakfast this morning."

"But you did eat breakfast this morning, father."

"You are a blessing, Kwaku."

The young man stuck a hand inside his robe and pulled out an envelope. Etienne opened it and read the two-line message. "You will receive an invitation. Do not attend." It was signed by Natas. A warning bell went off in his head, but he stuck the paper back into the golden envelope and closed his eyes.

"Kwaku, my son, come pray with me."

Kwaku knelt next to the bed, and Etienne placed his hand affectionately on the young Ghanaian's head, thinking, not for the first time, how isolated they were in this Italian city. In his mind were several questions. What invitation would be sent to him? Why should he decline? What was Natas Branniff up to now? Pushing these questions aside, however, was a fearful image. As he had fallen, the pain in his chest stopping his breathing, the earlier pain in his bones had returned. It was different from the chest pain, and in his mind, a reptilian image had formed.

Almost as if it was inside me.

After Kwaku left, Etienne felt the bone of his jaw. It was strong and not in any way misshapen.

"Now is not the time for fantasy, Etienne."

He drew the blanket up over his chest. It was a long time before Pope Celestine fell asleep.

Chapter 39

*S*idoti squinted through the occasional breaks in the heavy fog at a world that even from the ship's porthole looked frightening.

Antarctica. The last mystery on the planet.

The air was frigid. For weeks, they had ploughed through heaving seas, heading this way and that as their instruments provided contradictory signals about the possible location of the heat signature. Generally, they were moving farther southwest, and that was a problem because the captain did not want to take his ship any farther below the Antarctic Circle. With winter coming, he was worried about being trapped in the ice. General Blount came to Sidoti's defence, but it took a direct order from the secretary of the navy to move Captain Schmidt.

Staring out the window, Sidoti could understand why Schmidt was worried. The water, when he could see it, looked alive. The seas were fairly heavy at the moment, and ice floes were being pushed aside by the boat. Occasionally appearing through the mist was a uniform whiteness in the distance. Soon, they would turn toward that pallid icescape. They had no choice. Sidoti's mission was to find, control or destroy the energy source. The presence of the soldiers on the ship now made sense. When Schmidt had argued with him, the major made it clear that the soldiers were there for the protection of the mission and that they were perfectly willing to take over the ship if necessary. Sidoti felt for Schmidt, but the man did not seem to get it that the safety of his ship was a minor consideration. He turned as Dr. Faison joined him at the porthole.

"Awesome, isn't it?" the scientist said.

Sidoti nodded. He did not have much of a relationship with Dr. Faison, who seemed better at interpreting Metzer's findings than in coming up with breakthroughs of his own. Metzer believed that Dr. Faison was a second-rate brain, and, given how little the man was contributing, Sidoti was beginning to think that Metzer was right. As usual, Dr. Faison was immaculately dressed.

"Temperature's dropping. Did Dr. Metzer tell you he found another anomaly, Mr. Sidoti?"

"What anomaly?"

"His calculations now suggest that the heat signature is at a much greater depth than we at first thought."

"It's buried?" Sidoti asked.

"We're not sure. We're speculating that maybe it was built where the iceberg broke off."

"But I saw the first signature as the ice was breaking. It had to have been there before the break."

"Yes, yes. We're trying to make sense of that now."

Sidoti felt like asking Dr. Faison how come he was not in the laboratory with Metzer trying to figure it out but restrained himself. He needed both scientists. Metzer's behavior was becoming more erratic. Sidoti was trying not to push him too hard, but Metzer was his own spur. He cared little about the politics, and it did not seem to matter to him that the United States was in danger. Sidoti had the impression that Metzer saw all political systems as pretty much the same—annoying. He turned as Captain Schmidt called from the doorway of the cabin. For the first time in several days, he was smiling.

"Come. You'll want to see this."

They followed him through the convoluted corridors of the ship until he climbed out on to a protected deck.

"Oh my God!"

Sidoti's eyes traveled upwards. Before him was the strangest sight he had ever seen. The iceberg was still some distance away, but it was so big that it seemed close, crowding the ship.

"Big sucker, isn't she?" the captain said. "Not too many have seen it up close. Branniff's 'keep off the grass' notice, you know."

"It's beautiful," Sidoti whispered.

The iceberg had broken off from Antarctica thirteen years earlier. Having expected it to be pure white, he was surprised by the blueness.

The combination of pasty white tinged with blue created the impression it had fallen from some ice planet.

"It doesn't appear to have moved too far from the continent," Sidoti said.

"Actually, it's moved quite a bit. We're still a ways north of the continent. What you see on the other side isn't Antarctica proper. It's the ice cap. That's already reaching out from the continent. In a few weeks, it will be solid."

"Still doesn't seem very far for it to have drifted in thirteen years."

"Remember, Mr. Sidoti, this is a block of ice, and it floats, but it is a very large block. Almost one-third the size of the United States."

Sidoti nodded, his eyes traveling up the impossible height of the great iceberg.

I wonder how tall it is. Looks like a mile high.

They stood for a long time, the cold forgotten, staring at the iceberg until it again slid behind the mist. Even then, Sidoti remained on the deck, hoping for another glimpse. It had been simultaneously the most beautiful and the most frightening thing he had ever seen.

Turning to Captain Schmidt, he said, "Does that mean we'll be tacking to the south soon?"

"We already have. Soon, you'll feel the ice."

"Meaning?"

"We're equipped to plough through the ice. If we're caught, we can withstand any pressure it might exert over the winter."

"What are you talking about?"

"Mr. Sidoti, we could be here for the whole winter. Once we move into that ice, we are committed. You won't just jump off my ship and find whatever you're looking for. That will take time. It's possible we won't be able to get out of the ice."

Sidoti stared at the captain. He had not thought of being trapped in that god-forsaken wasteland for the whole winter. And winter in Antarctica lasted a whole lot longer than in the United States. He turned just as the mist broke. In the distance was the achromatic dullness of the approaching ice cap. It no longer looked beautiful.

Chapter 40

Andreas jumped, body turning in very rapid revolutions as his legs snapped out powerfully, breaking the limb from a tree. The contact seemed to propel him back into the air, and as his body assumed a vertical position, the golden staff lanced out, almost like an extension of his arm, slicing effortlessly through another branch. Instantly, it was retracted, and his body curled into a ball before he snapped his feet straight backwards into a kick that seemed to rip the air apart. He landed in a full split, before springing back to his feet.

"You're becoming a menace to the forest. No tree is safe when you practice *tusiata*," Eurydice said.

She observed his chest which moved slowly in and out. Andreas smiled sheepishly, but she could see that he was proud of his effort.

"What was that last move? The one where you tucked and then kicked backwards? I've never seen that."

"It doesn't exist in the art. It came in a dream."

He placed the staff against a tree. Eurydice nodded in appreciation as he raised his leg until it was flat against his face. He lifted his arms next to the raised leg and froze in that position. There was no tension in his body. Eurydice moved around the still figure, noting how dark Andreas' skin was. She picked up the staff. It felt alive in her hand. Suddenly, she jumped at him, the staff extended. He never moved, but the staff struck something and recoiled in her hand.

"Remarkable," she said.

He relaxed, slowly returning his leg to the ground as she examined his body, noting its strength.

"Did you do that, or did it just happen?"

He picked up his robe.

"It's odd. In some ways, it was both, as if a part of me saw the blow and knew I couldn't move in time. Another part of me sprang to my defense because it had seen … actually, 'seen' is not quite right. It was more like it anticipated the attack and moved to deflect it."

Eurydice nodded.

"Andreas, are you aware of anything, other than you, inside you? I know that's a strange question, but trust me."

"Well, I'm aware of the dying boy being with me somehow. I don't exactly think of him as being inside me. That's way too weird."

"And the rest of this is not?" Eurydice said, laughing.

That laughter made Andreas happy because there was precious little of it since she found out about Lona's death. It was as if the boy inhabited a wholly private and inaccessible part of her. When she asked about something inside him, he thought of her pain at the loss of their son.

"Strangely enough, this is beginning to make all the sense in the world," he replied.

"Thinking can get in your way. It's something that Mother Mutasii had to teach me. In the early days, she called me *fal se na*, thought then action. It's so normal for us in the world above that we never become what Mother Mutasii calls *na isi,* action in itself."

Andreas nodded, thinking of his time of trial and initiation in the desert. In the Hall of the Onyes, it was only when he stopped trying that his mind sense had slid into the tumblers, finding the electrical impulses that opened the door. *Na isi.* Action in itself. He liked the idea.

"You said it came to you in a dream. What about the goddess?"

"Almost every time I sleep."

"And your dreams are no longer confused?"

"No. They're more like conversations now."

"That's because she lives in you. You are aware of the dying god's presence, but is his voice clear?"

"I don't hear a voice at all. I sense his presence and that excruciating pain of his. I can only stand it because you showed me how to isolate it in my mind sense."

She was quiet for a while and then said, "It is no longer his pain, Andreas."

"I know."

Andreas moved to the small fire and popped a handful of roasted berries into his mouth. Some property in the fruit darkened their skins.

"Eudy, I'll tell you the strangest thing of all. I'm a scientist, but I had to give up my science to grasp what's happening here. Something magical is happening to us, and yet, it does not feel illogical. I find myself wondering if perhaps some sort of divine physics underlies all this."

She made a face.

"Magic. Science. What truly is the difference?"

"It is science that has pushed us forward as a species, Eudy. We can't deny that."

"Yes. Yesterday's alchemist becomes today's chemist and then denies the value of alchemy. The truth is, Andreas, they both search for ways of understanding the divine physics, as you call it. Sometimes we get it, and, like children, we celebrate our brilliance, but always, there's another veil, and there we are, alchemists all over again."

Andreas went to the river without replying, investigating his reflected image in the water. Whatever property in the berries darkened his skin also caused loss of hair. There were only a few remaining blond strands. Soon, it would all be gone, and he would be indistinguishable from the First People. Then, they could leave the forest. Andreas returned to the fire and pulled out a tuber. Absorbing the heat, he handed her half.

"Is the pain more frequent now?" Eurydice said.

"Yes. I'm not sure how to explain this, but it's taking up more and more of my mind sense."

"We must return to the world above. That is the pain you feel. You must extinguish it."

At the word "extinguish," something tightened in his stomach. Maatemnu. The Great Slayer. Andreas tried to keep the images of destruction out of his mind but failed.

"Eudy, how did you and Natas come to be brother and sister? You don't seem anything alike."

She searched his face for the question behind the question. When she answered, her voice was no longer Eurydice's, but Empheme's, the high priestess of Tiamat.

"Know, Tama, that in the time before time, the god to whom the people give no name ordained that his offspring, the goddess Tiamat and his sons, Baal and Chango, should stride across the universe. Chango grew lonely upon the earth, and for him was created the First People. Chango nursed them, and they increased in size and power, their passage through time shaped by the union of Empheme and Ghalib. That union always produced the Onye who walked in the footsteps of the god Chango.

"In time, the Onye grew jealous of that unity and sought to break it by deception and guile, interposing himself between Chango and the woman Empheme. This act of the Onye weakened the god Chango, and he was replaced in power and majesty by the goddess Tiamat. The Onye's action also let loose upon the earth the spirit of dissension and strife, and the First People saw each other not as brethren but as foes. The air was darkened with spears; stones pounded the life from men, and the First People knew death.

"Then was Maatemnu, the Great Slayer, created, he of the withered arm who had placed his hand in the fire, the voice of the god Chango. In his new-found strength, he spoke harshly with the Onye, and they fought. The gods made certain that neither would prevail, and in the end, they parted. The Oyne, led by the will of the god to whom the people give no name, journeyed to the Land of Tiamat. Maatemnu, the Great Slayer, went north to the ancestral lands of the First People. This was the Great Parting. In the time since the First People left, the ancestral lands had changed, and Maatemnu found a strange people whose heads did not resemble the First People's. These he slew. One woman only he spared because his heart leapt from his body, and she possessed it.

"The Onye's remnant of the First People flourished in the distant, magical land of the goddess Tiamat. The madness of the Onye did not die but walked with him in time. He lusted after the woman Empheme and took her for wife when Ghalib was slain by the people of the Ilegu Forest. The goddess Tiamat, who loved Empheme, was angered, and she fought against the Onye until he died of a broken heart. The goddess was pained at the separation of the First People, and she sent Empheme to Maatemnu's followers who now lived in what the First People called the land above.

"So much had changed since the Great Parting that Empheme almost did not recognize the Descendants. Now numerous, they had developed many voices. Empheme tried to walk in the way of the goddess and lay with the Son of Ghalib who had accompanied her to the land above, but his seed was weak, and there was no provenance. Seeing the Son of Ghalib's weakness, the goddess led Empheme to the descendant of Maatemnu. He was strong and gave her a child. The two groups of the First People were rejoined in the offspring of Maatemnu and Empheme, and they played in friendship, planning the Reunion of the First People of the two lands.

"It was then that the fiery god Baal entered history from his place outside of Time. He looked upon the creation of his sister, the goddess Tiamat, and his anger blew up the mountains and destroyed the cities of men. His long imprisonment had maddened him. He cast his baleful eyes from the mountain down and saw the children of Empheme and Maatemnu. And Baal said, 'Surely this is an abomination, for always Empheme, the child of Tiamat, has been given to Chango through Ghalib. Who, then, is this Maatemnu whose arm is withered from his contact with the fire of the gods?'

"And so, he sought out the Son of Ghalib and found him drunk, the spirit almost departed from him. Baal raised him from the earth and gave him strength. The Son of Ghalib, the fire of Baal in his eyes, searched for Empheme and found her in the land to the north, which is called America.

"Baal's entry into time created a fracture in the world of the gods. He who had been Empheme's guide in the land above when she came from the Land of Tiamat, and who had gone to sleep in Time, was awakened. The Father of the Ilegu Forest strode out of the land of the ancestors, from this place called Africa, seeking Empheme and the Son of Ghalib. His heart was heavy because trouble lay between the Son of Ghalib and Maatemnu over the woman who was precious to the goddess. He proposed to the Son of Ghalib an agreement. He must accept for a time the role of brother. The Son of Ghalib, confronted by the Father of the Ilegu Forest's strength, was forced to accept. Also, Tiamat still cared for her daughter Empheme, and the Son of Ghalib did not wish to feel her might again.

"So, through time, they have traveled, the Son of Ghalib, fired by Baal, still angry but subdued, and Empheme, the daughter of the goddess Tiamat, drawn to the sons of Maatemnu. As Eurydice was drawn to you, Andreas."

The voice stopped, and to Andreas' amazement, the woman before him changed. No longer was she Eurydice or even Empheme. She was the goddess he had seen in his visions for so many years on the distant, cantering horse. She was beautiful, her skin having the delicacy of dark satin. Around her, the air was still. He had many questions, but he could not voice them, wanting only to lie in the embrace of her smile that seemed to comfort the universe.

"You are not really here, are you? Andreas asked.

"I am as much here as I am anywhere else, Tama. Time can be a line with a direction. That is how you experience it. For us, it is different. Think of a flat piece of string along which you walk. Then, think of that string being bent upwards so that it is no longer flat, but a series of bows or loops. If you walked along the string, you would experience a series of hills and valleys. Time slowing down and speeding up, but you would still cover the same distance in the same lengths of time."

"Yes. That makes sense," Andreas responded.

"But what if at the top, the loops actually touched? You could step from the top of one loop to the other. Then, if the string of time were stretched out again, it would appear that you had avoided a considerable amount of time. Add to that an infinite number of time strings, and you will understand what I mean by being as much here as anywhere else."

Andreas thought for a moment, realizing that as the figure before him explained it, the concept of time shrinking or expanding actually made sense. An infinite number of timelines would also mean no fixed past or future, only a lived present. Things already lived and to be lived would be accessible if one had a 'map' across the timelines. It would certainly explain the way the First People experienced their history. Nothing they described seemed fully in the past, and yesterday's actions appeared again today in their stories. Could it be that what he had thought of as mistakes in the stories, those slight changes in detail from telling to telling, were not mistakes at all? What if each story was true, from the "experience" of a different timeline? The theoretical physicists had some pretty strange ideas about how time worked. What if he was actually experiencing some of these strange notions, like time folding? As he thought, the figure waited without any sign of impatience.

Not aware of how much time had passed, Andreas asked, *"Something is about to happen, isn't it?"*

"Yes," she said with a serene smile. *"Something, as you so prosaically put it, is about to happen. My brothers and I are all here now, and so the repulsion begins."*

"But it is destructive. Why are you so happy about it?"

"It is both an end and a beginning, Maatemnu. Baal has loosed his spirit upon the world. The balance must be restored."

"What will happen?"

Her smile broadened, and she said, *"You will decide."*

He started to ask another question, but she was no longer there. On the ground beside him, Eurydice slept, her breast gently rising. Andreas looked to the sky where the light was fading. *Pogosi* was returning, and a chill had come. He shivered, thinking that they needed to find warm clothes soon. Around him, the noises of the forest gave him comfort, so different from when he first came. Then, the slithering of snakes and the tramping of the *orlu'sii*, those big animals that walked with slow, ponderous steps, unafraid of anything, had caused him some anxiety. He had learned their step, and they his, so they lived together in this land that was not on any map.

Suddenly, the ground shook. Eurydice's eyes popped open. She stood, alert. In his mind sense was the sound of engines. They were far away, and they were numerous. Eurydice looked at him, a sadness in her eyes.

"It has begun," she said.

Chapter 41

*N*atas stood on the central hill overlooking LLehstan, the capital of the Land of Ghalib. For hours, planes had been taking off and landing. Teme stood next to him, her eyes impartial, observing the massive exodus of soldiers from LLehstan.

"How does it feel to be on the edge of history, priestess? Soon, the world above will be changed. The First People will be one again, and our god will rule their lives," Natas said.

Teme turned, her face not showing the turmoil she felt.

"Our god, Natas? Whose god is that?"

He chuckled, his eyes following an ungainly transport plane as it rose, quickly disappearing. Each one of the transports carried two hundred and forty military personnel to the fleet of giant ships that hid within the electronic web created by his scientists. The nations above were not able to penetrate that web, but they continued to try.

The fools thought it was to hide my extracting oil. They never guessed.

"Our god, priestess. Chango, the god of thunder and lightning."

Teme observed Natas' face. Her eyes were sad. She felt sorry for him.

It is as Mother Mutasii taught. The Son of Ghalib knows not whom he serves.

Teme wondered about her own role. She did not know Natas' purpose, and that frightened her. In the world above, Natas fostered the religion that was creating the bond between the descendants of the First People who occupied those lands, but that was not his only purpose. Natas used the stories of the First People, spoke of the Reunion with great authority, but his true purpose was masked behind the words. Something other than the desire for power drove him. In him, she saw Baal, the god of the fiery mountain. The stories spoke of Baal's anger, and Teme remembered a tale, banned by the sisterhood, that told of his struggle with the god to whom the people give no name. In that story, the god to whom the people give no name enfolded Baal in the spaces between time. There he wandered, his bitterness growing. Chango was the caretaker of Time and all its children—the children of the goddess Tiamat—and Baal hated that unity.

The night before, Natas donned the garb of Chango. Eventually, the lightning snaked down, striking him on the head, but though he shouted the god's name, Teme was not fooled. The god had not come, and seeing the look of perplexity on Natas' face, she knew that he was lost. When he first arrived in the Land of Tiamat some thirteen seasons earlier, the excitement was palpable. He was hailed as the embodiment of the promise. Empheme and the Son of Ghalib would unite, and Tiamat would be free, as the stories said.

And they did unite, she thought bitterly.

Images of Lusani, Natas coupling with Empheme, filled her mind. It was not the union of the priestesses' dreams. Soon after, Natas scattered the priestesses, and particularly the *leo-leos*, those women of the warrior caste, all over the Land of Tiamat, which he renamed the Land of Ghalib. Teme wondered about her sisters. She particularly missed Mother Mustasii who, as the young priestesses often whispered, seemed as old as the goddess herself.

I pray the goddess protects you, mother.

Teme's right hand went to her lips. Natas, seeing the movement, laughed.

"Still praying to your goddess, priestess? Is not her broken body enough to persuade you of her death?"

Teme's face did not change, but her heart quickened in fear. She had seen the fractured body of the goddess, the figure, even in pieces, still suggestive of grace. Several burial mounds surrounded the fallen statue. The *Ulumatua* had defended the goddess but were no match for Natas' new weapons.

The very blood of the gods taken for use in hatred, she thought.

She had prayed over Lona's mound after Marcus identified it, the grave having no marker. Her gaze went to the man who spoke the language of Tiastan with such a strange accent. Something had changed in Marcus. Until recently, despite his charm, she always sensed the deep hurt and hatred in him when he spoke of the "white world." She did not understand what Marcus meant until Andreas arrived at Lusani, that beautiful city dedicated to the goddess and destroyed by Natas. Marcus' pain had immediately become more acute, and his face grew hard with anger. He spoke with great bitterness of something called the Expulsion. Only then did she finally understand the truth of Natas' story in the temple many seasons earlier. Andreas had caused Marcus' people to be sent to the barren expanse of ice, cold and snow that Tiamatians knew as the breast of Tiamat, and which protected the Land of Tiamat.

Recently, Marcus seemed ambivalent. It could be that he had fallen out of favor with Natas, having been blamed for allowing Andreas to escape twice, first from Lusani and then from the castle. Natas' anger had not been pleasant to see. Marcus was observing the transport planes. The soldiers they carried were massing at the city built by Natas thirteen seasons earlier to house the African Americans expelled from the United States. Then, they were being transported to the giant ships that had been constructed in utter secrecy. Teme strolled along the catwalk of the castle to where Marcus stood. She understood his nervousness. Once, she, too, was responsible for a fighting force.

"The transport goes well, Marcus?"

"Quite well, Teme. We're ahead of schedule, actually."

"You go to the city on the breast of Tiamat. After that?"

Marcus' eyes narrowed.

"No tricks. I am simply curious," she said.

"Then you should speak with the Son of Ghalib."

His heart was not in the rebuff.

"He is not the Son of Ghalib, Marcus."

Marcus did not turn, but his body became rigid.

"Enough, priestess. The Son of Ghalib is the fulfillment of the promise. He brings about the Reunion."

"Do you know what that is, Marcus? What does it mean to you?"

The young commander looked uncertain for a moment.

"The First People will be reunited, and they will rule."

"Rule whom? The stories do not speak of ruler and ruled. Only the gods have dominion over humans."

He turned to her, and she again saw the great pain in him. When he spoke, his voice possessed a hard edge.

"You do not know my land, Teme. The land above, as you call it. There, not to rule is to be ruled."

"And you have been ruled too long. Now, you wish to rule. Is that it?"

"Yes."

Teme was silenced by the bitterness in his voice. She watched the transports climb upwards, and, thinking of the coming war, felt a deep sadness. Marcus wanted revenge for the wrongs of the past. Yet, the stories of the First People contained many wrongs. If everyone fought to right the wrongs of the past, what would become of the First People? Still, was this not exactly what Natas had reintroduced into their history? He whom they called the Son of Ghalib had come, and, for the first time in an age, called people to him in the name of the Onye and the god Chango. He whispered as the *malini*, those false voices of the night, did, and he told the forbidden stories of the battle between Tiamat and Chango. Natas, too, believed he was righting a wrong—re-taking the woman who was rightfully his and restoring the power of his god. For this, he was willing to oppose the gods themselves.

Is he heroic? Is it good to feed on the despair of someone like Marcus to achieve an end that may be no better? But if Natas is an instrument of the gods, how then can his actions be wrong?

Teme pondered these questions as the echoes of the planes and Marcus' bitter voice reverberated in her mind. The war in the land above would be terrible. She had seen their penchant for violence. The three seasons spent in the land of the ancestors, what those above called Africa, had been painful. She heard the hatred in those who came to the place called Bumba, the smiles on their faces a poor disguise for the malice in their hearts. Natas was admired, feared and hated, and these emotions were, for her, plain to see in the delegates who came from all over the land above. Those men's pride was stymied but not broken, and Natas was a fool if he thought that their coming to his palace was a sign of their submission. They would fight him, and the war would be fierce.

"Marcus, for what are we fighting?"

"For the Reunion, of course. It is told in the stories, Teme. You of all people should know that."

"But the stories do not speak of war. The gods are not fooled by men's speeches, Marcus. It is their hearts to which Tiamat listens."

"I saw your goddess die, Teme. I am sorry."

Teme, taking advantage of the moment, asked, "What happened in the land to the south?"

Marcus glanced at Natas who stood outlined against the castle keep and sighed.

"He chose to save me, Teme." At first, she thought he was referring to Natas, but then, he added, "He could have saved his son, but he saved me instead."

"Do you speak of Andreas, Marcus? Lona was not his son. Lona was given to Empheme by the goddess."

"I know that, but I also know that Andreas Prescod had a chance to save Lona, and he saved me instead."

Teme was in turmoil. Forbidden images jumped into her mind. She thought of Natas' story accusing Andreas of the same thing and Andreas' defiant admission of his paternity. She told herself that Lona was the goddess' gift, not the product of a man's loins.

Unless Andreas is more than man.

Teme considered that for a long time. The stories of the First People did not account for Andreas, so his arrival in Tiastan with Natas was a surprise. Even more surprising, he was allowed to live in the temple with Empheme while he whom the priestesses thought to be the Son of Ghalib, the partner of Empheme in the stories, went far away to the land of his ancestors. Teme uttered an involuntary prayer.

Nothing is as it seems.

Aware that Marcus watched her, she turned, smiling.

"Every person's life is written in the ledger of the goddess, Marcus. Andreas' choice places a *fata aigu* upon you."

His face soured at first, and then, he looked perplexed.

"I do not want this obligation, Teme. Andreas Prescod is my enemy."

"The stories of the First People are filled with enemies whose *fata aigu* overwhelmed their hatred."

"No," he replied sharply, staring ahead. "Prescod and I have too much history between us. It can end only one way."

"And what way is that? The Reunion?"

His face tightened as he recognized the irony. He would lead an army in the name of the promised Reunion but carry hatred in his heart. Angry at his own confusion, Marcus turned abruptly, striding to where Natas stood.

Images of Empheme and Andreas together filled Teme's mind. If, indeed, Andreas had fathered Lona, who then was he? She had heard that during the battle, Andreas absorbed the blood of the gods with no ill effects. She thought of the stories being whispered about the four soldiers who had guarded Empheme in the castle keep. They said that the Onye came to the corridor, commanding them to guard the woman more closely. They were not aware that she was gone until Natas arrived. Teme quailed at the thought of Natas' wrath. He killed the four guards himself, first knifing them and then throwing them from the battlements into the river.

He is changing, become more like the god of the fiery mountain.

Shaking her head, Teme strode toward the castle's keep.

Chapter 42

*S*idoti peered through the thick glass of the tractor's window at heavy snow. There were two other tractors, one behind and one in front, but it was impossible to see them. A taciturn ranger was driving. One week earlier, Sidoti had felt the ice for the first time as the ship stopped. All around, the whiteness stretched in empty silence, and he felt a primordial fear at the sight of that emptiness. When they left the ship two days earlier, the sun was bright, the ice flat and accessible. He had actually thought that the trip could be quite an adventure. Forty-eight hours later, his perspective was considerably modified.

The weather had changed, and the sunlight that seemed so friendly slid away, leaving the sky a pasty gray that, from Sidoti's perspective, looked like a version of Hell. The ice proved to be a surprise as well. This was not a flat land but one shaped by the pressures of the ice. It was hilly and broken, and Sidoti soon lost his sense of adventure. Worst of all was the cold. As they swung south, the temperature dropped and for the last few days had hovered around minus fifty degrees. The comparative warmth of the ship now seemed like paradise.

Apart from himself and the ranger, two others were in the small tractor. Metzer was, as usual, bent over a laptop, scribbling more of those indecipherable equations. Dr. Faison sat, a thoughtful look on his face. It had become clear over the weeks on the ship that outside of a lab where he could conduct experiments, Dr. Faison was less effective than Sidoti had hoped. He seemed capable of interpreting what Metzer was doing but provided few insights of his own. Sidoti occasionally wondered if he had made the wrong choice, but that was not entirely fair. He needed Dr. Faison to translate Metzer's ramblings. The strange world of theoretical physics was way outside Sidoti's area of expertise.

Metzer was becoming more reluctant to explain, apparently frustrated at having to search for real world parallels to the rather odd ideas that he was spawning with increasing rapidity. Sidoti had heard theories in the last few days that worried him because he could not judge their merit. He was a brilliant analyst, but analysis depended on knowledge and, in this area, he was woefully lacking.

He did feel a growing respect for the man who sat behind him pouring over his equations like a high school senior desperately preparing for final exams. Dr. Faison had explained that Metzer was working on a set of equations to demonstrate that something called a brane world existed. It seemed nonsensical to Sidoti, but he had heard so much about brane theory, quantum theory, general relativity and the existence of at least seven additional dimensions besides the four he was aware of—that is, left/right, up/down, back/forth and time—that he was beginning to develop some familiarity with the language, if no comfort with the ideas.

Two days earlier, when they regained satellite accessibility, the news from the north was all bad. A new war was brewing, and no one seemed able to explain what the objectives were. The war with China dragged on, but now, Sidoti noticed nervousness in General Blount's communications. A week earlier, something that General Blount referred to as the Black Fleet appeared on the radar screens of the world's nations. It was east of Graham Land at the northern extremity of Antarctica and moving northeast. So far, there were no aggressive moves, even when the United States sent an aircraft carrier to investigate.

Sidoti's face was grim. It was unlikely that the two things—the unrecognizable heat source and this Black Fleet—were unrelated. Glancing at Metzer, his heart sank. The man was disheveled and lost to the world. Sidoti made sure that Metzer ate at least one meal a day since the scientist seemed not to care about nourishment.

Aware of Dr. Faison's gaze, he turned just as the scientist said, "He could go on like this for weeks."

"We don't have weeks. Does he know where he's leading us?" Sidoti replied irritably.

They spoke as if Metzer was not there, and maybe, in some sense, he was not. Dr. Faison shrugged.

"His mathematics has become very exotic. I'm not sure he even cares about the original problem."

"What!"

"It's not that he's forgotten what you want. It's just that he's found a more interesting problem. That was his downfall when he was at the Center for Advanced Physics."

"In Pisa?"

Dr. Faison nodded.

"I didn't realize you two had worked together before."

"We didn't actually work together, but we were both at the Center."

"What do you mean by his downfall?"

"Dr. Metzer was responsible for the major lab in the Center. They were working on creating sustainable black holes."

"Black holes? I thought they were created by collapsing stars."

"Yes. When a star collapses, it retains its mass but shrinks to what could be a relatively negligible size. Its gravitational pull is not reduced, so nothing can escape from the black hole, not even light. That's why it appears black. It is theoretically possible to create small black holes using a particle accelerator. The problem is they are extremely unstable and degrade out of existence in fractions of a second."

"That sounds like a solution to me, not a problem. We gave that research up a while ago as too dangerous."

"Not everyone did."

"So who was funding this research in Italy? The Europeans?"

"Not exactly. They did provide some funding to the Center itself, but the secret research that Dr. Metzer worked on was funded exclusively by Branniff Enterprises."

Sidoti stared at the pelting snow. The ranger was studying the brightly-lit dials on the tractor's dashboard. Within the tractor's guts was probably the most sophisticated radar system on earth. On a screen, two small, red dots flashed as they moved across a longitudinal and latitudinal grid. These represented the other tractors. The lead tractor slowed and so did the others.

"Trouble?" Sidoti asked.

The ranger shook his head.

"Broken ice. There's a crevasse ahead that we have to negotiate."

He reached forward and hit a button. The grid dissolved, replaced by a detailed map showing a huge scar in the ice.

"Jesus!" Sidoti said. "How long will it take to go around that?"

The ranger fiddled with the controls, and the sound of the engine died away.

"We're not going around it, sir. We have to go across it."

Sidoti leaned forward, staring at the map.

"I don't see any way across, major."

"Actually, sir, you can't see it. We have to descend into the crevasse itself. There's an ice bridge, but it's several meters below the top of the crevasse."

"You mean we have to go down into the ice?"

This came from Dr. Faison. There was concern in his voice. The ranger nodded. The blip on the screen tilted, and they watched as it slid down at a frighteningly steep angle.

"Good Lord!" Dr. Faison said. "Is that safe?"

"Well, sir, nothing in this land is safe. There are more ways to die here than in just about any other place on the planet. These tractors are remarkable on the ice, though. They can practically hang upside down if we encounter a problem."

Sidoti could not help thinking that the soldier was just a little too enthusiastic in creating that image for them.

"Why are we stopping? And where the hell are we?"

"Hello, Karl. How's it coming along?"

Metzer stared at Sidoti without recognition for a moment. Then, he smiled.

"Oh, it's you. How long you been with us?"

The scientist's voice sounded controlled, like a drunk trying to make a speech. Sidoti did not respond directly to the question.

"How's the work coming along?"

Metzer's face became guarded, and he swiveled to stare at Dr. Faison who watched the mad man as if expecting an attack. Metzer grinned, and something in Sidoti recoiled when he saw the yellowish film over the man's teeth. He would have to pay better attention to Metzer's hygiene.

Metzer punched the ENTER button on the computer and handed it to Sidoti. Sidoti stifled his anger as he studied the images. There were three rectangular shapes that, depending on how he looked at them, appeared to be either stacked one behind the other or next to each other. One was a cloudy white with intermittent dark spots on it, almost like a partially visible sky on a cloudy day. A second was a dark, slate-like color with a lighter gray—again sort of cloudy—in the center. The one in the middle was the most interesting. It looked like a representation of the universe with the characteristic flaring of distant stars and swirls of galaxies.

"Karl, what is this? I thought you were working on a more refined location of the power source."

Dr. Faison was peering over Sidoti's shoulder, his eyes running swiftly over the equations below the pictures. Ignoring Sidoti, he stuck his finger on an equation that read, $cl^2 a/dt^2/a = 4\pi3(p^+ 3p)$.

"This represents the scale factor of the universe, the energy density and pressure density," he mumbled.

"Stop!" Sidoti shouted. "What in God's name are you talking about?"

Dr. Faison ignored him, going on to a slightly longer equation and continuing to mumble. When he spoke, there was grudging admiration in his voice.

"Brilliant. Absolutely brilliant. How very elegant."

Sidoti was about to explode when Metzer, a shy smile on his face, replied, "Glad you like it, doc. It was good for me, too."

"That, in case you don't recognize it, is one of Einstein's equations. It shows that the universe's rate of growth will accelerate in time," Dr. Faison explained.

"And what has that got to do with anything?" Sidoti asked exasperatedly.

"It's the other equation that's the exciting one, Mr. Sidoti. Using Einstein's idea, Dr. Metzer has derived a second equation that proves—mathematically, anyway—the existence of the branes. Those are the rectangular images you see."

"The pictures were put in for your convenience, chimp. I knew the mathematics would be too much of a strain for that noodle you call a brain."

At least, Karl sounds lucid again, Sidoti thought, as he said, "Don't get me wrong. I'm happy for you both, but what the hell has this got to do with our problem?"

"Don't you see? Look at this," Dr. Faison said, pointing to a four-line equation. "Dr. Metzer's equation strongly suggests that your energy source is coming from outside the brane world with the stars in it. To put it crudely, the energy we're trying to find is not from within our universe."

Sidoti scowled. None of it made sense. He was just about to say so when the tractor pitched forward at a steep angle. His stomach lurched. Metzer screamed. Dr. Faison grabbed the back of his seat.

"Sorry," the ranger said. "Misjudged the angle."

Sidoti stared at the nothingness on his left and felt his lower intestine squeeze inward. The snow helped because visibility was low, but the beeping was a constant reminder of where they were. The image on the screen did not help. The ice bridge was represented as a single, white line in a sea of blue. It looked very narrow. All conversation stopped as the tractor gripped its way to the bottom of the incline and levelled out. The soft chugging was not a calming background to Sidoti's fevered imagination as he visualized the vertiginous depths on either side. The world was silent, white and frightening.

"How strong are these ice bridges?" he said nervously.

"Most are pretty fragile, but this one has been around for centuries. This is very old ice. Not brittle, sir."

Sidoti tried, without success, to ignore the word "brittle."

"How do you know about this stuff, major?"

"Geology Masters from CalTech, sir, but most of my information came from the military."

"Tax dollars well spent," Metzer said, an edge of hysteria in his voice.

"What part of the military do you belong to?" Sidoti asked.

"If I told you that, sir, I'd have to kill you. Let's say my training includes warfare in polar regions."

There was not even the hint of a smile on the ranger's face. Sidoti did not press the issue. His security clearance could extract the information in two seconds, but he did not need to know. The trip across the ice bridge continued. The tension remained palpable, but after a while, they began to climb. The tractor chugged its way up the side, and not soon enough for Sidoti's liking, they were on top of the continent again. The major waited until the third tractor came out of the crevasse. He zipped up his parka and stepped out, climbing down the external steps to the ice. The blast of cold was like a physical blow, and Sidoti clutched at his nose as air burned its way into his lungs. Fortunately, the door was soon closed. He turned to the two scientists who both looked a little whiter than usual.

"Now, can somebody explain to me again what the hell a brane world is?"

For the next twenty minutes, he asked questions, feeling like a fool whenever Metzer called him chimp, or Dr. Faison smiled superciliously at him. Still, in the end, he thought he understood, in principle, what they were describing.

"So you're saying we may be living in one of these brane worlds, and there may be others that we can't see?"

"Sort of," Dr. Faison replied. "Except it's not just we on the planet Earth. Our whole universe would be a brane world. The other brane worlds would be complete universes as well."

"And why can't we see them again?"

Dr. Faison squinted as he sought language to simplify the concept.

"Do you remember what Dr. Metzer said about strings, the fundamental element of the universe? Photons, that is, light, are open strings with the end parts trapped in the brane. Think of the brane as a kind of frame for the universe. Photons, light that is, cannot escape the brane, and since images are carried in light, we would not be able to see any additional branes."

Sidoti shook his head as the ranger returned, bringing a fresh gust of Antarctic air. Soon, they were moving again. The flashing dot on the map indicated that they were heading west-southwest.

"And it is your calculation that the signature of the heat source could not have come from within our brane."

Metzer nodded, a silly smile on his face.

"You got it in one, chimp. Somebody is doing the impossible. He, or she, has figured out how to move energy between branes."

"You said that nothing escapes the branes. Not even light."

"I know. I know. It's happening, anyway. I just haven't quite figured out how."

"But you think that the branes will touch at a single point in our universe, and that point is Earth. More specifically, a single point above Antarctica where the ozone has been ripped to shreds?"

"Yup," Metzer replied, laughing. "Ain't it beautiful?"

Sidoti ignored him, trying to get his mind around the ideas Metzer seemed so comfortable espousing. Metzer was nuts. Few people understood how his mind worked when he was sane, still less so when he was off in those worlds the insane inhabited. Was he mad now? Sidoti considered the other scientist. Dr. Faison possessed an impeccable reputation in the scientific world, and he was not contradicting Metzer, although Sidoti put this down to the natural caution of the experimental physicist. For them, if the experiment did not yield the same results after the thousandth trial, then something must be wrong with the equations. That was the way the experimental guys thought. Metzer did not have that restraint. His mind was like a frog on a hot stone. It just jumped from point to point, leaving others to figure out the patterns. Yet, he was saying something incredible. More than incredible, it was frightening.

Sidoti did not believe in little green men from space who had much better technology than humans. He hated movies that showed "Earthlings" to be technologically inferior, even if they eventually triumphed through their ingenuity. The last two decades had forced him, as it did so many others, to think about life on earth. He came to the conclusion that we were alone in the universe—no god and no little green men. We were alone. It was not a comforting thought, but it made him more aware of his humanity as well as his relationship to the planet and the others who lived on it. That thought took his mind to the report that led to the fiasco of the Expulsion.

Would I make the same recommendation today if faced with the same situation?

He was not sure. The United States was then threatened, and he had identified what seemed the logical action, the reduction of the nation's population. The politicians then decided how to implement that recommendation. The result was expulsion of the African Americans.

How am I different from Eric Stoltz?

He did not like the answer.

Andreas Prescod took the blame for the whole thing. His appointment as chair of the committee looking into the country's food supply was a set-up from the start, and the poor guy never knew.

Like Sidoti's analysts, Prescod's committee had come up with a number of recommendations, one of which was to reduce the population of the United States. That was the only recommendation put into effect. How much did Natas Branniff have to do with that? Ten years after the Expulsion, Sidoti discovered that the African Americans taken to Antarctica were not randomly selected but shared the same DNA, and he wondered what made this group of people special. The movement of black populations from other countries to Africa was also puzzling. The black people, it seemed, were being concentrated in Africa, and smaller populations, not black, were being invited. Why? Sidoti had no answer. He stared out the window at the haunting whiteness of the ice.

"There's a hypnotic beauty to this place," he said.

The ranger nodded.

"I've known people who repeatedly requested duty on the continent just to be close to something still pure. That was before the treaty with Branniff, of course."

"Yes," Sidoti replied. "That means, technically we are now trespassing. How does that square with you, major?"

"Uncle commands; we go. Let the lawyers worry about the legality."

Sidoti was about to respond when Dr. Faison said, "Actually, I am quite uncomfortable with that. The law is the law. We have no right to be here."

Sidoti turned slowly in his seat, and when he spoke, his voice was cold.

"You tell that to the parents of the thousands who died when those ships exploded or disintegrated or whatever they did. Don't talk to me about legality. If whatever did that is down here, then we have to get rid of it."

Metzer cackled, saying in a singsong voice, "You can't get rid of it. You can't get rid of it."

"Why not?"

"Because it is eternal. Second law and all that, you know."

"I know energy can't be destroyed, but the machinery that harnesses it can be."

"Maybe not."

Sidoti, losing patience, shouted, "Karl, do you know something you're not telling us?"

Metzer looked down at the computer, and Sidoti resisted the temptation to snatch the machine away.

"As a matter of fact, I do. Look at this."

Metzer's voice was normal again. Sidoti took the computer. It displayed three two-dimensional drawings that obviously represented three-dimensional figures. They looked like tall funnels. Wide and circular at the base, they bent inwards all the way to the top to form a circle about one-third the size of the base. They looked like bananas.

"What this? Are these nuclear plants?"

"No. I think that has to be the configuration of the machines that will draw in the dark energy. If my calculations are correct, these would also have to be their approximate locations."

"What locations?"

Metzer hit the space bar. The picture slid away, replaced by a Mercator's map of the world, with the difference that Antarctica was not squeezed off the lower end but was fully represented. The three funnels were located on different continents—Antarctica, Africa and the United States. Sidoti was vaguely aware of breath slowly escaping Dr. Faison, of the ranger sneaking a peek down at the computer, and of Metzer, with an ear-to-ear grin, looking at him like a puppy waiting for a pat. Most of all, he was aware of a question that burned in his brain. Had someone built a weapon on United States' soil without his knowing?

Chapter 43

"*B*ut why?"

Anne Ernsky sounded distressed, and Notah stared at his boots. He was dressed in a white elk-skin jacket, pants with matching fringes, and wore a similarly-colored cap. The buckskin boots came up to his knees and were topped with ivory tassels. Dressed like that, he could disappear into the landscape. Anne Ernsky noted how much more dignified he looked in traditional clothes.

"Why won't you come with us?"

"I cannot. I thought I could, and we—Olahl and I—have pondered it for a long time. We finally decided that it would be right to stay. Stoltz has become more active now that your people are moving away. I received word a few days ago that he's moved into Montana."

"Why is he attacking the Indians now? He never made much of the Indian presence before," Anne Ernsky replied.

Notah looked even more uncomfortable.

"It's me. Stoltz knows what I've been doing, and he wants to punish the Salish, my adopted people. I can't leave in those circumstances."

Anne Ernsky turned away, staring at the brightness outside. The snow had stopped, even though the cold remained, and she rubbed her forefinger along the windowpane where frost sat like a silent threat. Notah was right, but she was used to the big Indian, depended on him, and had assumed he would be in Africa with them. Now, because of Eric Stoltz, this good man would not be going east but west, most likely to his death. She had no illusions about how he would be treated if Stoltz caught him. Notah was not going back to Montana to hide. In spite of the hangdog look he now wore, there was something rebellious in the cast of his body. He was going west to find Stoltz.

"It will be very difficult. Almost impossible," she said.

"Very difficult," Notah replied, the beginning of a smile touching his lips. "And when there is a storm, you should never run in it because Thunderbird will strike you with his lightning."

Anne Ernsky grinned.

"More Salish wisdom?"

"Kootenai, actually."

Notah poured a cup of coffee from a pot sitting on the plain, wooden table and handed it to her. He poured another for himself, and, more relaxed now, sat.

"There's always a story behind your bits of wisdom, so what's this one?"

"It is the story of Coyote and Thunderbird. Coyote had three sons who, when they were grown, he took to the Nupika village to gamble. As they came to the Nupika village, Coyote started hollering, and Fox said, 'Coyote is cruel to bring his sons here. Thunderbird will win, and he will throw Coyote's sons in the fire.' Thunderbird heard Coyote's challenge, and he flew over, saying to Coyote, 'We will race tomorrow.' The next day, Coyote and his sons saw women piling logs together, and Coyote asked, 'Why are you piling wood?' The women replied, 'It is for you and your sons to be burnt when you lose.' Soon, Thunderbird came, and Coyote said, 'Here are my possessions that I will bet.' But Thunderbird replied, 'I only bet against lives. Your sons against mine.' The race started, and soon someone came and said, 'Thunderbird, your eldest son lost the race.' Thunderbird lit his pipe. Coyote did the same after holding his pipe toward the sun. After a while, someone came and said, 'Thunderbird, your second son lost the race.' Thunderbird looked angry but picked up his pipe and lit it with pitch wood. Coyote did the same, but he used sagebrush. Thunderbird was worried and angry, and the Nupika villagers said, 'This is getting serious. Coyote and Thunderbird are angry with each other.' The youngest sons raced, and Coyote's son was beating Thunderbird's son, so Thunderbird tried to strike Coyote's son with lightning. He missed, and young Coyote ran faster. He ran so fast that he almost reached the rainbow. When young Coyote returned, he had won the race."

Notah stopped. Anne Ernsky looked at him quizzically.

"I'm never sure what the point of your stories is."

"It's simple. Thunderbird is still angry about losing the race. When there is a storm, you should never run in it because Thunderbird will strike you with his lightning."

Anne Ernksy became serious. Notah had intuited what she intended and was warning her off in his gentle way.

"Well, Thunderbird will have to use his lightning on me because I'm coming with you. Stoltz has caused quite enough trouble."

"Just to be clear, Ms. Ernsky, I intend to hunt Stoltz and to kill him. For you to help, you will have to return to the United States. If they catch you, you will be executed. You know that?"

"Thanks for making it so clear, Notah. That certainly relieves any nervousness I might have had."

Two hours later, they walked out to the disguised tarmac the group used. The official airport was too exposed. The plan was to fly northwest, toward Calgary and then turn south, hugging the ground and hoping that the Americans would not find the flight path suspicious. Anne Ernsky had not seen Stoltz in thirteen years, but she remembered well the small, porcine eyes that always seemed to be seeing something particularly distasteful when he looked at her. His friendship with the man who made her secretary of state had always been a source of some unease between her and the then president. Stoltz's influence in the country was now exponentially greater. He no longer simply represented a block of votes but was a power in his own right. He would probably be the next president of the United States. Thinking about what America now represented, her heart ached.

Stoltz alone was not responsible for the Expulsion. Something drastic happened to the country when the waters rose and droughts came. She glanced at Notah who sat on the other side of the aisle behind Olahl. The ground receded as Rene brought the Beechcraft smoothly off the ground, and soon, they banked sharply to the left.

"How did we change so much, so quickly, Notah?" Anne Ernsky asked.

"We?"

"America. It seemed like one moment we were the most tolerant nation on earth, and the next, we were a boiling cauldron of hatred."

Notah chuckled.

"Maybe to you it seems that way, but I see little change."

Anne Ernsky raised an eyebrow, and Notah continued.

"Their tolerance was always based on the idea of limitless expansion. As long as they saw the possibility of growth, they could be tolerant of those within their political borders. Once the idea of expansion died, so did their tolerance. The rising waters reminded them of limits, and that notion had not been alive in America for a long time."

Anne Ernsky studied Notah's face as she said, "I had no idea you'd thought about this so deeply."

"Two years at Salish Kootenai College, and two more at the University of New Mexico. We spent a lot of time talking about how the Whites took our land and why. In some ways, Indian generosity in the early days of white settlement was also based on our belief that there was enough land to go around."

"I have often wondered why my people, the Salish, fought the Kootenai and the Blackfeet for so long but conceded our land to the Whites so easily," Olahl said.

"When did your people come in contact with the Whites?" Anne Ernsky asked, a note of sadness in her voice.

"We were the end point of the great Lewis and Clark expedition. The end of our life as a free people, that is," Olahl replied.

Anne Ernsky nodded. She wondered if Notah's explanation for the changes in America was right. Had reduced possibilities really destroyed American tolerance? What had gone wrong with the world?

The white landscape flitted by, the Canadian wilderness softened by fallen snow. Notah and Olahl continued to chat quietly, and Anne Ernsky marveled at the normality of the scene.

Four people flying west in an airplane. Who would guess that we were going to kill a man?

Chapter 44

*E*tienne Ochukwu slowly put down the newspaper. His hands were shaking. The front page of *La Repubblica* was chock-full of news, all of it bad, but dominating the page was the headline: **EDIFICIO STORICO INGLESE DISTRUTTO.** Historic English building destroyed. The picture below showed the Tower of London ripped to shreds, its smoking remains seeming to suggest it was climbing out of its own ashes. On the television, a young anchor, all coiffed and perky, was reporting on the war in central Asia. As she spoke, switching periodically to reporters who were near the battlefield, Etienne took a cup of tea and sipped slowly, his mind in a daze.

I could have been there.

His eyes wandered back to the picture of the disemboweled building. Just as Natas Branniff indicated, Etienne had been invited to attend a secret meeting of the Nine. Only seven were to attend because the meeting would be held without Natas, and no one had replaced Hargrove. Etienne took the invitation from a teak desk. The envelope had a 1 and a 5 in the top left-hand corner. Underneath the 1 and the 5 were four animals—a lion, an ox, a flying eagle and one animal that had the face of a man. Etienne rubbed his finger gently over the odd emblem, his heart heavy.

"Goodbye, my brothers. May God have mercy on your souls," he whispered, making the sign of the cross.

From the same drawer, he took the letter that Kwaku had brought him on the day of his heart attack. The warning. It was handwritten in Natas' overly cursive script.

He turned as the reporter's voice changed, taking on the professional concern it was trained to. She was reporting on the bombing of the Tower. Etienne waited impatiently as she gave the background of the building, its grisly role in English history and its ambiguous function as both palace and prison. At the end of the news segment, there was still no mention of any bodies except those of the Tower of London's night staff. Someone was containing the story. Etienne's attention wandered until the reporter's voice changed again. She was announcing the death of Sir Anthony Shays-Hawley, noted industrialist, scientist and advisor to several prime ministers.

"Kwaku, could you get me the major newspapers from France, Germany, Russia, India, England and China?"

Kwaku hurried out. Etienne sat, hoping against hope that his suspicion would prove false. Kwaku soon returned with the newspapers, and Etienne flipped through them, noting, with a sinking feeling, the individually reported deaths of six members of the Nine. Hearing a familiar voice, he looked up and saw the startlingly handsome face of Natas Branniff. On the television, the caption above Natas' head said, "Bumba, Africa."

People still can't be trusted to know where Bumba is, I guess.

He watched as Natas made the right noises about his sorrow at the world having lost a great man.

"Anthony Shays-Hawley was a wonderful man and a great humanitarian. I was tremendously proud to call him friend. Our projects together were always for the benefit of all."

The interview went on for some time, the young woman clearly prolonging the conversation. Then, Natas pointedly glanced at his watch, and the reporter asked him if he had anything else to add. Natas looked directly into the camera.

"There's too much death in the world. Let's hope this is the last of its kind."

The reporter looked perplexed but thanked him and smoothly switched to another story about the mysterious black ships that were making their way north out of the Southern Ocean. Etienne turned the television off. He was nervous. At Natas' last statement, Etienne's heart had fluttered again. It felt as if Natas was speaking to him. He placed the last of the newspapers back on the tray. Six of the Nine had been murdered, and Hargrove, the seventh, had died some time ago. Only he and Natas remained.

O Lord, be my strength. Natas knew about the plot to destroy the Nine. Now, they are dead.

Breakfast was brought in, and Etienne ate, thinking of the dead men. Natas was keeping him alive for some reason. The offer he received from the elder Branniff three years earlier had seemed a good one. The Catholic Church avoided the threatened strife; he was made pope, and the Church's coffers were enriched. There seemed to be no downside. Accommodating the new religion created severe stress between Rome and the churches in the United States and Europe, but that had been manageable until the last year when changes in the new religion proved to be too much.

Is this new tension in any way responsible for Natas' actions? Etienne wondered.

Natas was accumulating power by the day, but there was no compelling reason Etienne could see for killing the members of the Nine. He chewed slowly, palate insensitive to the food's taste.

Maybe the time for indirect control is gone.

The silver knife clattered against the plate as Etienne stopped eating, a frightening idea forming in his head. He picked up the London Times, turning the pages quickly until he found a story about the Black Fleet. There was nothing new. No one knew anything about its purpose or ownership, but a large fleet of ships heading toward the cross-Atlantic shipping lanes made everyone nervous.

"Natas' ships," Etienne whispered.

He dabbed his mouth with a burgundy napkin. Branniff possessed almost limitless power, and the corporation used it ruthlessly to eliminate competition. Most nations accepted it because the monopoly in supply and production had not resulted in a significant inflation of prices. Branniff employed their people, paid taxes and was generous. As long as the world's leaders got their weapons and their people were not too restless, most went along.

Etienne looked out the window at the beautiful purple flowers he had nursed back from history's grave. Africana Incognito. The unknown African. The flowers hid their true color under the royal purple, but when wet, they turned black. It was quite startling the first time one saw it. Africa. Natas' presence made that continent the center of the new religion. Bumba now competed for financial dominace with London, New York and Hong Kong, but countries had consoled themselves with the thought that Natas did not control a major military force.

"Now, it looks as if he has that as well."

Natas had not killed him, and there could be only one reason for that. He was still needed for some purpose. Natas had earlier invited him to lead the new religion from Bumba. Could it be that, in spite of his power and new-found military might, Natas was nervous about his control over the masses? That would certainly explain the offer. It also signaled Natas' contempt for religion as he clearly expected Etienne to change hats without any regard for the content of the doctrine.

"And their doctrine is blasphemous."

He flipped open the new liturgy. In it, Christ's humanity was emphasized, his divinity denied. The liturgy had to be denounced. Christianity depended on Christ's rising from the dead to sit on the right hand of God.

"Yet the new liturgy would have men believe that Christ was merely a good man."

Sighing, Etienne put the liturgy down, aware of the weight of his decision. If he did nothing, the United States and Europe would break from Rome, but if he tried to excommunicate those of the new religion who flocked to Catholic churches the world over, there would be war. The non-European Catholics would rebel against the excommuni-cation, but the change in vestments and the offensive genealogy that placed Jesus in a line that went back to the ancient gods of the Middle East could not be ignored.

"On the other hand," Etienne said, "there is no question that Africa has benefited. The place has changed almost overnight. And Bumba. What a lovely city!"

Part of Bumba's charm was the cathedral, with its ultra-modern, funnel-like appearance on the outside and the perfection of the ar-chitecture on the inside. It was huge, having the capacity to hold two hundred and fifty thousand people.

They need the space, too.

Etienne saw crowds like those in Bumba only on Vatican state occasions such as Christmas when St. Peter's Square would be packed. Bumba seemed to attract those crowds every day. They came from all over the world because they believed. He thought of the commercial aspect of his own world where most of the visitors came as tourists to snap pictures and carry with them a story of their tour of the Vatican. In Bumba, it was different. There was a quietness that seemed to speak with the assurance of the ages, and though the cathedral was recently finished, it inspired veneration.

How could the same man who created that cathedral take the lives of six men he had known?

It did not add up. Now, Natas had a continent, an army and hundreds of millions faithful to a religion that he had given them and to which they were fanatically attached.

"What more could Natas possibly want?"

In his mind, he saw Natas' beautiful face and smiling eyes. He also remembered the older Branniff whose face looked like something from a nightmare but whose voice was soothing. They already had more power than anyone should have. What was it they still strove for? Why did they need him? Etienne had no answers. He picked up the phone.

"Could you track down Miss Ernsky, please."

The sun was high in the sky. It was still early in North America, but he would go mad if he did not talk to someone. It took almost two hours to find Anne Ernsky.

"Well, Etienne, my friend. How can I help?" she asked, genuine pleasure in her voice.

"I am in need of an ear, Anne."

"Am I to be mother confessor to the pope? I think you have come to the right place."

Etienne chuckled briefly, but when he spoke, the laughter died. Etienne introduced a subject that he sensed also troubled Anne Ernsky. They spoke for a while, and when Etienne finally hung up, he was no wiser but felt better.

Turning from the phone, he froze. *Something was in the room.* His eyes involuntarily went to the deeper shadow created by the curtains.

There, he saw Branniff. The light in the room seemed to be repelled by him, and Etienne uttered a brief prayer.

"Too late for that, dear boy. It is time."

Instantly, Etienne heard the penetrating sound that he thought of as the Voice of God. It sliced through him, and, in spite of his fear, it soon soothed him. He did not see Branniff move, but the man was beside him, the horrific face changing to something even more frightening, something that reminded Etienne of a crocodile and yet was not.

Pain exploded in his bones. It felt as if he was dying, but the pure sound of the silent Voice of God told him otherwise. He was losing consciousness, but as he did, something frighteningly alien crawled into his brain. Branniff's mind was inside him, searching for something. Etienne was immobilized, a part of him anticipating the contact. Then, it happened. The pain was remote, but the bones of his face seemed to be moving, reshaping themselves. Before him was his father, dancing in a powerful invocation to the god Chango. Something in Etienne gave way. The pain dissipated. As he lost consciousness, his last thought was that his body had changed shape, becoming like Branniff's.

Chapter 45

*X*u studied the photos of the Black Fleet, fascinated by the size of the leading ship's bow wave. The giant ships were proceeding northeast, apparently oblivious to the turmoil their appearance caused.

"Is that the *Rhode Island*?" he asked, pointing to an American carrier.

"Yes, sir," a general answered. "It approached the fleet a little while ago. There was some electronic chatter."

"Did the fleet respond?"

"No, sir. The physicists have been working on identifying a signature for the ships."

Xu leveled his gaze on the one man in the room not wearing a uniform and asked, "What did you find out, Tung?"

A bespeckled man blinked owlishly, adjusted his glasses and stepped forward. While attending the University of California, Berkeley, Tung changed his first name to James. Xu hated the sound of that western name, and Tung was not unaware of that.

"Well, General Xu," he began in a high-pitched voice that betrayed his nervousness, "our tests suggest an unknown heat signature coming from Antarctica."

"Unknown, you say. Have I come from the war to hear you speak of unknowns?"

Tung gulped and hurriedly replied, "No, sir. The heat signatures of the ships and the one in Antarctica are the same." Xu did not respond but continued to glare at the scientist, who swallowed and added, "And the same as the explosion that destroyed the American ships."

Xu nodded. That is what he had been most anxious to confirm.

"So, we know that whatever it is can power ships as well as blast them out of existence. What else do we know, Tung?"

"Not much more, sir. The team at Beijing University of Technology is following a number of possibilities."

"Such as?"

"Several, but the most promising is that it may be based on a technology that can create black holes, using dark energy as the power source."

"How would this become a weapon?"

Tung, confidence growing, approached the long table where the generals sat.

"General Xu, this is very exotic material," he said hesitantly.

"Indulge me."

"Well, it is important to understand that only about five percent of the universe's density comes from observable matter. Twenty-five percent comes from dark matter."

"That's thirty percent. What's the rest made up of?"

"Dark energy."

"What's that?"

"No one knows for sure, and until now, no one had observed it."

"Until now?" Xu asked.

"We are fairly certain that dark energy is the power source, and if it is, then whoever controls it has an inexhaustible supply of energy. Theoretically, that nation would have seventy percent of the universe available as an energy source."

Xu hunched forward, pushing aside the cup of unfinished tea.

"Inexhaustible?"

"If we could find a way to mine, store and covert it to usable energy, sir. That's a big if."

"Is there any way for us to overcome that if, Tung?"

"There may be, sir, but there is a problem."

"What's that?"

"The findings we have were the result of a joint project with the Americans' Lawrence Berkeley Laboratory. It is called the Super Nova/ Acceleration Probe. SNAP for short. Unfortunately, we have had little communication since the breakdown in our relations."

Xu frowned, thinking that scientists were like children. Give them their science toys, and the realities of the world just disappeared. He could hear the accusation in Tung's voice. Daddy no longer allowed him to play with his American friends. He hated the scientist's characterization of the conflict. "Breakdown in our relations" was not the way he would describe a war that had, so far, cost close to twenty thousand Chinese lives.

"In the past few years, we have tapped into the SNAP project by eavesdropping on their satellite," the scientist continued.

"Their satellite?"

"Yes. SNAP is a satellite-borne telescope that measures supernovae. I have to assume they are doing the same with our satellite."

"What does all this add up to?" Xu said impatiently.

"We have confirmed that dark energy does exist, sir. It is transported through the universe on the backs of gravitons, the elemental constituent of gravity. If we had the engineering to tap that source and squeeze it into much more restricted space, it would be possible to use both the force of gravity and the dark energy."

The scientist's voice became excited as he related the possibilities, but he was immediately crestfallen when Xu asked, "How?"

"In theory, we could use the dark energy for fuel and the force of gravity as a weapon."

"How? I thought gravity was one of the weakest forces in the universe. That has not changed, has it?"

"It is a very weak force over the immense distances of the universe. As you know, sir, its force decreases as distance from the source increases, but our research suggests that gravity is tremendously powerful over short distances. For example, think of the gravitational pull of a massive collapsed star. It is so powerful that not even light can escape."

"Do we have the capacity to create a massive collapsed star, Tung?"

"No, sir, but, from our calculations, someone has."

"Who?"

"We are not sure," a general answered before Tung could respond. "We have some clues, though. The leading scientist in this area of study has disappeared from the lab at the Astroparticle Physics Institute in Maryland in the United States."

He walked to the head of the table and handed Xu several satellite photos. In one, three tractors were making their way across the stark whiteness of an icy land. Another showed a group erecting a tent. There were seven persons in the photo.

"What is this, and who are they?" Xu asked.

"These were taken by our satellite overflying Antarctica. Two are scientists we know. That one's Dr. Antonius Faison who heads up the Advanced Physics Lab in Princeton. The other is Dr. Karl Metzer, who, when sane, is probably the most brilliant physicist in the world. No offence, Tung."

The bespeckled scientist grinned but did not dispute the assessment.

"Who are the others?

"It looks as if they have a squad of military people with them. The third civilian, we don't know. He could be another scientist, but Tung doesn't know him, so we think he may be one of their political officers. The Americans would never allow two of their major scientists to get too far afield without a handler."

Xu, having studied the photos, said "Good work, General Wang. You too, Tung. You did the right thing to call me."

Xu dismissed the scientist and offered everyone tea.

Then, he said, "Gentlemen, unless we move quickly, we are buggered."

For a long time, he spoke quietly but with great passion about the fate of the war and felt the greatest satisfaction when the generals rose and raised their teacups to him. Three hours later, a plane left Tongxian Air Base on a trip that would see the passengers transferred to an aircraft carrier in the South China Sea. From there, a small group of military and scientific personnel would be ferried to Antarctica. Whoever possessed the recently discovered technology had a power never before seen in human history. That power contained unlimited possibilities, and Xu was determined that those possibilities would belong to China. The hunt was on.

Chapter 46

The pain became more intense. Trying to control it, Andreas felt drained of energy. And they had only just begun to climb out of the valley. It was a beautiful vista, with two rivers meeting in the middle. One was the source of the River Wilongo, the giant waterway that ran the length of the Land of Tiamat. Andreas thought nostalgically of the many times he had sat on the lawn of the temple in Tiastan, watching the broad River Wilongo. Why everyone referred to it as "the broad River Wilongo," he did not know, but there was affection contained in those words. A powerful feeling of loss overcame him as he admired the Valley of Sidemia, with its fields of golden *Q'emi*, the flowers whose scent filled the air. They stretched like a flaxen blanket into the distance. Having never seen anything quite that color before coming to the Land of Tiamat, he would miss it.

Somewhere far to the southeast was the ancient capital city of Tiastan, battered by Natas' armies but still standing. Eurydice cried when they passed the city. Though it was not visible, their mind senses detected the life there. And the pain. Natas had not been kind to the city that was dedicated to the goddess. Eurydice's escape brought a fresh round of reprisals, and smoke hung above the city. That was several days ago, and though quiet for a long time after, Eurydice was beginning to smile again. She was standing on an outcropping, staring at the valley, the last before they began the ascent from the Land of Tiamat.

How do I feel? Andreas wondered.

His eyes followed the path of a darting bird that children called a *scr'ee-scr'ee* because of the sound it made. Would he ever see this land again? Not sure, he was filled with a sense of foreboding. The Land of Tiamat had survived in the most improbable way over tens of millennia, and there, he had met some of the gentlest souls. Until Natas' attack, Andreas had known peace, a kind of forgetfulness that allowed him to heal. At the thought of Natas, the involuntary hatred sprang up, but he calmed it, as if it was a separate part of him. That battle was not for today.

I have changed so much.

The most important change was the new power he possessed. From time to time, he wondered if this was all a dream, some grand illusion from which he would be set free. Running his fingers across the furrowed ridges of the cuts made by the crocodile's paw, he knew his experiences were all too real. The cuts had healed, and sight came back to his eye. His arm, though it tingled from time to time, lost its withered look and was stronger. Andreas flexed it, noting the corded muscles. The staff was now almost an extension of his body. He observed Eurydice, who raised her arms to the cloudy sky and then bent low, her head almost touching the ground.

Obeisance to the goddess. Such a delicate movement and yet, so powerful, he thought.

Her body was outlined against the sky, and Andreas, seeing her strength, was glad to have her at his side. He had lost her, then found her again, and gazing at the dying light of *malamalama* and the approaching darkness of *pogosi,* he swore that he would never lose her again. As if she sensed his pledge, Eurydice turned and waved. He was on the verge of responding when his mind sense tingled. His eyes searched the distance. Eurydice's laughter greeted his alarm.

"I wondered how long it would take before you were aware of them."

"Of whom?" Andreas said, perplexed.

"Usai and Meldana."

"Your personal guards?"

She nodded. Andreas felt joy because, for the first time since she had found out about Lona's death, there was no heaviness behind her smile. The *leo-leos* were quite a way off, and Eurydice started a fire, preparing a meal for them. Hours later, they arrived, their beautifully taut bodies exhibiting a silvery sheen. They struggled to control their faces, and Andreas was perplexed until he remembered that the berries were changing his and Eurydice's skin color. That proved very useful as they passed village after village. Security was tight, but their changed color and the gentle ministrations of their mind senses made what could have been a truly dangerous trip somewhat less so.

Eurydice must have been able to send a message to the leo-leos, Andreas thought.

Each *leo-leo* carried a bundle. Eurydice opened her arms wide, and they came to her. She kissed them both on the tops of their sweaty heads, then on each cheek and finally on their mouths. The two young warriors glowed with pride.

The supreme honor from the high priestess.

So far, they had not looked directly at Andreas, and he thought how uncomfortable it must be for them. They were reared in the temple, and, except for Lona and himself, no men were allowed there. He was startled, therefore, when the *leo-leos* disrobed. Naked, they walked to a rivulet and quickly bathed, lathering themselves with the juice from the *scruc'i'nele,* a prickly plant with wonderful cleansing properties. Andreas admired the tall, muscular bodies, but he walked away. Eurydice followed him.

"They have no fear of men's eyes, Andreas, because they have never had men's eyes on them. The embarrassment you feel is yours alone."

Andreas, wanting to avoid the subject, asked, "How did they know where we were?"

"They didn't. They simply came to the pedestal of the Goddess' Footsteps."

"What's that?"

"Do you remember that before Natas attacked three years ago, I was supposed to make an ascent to the breast of the goddess? I did not because we went to Lusani. Usai and Meldana did not accompany me to Lusani because they had already left to prepare for my ascent. They have been returning here each season at the approach of the time of *pogosi,* awaiting me."

"So, they didn't know you'd be here, but you knew they would be. And they would have done this each year until you came? What if you never did?"

"Empheme has always come, Andreas," she replied, adding after a moment, "Plus, I sent word by the priestesses in the forest."

She laughed at the look on his face as she placed an arm on his shoulder.

"Don't think so much about reality and fantasy. The difference is often simply a matter of the depth of our imaginations. Come. They brought you a change of clothes."

They brought equipment, as well as a new robe and a synthetic heat suit. Encouraged by the *leo-leos'* earlier actions, he stripped and took a bath in the river. Later, they ate, and after the steady diet of tubers, never had processed food tasted so good. One of the women gave him a small bottle of a blue liquid. He took a sip, and the flavor exploded in his mouth, exciting his taste buds and quenching his thirst.

"What's this?"

"Something they brought from the temple," Eurydice replied.

That night, he slept soundly, reassured by the presence of the *leo-leos* who carried staffs and the short guns that fired almost without recoil. The next day, they sat at lunch, watching the last of the valley that would soon be hidden by clouds.

"We are going to run out of food, and there's nothing to hunt once we leave this valley," Andreas said.

He gazed at the west wall of the valley. Soon, they would leave that rock, and he thought of what lurked behind the clouds. Ice. It would be the enemy as they climbed higher. Thirteen years ago, having the latest technology at his disposal, the descent was still hell. He stood, surprising the women. The *leo-leos* glanced at Eurydice, and she nodded. They tidied the site and soon were on their way. *Pogosi* came as they reached the pines.

Andreas awoke to the sound of grunts, and crawling out of the sleeping bag, he saw the *leo-leos*, stripped to their undergarments, in full combat. He noted the speed and power of their movements, realizing, after a while, that he could anticipate their moves. He admired the women's skill and strength. When they jumped, it was as if the air itself provided a suction that drew them upwards and then supported them in their turns. They fought for a long time before resting briefly. Then, they picked up their staffs. Andreas followed their moves, and while his brain told him that the staffs were flying around in a blur, his mind sense saw each stroke clearly. Soon, the *leo-leos* worked up a sweat.

Eurydice, a little too casually, asked, "Do you wish to join them?"

Andreas laughed and demurred. The women warriors stopped, their staffs held erect, looking at him.

"I don't want to fight them. They're probably too good, anyway."

"Do not confuse them with the women you normally meet, Andreas. They are *leo-leos*."

Andreas studied the two women, and what he saw was their breasts rising and falling in ways that dragged his eyes with them. He was also uncomfortably aware of how skimpy their undergarments were. The two women stepped sideways. Their movements were fluid, reminding him of *tusiata* fighters seen in the *falalalaga*, the gyms where the art was taught and the matches took place. Andreas reached for his staff, and it leapt into his hand. Immediately, both women were in the air, their staffs making a whirring sound as they jumped. Andreas did not jump. Instead, he took two steps forward, shortening the distance between him and the flying *leo-leos*. Their staffs were still raised above their heads when Andreas' staff connected with their shins. They fell forward, rolling back to their feet as one. Without pause, they attacked again, one from the left, the other from the right. Andreas recognized the encircling movement known as *lotaifale* and bent forward sharply at the waist, leaving the staff aloft, held by one hand. Hearing the sounds of the *leo-leos'* staffs smacking into his staff, he rolled forward, flowing to his feet in the defensive position, one arm straight forward, with the fingers bent upwards and the staff held at an acute angle to his body. They could not hit him, and confidence growing, he shifted to an attack position.

"Enough," Eurydice said.

The two *leo-leos* instantly relaxed, but Andreas remained alert.

"Enough, Andreas."

He exhaled. The *leo-leos* bowed, and Andreas returned the honor. Eurydice handed water to each of the fighters, and they drank deeply.

"You fight well, Tama. Unorthodox, but well," Meldana said.

She looked embarrassed. They were Empheme's personal

bodyguards, and they had lost. Worse, they had lost to a man who, only a few seasons earlier, knew nothing of the *tusiata*.

Recognizing this, he said, "You, too, fight well, Meldana and Usai. Maybe one day, we will fight together in defense of Empheme."

They both nodded and, bowing, walked away. Soon, they were climbing again.

"You did very well, Andreas," Empheme said.

"Yes," he responded excitedly. "It felt as if I was moving so much faster than they. I—"

"I do not mean that. I was speaking of your courtesy in acknowledging their skill. The *leo-leos* are dedicated to me from birth. My personal guards are the best of the *leo-leos*. Meldana and Usai will not forget this day, nor will they forget your statement at the end of the fight. Do you know how you won?"

"I was faster."

"Put down the staff. Meldana, come."

The tall, imposing woman strode over, appearing not to touch the ground.

"Now hit her," Eurydice said.

Andreas shrugged and suddenly lunged at the woman. When his foot arrived, there was only air. He felt the light tap of a hand against his neck. The *leo-leo* was behind him. He had not seen her move.

"OK. That's enough," Eurydice said, laughing.

Meldana walked away.

"Have you figured it out?"

"The staff."

She nodded.

"Confidence is a good thing. Overconfidence can be the end of you. Those are Teme's words, not mine."

Andreas surveyed the staff, false pride draining out of him.

"The staff amplifies my mind sense, so I was not simply reacting to Usai and Meldana's actions. The staff was anticipating them for me. Without the staff, I'm no match for a *leo-leo*."

"Something has changed in your relationship with the staff. I've suspected it for a while but was only sure when I saw your reaction to Meldana and Usai. Keep it close to you, Andreas. It is the goddess' gift."

When they came out of the pines, Andreas looked back, but clouds now covered the Land of Tiamat. They stood for a long time, staring, hoping the clouds would break, giving them one last view.

Eventually, Eurydice said, "Come. We must concentrate on the land above now."

At those words, Andreas felt the sharp pain in his body, but he mastered it, pushing it away. Above him, the path steepened.

Chapter 47

They encountered the first ice on the tenth day of the climb. It became noticeably colder, and they changed into the synthetics brought by the *leo-leos*. The cuffs of the sleeves had adjustable heat monitors. Once again, Andreas marveled at the contradictions in a Tiamatian society that could develop the technology used in the heat suit and still believed so firmly in its gods. He wondered what would happen when that society met his. Would the First People understand the violence, the irrationality, or the secularism of his people? Andreas realized that, for the first time, he was thinking of the whole world above as his people. Was that what it would take to create unity above? Would they need the presence of an external enemy? The terms of the contact between the two worlds were already being determined. Weeks earlier, they had heard sounds suggestive of an exodus. He caught up to Eurydice.

"What exactly is the Hall of the Onyes, Eudy? When I found it in the southern Plain of Sotami, it was more than a hall. There was a power plant and a bunch of computers beneath the building. Any idea what that is?"

"I've been thinking about that since you mentioned it. Obviously, Natas has moved the Hall of the Onyes from the Marble Mountains to the south. I can't think of any reason why he would do that."

"You once said that he needed the Onyes to consolidate his power in the Land of Tiamat. Wouldn't having the mummies on display be to his advantage? Why hide them away?"

Eurydice scrambled over some loose shale before she answered.

"Actually, the Hall of the Onyes has always been hidden away. Even in the Marble Mountains, few knew its location. Natas' power would have multiplied when word spread that he possessed the bodies of the first and the last Onye. The people don't need to see the mummies of the Onyes; they would simply accept it."

"If it doesn't matter where the mummies are housed, why move them to such an inaccessible place?"

"I don't know."

"And another thing. The computers seemed to be measuring the temperature of the continent."

"Why would Natas need to do that?"

"No idea. The readings were constantly changing, but around a constant value."

"You mean like plus or minus one?"

"Yes."

Leaning forward as the gradient changed, he smiled, pleased at the feeling of reserve power in his legs.

"I was wondering if maybe he'd discovered oil."

"We've never found any in the east of the Land of Tiamat. The oil fields we know are in the center and toward the southwest. Tiastan sits on a very rich oil field."

"What could demand the kind of technology that was below the Hall of the Onyes? It was huge, many times bigger than the hall itself."

She shook her head. Soon, the land became steeper, and they spoke no more. That night, the cave was stocked with supplies.

"You're full of surprises," he said.

"I told you I had to make the ascent. There are thirteen of these stations on the way. Each is designed to give a place to rest, to provide food and equipment."

"And they just happen to have my size."

He held up a pair of hiking boots, and Eurydice grinned.

"The goddess provides."

"You knew that I was going to be here? Is that why it's laid out like this?"

"The stories speak of Empheme's escape to the ice above. There, she is picked up by a stranded ship. We prepare for all contingencies."

"In the stories, Empheme escapes with the Son of Ghalib."

"There are many stories, Andreas."

"That's what Mother Mutasii once said to me."

"Mother Mutasii is wise."

"I hope she's all right. When I saw her last, she was among the *Ulumatua*."

"But you never found her body. She's all right. You will see her again."

"Who is she, Eudy?"

"The First People have asked that question about her and the Father of the Ilegu Forest from time before time."

"Are they immortal?"

She smiled and with her priestess' voice, said, "Would you know the time of your death, Maatemnu?"

Andreas was quiet for a while, his eyes straying to the two women who were bedding down near the mouth of the cave. It was colder there, and he suggested they invite the *leo-leos* inside where the fire burned.

"Meldana and Usai will create their own warmth."

He did not ask what she meant.

"What do you think it's like above now, Eudy?"

"Wars, rumors of wars, theft, larceny, murder and occasionally, very occasionally, a good person walks by."

"That's pretty cynical. Sounds more like me," Andreas replied, chuckling.

"Not cynical, merely honest. Natas is sending an army above, so there's bound to be conflict. The world was already pretty tense when I left."

Andreas glanced at the *leo-leos*. Then, seeing Eurydice's smile, he leaned over, hugging her to him.

"I'm so glad I found you, Eudy."

"I'm glad you found me, too, my heart."

She raised her face, and they kissed softly. Then, they were quiet, each enjoying the other's warmth.

"There will be conflict. When I left, China and the United States were already pretty close to war. Maybe that's over by now, but if Natas brings an army, he must have somewhere to station it. Who would let an army of that size on its territory?" Andreas said.

"Africa would be the logical place."

"Why?"

"Think about it. A black army suddenly appearing from nowhere; a weak, fragmented continent; Branniff's massive investment in Africa over the last few decades. What better place to go? There may be an even more compelling reason. Natas' army is made up of troops from the Land of Tiamat and African American *expulsees*. They will both recognize in Africa a homeland of sorts."

Andreas nodded.

"It is possible Natas arranged the Expulsion to create the conditions we now have. He has an army with an ancestral claim to the African continent and a world weakened by a quarter century of environmental tragedy. Unless things have changed radically in the time we've been down here, above is still a land of drought and famine, homelessness and death. Very few countries were able to hold themselves together as political entities. If into that breach steps Natas with a powerful army, limitless wealth and a supply of energy, what could stop him?"

They were both silent for a long time, but Andreas was experiencing a fear that Eurydice was not. He thought of one character who was even more enigmatic than Natas. Himself. Maatemnu, the Great Slayer. Whom would Maatemnu slay? And why the adjective "Great"? Natas was mentioned in the stories of the First People as the Son of Ghalib, but it was Maatemnu who was called "Great." His mind spun round and round on the conundrum, but the future remained opaque. When finally sleep came, he was clinging to Eurydice.

Chapter 48

*E*ight days later, the first snow came. Worse, a lone war plane flashed by overhead, a stark reminder that the quiet of the mountain was no protection against Natas' searchers. The sheer climb up the ice had not yet begun, but at the end of that climb was probably the most inhospitable region on earth. The short summer was ending, and a darkness that would seem like eternal night was approaching. In a few weeks, the temperature could drop to minus seventy degrees, and they had no protection against it.

Andreas glanced at Eurydice who walked at his side. As always, he was ambivalent about her faith in the stories. Having passed two of the thirteen stations up the mountain, it was clear that someone had prepared for his presence. There were warm clothing and boots at both stations. The mythical story of Empheme's escape with the Son of Ghalib in some remote past seemed to be determining their actions now. Ahead of them, the *leo-leos* strode powerfully upwards.

"Is there anything they don't do well?" he asked.

Eurydice turned to him, eyes playful but proud.

"They're trained for any circumstance. We're very fortunate to have them."

Their brown coats were starkly outlined against the snow, which had come more quickly than anticipated. A certain urgency was added to their climb.

Eurydice, noticing his look, said, "A few more hours and we'll reach the next station. There are white snow suits there."

Before he could respond, they both sensed the plane, and Eurydice yelled something to the *leo-leos*. Immediately, they dropped, piling snow on top of themselves.

"What are they doing?" Andreas asked, falling to the ground himself.

"Cover yourself with snow. It makes it more difficult for them to spot us from the air."

"Why not use our mind sense to distract the pilot?" he asked, as he complied with the order.

"No effect on a surveillance camera if they're using one."

They quickly covered themselves and waited as the plane, beautifully delta-shaped, came out of the clouds, looking like a bee against a white background. It moved slowly for a fighter plane, and Andreas surmised that it was a VTOLM—a vertical take-off or landing machine. It had the speed of a fighter plane and the flexibility of a helicopter. The plane came over the mountain. Eurydice's mind sense joined his, and they reached out to the pilot. The plane speeded up and, banking left sharply, was gone.

"Why couldn't we have done that earlier?" Andreas asked, as he brushed snow from his face and coat.

"I tried. Whatever Natas has created that weakens our mind sense in Ghalib's Land is portable. It was on that plane."

"That explains why we didn't sense it until it was almost on top of us."

"Natas isn't standing still. He doesn't yet know how we'll get to the surface, but he intends to stop us."

"Why? What can we do to him?"

"Not we. You. He knows who you are now."

"How would you know that?"

"Teme."

"Teme? Are you in contact with her?"

"No. Unfortunately, she has no mind sense. One of the oddities of our culture. Some have the ability, and others do not."

"Then how could she have communicated anything to you?"

"By now, she would have told Natas that you're Maatemnu."

"And why would Natas care about that? He's—"

"What? Too sophisticated? Too modern? Andreas, you must believe. Your ability to win is going to be dependent on your faith. You are Maatemnu, and your inability to reason it out changes nothing.

Natas is modern, but he is also the product of a cultural bloodline. He believes in the things that you struggle to accept. You can't pick and choose what you will accept and what you will reject. You can't take the mind sense and the staff but reject the goddess. It's all one thing."

Her eyes bored into his as she added, "If you falter, Natas will kill us both. And not just us. The world you know will cease to exist. You must believe in Tiamat, my love."

He sought to find her faith, but it was hard. Something else bothered him.

"Eudy, you said that Teme would have told him by now. How would you know that?"

"I sent her, Andreas. Natas wanted to show his contempt for me, so I took advantage of that. I sent her to him. Teme whispers words of confusion in Natas' ears. She tells him who he truly is, and she reminds him who you really are and what you have done in the past. This knowledge will unsettle him. It is for this reason Teme suffers in Natas' bed."

"Natas' bed? I thought the priestesses didn't ..."

"They don't. That was Teme's *fata aigu*," she replied bitterly.

Eurydice resumed climbing, and Andreas followed, his mind in turmoil. He wanted to hold her, but now she seemed less like his wife than the high priestess Empheme.

How much did it cost her?

In the last three years, she had lost her temple, seen her goddess defeated and broken, lost her only child, been forced to hand her closest associate over to the enemy for his repeated violations. In all that time, through everything, she had never questioned her faith, never shied away from what her goddess demanded. Andreas wondered where the strength came from.

I'm like a cork on water, pushed this way and that. She's like a rock.

"Ah, but you are a different kind of rock, for you will never break, Maatemnu."

The voice slid into his brain. At first, he thought it was Eurydice, but the texture was different. He was in a cave. Eurydice, Meldana and Usai were sitting at the far end, in conversation. Near to him, something shimmered. He recognized the goddess. The figure reached out, and Andreas screamed when its finger touched the scars left by the crocodile. Instantly, he saw a dying world, and pain shot through him. At one extreme end of his sight was a black mountain, at the other, a group of shimmering peaks.

The Marble Mountains, he thought.

The goddess answered, "*Yes.*"

On the first mountain, Natas, barely recognizable, stood, a staff in his hand. It was the dancing god of Andreas' earlier dreams, but now, Natas was not dancing. His face was grim. Between the two mountains was a dead valley.

The desert of my visions.

"*Not quite, Maatemnu.*"

The vista changed, and the valley became the solar system. It was dying. Slowly, from where Natas' mountain reared up, the solar system was being folded up like a rug, and the death cry was horrible in Andreas' ears. He was on a hillside, golden staff in hand. His anger shook the mountains, and they flew together, colliding with a mighty crash. He shouted something, and his arms smashed into Natas'. For a moment, the folding of the solar system stopped, as if all now looked at the two mountains.

Then, he heard Eurydice say, "Wake up. It's time to be going."

Andreas blinked, still seeing images of the holocaust. He shuddered. "A vision?"

He nodded.

"What do you see, Andreas?"

The familiar question prompted his memory, and he told her all that he remembered.

"How did I get here?" he asked, looking around the cave.

"Same way we did. Don't you remember?"

"No. One minute I was on the mountain, and then, I was in this cave."

"The goddess speaks to you directly now, Andreas, and much more personally than she ever spoke to me." Eurydice shook her head, adding, with wonder in her voice, "It is to Maatemnu she speaks."

"What was it I saw, Eudy?"

Eurydice slowly zipped her sleeping bag up and stuffed it in one of the four large, synthetic knapsacks found in the cave. Judging from the equipment, the assault on the ice cliff was about to begin. There were fur-lined boots with the associated crampons for climbing and another set of synthetic suits. Eurydice packed hers before answering.

"What do you believe about the end of the world, Andreas?"

"I don't know," he said, frowning. "As a scientist, I suppose I believe that at some point our sun will supernova, and it will wipe out everything in the solar system. I can't say that I have fully escaped the teachings of my Catholic upbringing. You know, someday God will judge us, and the righteous will go to heaven, etcetera, etcetera."

She was quiet for a moment and then said, "Do you realize that in south Asia, there is no tradition of a cataclysmic end like in the Abramic traditions of Islam, Judaism and Christianity? There is, instead, a gentler recycling of our lives. They end and begin again in a cycle of regeneration and improvement. Do you think that both traditions could be right?"

"Well, science has attempted to reconcile the two. We accept that energy can neither be created nor destroyed. Forms change, but the amount of energy remains the same."

"Science," she said with a trace of anger. "It is both our salvation and the bane of our existence. We have discovered so much that we do not understand, and it now threatens to kill us all."

"Is that what I saw in my vision? Some scientific experiment that goes wrong, that destroys the world? What about the mountains and Natas and me? What's that all about?"

The *leo-leos* heaved packs on their backs, and Andreas lifted his, surprised at how light it was.

Science gave us this capability.

Outside the cave, they looked up. Newly-fallen snow was everywhere, but high above, something glinted. Ice. Andreas' stomach tightened. After a while, Eurydice responded to his question.

"In many ways, Andreas, I am blind. Except for my obedience to the goddess, the path is no longer clear to me. That is why your ears must be open. You must hear her voice. She speaks to you now with an intimacy that the stories say the first Onye experienced when he walked with the gods."

"But what about the images, Eudy? What are they? The valley I saw was dead, barren, and it was being folded up as if it was to be disposed of. Could it be the end? Could the gods be so cruel?"

She touched his face, running her thumb gently over the scars.

"You have been changed in so many ways, Andreas. In name, appearance, and in strength, but still your mind remains the same."

"Can a man truly change, Eudy?"

"Yes, but acceptance of that change is hard, my love. What is the central story of your religion?"

"The crucifixion of Jesus Christ."

"A human sacrifice," she responded quietly. "But is the sacrifice all?"

"As you know, Christ rises on the third day."

"So, it is both sacrifice and renewal, crucifixion and resurrection, that is the full story, no? The two actions can't be separated, though adherents to the religion seem to glory in the sacrificial part more than the renewal. Yet, it is there, just as the south Asian idea of a renewable cycle is there. Isn't that interesting? Two cultures, seen as separate and distinct, having at the center of their cosmology the same idea."

"It's humans' instinct to find meaning in their lives. It's hard to accept that this thing we hold to be so precious could be meaningless after all."

"Or the myths could contain the kernel of a larger truth, something we have intuited throughout time, something that the universe itself seems to be trying to tell us. The sun rising and setting, tides going in and out, the recurrent cycles of the moon, the seasons. Everything begins, ends, then begins again. Why should human life be different?"

"Finite lives also, by definition, mean finite knowledge," Andreas responded. "If I die before a cure for cancer is discovered, then I cannot know of the cure. It's almost as if God, if such there be, or the gods did not want to overburden us. Yet the acquisition of knowledge continues, not in the single human but in the species. Our immortality is not that of the individual but of the group which continues forever. Right?"

"Is it?" Eurydice asked, her voice penetrating.

Andreas felt her mind sense slice into his, bringing a brief pain. He recoiled, but she pushed into him, and he felt faint.

"What are you doing?" he gasped. "Stop it!"

"*See, Maatemnu,*" a voice ordered.

He looked into her and saw ... nothing. Then, she was out of him.

"My God, Eudy. What the hell was that?" he said.

"*Choices,*" a hard voice responded from the mouth of the woman who was his wife. "*Come into me.*"

His mind sense slid easily into hers, and this time, he saw Cybele, with sickle-shaped knife designed for ritual castration, standing over the resurrected god Attis; he saw Anubis, the Lord of the Sacred Land, weighing the hearts of the deceased, and then guiding them to the throne of Osiris. Ammut, Devouress of the Dead, sat next to the seals, waiting for Ma'at, the goddess of Truth, to declare the dead either true of voice or untruthful, and then opening her crocodile jaws to devour the untruthful. There was, too, Adonis, the Lord, whose annual death and resurrection were celebrated at Byblos and Pathos. Jesus was dying on a Roman cross and climbing from a tomb with his message of hope not for this earth but of a Heaven to come. Maatemnu walked with Ajok who was at first a benevolent god but who was changed by man's selfishness and pride. A mother begged Ajok to restore her child to life, but when he did, the woman's husband chided her and killed the child again. From that moment, death became long-lasting, for the god had turned his back on humans. Andreas saw Andriambahornanana ask his god to let him die as a banana plant which quickly grew back after its death. And Azra'il, the angel of death, who when he heard of a virgin who had lived for five hundred years was so impressed that he brought her back to life in order to meet her. Bumba, the chief creator god, came next, appearing to Keri Keri in a dream and showing him the secret of fire.

Then, he saw Cagn who when he was killed by the Thornbushmen, his bones rejoined, and he lived again. Next was Chuku who sent a dog to his people with the message of eternal life, but since the message was garbled, the people found death instead. Then came Harri-Hara, the creator/death-dealer, who reconciled the opposing principles of existence. There, too, were the Hsien, overseeing the separation of the soul into its two parts, the *hun* returning to the heavens and the *pho* to earth. Then, came Izanagi and Izanami, the brother and sister creators, who accidentally created monsters and the fire-god Ho-masubi, whose birth killed his mother. Izanagi followed her to Hell, but she was angry because Izanagi saw her decomposing ugliness, and she sent demons after him. This caused Izanagi to close the door to hell.

Finally, Maatemnu saw Abassi, the creator sky god, who when he created Earth wanted it to be barren but was persuaded by his wife to allow a human couple to live upon the earth. His fear was that they would soon surpass him in wisdom and capacity. So that this should not happen, he forbade them to grow food, to work or have children, summoning them to heaven each day to get their meals. The two humans ignored the laws, grew plants and had children. Abassi sent dissension and death to the humans. Then, Maatemnu saw himself, with cruel spears ending the lives of the hairy creatures, and also an age.

"And so, the lesson is clear, Maatemnu. Humans have always confronted the gods, who have always punished humans. The price of your knowledge has always been your mortality," the voice said.

Andreas looked around. Again, he was in a cave, this one somewhat smaller than the last. Eurydice was holding a damp cloth to his lips. When he tried to speak, no sound came.

"Hush, my love," she said.

Andreas leaned back, accepting water.

"I have kept you from climbing."

"No. Meldana and Usai carried you."

"Carried me?" Andreas said, surprised, his eyes going to the tall women. "How far?"

"Two days."

"Two days! I remember nothing of that. I thought I was in your mind sense."

"No. The goddess guided you."

She observed him, the question obvious on her face, but she did not ask.

"You said all things begin and end, then begin again, but that is not true only of individual human life, is it? Civilizations behave in the same way, each civilization's life propelling the species forward until it tires and is replaced by another. They can, however, come round again. Am I right?"

There was a smile on Eurydice's face.

"Yes, my love."

"And this is such a moment," he said almost to himself. "You said that the First People awaited the freeing of Tiamat, but she is not simply goddess, is she? Not simply the sister of Chango and Baal. She is everything."

"Is that what she said, Andreas?"

At the cave's entrance, the tall *leo-leos* stood staring into the cave at the high priestess.

"When all three divinities are together in any moment of time, they act as repulsive forces. They destroy all until they are entrapped in the singular godhead that is the god to whom the people give no name?"

In response, Eurydice said, "What do you see, Maatemnu?"

Andreas looked and saw the struggle between the goddess, who had given birth to Time, and her brothers. The universe was crimson yet completely black. He did not understand. The horror of that time-less struggle caused him to cringe and shudder, for the weapons of the gods were the very elements of the universe itself. It was the moment of the Repulsion, when universes collided. Tiamat, unable to subdue her brothers and draw them into herself to create unity, gave in to Time and volunteered to retreat, folding herself in the hardened waters of the universe. Order returned, and the horror left. Tiamat cried for the loss of her brothers, Chango who walked the earth like a vagabond and Baal whose anger burned the mountains with his fire. Now, Tiamat was free, and the Repulsion was beginning.

"There is more. You must find it," Eurydice said

"I know. 'Choices', you said. Two possibilities, I see now. The Reunion of the First People, uniting all of humankind, or the Repulsion, the destruction of all that we know."

"And much that we do not, my love."

Andreas was afraid, and his body became chilled.

"I can't," he said hoarsely, clutching at Eurydice's arm, his eyes wild.

"You must, my love. No one else can."

Andreas saw again the dead valley, the galaxy being folded up like a rug for disposal, and he shuddered. When Eurydice's mouth moved, her tone was tender, suggestive and careful, as if it had joined her mind sense.

"You have stood here at the end of every age, Maatemnu. You have stood here at the beginning of every age. You decide whether worlds live or die, and always you have chosen their deaths. You are the Great Slayer. There's nothing to be done."

A memory came to him, and he asked, "Do you remember when I first spoke with the goddess, that time when I lost five days?"

"Teme and I found you. Even then, Mother Mutasii said the spirit of the gods was strong in you."

"After that, I told Lona about the vision, and he said that he had also seen it. He, too, had been on the mountain, but there was a difference. Where I could find a path only to the Marble Mountains, he, in his dream, found a path down to the green, grassy valley. Why was that, Eudy? Why did Lona have a path that I could not find?"

Even as he asked the question, he knew the answer. Lona found the green valley of peace in death. For him, it was a different path, of hardship, pain and despair. Eurydice continued to press the wet cloth against his forehead as he interpreted the signs of his life, struggling to make sense of them.

"We must hurry, Eudy. Natas' strength grows, and I must confront him."

"You must defeat him. Baal grows in Natas, and now, only he is free."

"What do you mean only he is free?"

"Look into yourself, Maatemnu," the frightening voice said. *"There you will find me in my many names, save one. I am Tiamat, as well as the god to whom the people give no name. I am Chango, and I am the dying god. I am purity, and I am whore. I am all, save one. That one is Baal. If Baal is free at the moment of the Repulsion, then all that I have created dies. At least, as you understand it. Baal must be subdued by you, Maatemnu. Do not fail me, for my wrath has destroyed many times and will destroy again."*

Andreas cowered before the voice, and a part of him wondered why the three women in the cave were so calm. Could they not hear the voice's fury? But the voice spoke only to him. Weakly, he extended his mind sense and touched Eurydice. With that touch, his breathing slowed, and he slept.

Chapter 49

"Again and again?" Dr. Faison said scornfully. "That is pure fantasy, as I wrote four years ago in my paper 'Rejecting the Brane Universe.'"

Sidoti sighed. The two scientists had been arguing for hours, and he was beginning to get a headache. Still, there was nothing else to do. They had to take rest stops, and since crossing the ice bridge, they were making pretty good time. He was more worried about what General Blount had sent to him. The photograph of what they were calling the Black Fleet was ominous. It was huge. How could anyone build a fleet of that size, and ships of those gigantic proportions, without the nations of the world finding out?

Everything pointed to Branniff Enterprises, but no one understood how Branniff could have found the materials or the manpower in Antarctica. The whole world was on high alert. The aircraft carrier, U.S.S. *Rhode Island,* had approached the fleet, but there was no response to the hail, no acknowledgment of any kind. In General Blount's words, it was "like a destroyer gliding past a goddamn toy boat."

"The work done with the collider at the Centre Européène pour la Recherche Nucleaire suggests that it is possible," Metzer said.

They're so naïve. Not even aware of what's going on, Sidoti thought.

The two scientists were arguing over the brane world hypothesis, and he allowed them to go on since their more orginal ideas sprang from the arguments. At least, Metzer's did. Dr. Faison spent most of his time trying to show why Metzer's theories were wrong.

That's like spitting into a typhoon.

Another area of contention was black holes and the capacity of their colossal power to bring two brane worlds together. Sidoti tried to follow the argument.

"The idea of a cyclical universe has been around since the 1930s when Richard Tolman at Caltech proposed it. The notion of the universe expanding until it runs out of energy and then collapsing back on itself is unfathomable," Dr. Faison was saying.

"Actually, Tolman said there would be some kind of bounce after the universe contracted into a submicroscopic piece of matter," Metzer replied smugly.

"I know that. It's the same principle," Dr. Faison responded with barely concealed anger.

"Not at all. Tolman introduced the idea of the universe continually beginning again. Expansion, contraction, bounce, expansion again, and so on. What I'm saying is that brane worlds—and I should give credit here to Steinhardt and Turok—do exist, but because they are in different dimensions, they could exist side by side, literally not more than a fraction of a centimeter away, and we wouldn't know it."

"Why?" Dr. Faison snapped.

Metzer, who, Sidoti noted, was having a good day, was the soul of restraint.

"As of the last few weeks, that has become less clear. We previously thought that light would never exit the branes—"

"That was an assumption. None of this has been experimentally proven."

"True, but that's why you experimental boys leave the really brainy work to us."

Dr. Faison flushed but said nothing.

"Anyway, given what I now know is happening, I've been working on a second set of equations. Gravity."

"What about it?" Sidoti asked.

"It is the only force of which we are aware that could possibly travel across the brane borders. However, in crossing that frontier, it becomes so diffuse, we would have no instruments to detect it."

"How very convenient," Dr. Faison said.

As Metzer was about to reply, Sidoti asked, "Is there a point here?"

"Yup. My mathematics shows that we may be heading for an astronomical event of some magnitude."

"Yes. In a trillion years. I've heard of it," Dr. Faison scoffed.

"Explain what you mean to Sidoti. He's looking a little fish-eyed," Metzer said, snickering.

"Well, Mr. Sidoti, the theory, if it can be called that, suggests that after the so-called 'bounce' in his model, the universe expands at a specific rate for seven billion years. Then, it accelerates for another trillion years—"

"Trillion? With a 't'?"

"Yes. And after that, it collapses as if you had let go both ends of a stretched rubber band. Except, unlike the rubber band which returns to a state of inertia, the contracting brane world 'bounces' against another brane world—in another dimension, mind you—and starts the whole bloody cycle all over again."

"Sounds pretty silly to me," Sidoti responded, shrugging.

Metzer pointed to the wilderness around them.

"That ice is really water, which is really made up of two hydrogen molecules and one oxygen molecule. These molecules are made up of something even smaller, protons and neutrons, and they are made up of something even smaller, all the way down to neutrinos and the Planck size. All of this is counterintuitive. Why the hell is the brane world so hard to understand?"

Metzer's voice rose, and the ranger looked up. Metzer had occasionally drifted away from reality in the last few days. Dr. Faison was feeding him pills, and that seemed to help for a short while. The severity of the episodes was increasing, but at that moment, he seemed as normal as he ever got. Sidoti touched Metzer on the arm.

"Calm down, Karl. All I'm saying is that it sounds pretty far-fetched. I'm still not entirely sold on the bit about atoms, either."

Metzer laughed, and the mood lightened. Silence descended. Sidoti thought of the improbability of what was happening. He was in the middle of Antarctica. Antarctica! The days were still very long but becoming shorter. He hoped they could find the power source and either make use of it or destroy it before the long nights began. Not normally a superstitious man, to him, twenty-three hours of darkness seemed the embodiment of evil.

With the warm suits on, it was actually quite tolerable inside the tent. Sidoti munched an energy bar, thinking of what was going on in the United States. He wondered how they were doing in the search for the ... what was it? The only thing he could think of was "conductor." After Metzer indicated that the United States was a probable site for one of the conductors, Sidoti thought of the ship he had discovered, three years earlier, sneaking up the northwest coast of the United States. That ship off-loaded something on to trucks that disappeared in Montana. He immediately sent that information to General Blount. The area around Missoula was probably swarming with national guardsmen searching for anything unusual. Africa, the other projected location, was a more difficult proposition. Branniff allowed only a small number of diplomatic personnel into Bumba and the other major cities in Africa, but the CIA had done the best it could, substituting experienced information gatherers for diplomats. America needed to know what it was dealing with.

"I can't thank you guys enough for volunteering to do this," he said.

Dr. Faison made the appropriate demurral, but Metzer quipped, "Volunteer, my ass. You threatened to send me to the sanatorium if I didn't come."

They all grinned.

"Now, you know that's not true, Karl. By the way, what would happen if these brane worlds collapse and bounce off each other? 'Bounce' sounds gentle, like two balloons or something."

"It does, doesn't it? Actually, it's more like your fire and brimstone stuff. Truly biblical, man. The whole universe collapsing, eating up planets and galaxies as it contracts. It would be the biggest goddamned July Fourth and Cinco de Mayo rolled into one. If you had a camera and the right point of view, you'd have one hell of an end of the world movie."

"Except it wouldn't be just the world but the universe, and, apparently, you'd have to wait seven billion years or so before you could sell the rights to the movie."

"Why, chimp, you have been listening," Metzer said with elaborate affection.

"And you think that the power source we're searching for is connected to your idea of brane worlds?"

"Yesiree Bob."

"So, in theory, we have a mechanical device that could initiate this collapse of the universe?"

"Well, Mr. Sidoti, that's quite a stretch. Dr. Metzer has only developed mathematical models of this possibility. It's actually quite improbable. There's not a shred of evidence to support either the existence of brane worlds or cosmic circularity."

"What's cosmic circularity?"

"His idea that the universe begins over and over again."

Sidoti nodded. It was confusing having his two experts contradict each other all the time, but it was healthy, too. He was getting feedback to each proposal, and this he could weigh.

"Well, major, how much farther?" he asked.

The soldier hooked up his computer and did some calculations. He frowned.

"That's odd," he said.

"What is?"

"Something must be interfering with the signal. The location of the heat signature seems to have changed again."

"What the hell do you mean changed? Gi'e me that," Metzer said.

He grabbed the computer and fiddled with the keyboard while the others waited. Then, he handed the laptop to Dr. Faison.

"What do you think?" he asked.

Dr. Faison studied the screen for a couple of minutes.

"I don't know. It could be right."

"What are you two talking about?" Sidoti said.

"It seems that the location has both changed and not changed," Dr. Faison replied.

"Explain."

"Well, its latitudinal and longitudinal position is unchanged, but according to Karl's calculations, it's well below sea level."

"Why didn't we see this before?"

"It could be anything, maybe even whatever interference Branniff has built to protect its secrets. Anyway, I'm sure that whatever created the heat signature is below sea level," Metzer said.

Sidoti stared at the computer, a disturbing thought forming in his mind.

"Any chance at all you're wrong? Has the level changed over time?"

"Hell, anything has a chance of being wrong, but those calculations are solid. As for changing depth levels, I can't say for sure, but my gut says no. Whatever is down there has probably been there for a while."

"Karl, this is very important. You said before that this heat signature is different from the first one. Could its being underground cause your equipment to record the different heat levels?"

"Hard to tell, Sidoti, but I think not."

Sidoti thought for a moment and then said, "Major, I need to use the tractor. Could you open it for me?"

The three tractors were locked at night, and the ranger held the keys. They bundled up and went outside. Sidoti climbed in and closed the door behind him. The darkness was solid, although there was a hint of something not quite luminescent writhing in the sky.

The Aurora Australis, he thought, booting up the satellite phone.

"Yes, Sidoti," General Blount said.

"Sorry about the time, sir, but I thought you needed to know this as soon as possible. I just found out that the heat signature is quite some distance below sea level."

Sidoti paused, but when General Blount did not react, he continued.

"When I saw the heat signature thirteen years ago, sir, it was clearly visible before the iceberg separated from the continent. The break had just appeared in the ice when the flash came. Then, it was gone."

"What are you saying, Sidoti?"

Sidoti hesitated. He was going out on a limb.

"Sir, if the heat signature was there before the break in the ice, then something must have been below the ice."

"Or on top of it."

The general's voice lost some of its antagonism.

"Then where did it go, sir? There's no evidence of anything being on top of the continent now, nor is anything on the iceberg."

"I seem to remember your saying that the first signature was different from the later ones. How do you explain that?"

"I can't yet, sir. Maybe it took whoever is down there that long to improve the technology. There is a thirteen-year gap between the occurrences. A lot could have changed with the technology in that time."

The general was quiet for a while.

"Is there a specific direction you're going in?"

Sidoti hesitated. He was not accustomed to making decisions. He provided facts for others to do that.

"General, I have a really bad feeling about this."

"Feeling, Sidoti?"

"We've been on the ice for weeks, and we're close to the edge of the break, but our assessment was based on the heat source being on the surface. If it's as deep as Metzer thinks, then we could have a long descent. The rangers may be able to do it, but the scientists certainly can't. Nor can I. We have no experience climbing ice faces."

"What you are implicitly suggesting violates international law," the general said with a trace of laughter in his voice. "If we send a force in, there's going to be a reaction from Branniff, and that damned Black Fleet is still out there. I'll run it by the chairman, however. Anything else?"

"Yes, sir. Have you found anything in the northwest?"

"No. It's beginning to feel like a wild goose chase. We have the National Guard in Montana, Idaho, Wyoming and Washington out searching. So far, they've found nothing. And remember, those states are practically deserted now."

"Metzer says his calculations prove that something's there."

"You trust that guy? I mean, he is a little off."

"I do. Karl's odd, but he's a brilliant physicist, sir."

Sidoti wondered if he should mention Metzer's theory about brane worlds and universes collapsing, but he did not want to strain General Blount's credulity.

"OK. I'll see what I can do about getting some support for you."

With that, the general hung up without saying goodbye. Sidoti returned to the tent.

Chapter 50

Anne Ernsky gazed at what surely was paradise. From the sharp rise outside the town of Polson, Flathead Lake dominated the landscape. She whistled softly at the expanse of water, the blue of which was so sharp it almost seemed painted.

"It's beautiful."

Puffs of condensation escaped her lips. The valley was long, bowl-like, and she felt a renewed anger at having to leave her land. Her eyes rose to the heights of Flathead Range, noting the peak that Notah said was named after Olahl's grandfather.

"Yes," Notah said. "Once, it was our gift."

Anne Ernsky did not comment, but she understood. The night before, the Salish had danced. She had eaten dried huckleberries and salmon. There was a simplicity to the evening, and she had felt included. Though she did not dance, the beautiful lyricism of the Salish language enthralled her. One phrase Notah used stuck in her mind. Now, admiring the startling beauty of the tall mountains framing this valley of light and shade, with its greenery stretching as far as the eye could see, divided only by the surprisingly blue lake, she took out the piece of paper on which Notah had written, "Tutsqsi neti l es milk" ye st'ulik' u es tuk'" tu malyémistis l us sqélix." The translation was, "A long time ago, all over this land, the people's medicine was put here." She agreed with the sentiment.

Her eyes shifted to the reason they had pulled the pickup truck into the turnoff. The rumble alerted them just in time, and she hoped that none of the soldiers would see the dust raised by the truck Notah had borrowed. Route 93, high up in the mountain range, was choked by a convoy of camouflaged green vehicles.

Notah, squinting against the sun's glare, said, "These are definitely not Stoltz's Raiders. Looks like the stories are true."

Anne Ernsky, returning the paper to her pocket, nodded, her face reflecting the questions in her mind. A massive search was underway throughout the northwest, and an Oglala Lakota had told them that the search was as far east as the Dakotas. The military's presence was keeping Stoltz's Raiders quiet. After following every lead as to Stoltz's whereabouts for the last few weeks, word came to Notah that Stoltz was spotted in Missoula. That was where they were headed.

Below them, the long line of trucks slid into the valley, going in the direction of Kalispell. They had driven through the town less that an hour earlier. It was practically deserted. The boards on many of the windows, placed there when the Whites moved south, had partially fallen off, and looked like scabs on a wound.

"What do you think they're looking for?" Notah asked.

"I don't know. Even if they found out about me, this is too big a reaction. And it started before we came."

"There are only two reasons why anyone searches. Either something is lost or something is hidden," Notah said.

"True, but what could the Americans have lost, or what could be hidden from them?"

Notah shrugged.

"I wonder if this has anything to do with the object you and Rene found a while ago," Anne Ernsky said.

"How?"

"Don't know. I just can't think of anything else that would have mobilized this many troops in the area."

"The Lakota in Kalispell said something about the white soldiers searching for the blood of the gods, but he was possibly just drunk."

"The blood of the gods?"

"Yes. There are lots of stories among the tribes about visits from gods."

"I know. The whites who showed up during the discovery period capitalized on those stories."

He turned, and there was a fierce pride in his voice when he said,

"If you mean when the Spanish stumbled upon us, then that was no discovery. However, I'm talking about long before that. There's a common thread in the stories of the two American continents about gods coming from the sky and giving the Indians understanding."

"I've heard those stories. What about the tales of people coming from Mars when it was threatened by a comet? Those seem to be cropping up now more and more."

"Our stories do not stipulate Mars, but many speak of contact between gods and Indians."

"Probably the result of a single point of genesis. All your people coming from a common location, and, in spite of the dispersal, keeping the same gods, even if with different names."

Notah kept a watchful eye on the convoy as it turned at the bottom of the steep hill. Soon, it would be out of sight, and they could move.

"I had a vision about it," he said.

"You dreamt about a contact between Indians and people from outer space?"

"Not a dream. A vision. There's a difference. In the vision, I saw a fertile land, and my people walked upon it. Giant beasts roamed the land as far as the eye could see, and all the world was green and brown. The green was the earth as it was; the brown was its potential. The antelope walked at the top and the bottom of the world."

"Do you mean the south and north poles? How could antelope walk there? Both places are freezing."

"Not in that time. Then, the sky turned to silver, and the silver fell on the top and the bottom of the earth. The earth shook mightily and flipped over in the sky."

"What has this to do with the blood of the gods?"

When Notah answered, his voice was solemn.

"It was then they came in their ships of fire and silver. Their faces were like Coyote's, but in their eyes was death. They commanded the Indian to shape the silver at the ends of the world into mountains of ice. When this was done, they fired the sky, the ice melted, and they drank. Thirst quenched, they left."

Anne Ernsky observed the big man's fierce, rugged face, wondering what he had really seen.

"Before they left," Notah continued, "they again seeded the world with their silver that was to become ice."

"Every culture in the world has a story, a myth if you will, about the floods and a god, or gods, saving them. It's universal."

He turned, eyes piercing.

"Exactly."

Anne Ernsky nodded toward the disappearing trucks.

"We'd better get going. The convoy's gone."

"The Indians weren't asked to shape the silver into ice. They were forced to do so," Notah said quietly.

"Forced? How?"

"By the blood of the gods. Some Indians resisted, but they were wiped out."

"Killed?"

"That wasn't clear. There were no bodies. They were simply touched by the blood of the gods, and they disappeared." He stopped, staring directly into her eyes as he added, "Just like the American ships the Black Fleet attacked."

Anne Ernsky, not sure what to make of the comment, said, "Was the dark force, this blood of the gods, from the stories of the Indian people?"

"No."

Notah stood. It was like a mountain rising. They went toward the rusted-out pickup truck.

"There's more, isn't there?"

"The vision suggested they would return when the water-carrier's jug is full."

"The water-carrier? Oh, Aquarius," she said, taking in the landscape and the expanded lake. "Well, we're definitely in the age of Aquarius now, although technically, Aquarius is an air, not a water, sign. What are you not telling me, Notah?"

"The Whites have appropriated the stories of the Indian for their own purposes. They say that when they arrived in our lands they were treated as gods because the Indian had been visited by superior white men before. Sometimes, they say those white men came from outer space. Whites seem not able to rid themselves of notions of their supremacy. Still, there is some truth to their stories. Indians did see them as the returning beings who looked like Coyote, but they soon proved not to be. That is why we made war upon them from the tip of South America to Canada."

"How did the Whites prove not to be who they said they were?"

"They did not know what the stories did not tell but what the Indian knew. The whiteness the Indian first saw was not a skin but a covering. When the Whites could not remove their cover, the Indian knew they were false."

"What was below the cover?" Anne Ernsky asked.

"They looked like you. And remember the Salish said the beings who built the object Rene and I investigated looked like you, too."

Notah started the truck.

"Before the beings from the sky left, they changed some of the Indians into creatures who looked as they did. These were to tend the ice fields that had been created."

"Where are they now?"

Notah put the truck in gear and shook his head.

"You think that's why Branniff was trying to get the Indians to join us? Because there are descendents of the ones who have been changed among them?"

Anne Ernsky had gone from disbelief to at least accepting the premise of Notah's statement. Many African Americans claimed Indian heritage, and some claimed that was to escape the stigma of being black in America. To her, that had always seemed only a partial explanation. Though Notah's story was too incredible to accept, she was intrigued by the possibility of a descent other than that the Whites assigned to her people.

"The vision indicated they would have the light of stars upon them," Notah said.

"The light of stars. I like that." Then, something occurring to her, she asked, "Is that why you came back? Not for Stoltz?"

"Oh, I came for Stoltz, but I was searching for them, too. The vision said they're still here. The ten thousand who came to you are not the ones."

"They don't have the light of stars upon them? Just kidding."

They drove in silence, each deep in thought. The pickup truck rushed past Salish Kootenai College off Route 93.

"Notah, I know Stoltz deserves to die, but what will you do once he's dead?"

Before he could reply, her phone vibrated.

After a moment, she asked anxiously, "Etienne, what's the matter? You alright?"

Chapter 51

*D*arkness descended like a diaphanous gown falling over a virgin's head, and Anne Ernsky felt some of the tension of the last few days seep from her. It had been a hectic flight back to the Canadian east coast after Etienne's call and then a swift trip to the island of Tortola where Etienne had asked that she meet him. The place was quiet. The few remaining inhabitants were fighting the rising ocean. The capital, Road Town, was now relocated farther up the mountain, and lower down, there was a seawall. She wondered how long they would be able to keep the ocean at bay.

In the encroaching darkness, a large yacht dropped anchor. A man of medium height walked across the deck and descended the steps to a waiting tender which made for shore. It was not Etienne, and she turned away. Light sparkled on the neighboring island of Jos Van Dyke, and to her left was what the proprietor of the restaurant, a friendly man with dreadlocks, informed her was St. Thomas.

She was not sure what was on Etienne's mind, but his role in holding things together was still important. He asked her not to say anything to Natas Branniff. Oddly enough, she had complied. He also told her not to use the Lear jet that Natas had given her. Etienne was worried about Branniff, and given her own not fully formed concerns about what had happened in the last few weeks, she was willing to go along.

The young man, dressed in a dark nautical jacket and well-cut, gray slacks, reached the dock. There was something familiar about him. He climbed the steps briskly and made his way over to her.

"Good evening, Madam Secretary. His Holiness sends his regards. I am Kwaku Armah."

"I remember you. Where's His Holiness?"

"I am sorry, Madam Secretary. I have been asked only to bring you to him."

Anne Ernsky stood, leaving a large bill on the table. The tender quickly covered the short distance to the yacht, and soon, they were sliding past Jos Van Dyke, headed out to sea. Anne Ernsky, shown to a stateroom, was offered a drink. She recognized the delicate body of a wine from Etienne's personal vineyard south of Rome. Kwaku stood quietly at the door.

"You guys live well. This is beautiful."

"It belongs to a friend of His Holiness. It is discreet."

She smiled, wondering how discreet a hundred and twenty-five foot, three-deck yacht could be. The boat slid into the darkening evening, the islands' lights creating an odd Christmas tree in the ocean with their pink, golden flickering. An hour later, the sound of the engine changed.

"Will you come with me please? We will be leaving this boat now," Kwaku said.

Anne Ernsky took a life jacket that the young man handed her. Once on the deck, she saw that a sleek boat had pulled alongside. They climbed down carefully, and Kwaku settled her in the rear jump seat. As soon as she was comfortable, the boat's engine roared to life. Her body was pushed back against the seat, and she experienced that exhilarating feeling of almost flying. The bouncing took a little getting used to, but she soon adjusted and relaxed into the sense of power. It was pitch black. Eventually, tiredness overwhelmed her, and she dozed. When she awoke, they were pulling into a tiny port. Kwaku helped her on to a pier, and after a short walk, she saw an airplane. Within minutes, they were airborne. The flight did not last long.

Back on the ground, she was whisked to a large American car, the windows of which were dark. A couple of hours later, the car pulled on to a private road. The entrance was guarded by two armed men. Not long after, the car slowed, and they entered a driveway. The car stopped, and she stepped out. Etienne's giant figure, standing at the top of very high steps, greeted her. He walked down, a strained smile on his face.

"Welcome, Anne. I trust the trip was not too uncomfortable."

"Intriguing, Etienne. I didn't realize you were into this cloak and dagger stuff."

He smiled apologetically, taking her arm as they climbed the steps. Inside, he invited her to freshen up, and, to her surprise, she found a pair of slacks and a blouse in a bedroom. A little later, feeling refreshed, she came out. Etienne had set a pot of tea on the table in a room that, with its Louis XV-styled desk, dark marble busts and heavy mahogany settee, seemed to belong to the seventeenth century. That it belonged to someone of great wealth was equally evident.

"Very nice," she said, looking around.

"Yes. It's been in our family for a long time."

"How old is it?"

"It was started in 1670 or so. It's been expanded and modernized from time to time."

"In 1670, blacks would have been slaves in these islands," she said quietly.

"Many would have been," Etienne replied, not explaining. "Come. We must talk."

They went down a long corridor with several old paintings on the wall, and soon reached a door that Etienne unlocked. Immediately, the sense of the seventeenth century evaporated. This room looked as if it had been constructed of stainless steel. The furnishings were modern and functional. Etienne pressed a recessed button in the wall, and she felt a slight vibration. Then, the room itself began to descend. When it stopped, they stepped into another well-appointed room. The lighting was subdued and comforting.

"Where are we, Etienne?"

She noted the paintings that adorned the wall. Three were by Dutch masters, but one in particular, *King Caspar,* caught her eye. It was by a lesser-known Dutch painter, Hendrik Heerschop. She nodded appreciatively.

"We are in Cuba, Anne. More specifically, we are in a home that has seen much of what shaped this region and the world. Please, sit down."

"I'm too curious to sit. What's going on?"

Etienne sat in a chair that had wings which flared behind his head. It dwarfed even his huge frame.

"I have invited you here to tell a story you will never be able to repeat. It is also a story of which, until very recently, I was entirely ignorant."

Anne Ernsky nodded.

"Do you still have faith, Anne?'

"I suppose," she replied, not sure what he meant, or of her feelings.

"Then swear on whatever you hold most dear that you will never repeat what I say. Your life will be worth nothing if you do. In fact, it is only fair to let you know that simply knowing endangers you."

Anne Ernsky smiled.

"Don't forget what I was, Etienne. The root word of secretary is secret. I've had to keep a few as secretary of state, but if you want me to swear, I will."

"Of course, Anne. I am sorry, but the secrets you keep, or kept, are nothing like what I am entrusting to you, and you do not have a nation's power to protect you now."

She nodded.

"I swear to keep your secret, Etienne."

He took a deep breath.

"We live in a world of shadow and substance, Anne. Much of what we think to be true is not, and much that we have denied actually is. We have learned, and therefore lived, a history that is simply the shadow of the reality."

"What do you mean?"

"I am talking about a bargain we made so long ago that few to-day know or even suspect the origins of our existence and the circumstances that formed it. Humans have always worried about their shadow selves, whether we call it numina, spirit, soul, other dimensions or the occult. The list is practically endless, but the sense of someone or something being there as an alternative to our reality is a constant in human existence. Humans have tried to explain that vague sense of unease in a thousand ways, often through the creation of gods who, by being placated, would not be vengeful. In this way, we have eased our fears, sought to manage that unseen malevolence we sensed in the universe around us."

He stopped, and Anne Ernsky, amused, asked, "Does that mean the Church and religion are a sham, Etienne?"

"Don't be flippant, Anne. Religion is not a sham, but what we seek to placate is somewhat different from what the Church publicly says."

He hesitated again, as if seeking the right words to use.

Looking at her fiercely, he asked, "Have you ever wondered why people from the same family groups always seem to be in charge of things? Why, in spite of their location in different countries from age to age, the same families dominate the world throughout time? Why they almost always see themselves and describe themselves as favored by God or the gods? You don't have to answer these questions. The answer is they do."

Anne Ernsky frowned.

"That's not new, Etienne. People who are successful have always felt that way."

"No, Anne. What I am describing is not simply how successful people feel about themselves. There is a moment in our history as humans when everything changed, when our whole arc of development just stopped and changed direction. That time was around the last ice age. Thirty thousand years ago, humans went from being the frightened underdogs on the earth to being the dominant force. Why is that?"

Anne Ernsky shrugged, shaking her head.

"It is because we didn't evolve from one being into another. One being was replaced by another."

"Replaced? By whom?"

"That, Anne, is the greatest mystery we face. Some may know, but they are not telling. First, before I go any further, I want you to know I am fully aware you have been keeping an eye on me for Branniff. What you do not know is that there are circles within circles, and they all lead to the same place. Branniff Enterprises. I have been manipulated, although not in the way you may think. Much of what has happened was planned a long time ago."

"What has been planned?"

"It is unbelievable, Anne. This plan is at least thirty thousand years old. I don't know the details, but I believe it has to do with this planet being used in some way by a group of beings."

"Come on, Etienne," she said with a humorless laugh. "Little green men? Really!"

"Actually, quite big, black men."

"Big, black men?"

"In truth, 'men' is simply a rhetorical construction. The term doesn't apply to these beings."

"Strangely enough, I heard something similar from an Indian a little while ago."

Etienne looked up, his eyes bright.

"An Indian? A North American Indian? There are accounts of these beings' visits all over our records. Three extraordinarily holy sites. One in the Southern Ocean, most likely Antarctica; one in central Africa and a third in North America somewhere. No one knows where the sites are. The world would have changed very much since then."

"I'm aware of that, but could you get back to the beings? What did they want? Why Earth?"

"Its water."

"What about its water?"

"The symbol for the earth among these beings is the jug-carrier Aquarius."

"Notah mentioned Aquarius, too," she said, frowning.

"There is much wisdom among the ancient tribes, Anne. Are you familiar with the concept of precession?"

She shook her head.

"It is a mathematical or astronomical calculation that accounts for the effect of the earth's wobble in relation to other star systems. This gives the impression of the earth "looking" at different parts of the sky at different times. In astrology, these impressions are called "houses," and the earth is oriented to each house at some point in the cycle."

"What has astrology to do with all this?"

"Everything, Anne."

"I thought the Catholic Church banned belief in astrology."

"Of course, we did."

"I don't understand."

"I said that our history is both shadow and reality. Reality is a dangerous business. In any case, we are completing a cycle through one of the astrological houses right now."

"How long did that take?" Anne Ernsky asked.

"Twenty-five thousand, nine hundred and twenty years."

"But that's—"

"Right about the timeline of the last ice age."

"Are you suggesting there's a relationship?"

"There are no coincidences in the universe, Anne. Of course, there is a relationship. There is every evidence that we are in store for a major event again."

"What event?"

"I am not sure."

"You know, Notah talked about the ice at the poles having been brought by beings from outer space or somewhere."

"They brought many things, not all of them good. From all accounts, they brought strife, for example. Before they came, all on the earth spoke the same language and lived in harmony. They came with different languages, and soon humans could no longer understand each other."

"The Tower of Babel?"

"Indeed, but beyond that, the whole Old Testament story is a metaphor. The conflict between Cain and Abel, for instance, is a record of that first conflict between the humans and the beings, and the Garden of Eden was the period of harmony before the beings came."

"I can understand the metaphor, Etienne, but why, if this is true, is it necessary to cover it up? Why can't people know?"

"Because, Anne, knowledge is power. Power is dangerous."

"Dangerous for whom?"

Etienne hesitated and then said, "Dangerous for us."

"Us?"

"Yes. Look at me closely."

She stared as Etienne changed before her, his face becoming blacker and more elongated, like a crocodile's. Then, he was himself again.

"Do you understand now?" he asked softly.

Anne Ernsky had instinctively drawn back in her chair.

"No. I don't."

Her voice was husky and strained as she struggled to control her terror.

"Please, Anne. You have nothing to fear from me. I would never hurt you. I only show you this so you can trust me. Until a few days ago, I did not know of this either."

"But you're the pope."

When Etienne answered, there was agony in his voice.

"How do you think I became pope?"

Anne Ernsky shook her head.

"I don't understand. Are you ... are there a lot of you?"

"Much of the leadership of the planet, though not necessarily the visible leaders. They have had one task for the last thirty thousand years, and that is to prepare for the return, or as I have discovered it is called in the secret texts, the Repulsion."

"Slow down, Etienne. The return? I thought you were already here."

"No. Those who were left to manage the earth are mostly human now."

Anne Ernsky stared, her face a mixture of skepticism and horror. When she spoke, her voice shook.

"Etienne, you sometimes say 'we' and sometimes 'they'. Are you one of them or not?"

Etienne leaned forward, head in his hands. When he looked up, his face was haunted.

"Until a few days ago, I had no idea what was inside me. Even now, it is hard to believe."

"How did you find out?"

"Branniff. He came to the Vatican, and it was as if he turned some switch inside me. One moment, I was Etienne Ochukwu, and the next, I was this ... thing. Suddenly, it felt as if I inhabited a new body with a new mind, possessing knowledge that had lain dormant for thousands of years."

"This is madness."

Anne Ernsky turned away, but she could not deny what she had just seen. Something else bothered her.

"Much of the world's leadership is white. Yet Notah said that in his vision, the beings looked like us. Now, you say that you were left behind. Why would the leadership be white if they looked like us?"

"First, Anne, as I've said, the leadership is not necessarily what you see. Second, don't apply your categories to them. Race, in the sense you experience it, means nothing to them. They simply came in touch with black humans first and assumed their shape."

"So, the archaeological evidence is only accidentally correct?"

"Yes. The change did take place in Africa. Humans there did become something different, more intelligent, more in charge of their environment, but it was pure serendipity. It could have been anywhere."

Anne Ernsky was disappointed to hear this, but she pressed on.

"What about Whites?"

"According to the secret texts, at that time, they lived in the Caucasus mountains where they had gone to escape the flooding from the melted ice. Africa, it is said, was protected by the blood of the gods, and—"

"Did you say the blood of the gods?"

"Yes. Why?"

"Notah said that those Indians who resisted the beings were killed by the blood of the gods. And the other day, a Lakota told him that the National Guard is searching all over the northwestern United States for the same thing, this blood of the gods."

"He used that exact phrase? The blood of the gods? This is very important, Anne."

"Absolutely the same."

"Then someone must know. If the Americans are searching for whatever it is, then it could not be Natas who informed them. He would certainly know where it is."

"Etienne, where does Natas stand in all this? Is he friend or foe?"

"That's difficult to say, Anne. Let me explain. I now know that there are knowledge areas, called veils, into which they ... we are initiated. There are seventeen levels. I discovered that I am an initiate into the sixth level, the Veil of the Celestial Dragon. As far as I can tell, only three persons on earth have been initiated into the seventeenth level, the Veil of the Marble Mountains. Maybe one of them is Natas. His purpose, therefore, is beyond my knowledge. Whether he is friend or foe, or simply acting out a purpose I don't understand, I don't really know."

"But you're worried?"

"Very. There is something dark about his purpose, and I don't quite sense its rightness. It seems beyond all scale, and its geometry is flawed."

"I won't ask what that means. The Whites? You were saying they had hidden in the Caucasus Mountains."

"Yes. After the waters were taken, or, as your stories say, receded, those you think of as Whites moved down from the mountains just as the black-skinned people were moving north. They met on the plains between the Tigris and Euphrates rivers in what would become Iraq. It was there, not in Egypt as so many now claim, that we passed our knowledge on to those from the Caucasus. For a time, we flourished. We even interbred with them, passing on the genes of those who had been transformed by the beings. In this way, they became strong. After some time, in an act of treachery, they attacked us and almost wiped us out. You know this in popular history as the struggle between the Hyksos and the Egyptians."

"But that is an actual historical event, isn't it? It can't just mean something else."

Etienne smiled sadly.

"Most of our ancient history should not be taken literally. It is a series of stories constantly repeated under different guises. Christianity refers to Satan as the Prince of Lies. That is another metaphor for the voice of history, which deceives always."

Anne Ernsky listened to the man she had known for so many years, aware that something was different. Not only had Etienne changed in the physical way he demonstrated, but his thinking, the very nuance of his ideas, was alien.

As if sensing her questions, he said, "I believe, Anne, as all who came before me have believed, not in the metaphors, but in the truth behind them."

"And what is that truth, Etienne?"

"That life is purposeful but not moral; that we serve a purpose we do not fully understand; that we are a means to some end another race of beings has determined."

"Ignorant slaves, Etienne? Is that what we are then?"

"Is that the way you think of the cow who gives you beef or the dolphin whose flesh you eat?"

"I am not a damn cow or dolphin."

Etienne, seeing the taut lines of her body as she stood, guessed at her feelings. Still, it was not over.

"Anne, you asked me if I was worried about Natas, and the answer is yes."

She turned, her face rigid with anger.

"And what is the difference between you and Natas? What are you both? Overlords?"

She swore, and he allowed her to go on, aware of the fear and the profound sense of betrayal she felt. He understood, too, that she experienced his betrayal more deeply because he shared her skin color. Later, analyzing this, she would no longer simply see him as a black man, but for now, trapped by her history and pain, hate was visible in her eyes.

"What now, Etienne? Will you kill us all? Is there some new enslavement coming as a result of this Repulsion?"

He recoiled in the face of her fury.

"That is unknown, Anne. The Repulsion has more to do with them than with you. As I understand it, for a moment in time, all of their force will be concentrated in one corner of the galaxy. The competition for that space could be the cause of the Repulsion."

"You mean they fight each other? They're not all on the same side?"

"Competition exists everywhere, even among gods. That competition frequently breaks out in visible wars on this planet."

"Is that what's going on now, a competition between you and Natas? Do you represent different factions among these beings?"

"Not quite in the way you mean it. There has been, since time immemorial, a means of managing the affairs of this planet. Though never fully effective, it has kept the place from going completely mad.

The Catholic Church has been an important part of that process for thousands of years, but before that, there have always been cults, religions and orders to manage the emotional dissensions introduced by the beings so long ago. These religions have, like history, always been shadow and reality, too. They have both kept information secret and have dispensed it as needed. The secret world behind the religion has been guarded by nine men, each responsible for a sphere of the earth. You have known some of this because your world has always been awash in rumors about secret orders, witches' covens and the like. Your father and grandfather were very high in the Freemasons, as you know."

"What has this to do with your purpose?"

"Patience, Anne. The latest iteration of this very secret order was called the Nine."

"Was? What happened to it?"

"It was destroyed."

"Destroyed? How do you know?"

"Because I was a member, as was Natas and Ambassador Hargrove."

"Hargrove? Was he like you?"

"I don't know, but since he was a member of the Nine, he was clearly a descendent."

"You and Natas are both alive."

"Yes. Natas warned me not to go to a meeting that was called by the others. He had not been invited. They died in that explosion in the Tower of London."

"I didn't hear of any bodies being found other than staff."

"And you won't, but if you check for the wealthiest, most powerful figures in the most powerful countries, you will find that they are reported to have all died a few weeks ago from natural causes. You don't have to believe me, Anne. You can check this yourself."

"And I'm guessing you'll say that Natas is responsible."

Etienne nodded, his eyes willing her to believe. She was silent for a while, confusion evident on her face.

"Natas is helping our people. He's taking them out of the condition of deprivation they have been in for so long. And he's restoring Africa to prominence, Etienne."

"Shadow and reality, Anne. Something very dark is happening, and I feel certain Natas is preparing for it."

"But he warned you. Why would he warn you?"

Suspicion was back in her voice, and Etienne, aware of the weakness of his response, shook his head.

"I don't know. Some things have been revealed to me in the last couple of weeks, but as to the purpose, I know no more than you. I do know that Natas is not what he seems. His purposes may no longer be part of any plan that these beings created."

She was confused, and he waited as her brain sought to make sense of the incomprehensible.

"Why are you telling me this, Etienne?"

The big man walked across the room to where Anne Ernsky stood. He gently took her hand and kissed it.

"Because I am afraid for you, Anne. I do not know why Natas wants all of our people in Africa, but it frightens me. He seems not to be restrained by even the arrangements that have held the planet together for millennia. His elimination of the Nine, I fear, signals something montrous."

Anne Ernsky eyed the man whom the world knew as Pope Celestine VI, wondering who or what he was. She wanted to run away. He was nothing she understood, nothing that in the normal bounds of human interaction she could embrace. She had seen him change, and she shivered at the remembrance of that elongated, black face with the red, saurian eyes that had glared at her for a second. Etienne claimed to be her friend, but could those eyes truly understand friendship? When the creature looked at her, it had seemed merely hungry, uninterested in her as a person. If he was a friend, then how would an enemy look upon her? Now, though, the tall, gray-haired man was a far cry from that saurian figure.

"Etienne, you've always spoken of your love for the church. Was all that a lie?"

He smiled gently.

"I know you seek a logic that would make sense of this experience. I understand because I, too, have struggled to make sense of it. Try to understand that I was as fully the Etienne Ochukwu you knew as I am this ... whatever it is I am today. Branniff did not change me. Rather, it feels as if he liberated some part of me that was hidden in shadow. I do love the church. As you mean it—a congregation of human souls—the church is solace, though not truth. It helps with blinding you to the nightmare that lies behind the veil. For me now, she is Mother, for behind her is the Great Goddess."

"But the Church has been anti-woman from its inception," Anne Ernsky said.

"Another circle within a circle. Not only black-skinned people lost the battle in the Nile delta. The Goddess had to be restrained as well. That feminine energy, the creative spirit of the universe, was also subdued, and though Woman and the Universal Feminine are not one and the same, women have easier access to that energy. Those Hyksos who won in the Nile delta had need of it. Woman had to be suppressed so they could use her energy. In time, that feminine energy was contained within the Church. You had to be kept out, so you would never know this."

"Slavery again. Does everyone live off of everyone else?"

"It is the way of the universe, Anne. It is only heartless if you think of your consciousness as unique, worthy of immortality. If you accept that your existence is simply a gift, an arrangement of the universe's energy, then you will know that you can never not exist. You simply change form, but the energy is immortal."

That did not bring her much solace.

"So, what now, Etienne? What do I do with this knowledge?"

"Things will go as they are designed to, but be careful of Natas. He is no longer constrained, no longer a part of anything you can comprehend. He has become a singular power, and he was never supposed to be that."

"But if you're right, the world will oppose him. He can't defeat the whole world, no matter how strong he is."

"Can't he? I am not sure of that. He has power you cannot appreciate. The destruction of those American ships was nothing for him. He can do that on a much larger scale. And worse, he may not have to. The new religion, which he has misnamed Changoism, is the most powerful force in the world today."

"True, but most of the adherents are still Catholics. You have influence, don't you?"

"You have seen them in Bumba. They have the certainty of the faithful," Etienne said sadly. "In that, too, I was manipulated. I had no idea of the scale of Natas' betrayal. Still, I wanted to let you know, though it may already be too late."

Anne Ernsky felt helpless. Her body was rigid, and Etienne, knowing how shocked she was by his revelation, did not try to comfort her.

"Goodbye, Anne. Please be careful, and do not trust the man you know as Natas. He is very different from what he seems."

Anne Ernsky did not answer. The door to the elevator that was disguised as a room was open, and she stepped in. Etienne Ochukwu disappeared.

Chapter 52

Two bodies, dressed in loose-fitting leggings, flashed through the air, the legs performing kicks at a rate that made them a blur. As they passed each other, the taller one bent at an acute angle, and the foot flicked backwards, thumping into the smaller person's hip. Teme twisted away, lessening the impact of the blow and, landing, rolled with lightning speed into a standing defensive position. Across from her, Natas stood casually, feline, smiling eyes gauging the damage he had done.

"Come, priestess. Surely, you have more skill than that."

He attacked effortlessly. One second, he was standing, his laughter floating around the room; the next, he was on her, feet driving with fearsome power toward her midriff. Teme lunged forward and to the side. Again, the blow glanced off her hip. It would not take much more. Natas' kicks seemed almost lazy, but a direct hit would crush her bones. She had never fought anyone with such power and speed. Natas reminded her of the stories told about Ghalib, the greatest warrior of the First People. He was the only man who had ever performed the *Sa'a vili*, the twelve turns in the air. Natas had not done that yet, but the ease with which he performed the *Ne vili*, the eight-turn move, was a sign that there was plenty of speed and power in reserve.

He was arranging his feet for another flying attack when a door opened. An acolyte wearing the brightly-colored robe of the new priesthood came in. Natas turned to the man, ignoring Teme. He took from the acolyte a small object that carried a series of pictures on it. Teme could not see the images, but as Natas scrolled down, his face changed. No longer handsome, he looked savage, atavistic.

"The betrayal begins," he said.

Turning, he stared at the priestess. Teme felt her heart accelerate.

When Natas was like that, he was particularly dangerous. He waved the acolyte away, and as the door soundlessly closed, threw the machine on to the mat. Without appearing to change position, he flew at her, his feet spread wide and closing like a pair of scissors. Teme recognized the *Pa sati* but could not defend against it. She swiftly tucked her body. Still, both feet slammed into her head. Everything went black as her body fell to the mat. Above her, the handsome, oddly repulsive, face of Natas Branniff looked down impassively.

A throbbing headache woke her. Uttering a prayer to the goddess, Teme got to her knees. The world wobbled. Fighting for balance, she moved stiffly toward the door, picking up the discarded machine from the mat. There were several pictures, but one in particular caught her eye. It was of the man they called Pope Celestine VI and the stern-faced woman who led the tribe being brought to the land of the Ancients. She stared at the woman's face, noting the chiseled cheeks and the dark, curious eyes.

So much like the First People, she thought.

Replacing the machine, she limped from the room. A warm shower took some of the pain away. Natas was taking greater pleasure in hurting her, and she often had to soak after their encounters. Thankfully, these had become less frequent in the last few weeks as preparations for the Easter festival took more of his time. The atmosphere inside the cathedral, where hundreds lived within the grounds, was electric, and worry lines had appeared on Natas' face. Since Andreas' and Empheme's escape, Natas' cruelty was more on display, and the inhabitants of the cathedral gave him a wide berth. In spite of having crushed the *Ulumatua,* he was still very cautious in his dealings with the people of the Land of Tiamat. This was particularly the case as more of the inhabitants were brought to the world above. Once, seeing the Father of the Ilegu Forest in the cathedral, she had been shocked when Natas shouted at him, ordering him away. The Father of the Ilegu Forest had said, "You endanger all with your actions. Let us save the fragment." She had no idea what saving the fragment meant, and questions buffeted her mind.

Does Natas intend to destroy the First People? Is that why he is bringing them to the land above? Why did Natas say, in response to the Father of the Ilegu Forest, "All or nothing"? Teme wondered.

As the elements of his plan came together, Natas seemed not to need sleep. The world outside was frenzied, and, on television, she noted the increase in the number of "priests" who preached about something they called the Rapture, through which they seemed to believe they would be taken up by their gods to some place called Heaven. At first, Teme smiled at this idea because the people owned, for all time, the land the goddess had given to them. Although there was a story about being taken up, she knew this was the goddess' way of reuniting the two groups of the First People. It was not the physical ascension about which the "priests" seemed to be preaching. Who would tend the fields of the goddess if the people were taken up? It made no sense, but she also saw the power of the belief and how Natas was able to capture it, making it his. Many wanted this death they called the Rapture, and Natas became the guide to the place of execution. Only priests now served the people. She had no role and so, no information about what was planned. There was an air of expectancy among the priesthood, those dark men in brightly-colored robes who gave to the people the body and blood of their god.

At first, Teme was horrified by this act of symbolic cannibalism, but she became less agitated after considering the alternative—actual human sacrifice. Thanks to the goddess, the First People had left behind that time of darkness. These people, however, seemed intent on returning to the ecstasy of that ancient time. The wine became darker and the wafer more brightly red. There was a gentle but insistent shoving to reach the altar, as if the people could not wait to drink the blood and eat the flesh of their god. Something else was brewing, and it frightened her. Natas' physical cruelty was a problem, but more so was the fact that the god of the fiery mountain had hold of him now.

When Teme stepped from the shower, her body tingled. She slowly oiled herself, allowing the aches to recede under the ministrations of her experienced fingers. Wondering what had happened to Empheme and Tama, she uttered a prayer. Teme wished she possessed the mind sense. She needed contact with Empheme. Doubt had come when she saw the broken statue. The goddess could not die, but the sight of the marble face, split in half, still serene but lifeless, frightened her.

"Empheme, come to me now. I weaken," she said.

The large room was silent. The soft murmur of the pumps that pushed the river away from the cathedral formed the background to her thoughts.

If the goddess is free and her waters are broken, how can she be dead?

She pulled on a simple white robe and walked from the room. In the cathedral, she had no status, and most of the priests frowned on her presence.

So different. It is as if they hate me. Then, thinking of the fierce *leo-leos* she had commanded, she smiled. *Maybe the priests are not so different.*

She strode along a dimly-lit corridor, limbs loose, moving with the powerful, athletic stride of the *tusiata* fighter, yet with a distinctly feminine grace. Stepping outside the building, she was deep in thought when a low hiss caught her attention. Her eyes darted to a pillar.

"Marcus. Why are you skulking around?"

Banished from Natas' sight, Marcus was not often seen anymore. He signaled her to be quiet and to follow him. They hurried from the portico to the pool room and quietly stepped inside. The water glistened darkly. He stood close to her. Teme searched for any sign of aggression in the cast of his eyes or the angle of his body. All she saw was fear.

"Well, Marcus, what is it?"

"I know what Natas intends, Teme."

Chapter 53

*I*nformation had been streaming in for hours. Metzer's prediction of an astronomical anomaly proved prescient, and over the previous two days, the sky changed, and the temperature rose. Sidoti had received a report from General Blount that a rash of sun spots were being monitored. Now, radiation was wreaking havoc with the satellites' capabilities. Three years earlier, they had observed a dark spot that obscured Mintaka in the Orion system, and Sidoti was downloading all the information on that astronomical event. Although Mintaka was again visible, he hoped to find some clue as to what was now happening.

"Temperature's gone up another five degrees in the last hour, Mr. Sidoti," the ranger said, unzipping the top of his suit.

"What's that now, an increase of forty degrees in the last day?"

The ranger, face impassive, nodded. Sidoti glanced at the computer, noting the infinitesimal movement of the gauge indicating the proportion of the document that was already downloaded.

"Looks like we still have thirteen percent to go," he said to Metzer and Dr. Faison.

The two scientists looked frightened.

I should be scared, too.

Sidoti picked up an energy bar and chewed absentmindedly, thinking about the occurrences of the last forty-eight hours. His call to General Blount prompted the launch of several ships from the Pacific Fleet to Antarctica. As the American fleet steered south, four ships, previously unobserved and of similar dimensions to those in the so-called Black Fleet, appeared in the South Pacific Ocean, shadowing the Americans. Three Hornets sent to buzz the mysterious ships were snatched out of the air by the unknown force. Sidoti told General

Blount about Metzer's dark energy/brane world speculations, and since then, the considerable talents of the American physics establishment were devoted to making some sense of Metzer's exotic theories. They were also trying to figure out how to counter the weapon the Black Fleet was using. American ships were headed to the Southern Ocean, but no one was sure what they could do once they arrived. The Black Fleet, having offloaded a large number of people in Africa, had sailed back into the South Atlantic. Sidoti again glanced at the computer's gauge.

Almost done.

The American ships were scheduled to arrive at the northwestern extremity of the ice cap late that night, and he could sense the scientists' nervousness.

As if reading Sidoti's mind, Metzer asked, "What happens if the ships are attacked by these people and get blasted out of the water? Does that mean we're stuck here?"

The question was addressed to Sidoti, but it was the ranger who answered.

"We hike it back to where we left our ship. In fact, we will have to make that decision very soon. We're getting close to our limit on food as well as the life of the batteries that power the tractors."

"What do you mean close?" Metzer said.

"I mean we have three days to find whatever is here, or we turn back. Survival on this continent is simply a matter of mathematics, gentlemen. You either have the means to survive or you die."

"Seems stupid to come all this way and not get what we want."

This came from Metzer, and Sidoti wondered what prompted the man's sudden concern. Then, he realized that Metzer was probably not as interested in national security as he was in getting his hands on the machine that converted dark energy to a force capable of destroying ships. Suddenly, the ranger tensed.

"Hold up," he ordered.

At first, Sidoti heard nothing. Then, the low rumble of warplanes became audible.

"Thank God," he said, relieved. "It looks like we got some planes off. Maybe the Black Fleet won't interfere after all."

The soldier picked up a Heckler and Koch MP7 sub-machine gun. "What is it?"

"Those are not F-37s, Mr. Sidoti. Wrong sound."

"What are they?"

"Sound like FC-1 Super 9s."

The tension was palpable as the ranger slipped outside where the other three soldiers, also armed, were staring at the sky.

"What's an FC whatever it is he said?" Metzer yelled.

"Chinese fighter planes. They must have a carrier close by."

As they were speaking, the thunder of the warplanes grew.

"There."

The ranger pointed to the sky. Sidoti followed the man's finger, and just coming into sight were three planes, flying in close formation. In no time, they roared past and banked, making a giant circle above the men on the ground.

"Damn! They must have spotted the tractors," Sidoti said.

"Doesn't matter. They know we're here, but I don't think they're looking for us. I suspect they may be looking for the same thing we are," the ranger responded.

"How the hell could they know about it?" one of his soldiers asked.

"Probably the same way we found out. There are some pretty smart guys on the other side, too."

Sidoti hunched against the cold. The temperature might have climbed forty degrees, but it was still minus fifteen. The cold, however, was not his main worry. In all the concern with the mysterious Black Fleet, he had forgotten the Chinese. It was likely that they, too, had compared the energy signature from Antarctica to that which destroyed the American ships. He watched as the three planes banked left and plummeted downward toward the surface of the continent. There was something wonderfully graceful about them as they moved at those incredible speeds in tight formation. It was, therefore, an utter surprise when one of the planes suddenly spun away from the others, its movement erratic. There was a terrible screeching sound, and all of the planes seemed to stretch, taffy-like, for an instant. Then, they were gone.

"What the hell! Did you see that?" Sidoti yelled, staring at where, only a moment ago, the planes had been.

The ranger did not answer, but turning to one of his men, he said, "Henderson, run an analysis."

A short, sharp-faced soldier ducked inside a tractor.

"What kind of analysis, major?" Sidoti asked.

The ranger's eyes were narrowed when he answered.

"We're your back-up, Mr. Sidoti. Henderson has a PhD in physics."

Damn Blount.

The soldiers were there not only as protection but because General Blount did not trust civilians. The ranger looked to the sky.

"Is it me, or is it getting warmer?"

High above, the sky looked not blue but whitish, and Sidoti wondered if it was reflecting the color of the ice. The major was right. It was warmer. He flipped the lined hood from his head. The sky seemed to be shifting.

Maybe it's the daytime electromagnetism in the air.

The color gradually changed from white to cream and then slowly back to white again. It finally became blue. The soldier returned, and the ranger took a printout from him. His eyes narrowed.

"This can't be right. Are you sure?"

"I ran the analysis four times, sir, but we should send it to the house for verification."

"Do that."

He handed the paper to Sidoti who looked, uncomprehending, at the numbers.

"I'd like to show this to my guys."

Metzer and Dr. Faison quickly looked it over.

"This is incredible," Metzer said.

"What is it?" Sidoti asked.

"According to the calculations, this energy has the same heat signature as the others. This make sense to you?"

Dr. Faison studied the numbers for a while.

"It's counter-intuitive, but I can't see anything that suggests a problem with the calculations."

"What do the figures say?" Sidoti asked irritably.

"Hold on to your hat, ole buddy. These numbers say that the energy came from somewhere that shouldn't exist."

"What are you talking about?"

"It's tough to explain. The direction of the force is from the sky, meaning it came down, not up from whatever is the source on the ground."

"Is Branniff using satellites to project this energy?"

Metzer hesitated and went over the numbers again.

"Actually, Sidoti, the energy appears from nowhere. There does not seem to be a point of origin."

"From nowhere?"

Metzer, face wrinkled in concentration, did not immediately answer. Sidoti, throat dry, waited impatiently.

"Incredible," Metzer whispered. "This can't be, and yet, it is." He looked up, his eyes bright, a childlike smile on his face. "I was right, Sidoti. I was right. We have to get better verification of these numbers."

"Karl, listen to me. This isn't an experiment. Whatever you're seeing there just destroyed three Chinese fighter jets in front of our eyes. We didn't even see a flash. There's a threat here to us all. I need to know what you know."

Metzer's eyes glistened with excitement.

"Whoever is using this energy must be so evolved, so sophisticated, that we couldn't be a threat to them."

"In other words, you don't understand it. It is destructive, Karl. Whatever you may think, we need to know everything, and we need to know it now."

Metzer opened the neck of his suit.

"I don't think the energy came from space. I think it came from another dimension," he said.

Sidoti almost laughed, but the look on Metzer's face stopped him. The man was practically glowing.

"Another dimension. What nonsense," Dr. Faison said.

Metzer's head jerked around as he glared at the other scientist.

"Then explain the anomaly. Explain an energy that we don't recognize and that has no origin in space, only in time. Did you notice the reduction in force?"

"There was none," Dr. Faison replied.

"Exactly. After the planes were struck, there was no decrease in the energy. It just disappeared. What we have recorded as the start point of the burst of energy cannot possibly be its origin. It had to be traveling before we picked it up, and it must have returned to its point of origin since it was immediately lost to our instruments."

"There are any number of reasons why that could be the case. For one, we don't have the most sophisticated instruments here," Dr. Faison responded.

Turning to the ranger, Metzer said, "You got this from the U.S., didn't you? Your man could not have pulled this information directly from the air."

"To all intents and purposes, the answer to your question is yes. If you are going to ask us to get verification, Henderson's already doing that."

Metzer's face was somber when he turned to Sidoti.

"I need access to a super-collider and a dedicated super-computer. Would that happen to be in your bag of tricks, ole buddy?"

"Tell me what's going on, Karl."

"You won't believe it."

"Try me."

"Well, here goes. I think we're experiencing the early phase of a brane world collision, and—"

"Oh, God! Not that rubbish again," Dr. Faison said.

Metzer ignored him.

"I do believe that as those dimensions approach each other, it's causing distortions in the electromagnetic field in our galaxy. That probably explains the extraordinary activity in the sun. That's why the solar flares have increased so dramatically."

Sidoti studied the bushy-haired, unkempt man, a sliver of doubt in his mind. Karl Metzer was brilliant. Everyone acknowledged that. He was also ill-disciplined and capable of the wildest flights of fancy, to say nothing about being certifiably insane. Dr. Faison was respectability itself, but apart from criticizing Metzer, he had contributed little. Sidoti knew he had to trust Metzer, though the man was operating in a world Sidoti did not understand and which was very dangerous.

"You're not going to waste time listening to him, are you? He's quite mad, you know."

Dr. Faison's voice was like a buzzsaw. Sidoti looked directly into Metzer's eyes.

"Karl, are you sure? I was sent here to take possession of this thing or to destroy it. Are you saying it makes no difference if we find it because the power is coming from somewhere outside our dimension?"

"Yes, but I need a lab to verify some things."

That was enough for Sidoti.

"Major, can we get faster transportation back to the ship? I need to get Karl to the States."

Dr. Faison groaned.

"Mr. Sidoti, this is nonsense. There's no such thing as a brane world. We're wasting time."

"Maybe, Dr. Faison, but there's something here I can't explain. Karl's is the only hypothesis I have, unless you can give me an alternative explanation."

Dr. Faison turned away angrily, stalking toward the tent.

"There's one other thing, Sidoti. I need someone," Metzer said.

"Someone?"

"His name is James Tung. He's brilliant. Probably the second smartest physicist on the planet."

Sidoti nodded. At least Karl's insanity had not destroyed his ego. Out of the corner of his eye, he saw Dr. Faison duck into the tent.

"I can get him moved to wherever you want him. Which lab is he at?"

"He's in Beijing," Metzer said nonchalantly.

"Beijing! It may have slipped your mind, Karl, but we're at war with China."

Metzer stared at him. Sidoti had never seen the man look more unstable, but when Metzer spoke, his words were eminently sane.

"It's a stupid war. If I'm right, you have a much more serious problem. I don't know how you do it, Sidoti, but I need Tung to help with the mathematics."

The fact that Metzer admitted he needed another scientist's help persuaded Sidoti. He was about to address the ranger when Dr. Faison emerged from the tent. Sidoti's eyes widened. In the scientist's hand was a short, deadly-looking machine pistol. The Ingram MAC-10 was very steady.

"What are you doing, Dr. Faison?"

"I'm sorry, Mr. Sidoti," the man replied, his eyes on the three soldiers. "Major, would you be so good as to have your men come this way? And please, no tricks. I'm a very good shot. To answer your question, Mr. Sidoti, unfortunately, Dr. Metzer cannot be allowed to live."

"What the hell are you talking about, Faison?" Sidoti asked.

The gun was trained squarely at Metzer, but he seemed unaware of the danger.

"I'm right, no? I knew it. I knew it."

Dr. Faison nodded.

"You're right, Metzer. Although how you get your inspiration is a mystery to me. The pills I've been feeding you should have incapacitated you long ago. Instead, you seem to be gaining more insights. Ah, well. You'll all have to die. It cannot be stopped."

"What cannot be stopped?" Sidoti, aware of the gun, asked quietly.

Dr. Faison looked ecstatic.

"It is as Mr. Branniff said. They're coming to take us up."

Another religious kook, Sidoti thought as he said, "Who's coming, Dr. Faison?"

"Those who made us. It is time for the return spoken of in the sacred texts. Mr. Branniff said you'd interfere. You especially, Metzer. For years, you have poked at things we should not trouble ourselves with. I have watched you claw for the secrets that should remain hidden. Your curiosity endangers us all."

"I know it's hard to understand, but it's called science, yuh stupid jackass."

Metzer sounded disgusted. Dr. Faison's finger tightened on the trigger.

"Are you an adherent of that new religion Changoism?" Sidoti asked.

Before the scientist could answer, Metzer giggled.

"It would be just like the twit to believe in a bunch of religious crap."

Dr. Faison's eyes glinted, and his finger started to depress the trigger. Sidoti would never explain what made him do it, but he jumped as the gun spat. Almost instantaneously, he was aware of two things. One, the day exploded, as from somewhere, other guns began to fire in rapid succession. Two, there was a burning pain in his chest. As strength drained from him, and he fell, Sidoti saw Dr. Faison's body, half-turned away, his hands clutching at the air. There was a neat hole in his forehead. Then, everything went dark.

Chapter 54

*A*ndreas pushed himself up the last few steps of the climb. His mind sense revealed the cave just beyond the bend, and he hurried forward, moving powerfully over the ice. Behind him, the three women climbed in silence. When the steps became ice-covered, they changed to climbing boots, though the pathway, cut for Empheme's ascent to the breast of Tiamat, was shielded from the murderous cold above. Someone—Andreas did not even bother to think how long ago—had cut those steps. Heat vents were installed along the way to keep the pathway relatively clear, but between the eleventh and twelfth stations, the women slowed.

The ice did not bother Andreas. His hands and feet were sure. The air was warmer, and he glanced at the sky, pondering its writhing whiteness. It had been like that for a while, and as the temperature rose, the sky became more disturbed. Andreas sensed something there, but it was beyond his comprehension. At the eleventh station, he had tried to combine his mind sense with Eurydice's in an attempt to penetrate the roiling mass, but they gave up after a while. The sky was opaque, almost reflective as Andreas looked over his shoulder.

Strange how they seem so slow all of a sudden.

For days, the women had outpaced him, the long, flowing strides of the *leo-leos* gobbling up the ground, but as they climbed higher along the cliff face, they experienced more difficulty. At least, it became easier for him. At each station, the goddess came, and the contacts strengthened him. Now, as he approached the twelfth station, Andreas anticipated the contact. He waited until the three women caught up.

"It's just around the next bend," he said.

Above, the colors changed until the sky was again blue. The four stared. Only a moment before the sky had seemed to be boiling.

"Odd," Andreas said.

They rounded the bend on to a wider ledge. The *leo-leos* began to set up their lightweight tents.

"Aren't we using the cave tonight?" he asked, peering into the small, dark entrance.

"Only you will enter here, Andreas. There's space for only one."

"Why don't you take it then? I can sleep outside."

"Thank you, my sweet, but you must enter here."

She touched his face and pushed him gently toward the entrance. It was small, so he had to crawl in. Once inside, he could not stand upright. It was warmer than outside, and he unrolled his sleeping bag, wondering why the women did not come inside. Fortunately, it was not too uncomfortable on the ledge.

As soon as his head touched the sleeping bag, he noticed the smell. It was stale and suggestive of a sour-sweet rot. He sat up, staring around in the dusk. Eyes glinted. Andreas started up, but his mind sense told him that the roof was too low. He sat still. The red eyes did not blink. They slithered sideways, and the light from outside disappeared. The old wounds from the crocodile's claw throbbed. When the eyes moved toward him, he backed away but soon came up against a rock wall. The creature's breathing was a harsh rasp. The rotten smell, evidently coming from the creature's mouth, grew stronger.

His mind sense contracted. He was outside the cave, flying down a poorly-lit chute, accelerating past unfamiliar objects. A deep blackness appeared. For many years, a black mass had tormented his dreams, but this was not it. Instead, individual elements of blackness filled the sky, and everything moved with them. The mass folded on itself, crushing everything in its way. Its projected path, a golden light, ended at a small, watery planet that shimmered brightly blue in the distance. A figure was astride that world. Natas. Across the distance, the figure grinned, its long, black, saurian face a taunt. A huge white crocodile swam out from the stream of black motes. Andreas hovered between the blackness and the blue planet in the distance.

"Maatemnu," the crocodile said, "what do you see?"

The voice was low-pitched but powerful. Andreas looked inside himself and saw his body, lifeless and floating in the cosmos, a brightness surrounding it, and the black mass retreating. There was something odd about his body. It seemed to be more than his, but he could not be sure.

Suddenly, the crocodile struck, its paw raking murderously at him. This time, Andreas anticipated it, and his staff flashed, knocking the great paw aside. The fiery, red eyes blinked, and it attacked. Again, the staff was pushed by a vital force that flowed along Andreas' arm, through the staff and into the crocodile. It grunted but did not retreat, its own energy flowing outward, enveloping him. For a moment, unable to breathe, he struggled, the staff moving haphazardly, like a drowning man fighting the water. Then, through the fog of his mind sense, came the pure strain of Eurydice's voice. Breath returned to him.

In the blackness, the crocodile watched. When he attacked, it did not move, allowing the staff, which now seemed a spear, to penetrate its body. Andreas felt the pain. Having felt it before in a desert as he bent over a dying boy, it did not overwhelm him. Beyond the pain, there was sadness, a sense of loss so deep that, at first, he could not understand it. Three entities floated before him. His mind sense came alive, streaking along the staff. He felt the dying god, with his pain and sadness. There, too, was the goddess, her eyes as still as the unenlivened universe in potential, lovely yet remote. She was the being he knew as Mother Mutasii. There was, as well, a deeper darkness he had never seen before and yet knew instinctively it was the god Chango. Andreas also recognized that it was Branniff, the Father of the Ilegu Forest. An image formed in his mind sense—dark energy flowing into him in the southern desert as the explosion from the truck killed his son.

Tiamat, Chango and Baal, he thought.

Still, he was perplexed. Baal was not a child. A thought seemed to come alive in the universe, and the dark presence assumed a form. Chango became material. Andreas was almost blinded by the beauty of the divine figure filling the sky.

"We meet again," Andreas said.

Or Chango said. It was not clear to Andreas who had spoken, but the voice was sweet, like a single note that contained all the sounds in the universe.

Including silence.

His body tingled as the figure turned its head. The galaxy both wheeled and contracted. The sun and eleven planets spun wildly around. The number struck Andreas as wrong, and he looked to the god whose form seemed perfection.

He looks like Natas.

His surprise caused the whirling planets to wobble, but he steadied them with a glance, aware, in that instant, of a twelfth planet that was he.

"Will they die?" Andreas asked.

"All things die, Maatemnu, yet do not die," the god replied.

Andreas' perplexity deepened.

"We have failed again, and my brother does as he must," the god continued.

"Your brother?" Andreas asked, his whisper like the solar wind.

"My brother Baal. He who comes as confusion, deceit and death."

"Natas!"

"Baal lives by a thousand names. Now, you call him Natas."

Andreas turned to the third planet, feeling the pain of its loss.

"This has always been my favorite home," the dark god said.

There was sadness in his voice.

"Then why are you destroying it?"

"Is that what you think, Maatemnu? What do you see?" the goddess asked.

Andreas saw the many beginnings and the many endings, and the many beginnings again. Always, the divinities stood outside of Time, Tiamat's child, watching, a certain sadness in their failure evident, and he, Maatemnu, was the spear to end it all.

"You cannot reproduce your own perfection, and so you create and then destroy what you think of as failure. You bastards! You heartless bastards!"

Andreas felt no reciprocal anger in the god. There was only a kind of bewilderment as if the universe had asked itself a question.

"You have always been different, Maatemnu. When Tiamat formed you with her own hands, she said you would be. Your questions give us hope that we will succeed in creating perfection. But you, too, always fail."

"What do you mean 'fail'?"

The solar system surrounding them disappeared, and, seeing his life, Andreas felt ashamed. It was replete with ambition, callousness and death. He saw his spears again and again thumping into the chest of the Neanderthal. The faces repeatedly changed, but always there was death, and it was his hand that guided that laughing god to humans' hearts.

"Am I companion to Baal? Am I evil?"

"Look again, Maatemnu."

He looked and saw himself in a wide desert. The mighty sphinx sat staring into a future that seemed distant but certain, or was it a past that was equally distant but unknown? He found the mummy, and at the moment of his greatest achievement, all he felt was excruciating pain. There he was, stealing the scroll that turned out to be a homing device, sneaking it out of Egypt, thus handing it to Natas. He saw, too, Natas and his priests/scientists pouring over codes that would create instruments of war.

"I led him to it. You hid it, and I led him to it. It was my greed, my need to hold on to something of my find in Egypt that let Natas loose upon the earth."

The dark god Chango, voice soothing, said, "You are Maatemnu, and you act according to our dictates. Our flaws motivate you. You are our imperfection."

"But I do it. Every man is responsible for his actions."

Andreas sensed that the god and goddess pondered this, and as they thought, his anger grew.

"Why do you need us?"

"To tend the fields we have created."

The voice sounded mildly surprised, as if the goddess Tiamat had answered that question before. It occurred to Andreas that she had. How many times had this conversation taken place? How many creations? How many Armageddons?

"I will fight you."

"As you always have, Maatemnu," the god Chango said.

"And I have always lost?"

"Except once."

"Then, is my world doomed?"

The god and goddess smiled, and Andreas saw not simply his planet but millions of systems. He heard the screams as their suns grew too hot and exploded, folding themselves into the dark energy that was speeding from all corners toward where he watched.

"How many trillions?" he asked, a catch in his voice.

The god did not react, staring instead at the watery, blue planet that blazed like a beacon in the sky.

The goddess Tiamat, turning to Andreas, said, "All is not lost, Maatemnu. You can save a fragment."

"How?"

The god Chango seemed to have lost interest, smiling at the goddess Tiamat and the child god who lay dying on her breast.

"You will face your choice, Maatemnu. You, whose name means "set apart," will know then the nature of your sacrifice," the goddess answered.

Andreas wanted to scream that he had already sacrificed too much. He had lost his life to this path he had not chosen, had lost his wife to the goddess Tiamat and his son to the god Baal. His heart cried out, have I not given enough? Below him, the black motes streamed toward the blue planet that spun in the distance, and he knew his sacrifice had only just begun. His mind sense slid along the golden path, outpacing the black motes, and he saw the tear in the ozone layer, the weakness in the shield. Branniff's technology, promising progress and the provision of more comfort, had created the hole. Now, Natas waited at the end of the golden path for the coming of the black motes. At the poles, the white of the melting ice glinted, and he understood.

"You need us, don't you? 'To tend the fields we have created,' you said. We are your food, and our sacrifice of ourselves has always been simply the symbol of your true need."

He heard what Empheme must have heard a thousand times—the silence of the goddess. His mind sense was full of images, and he created order within it, separating what was from what is and what might be. The strands of time stretched before him in lines that went in every direction. From time to time, they intersected. At each of those intersections, darkness flared for a brief moment, caught for all eternity, an innumerable series of dots that lived as singularities. Andreas focused on a dot that he recognized as the beginning of his planet, a fiery, puny thing that three giants moulded into a sphere.

"You?" Andreas asked of the beings before him.

"You were given life, Maatemnu. How can taking you back into ourselves be worthy of your condemnation?"

The goddess' voice carried a deep sadness, but Andreas was not satisfied.

"You harvest our fear? Is that your food?"

He knew his disgust was futile. He also instantly knew that his deduction was not quite right. A thought formed in his mind.

All energy is consumable.

He wanted to scream that he was not energy, but life, that his consciousness made him unique, but looking at the faces before him, he knew they would not understand. He was simply their failure, their imperfection. They would start over, create a newer, better version of him. With a final glance at the placid faces, he turned toward the blue water planet that glowed in the distance.

Instantly, he was on the ledge. The two *leo-leos* rose, observing him. His mind sense reached for Eurydice as she opened her eyes. Sensing something unusual, she climbed out of the sleeping bag and stood next to him. Lifting the golden staff, he glared at the *leo-leos*.

"The mask is no longer effective or necessary," he said.

The *leo-leos* grinned, and the oddest thing happened. The two bodies merged into one and then changed shape as the bones rearranged themselves.

"The Father of the Ilegu Forest. How?" Eurydice whispered.

Andreas placed his arm protectively around his wife's shoulder.

"Much more than that, Eudy. He's the god Chango."

"It is a very useful trick," Branniff said. "It allowed me to monitor your progress."

"And Meldana and Usai?" Eurydice asked.

"They are unharmed. Wandering around lost somewhere near the bend in the River Wilongo but quite safe."

Andreas held his staff at the ready. The short, powerful, black god chuckled.

"Do you think you have the skill to defeat me, Maatemnu? You survived the white crocodile, and your skills are much improved, but do not deceive yourself."

"Will I have to fight you?"

Andreas' voice was cold, and the thick-shouldered god shook his head.

"I know you would like to test your strength against mine, but no. You will not have to fight me."

"What now?"

"The time of the Repulsion comes."

"I saw its coming. The goddess said I could still prevent it."

"Did she? I believe she said you can still save a fragment."

"How?"

"You must find your way, Maatemnu."

Andreas hesitated and then asked, "Will I win?"

Branniff grinned, the horrid angles of his face sliding around like plates of rock on top of magma.

"If you did, your myths would speak of it for an age."

Eurydice, baffled, listened to the enigmatic interplay between the two.

"Of what do you speak, Father of the Ilegu? You speak of myths. Are not then the gods real?"

Andreas did not wait for Branniff to answer.

"They are real, Eudy, but not in the way we thought. They are stronger and more advanced than we are, but they lack the fundamental quality we have sought in our gods."

"What is that?"

"Involvement. They have only a passing interest in us. We are simply food."

"Is that what you think, Maatemnu?" Branniff asked. "Do you not see the care we take to make you perfect?"

"Perfect? How can you create perfection when you are yourselves imperfect?"

"You do not understand."

"What is there to understand?" Andreas shouted.

"You are our hope. We seek our perfection in you."

Andreas was on the verge of an angry response when Eurydice said, "Yes. I understand."

Andreas stared at her, incredulous. She touched his face.

"Don't you see, Andreas? They are unchanging, not perfect and not capable of change. Yet, they have seen something that is perfect in their past, and it is this they try to recreate." She looked directly at Branniff. "The stories of the First People are not really our history, are they? Or only partially ours. They are your stories. It is your failures we have chronicled in our myths."

Branniff, his body a deeper darkness against the rock, nodded.

"Very good. Even your most powerful idea—that of the Great Parting—we gave to you. It is the story of our split from the unity you call the god to whom the people give no name. The act of generation that created Baal, Tiamat and me also doomed us to the imperfection of separation. Your impulse toward a joining comes from our similar impulse, but like us, you, too, are doomed to conflict and destruction at every attempt."

"The Reunion that the stories have instructed us to pursue will also lead to our destruction?" Eurydice asked.

"As our coming together is known as the Repulsion, so is your movement also a paradox."

Andreas was angry, and he gently pushed Eurydice away from him, his golden staff moving into attack position. Branniff chuckled.

"Do not be hasty, Maatemnu. Someday, you may be able to match me, but today is not that day."

Andreas heard the truth of those words and hesitated.

"I am not your enemy, Maatemnu. Indeed, my task is all but done."

"And what is that task?" Andreas asked.

"What it has been for each cycle. I guard the dying god whose life is restored at the beginning of each creation. I ensure that the matches are made to enrich the bloodline. I am the guardian."

"You protect Natas," Andreas said harshly.

"He is my brother," came the quiet reply. "I also protect Tiamat and Empheme. I protect you, so that you may effect your purpose."

"My purpose?"

"You, Maatemnu, will end the cycle. You have always had that purpose."

"And I have always failed."

"Except once when you gave the First People hope by your sacrifice. Then, a fragment was saved."

"My sacrifice?"

"Yes, Andreas. Your sacrifice," Eurydice said, her voice betraying her excitement. "They want the same thing we do, to end the cycle. Our instincts are the same. They seek the unity they once enjoyed, and we want a world free from the fear of endings."

"Why can't they just stop it?" Andreas asked angrily.

"Because they can't change. They are whatever they were created to be. That's it. Oh, my goddess, why did I not see this before? We, imperfect as we are, have the capacity to change. That means we may become perfect. Am I correct, Father of the Ilegu Forest?"

"Tiamat always said that this generation was the best we created. You have often proven that, Empheme."

"That is what they meant by us taking care of the fields they planted. You thought they were talking about using us as food, but it's different. The fuel we provide to them is the frequent changes we undergo. They live off of us in that sense. Yet, ironically, they're seeking their original unity, in which they will eternally be one."

Eurydice's voice was speculative, but there was admiration contained in it, too. Andreas, remembering the image of the galaxy being folded like a rug and the terrible sound of worlds dying, knew that her admiration was misplaced. That horde of dark motes was coming, and Earth, too, would be swallowed up, its last gasp the silent scream he had heard across the cosmos.

"Come," he said.

His arm went around Eurydice, and instantly, the cave and Branniff disappeared. Beneath Andreas' and Eurydice's feet was the stark whiteness of Antarctica.

"How did you do that?"

"I don't know, Eudy. My mind sense seems to have strengthened since I spoke to the three beings, but I think it is Branniff who sent me here."

"The three beings?"

"I'll explain later."

They stepped forward. In front of them were three tents, outside of which five men stood. Four had guns and carried themselves like soldiers. The fifth had a mad look in his eyes and was disheveled. They were staring at two bodies on the ice. A red stain had already crystallized in the cold. Andreas recognized one of the bodies. It was the fellow who had written the NSA report that started the whole nasty business of expelling the African Americans. The soldiers trained their guns on him and Eurydice.

"Good day, gentlemen. I am Andreas Prescod, and this is my wife Eurydice. Unless I'm mistaken, you are United States military. Who's in command here?"

A young, hard-faced man took a step forward.

"I am, mister. Who the hell are you, and where the hell did you come from?"

"That's a long story, and we don't have time. I need to get to Washington as quickly as possible."

Andreas seemed sure of himself, but the major was uncertain.

"Why?"

"We don't have time. I'm a scientist, and I have been in Antarctica for a long time. I have information I need to get back to Washington."

The major was not convinced, and Andreas, losing patience, reached out with his mind sense. It did not take long to break camp. Within minutes, the three tractors were trundling north. The major radioed the ship, asking that the helicopter meet them at the extreme end of its range.

Inside the lead tractor, Andreas and Eurydice sat with the major. The second tractor carried two of the soldiers and the mad-looking scientist. The third, driven by a fourth ranger, carried the bodies of two dead men. Andreas was tired but could not sleep. He held Eurydice's hand and watched a sky that was turning a putrid shade of cream. His mind was filled with images of disaster.

Chapter 55

On the first day of March, the Sino-American war effectively ended. When disciplined soldiers' eyes are turned to the sky, it is difficult to fight the enemy, and for almost three weeks the world had looked skyward. Xu stared down from the top floor of the Ministry of National Defense in the heart of Beijing at the madness below. The streets were jammed with people, all looking at a sky that, though beautiful, was no longer familiar. It was vermilion tinged with blackness but did not at all seem threatening.

Xu felt the pull of its beauty. Every place of worship in Beijing was full, and no one was working. His society was crumbling and not because of American might. It was the same in the United States, Europe, South America, everywhere. Everywhere, that is, except Africa. There, from all reports, life was proceeding with a normality that suggested madness. By any objective measure, Africa was becoming the center of the world, its economy having tripled in size during the previous five years. That was why Liu's coded communiqué about the placidity of the continent was so disturbing.

Xu was not thinking about Liu's message as he stared at a sky that, ranging through the colors of the spectrum, was now becoming a deep shade of blue. Everyone was spooked, including the generals who sat behind him.

"General Wang, do you think they can be trusted?"

Wang cleared his throat.

"Sir, it seems to me that the Americans are simply accepting reality. A thirty-day ceasefire would give us time to recover from this ... this ...."

Wang, glancing through the window where the colors were again shifting, shook his head. Xu nodded.

"No one knows what this force is. We lost three more planes trying to analyze it in Antarctica. When the force attacked the American ships, we assumed it had come to our aid. Now, it has struck at us, too."

Xu stood straight, his granitic face showing nothing of the turmoil inside him. These men would act as he did, and China needed strength now.

"This attests to American fear, gentlemen. I do not say this in condemnation, but it is a fact. We both have the same fears. That is why they have proposed we cooperate."

"Why cooperate, sir? It is only a matter of time before we become the most dominant power in the world. The Americans simply seek to delay the inevitable," a thin, bespectacled general replied.

Xu smiled. It was good they still believed in a future that promised much. The secret communiqué had come to the political bosses of China and was sent directly to him, the effective ruler of the country. The president of the United States was suggesting a joint project. They wanted James Tung, China's leading physicist, who had worked with their scientists before the destruction brought about by the rising waters and, later, the war. Xu called the meeting, recognizing the value of the proposed collaboration. For weeks, no soldier on either side had paid much attention to the war.

The ceasefire provided a welcome pause because he was worried about his ability to win the war. They were now less dependent on Branniff Enterprises for the equipment necessary to prosecute the war, but China still had needs it could not fulfill. Branniff Enterprises was becoming miserly in its supply of technology, replacement parts and the advanced weaponry China needed. When he had tried to contact Branniff Enterprises, those at the top of the corporation seemed never to be available. He suspected the Americans were facing the same problem. The ceasefire was a relief, but this business of lending them China's leading physicist created a bit of a conundrum.

And yet, he thought, glancing at the frightening sky, *we are fighting the same enemy.*

"Have Tung come in," Xu said.

The scientist entered, his eyes darting from one grim face to another.

"Well, Tung. What do we know?"

There was an empty chair at the table, and Xu indicated that the scientist should sit.

"What do we know? Well, we have not been able to take direct measurements of the phenomenon. None of our instruments can measure what is there, sir."

"Is there nothing to measure?"

"It's not that nothing's there. Something definitely is, but we can't measure it. However, the satellites have picked up something."

"What?"

"A kind of bow wave, sir." Tung turned to a junior officer and asked, "Do we have the images I sent?"

The room darkened as a projection system was activated.

"Oh, good," the scientist said. "In that photo, sir, you will notice that our satellite is depicted. Look at the numbers in the sequence at the bottom going from right to left, the direction in which the satellite is moving. Note that the numbers are of a decreasing magnitude. In short, sir, our satellite, and every other one up there, is slowing down."

"Why?" Xu asked.

"We have speculations and some mathematical models but no certainties."

"What do your calculations suggest?"

The scientist adjusted his glasses and took a sip of water.

"Our best guess, which the mathematics strongly supports, is that dark matter is being pushed by some force we don't understand."

The room became very quiet. The image on the screen changed, showing what looked like a giant scoop, concave in shape, as it pushed through the blackness around it. In front of it were tiny, black dots with white arrows showing the direction in which they were moving. Another slightly larger dot showed the position of the earth. The scoop was approaching that position.

"What is it, Tung?"

"We think some force is pushing the dark matter in our galaxy toward the center."

He signaled, and another image came up. This showed the sun with heat flares streaming out of it.

"That force is probably causing the strange lights in the sky. The odd thing is that sun flares are usually spherical in shape. You will note that the stream of the flares is on one side of the sun and goes counter to its direction through space. That suggests the force is pushing against the sun as well."

"Does that tell us anything in particular?"

"It tells us that we have an astronomical force sufficiently powerful to affect the sun's surface gravitationally but is so small or transparent that it is invisible to our instruments. It seems to be getting closer because the rate of spin in our satellite is slowing."

"I am not sure I know any more than before your explanation, Tung."

The scientist nervously shoved his glasses up on his nose.

"In brief, General Xu, we have something that is powerful enough to kill us all, but we can't identify what or where it is."

"Would the Americans have any better handle on this?"

"Possible, sir. They have invested more money in this kind of research, and with their labs and satellites, particularly the Gravity Probe B—"

"What's that?"

"It's a satellite with four of the most stable gyroscopes ever built. It measures something called frame dragging caused by the earth's rotation. They have been collecting data for years. I am sure they will have some idea of the degree of drag up there." Tung hesitated and then added, "If there was any way to work with their data, we might have a better chance of understanding this."

Xu had an odd feeling. He was not a pessimist, but the strange sky and the sudden fear around him had seriously shaken his faith.

Aware the generals were all waiting on him, he said, "Maybe you will get your wish, Tung. The Americans have invited you to join a project. You will not be allowed to go to America. The Americans realize that, and they are prepared to work through GEO600 in Germany. You will leave today."

Xu did not understand what the scientists did at the observatory, but someone had explained that it was designed to measure the degree of stretching a gravitational wave would create.

"By the way," he said as Tung rose, "there is an old friend of yours in charge of the project. A Dr. Karl Metzer."

Not even the thought that the general would certainly think him traitorous could prevent the smile that appeared on Tung's face.

"He is the best, sir. The very best."

Xu nodded, and the others left. He went to the window. For weeks, his smartest people had been trying to unravel a mystery. They had noticed that the thirty million Chinese selected by Branniff to go to Africa all shared the same DNA. It was rumored that the Americans discovered something similar with the population they had expelled to Antarctica. Xu frowned, wondering what he was missing.

Chapter 56

*A*nne Ernsky made her way through the streets of Bumba. It was just a few days before Good Friday, and the city was overrun with pilgrims. There was not a single hotel room available. Since she wanted to avoid contact with Branniff, she could not stay on the cathedral's grounds and was renting a tent from one of the hundreds of vendors who had opened businesses around the city. She was working her way slowly across Liberty Bridge and into a darker, less traveled section of town in response to Lui's cryptic communiqué. After all, the Chinese diplomat was providing her people with transportation to Africa. The instructions directed her to Merchant's Row, a seedier section of Bumba but perfect for maintaining invisibility. Struck by four gargoyles that formed capitals of the bridge, she stopped for a moment, admiring the artistry.

They're almost alive.

The communiqué surprised her because, like Etienne a few weeks earlier, Liu asked her not to say anything to Natas.

Everyone's afraid of Natas now.

There was no denying the changes in the man and the company. Always secretive, the corporation was now opaque, and its one humanizing element, Natas' playful image, was gone. It was almost two years since he had been seen on a magazine cover, and, lately, in his few appearances, he was serious, often giving a sober assessment of events in the world. She could no longer think of Natas without seeing the long, saurian face Etienne exposed to her. Who were these creatures? Where were they from? How could they do what they did? Etienne's explanation made Branniff Enterprises' success over its long history more understandable, given their head start in technology. When she served as secretary of state, every improvement in weaponry had come from a Branniff lab. The corporation made many other products, but its forte was war. Now, Branniff was apparently out of patience with its erstwhile allies.

Puppets would be more accurate, she thought, checking the name of a street.

The glass, steel and marble of Bumba's high-toned streets left behind, she moved carefully. After a while, turning left into a narrow street that was damp with effluvium, she saw The Dragon's Snout, its broken sign swaying gently in the wind. Here, people drank seriously, and there were no skygazers. As soon as she stepped into the threatening dimness of the bar, a graceful figure, head covered by a hood, rose, coming toward her. When the figure softly called her name, Anne Ernsky stopped.

"Do not be alarmed. There is one other with me."

Anne Ernsky allowed herself to be led to a table where a young man of medium height sat. He rose and bowed to her.

"Our savior," he said solemnly, remaining in a posture of submission.

Anne Ernsky, perplexed, said, "Sit, please." When they were seated at the round table, she asked, "Where's Lui?"

"Forgive me, my lady. I sent the message. Since you did not know me, we thought it best to use a name you recognized," the young man said in accented English.

Anne Ernsky nodded.

"What do you want of me?"

"It has to do with Pope Celestine, my lady. You are close to him, no?"

"I am."

"Then, please get me to him."

"Why?"

"He wavers. He attends Natas' cathedral. You must have Pope Celestine declare against Natas," the young man said urgently.

"Why? Who are you?"

"My name is Marcus. I am commander of Natas' military forces and imperial governor of the Province of Lusani in the Land of Ghalib."

Anne observed the earnest young man. He did not seem mad.

"The province of what in the land of where?"

The young woman lowered the hood of her robe. She was perfectly bald, but that did nothing to diminish the startling symmetry of her face. She was also the blackest person Anne Ernsky had ever seen.

"I am Teme."

"I remember you. You were with Natas in Salzburg."

Teme nodded abruptly, as if reminded of something distasteful.

"There is little time. Please, Miss Ernsky, listen to Marcus. He is who he says he is."

Anne Ernsky immediately trusted the woman. Maybe it was Teme's poise, the sense of quietude, or even her blackness, but she felt more comfortable.

"OK, Marcus. What can I do for you?"

"First, my lady, I must tell you a story. It is a strange story."

"My boy, it could not possibly be stranger than some of the things I have heard lately."

Marcus spoke for a long time. When he stopped, her face was wet with tears. She reached out and touched his arm.

"You are the first I've met. The first to return. Where are the others?"

"Everywhere on this continent, my lady. What you call the Black Fleet is emptying the Land of Ghalib. The stories say that, thanks to you, we survived. They speak of your bravery on the road to Najok," Marcus responded.

She had never heard of Najok but assumed it was some little town in the northern part of the United States. Marcus' narrative had a mythological quality to it. A tale of trial and survival, it was a fabulous, improbable story of gods and their return to earth.

Wiping her eyes, she said, "You said Etienne should be encouraged to declare against Natas. Why?"

"The man you call Natas does not have your interest at heart. This war, like so much of the dissension in your world, is created by Branniff," Teme said urgently.

"But why?"

"That is an even more complicated story. It is enough to know that, after the Repulsion, Natas intends to be worshiped as a god."

"A god?"

"Yes. Natas is now possessed by Baal, the god of the fiery mountain."

"And Baal is … what? Some sort of renegade?"

"If you wish. The god Baal has always stood aside from his sister Tiamat and his brother Chango."

"That sounds pretty nutty." Even as Anne Ernsky spoke, Etienne's saurian face filled her mind, and she said, "Sorry. It's just hard to take all this in. Let's see if I've got it. This god Baal is a rebel. He wants followers. He's picked a group of people, primarily black, because these are direct descendants of those who were shaped by the gods Tiamat, Chango and himself. These people are being assembled in Africa. Is that about right?"

The young man and woman both nodded.

"Why?"

Marcus turned to Teme who now seemed less sure.

"I don't think Natas acts of his own will."

"What do you mean?"

"I think it is the Father of the Ilegu—"

"Someone mentioned that name to me not long ago."

"It is the person you know as Branniff. It was he who directed Natas to assemble the descendants here in this place you call Africa."

"Why?"

"That I do not know. I only know that Natas and the Father of the Ilegu Forest no longer pursue the same ends."

Anne Ernsky was silent for a while before asking, "What is it you want Etienne to do?"

"Marcus organized Natas' army, so maybe they will fight as he commands. The pope is confused. His voice will be needed when the battle begins. He needs to be sure. He trusts you. Help him decide."

"Decide what?"

"To save us."

"You mean save the world? What can he do? He's not a military leader."

Marcus and Teme glanced at each other.

"We will not all be saved. Our stories speak of many beginnings, many endings. Sometimes a remnant survives, and our story begins again. There is no change," Teme said.

"That makes no sense, and anyway, doing nothing doesn't sit too well with me."

"Miss Ernsky, Marcus does not agree with me, but this battle will not be won with armies. It will be won by your acceptance of the goddess' will. In this way, Pope Celestine can be valuable. Always, the First People are given a good soul—man or woman—to stand against the gods. Our stories tell of Ghalib, our greatest warrior, who went to the Ilegu Forest to fight the dwarf people. There, the beings described as "from the east" came upon him, and he was slain. He has lived in the memory of the people since that time. Now, Natas assumes the name Son of Ghalib, knowing the meaning that title carries for the First People. He is doing the same here. His technology is superior to yours, but he does not want a war with you. This undermines everything Baal believes of himself. He wants to be worshiped. Your sacrifice must be voluntary. When you throw yourselves and your children into the yawning pit of fire, it must be with a cry of joy on your lips. He wants your souls, and he wants them without demand. The new religion may be preparing you for this. You must resist Natas. Your Pope Celestine can be the symbol of that resistance."

Anne Ernsky was quiet for a moment, and Teme reached across, touching her hand.

"This world as you know it will end. You must save those who survive."

"Nonsense. We will fight against what you describe."

Even as she said that, Anne Ernsky thought of the sermons proliferating on television. The Book of Revelation had become an obsession. Chapter six, in particular, was repeatedly heard. It read like a series of horrors, but the fifteenth through seventeenth verses were a particular favorite in most pulpits.

"And the Kings of the earth, and the great men, and the rich men, and the chief captains and the mighty men, and every bondman and every free man hid themselves in the dens and in the rocks of the mountains.

"And said to the mountains and the rocks, Fall on us and hide us from the face of him that sitteth on the throne and from the wrath of the lamb. For the great day of his wrath is come, and who shall be able to stand?"

Unconsciously, she had spoken out loud, and Teme, leaning forward, asked, "Is that from your great book?"

Anne Ernsky nodded, thinking that the world was already prepared for disaster. The priests had done their work well.

"It is said that within each generation, there is one who stands for the First People against the gods. One true descendant of the First People who does not know his name. We thought the man you know as Natas was the one, but we were deceived. I thought, perhaps, it was Empheme, the high priestess of Tiamat, but again I was mistaken," Teme said softly.

"Do you think it's Etienne who will stand for this generation?"

"It is not Pope Celestine, but there may be one. He came from your world, weak but pure in spirit."

"Who is he?"

"You called him Andreas. We call him Tama."

"Andreas? Andreas ..." Anne Ernsky said, brow wrinkling. "There was an Andreas Prescod who disappeared some time ago in Antarctica. His wife was also lost there."

"He sometimes calls the high priestess Eurydice."

"Are you saying that Andreas Prescod is alive?"

"He is, my lady," Marcus answered.

"Well, if it's the same person, he won't be much use to you. He became a drunk after his wife was lost."

"No, Miss Ernsky. He is stronger now," Teme responded.

"He saved me, and yet I hate him, as you must," Marcus said quietly.

"Must I? Why must I hate him?" Anne Ernsky said.

"It was he who caused us to be sent away. How could you not hate him?"

Anne Ernsky looked away. Marcus' words brought a terrible pain.

"Andreas Prescod was the fall guy."

"The fall guy? What does that mean?"

"It is someone who takes the blame. It was a setup from the start.

Natas used his influence to ensure that Prescod was appointed chair of the committee that looked into the effects of the changed weather patterns on the United States. Prescod's report correctly identified the problem of overpopulation, but the expulsion had been proposed by Natas long before the report was written."

Teme nodded, understanding showing on her face.

"In this way, the Son of Ghalib, Natas as you say, created an army, and with that army, he conquered the Land of Tiamat," she said.

"Why was that important to him?"

"The stories do not say, but I have thought that this was the only way to remove the First People from the Land of Tiamat and to bring them here."

"Why?"

Teme shook her head.

"So Andreas Prescod did not recommend the expulsion?" Marcus asked.

"No. His name was attached to it. Natas wanted it that way, and no one objected. It didn't seem important."

Teme rested her hand on Marcus' shoulder.

"So, Marcus, you have no reason to hate him."

Anne Ernsky saw relief on Marcus' face, but not sure why, she returned to the reason they had wanted to meet with her.

"I will speak with Etienne."

Her eyes held Teme's. Behind Teme's unconventional beauty, there was a deep sadness. Anne Ernsky wondered about the woman's relationship with Natas.

"Miss Ernsky, look to the sky. We are already on the edge of disaster. Impress that on Pope Celestine, please," Teme said.

Anne Ernsky soon left. Looking to the sky, a shudder went through her body.

Chapter 57

There must be over a million people here, Etienne thought as he made his way through the crowd.

He was once again in Bumba. The new Church had signaled its independence by making the Easter sacrament a fixed holiday, and so, Easter was being celebrated some days after the Vatican had done so. Though the announcement was made only four days earlier, the masses flocked to Bumba, anxious, it seemed, to atone for what they were increasingly speaking of as man's trangression. Natas now made appearances in the vestments of the new priests, and, in the last week, he was on constant display. Watching television a few nights before, Etienne was surprised by the change in Natas, whose former insouciant playfulness was replaced by a somber voice that spoke eloquently of "the last days." That night, Natas' face changed shape so that his beauty was obscured by his seriousness. Few who watched would have noticed, so subtle was the shift. It occurred to Etienne that Natas must be really sure of himself to change shape, however minutely, before a worldwide audience. The next day, the cathedral in Bumba announced the change in the celebration of the Easter mass.

The change stunned everyone. Having received notice of Natas' intent, the American and European churches were clamoring for immediate expulsion of the heretics from the body of the Catholic Church. Etienne asked them to delay their deliberations until after Rome's celebration of the Easter Mass. That bought him a little time, but he had to act. The beliefs of the Church could be stretched only so far, and with new vestments, a new liturgy and now the tampering with the sacraments, the new order had gone too far. He needed a final conversation with Natas. If Natas resisted, then excommunication would follow. Etienne observed the sky, appreciating the irony of a threat of excommunication when the world appeared on the edge of oblivion. Above, an unnatural crimson gave the impression of a worldwide fire, the flames of which were unseen.

Around him, too, was a potential conflagration. What would happen when he inflicted excommunication? How would the millions who followed the teachings of the new order react? Noting the discipline of the crowd, knowing that it reflected their faith, Etienne wondered if Rome would find itself isolated. The Americans and Europeans would embrace the Vatican, but would that be enough? Would over two thousand years of tradition and service crumble into dust? How had his own beliefs changed from that moment in the jungle when he saw his father praise the god Chango, to his evolution into a believer in the force that so many referred to as God? For him, the act became the reality. He sensed something more than the façade the Church presented to the world, and this seeped into his soul. He knew with certainty that something other than those beings who left their genes among the human race existed as a divine presence. In the last few months, his love for the Church had grown, and even the discovery of his true self did not threaten his loyalty. The first weeks had been hard, as his training fought against the new impulses, the new instinct. Thankfully, his humanity appeared to be winning.

There was a brittle quality to the crowd around him. The threat in the sky contributed to this, but there was something else. It was the new Mass. That action had energized the members of the new order. He entered through the giant doors of the cathedral, marveling again at the scale of the building. To his surprise, the aisle was not crowded. His arm was immediately taken by a friendly young priest who led him to the pews closest to the altar. He sat, taking the hood from his head, displaying the bushy beard he wore on his trips to Bumba. The silence in the cathedral, the vaulted ceiling of which towered somewhere in the dimness above, was absolute.

There must be two hundred and fifty thousand people inside, and yet, it feels as if no one is here, he thought.

Though primarily a black congregation, other races were represented. It occurred to him that their oneness of spirit accounted for the silence. At that moment, the organ started to play the antiphon, and Etienne allowed the familiar music to wash over him. He closed his eyes, humming the sonorous strains. The mass proceeded in conformity with the Roman sacrament. When the cardinal conducting the service reached the Rite of Blessing, Etienne listened more carefully. It was there that the changes were proposed. The familiar words sounded like a bell in his brain, and he whispered them.

The cardinal intoned, "Lord God Almighty, hear the prayers of the people. We celebrate our creation and redemption. Hear our prayers and bless this water which gives fruitfulness to the fields and refreshment and cleansing to man. You chose water to show your goodness when you led your people to freedom …."

Etienne whispered, "through the Red Sea," but the cardinal omitted those words.

"… Water was the symbol used by the prophets to foretell your new covenant with us. You made the water baptism holy …"

Etienne whispered, "By Christ's baptism in the Jordan."

Again, the cardinal omitted those words.

"… May this water remind us of our baptism, and let us share the joy of all who have been baptized at Easter."

This time, as Etienne now expected, nothing more was said. The cardinal made a sign that could have been the cross, except it seemed to have a loop at the top. The cardinal recessed from the alter.

The prayer should have ended "We ask this through Jesus Christ, our Lord," Etienne thought.

He sat uncomfortably, shifting as the First Reading proceeded with the same noticeable absence of reference to Christ. After the Second Reading, a hush came over the cathedral. Alerted by the air of expectancy around him, Etienne sat up. The organ began to moan. It was not anything he recognized, but it felt old and was deeply resonant. The lights gradually dimmed until it was impossible to see what was going on around the altar. There was, however, much activity. Suddenly, sharply-focused spotlights blazed, illuminating two crosses on each of which was a man whose body was scarlet. Etienne tensed, irritated at the confusion of the two sacraments—Easter and Good Friday.

What is Natas attempting to do? he wondered, leaning forward.

One of the men moaned. Etienne stared, hypnotized by the trail of a red bulb that slid down the man's chest. It moved slowly, in fits and starts, as if the body itself was grabbing it. He felt a tightness in his gut.

That is real blood.

He started to rise, but two priests immediately held him immobile. He sat, horrified, as the lights completely died. There was another groan, accompanied by the sound of someone falling. In the darkness, his imagination conjured up horrific images. The thumping continued, each fall followed by a groan. A spotlight suddenly pierced the darkness. There was a third cross between the others, and hanging from it was …

"Natas!" Etienne whispered fiercely.

He fought to rise, but hands gripped his neck. Pain exploded deep in his brain, immobilizing him. The expansive sanctuary was now a stage. Two men approached with hammers and spikes. Crossing Natas' feet, they placed a large spike against them. Etienne heard, as if in a dream, the sound of a multitude of voices intoning the words of the Penitential Rite. With one change.

"As we prepare to celebrate the mystery of Chango's love, let us acknowledge our failures and ask the Lord for pardon and strength," the triumphal voices rang out.

The break is complete. Natas has left our mother, the Church, Etienne thought.

The infernal pounding continued, the congregation wincing at each blow. Blood flowed freely. When, finally, the sacrificial figure's head fell forward in apparent death, the sanctuary resembled a slaughterhouse. There was a collective groan, and someone wailed, "My Lord! My Lord!" This voice, more than Natas' blasphemous act, seemed to signal the end of an age.

It was not the end. Dazed, Etienne watched as a man moved, zombie-like, across the sanctuary, a long spear in hand. His progress was slow, but there was an inevitability to the act. When the spear was thrust deep into Natas' side, the exhalation of breath in the cathedral carried no surprise, only a profound despair. Blood flowed down the shaft of the spear and into a cup that a cardinal carried. The cardinal raised the cup to his lips.

Etienne whispered, "God forgive us."

A procession of priests crossed the stage, each sipping the blood of the man who was slumped above them. Etienne wanted to be gone. As he attempted to rise, the lights went out. Strong hands pulled the fake beard from his face. The lights came back on. Etienne, greeted by the incessant flashing of cameras, cringed. Natas had found him out and exposed him in the most effective way possible.

Chapter 58

*A*s Etienne rushed from the cathedral, the rest of the world stared at a soundless explosion that was occurring. High in the southern sky, the light became more lurid. From its center, three lines snaked out, leaving fluorescent vapor trails as they dispersed, plunging down to the earth. Two men were unaware of the display. Metzer and Dr. Tung had been locked in a basement room with banks of computers for the last twenty hours, desperately trying to find a way to understand the physics of the astronomical phenomenon they faced. Their independent calculations gave the same results. Somehow, the invisible energy, the fundamental stuff of their universe, was being pushed, or scooped, in the direction of the earth by some force they could not analyze, measure or counteract. Metzer was sure they were witnessing a brane world collision. If that was true, then nothing in their technological arsenal could prevent it.

"What if the man in Antarctica is right?"

"What? That beings from space are behind this? Highly unlikely," Dr. Tung replied.

"Unlikely, yes. Impossible?" Metzer asked.

"Nothing's impossible. I just think we're better off trying to find a scientific answer."

"James, you know as well as I that the science we have does not explain what we're seeing. Maybe we should take data from Dr. Prescod's observations as well."

Metzer looked more sane than usual. He even wore a white shirt that had no stains. A transport plane had picked them up from the all but deserted city built by Branniff to house the African Americans in Antarctica. Metzer and the others were shuttled there by a helicopter from the ship, which had been freed from the ice as a result of the rising temperatures. Immediately upon landing on American soil, the scientist was whisked off to the Laser Interferometer Gravitational Wave Observatory in Hanford, Washington. Dead tired, Metzer, nevertheless, immediately began reviewing the observatory's data, which confirmed that gravity waves were increasing in frequency and magnitude. This was consistent with his hypothesis that they were witnessing inter-dimensional activity. Because the Chinese scientist was not allowed to go to America, Metzer was transported to GEO600, another gravitational wave detector near Sarstedt, Germany.

"Gravity's a weak force over distance, but its strength increases as distance diminishes. That's why we're seeing the slowing of celestial objects like the satellites and the sun. I think—"

He stopped as General Blount, just arrived from the U.S, pushed the door open.

"You boys will want to see this," he said.

"Hi, boss. You just got here?"

The general did not answer Metzer but strode toward an elevator. The ride terminated in an observatory.

"Holy shit!"

Metzer's eyes were glued to the heavens where the three fluorescent striations were moving in arcs toward the earth's surface. It was as if everything came together in his mind at that moment.

"The conductors!" he shouted. "They're going to connect to the three conductors. General, could you plot a projected end point for the three lines in the air?"

"Sure, but what difference will that make? It will only be an approximation. And what if they change course?"

"It's better than sitting around with our thumbs up our asses. Let's face it, General. We have no goddamned idea what we're dealing with. No goddamned idea at all. What we're doing downstairs, trying to figure this out scientifically, could take another century. What we're finding makes about as much sense as what that fellow who suddenly appeared in Antarctica was saying about gods from space and all that stuff."

General Blount was gruff, but he did listen to the people who worked for him.

"OK, Metzer. I'll get the projections for an Earth-fall. And the fellow who suddenly showed up in Antarctica was Dr. Andreas Prescod. He was quite a famous archaeologist a few years back. Not sure what happened to his mind in Antarctica, though. Anyway, he and his wife are here if you want to talk to them. I was all set to leave them behind in the States but changed my mind. They are on the fourth floor."

"I think we should talk to them, General."

Andreas and Eurydice were sitting at a long table when the scientists and the general entered. Tung was introduced, and they sat. It was impossible not to feel the calmness of the two. Metzer thought that, for the first time in his life, he was sitting with someone who could see the turmoil in his head and not be afraid.

Metzer was about to speak when Andreas said, "What you see in the sky is not they, simply the precursors of their presence."

"How do you know?"

General Blount's voice was gruff. He had not gotten used to the couple's dark skins. The photos on record showed that the Prescods were white. Andreas did not directly answer.

"Your weaponry will fail against them. They will turn your own men against you."

"Are you threatening the United States, Dr. Prescod?"

Metzer, eyes fixed on Andreas, surprised everyone by saying, "No, General, but he has seen much. Haven't you, Dr. Prescod?"

"What you seek is in my head. I have visited at least one of the destinations for the suctors. It is in Antarctica and provides energy for a whole civilization."

"What the hell are suctors?"

"They're here to harvest water from the planet, General."

"Harvest the planet? Have you lost your mind, Prescod?"

"No," Metzer said quietly. "He hasn't lost his mind. What we're doing here makes no difference, does it? We don't have anything that can stop this, do we?"

"No," Andreas responded.

"This is horseshit," General Blount said, rising.

"General," Andreas said as he and Eurydice also stood. "Something has happened."

"What?"

The dark-skinned, bald couple moved close together.

"Natas has achieved his apotheosis. He and Baal are one now," Eurydice whispered.

Andreas nodded, and turning to General Blount, said, "Do not seek the suctors. Your weapons would be ineffective."

"You two seem to know an awful lot about this. Maybe we should just squeeze what you know out of you."

Andreas smiled. The general blinked. When his eyes opened, Andreas and Eurydice were gone.

In Bumba, Eurydice and Andreas observed the people's frenzied worship. There was a buzz as they strode through the city. Men spoke of the god Chango's death and his imminent resurrection, and women boasted that they had seen the god give his life for humankind. Already, many were saying that the disturbances in the sky signaled the rise of the god, who would return on the third day. Beneath these hysterical claims was their terror. Eurydice held Andreas' hand as they moved through the streets.

Above, the sky blazed, making it unclear whether it was day or night. The heat increased appreciably, and perspiration poured off those who stood watching the heavens, ecstasy and fear etched on their faces in equal measure. In the distance, the cathedral towered over everything.

"He's there, Eudy."

"Can you sense him?"

"Not in my mind sense, but I know."

Something in her silence forced his head around. Eurydice was staring at him.

"Natas will not be the same as before, Andreas. He and Baal are one now."

"I know," Andreas, clutching the staff, answered grimly.

"Do you? I have often said that Natas does as he must. So do you. Do you know what that means?"

"Yes, Eudy. I understand. The gods you have served—Tiamat and Chango—will destroy all that we know in their insane desire to find perfection. They will create again, but that doesn't make me feel any better. I love this life. Not just my life, but this life I know, and I hate them for treating it so cavalierly. What would perfection be? They haven't said. Is it the perfect worshiper? A mental slave? Or is it a perfect human who sees everything rightly, even the gods? I can't believe that to be their purpose because they are themselves flawed."

"Do you see the irony of it?" she asked.

"Yes. Natas, or Baal if you like, is trying to save our existence. His motives are not noble. He wants to be worshiped as the only god. And yet, his ends are nearer to ours than Tiamat's or Chango's because they will destroy most of us, saving only a fragment."

When Eurydice spoke, it was with Mother Mutasii's voice.

"So, Tama, you approach the precipice. Maatemnu, the Great Slayer, stands at the crossroads of Time once again. Now, you must choose, as you have always had to choose. Are you a pure man, Maatemnu? Will your choice be for life or death?"

In the harsh light, Eurydice looked different, aged, something that had stepped out of time itself. Andreas stared at his hand, skeletal and large-veined, and knew that he, too, was beyond time.

"Three gods live in you, Tama. Tiamat, Chango and the dying god who breathed his life into you. The dying god is always on the way to death, as he is also always on the way to life. Natas seeks the resurrection, as is seen in his perverted Mass. His anger derives from the recognition that he is man, and if he dies, he is dead. As Baal, he cannot die and so, cannot live again. And yet, all things, except the gods, live, die and then live again, but they live again only in their reconstituted selves."

"So Natas' contradiction is that he wants to be both human and god, to relieve the tedium of existence but always to be himself."

"And such a thing cannot be."

"So, who is my enemy?"

Eurydice's face smiled, even as her eyes filled with tears.

"Enemy," Mother Mutasii's voice said as if weighing the sound. "That is a word of passion, Maatemnu. You must seek purity now. Only this will defeat Natas. Remember, in your distress, when your strength is not your strength, then you must call to Empheme."

He looked lovingly upon her for a long time, noting the subtle re-shaping of her face as she changed from the goddess back to Eurydice. There, in the middle of the street, with the cathedral louring above the bright, new city, he took her in his arms and kissed her fiercely.

"Always love me, Eudy. Always love me," he said in muffled tones against her cheek.

"I do. I will. Come. Let us find shelter. Natas will not be found today."

Chapter 59

A few miles away from Eurydice and Andreas, outside a small but comfortable tent, Anne Ernsky sat, staring at the descending streaks in the heavens. Not since the waters rose so precipitously almost twenty years earlier was there so much chaos in the world. Men's fears had overtaken them, and unable to make sense of their environment, they were in the process of destroying it. The images were coming in from everywhere as people burned their homes and attacked one another.

"Fear. Our lot. Always our lot," Etienne Ochukwu mumbled.

His voice was heavy with sadness.

"Our lot, Etienne?"

He stared at her owlishly, smiling after a while.

"Ah, Anne. You have been good to me."

"Etienne, focus. Can you help?"

"Too late," he said, making a dismissive gesture. "They are already here. When the suctors connect, the water will go."

Pointing at the television inside the tent, she said, "Are those the suctors, Etienne? What will they connect to?"

Even as she spoke, the television cameras switched to a squadron of warplanes slicing gracefully through the air, racing south.

"Those fighters are from the USS *Reading*. We are getting reports that the Pentagon has located a power source in the northwestern region of Antarctica, and these very brave pilots are headed there now," the professional voice declared.

Anne Ernsky stopped listening. This was the third such mission, but so far, they were unable to find anything. As soon as the planes got within firing range, their instruments went haywire. She felt certain this attempt would be no different.

Etienne had been with her for a while, ever since he stumbled from the cathedral, bent beneath the weight of the desecration he had witnessed. The sacrilegious act, broadcast worldwide, showed Etienne apparently worshiping at the new church that, in this supreme act of defiance, had declared its independence. The subterfuge worked because the crucifixion scene gave the faithful the comfort of familiarity while, at the same time, transferring their loyalty to Natas. The European and American churches had denounced Etienne within hours, and the cardinals in Rome were in conclave trying to decide on the next actions to take. In much of the world, however, Etienne's presence at the ceremony produced a different effect. In South America, Asia and Africa, people saw no betrayal. There, Etienne was being celebrated for his "decisive action in breaking with the false church in Rome."

Natas has what he wanted without Etienne ever agreeing. Etienne is viewed by the Changoists as a member of the new Church, Anne Ernsky thought.

She wondered about the effect on Etienne whom she had come to admire and respect. After the exposure, it seemed useless to mention her conversation with Teme and Marcus. Unwittingly playing the part given to him, Etienne had ascended the heights. Still, something in him was truly human. Like most, he accepted the created myths as a solace, and, in the end, the discovery of his true self tore him apart. Whatever was left of his humanity persuaded him that his visits to Bumba were exploratory missions on behalf of the Roman Church he led. However, Anne Ernsky suspected that, in some way, Etienne had been worshiping in the new church.

He tried to do the impossible, to straddle the fence dividing the worlds of myth and reality, and, in the end, he failed.

Anne Ernsky observed him, a man of incredible power who had lost the will to use it.

"Etienne, you must help others to understand."

"Understand what, Anne? That they have a choice between two lies? That they have been duped and controlled for millennia? Or should I help them understand that they are about to be duped again?"

"You said this has happened before. These beings have ended the world and started it again. Do they destroy everything?"

"I don't know. The stories are confusing. Some seem to suggest that they re-create the race; others say that if one worthy enough to sacrifice everything was found in the generation, then some could be saved. They would be changed, improved, so to speak, but they would be allowed to carry on."

"I have been thinking about that. Why has Branniff placed so much emphasis on Africa? He could have set Branniff Enterprises up anywhere in the world after he broke with the U.S. Why here? And why work so hard to get black people back on this continent? It was largely Branniff's exploitation of the environment that destroyed the ozone layer over the course of the last two centuries, and now that area over Antarctica seems to be the entry point for whatever is hurtling toward us. Natas was the one who picked Andreas Prescod to chair the food supply study; he was the one who came up with the idea of relocation to Antarctica. He also arranged for the relocation to Africa. Because of the cathedral, he now has not only black people here, but representatives of just about every racial and ethnic group on the planet. But why Africa?"

"Another beginning?" Etienne asked, his voice low. "Could that be the reason? A repopulated Africa, with all groups represented? His crucifixion act in the cathedral was recognizable and, in some ways, generic. Many of the world's religions have the sacrifice of a human/god figure at their center. Christians would have seen Jesus in Natas' act, but others would see their own central figure. That's the reason for the success of the new religion. All can read into it what they will since its basic imagery is so steeped in the ancient mythology of the human race."

"That's what I'm thinking."

She could not help but be horrified at the callousness of beings who could so cavalierly create and destroy.

"Maybe it's the nature of gods," she said, half to herself.

"'As flies to wanton boys are we to th' gods, they kill us for their sport.' How true," Etienne replied sadly.

"I met with two people today who claimed they had come from Antarctica, though they called it the Land of Tiamat or the Land of Ghalib, depending on which was speaking. They said that a group of people have lived there for millennia. They call themselves the First People."

Etienne's head came up.

"The First People? But that is just legend."

"You've heard of them?"

"Yes. I am sure you know that below the Vatican is the largest collection of esoteric literature anywhere in the world."

She had heard that somewhere but always assumed it was simply another attack on the authority of the Church. Those attacks, more frequent before the crisis created by the rising waters, had noticeably diminished since then.

"There is a text that speaks of the First People as survivors of the Flood. I dismissed it because, in spite of our explorations, no such civilization has been discovered. There is, though, a strand of belief that suggests the extraordinary exploration by Western Europe in the fifteenth and sixteenth centuries was the result of the Church having found this ancient text. It then used its power over the sovereigns of Europe to try and find these people. The reasons given—the search for a sea route to the east, pure adventurism—were simply a cover for the truth."

"This woman I met was believable. There's a quality to her that's almost other-worldly. I have never experienced such ... such ... beauty."

Etienne seemed to have come back to life.

"Where are they?" he asked anxiously. "We must find them."

"They were trying to persuade me to talk you into resisting Natas."

"Were they? Why?"

"They think you'll be needed in the battle to come. The woman—Teme is her name—lives with Natas. I didn't get the impression it was her idea, though."

Etienne stood, his giant frame towering over the tent.

"Do you know where they are, Anne? We must find them."

"They are both staying within the cathedral grounds."

He held out his hand to her, and she rose. In the distance, the cathedral stood, a marvel of lightness and strength. High in the sky, the stark luminescence denied primacy to the night. The three streaks continued their stately plunge downward.

Chapter 60

"I t is very sad about Dr. Faison," Dr. Tung said, fidgeting with his seatbelt. "I met him when I was at Berkeley."

Metzer snorted.

"He was a hack. A second-rate mind who was promoted because of his relationship to Branniff."

Metzer could not forget the look on the scientist's face when he pulled the trigger, the gun pointed directly at Metzer's heart. Only Sidoti's jumping in front of him had saved his life. As far as he was concerned, it was not at all sad about Dr. Faison.

"He was a brilliant experimental physicist, Karl. The religion drove him mad."

Metzer stared out the window at the city below.

"You say the religion drove him mad, and yet, we are going to the heart of Africa to find a man who talks about gods meeting in our solar system."

From the seat behind, General Blount said, "You requested the meeting, Metzer."

"Probably a waste of time."

General Blount did not respond. He understood why Metzer was being crabby. The work had prevented him from attending Sidoti's funeral. Having lost men himself, the general knew how strong the need for closure was. This would be even more the case with Metzer since Sidoti had saved his life. The plane suddenly dropped out of the sky and, within minutes, they were on the ground, landing hard. When Metzer said, "Must be a goddamned navy pilot," General Blount ignored him. Getting through immigration was a hassle. Tensions between America and Branniff were still on the rise. It was almost three hours later when they finally reached the American embassy compound. Not much given to ceremony, the general strode into the ambassador's office.

"Well, do we know where he is?"

The ambassador's face turned sour, but he said, "Yes. We've been keeping an eye on him and the woman. As luck would have it, they are all in the same place—Ernsky, the pope, Prescod and his wife. Ernsky has a tent in Ebonda. That's where they are."

"Do we still call that man pope now that he's disgraced?"

General Blount's voice had an edge. The ambassador remained silent.

"Well, do we get them over here or what?"

"General, we don't have a lot of leverage here. We can invite them, but if they come, it will be of their own accord. Of course, they may invite us to join them."

General Blount heard the unspoken question and nodded. They would go if invited. He was only interested in the Prescod fellow, anyway. If Prescod could help them, the general would make sure he did. He was mightily ticked off with the whole Branniff clan, and this Prescod fellow was one of them, as was his wife. Who was to say they were not responsible for what was happening?

The flotilla of black ships had slid out of the Southern Ocean like wraiths, snatching the initiative from the United States. No one was yet able to explain the masses of black people brought from Antarctica, and the modern army accompanying them was an issue. This was not his most pressing concern, however. The appearance of the phenomenon in the sky was.

Whatever is out there has certainly scared the bejesus out of us, he thought as the ambassador re-entered the room.

"I spoke with the major-domo to the pope … to Ochukwu. Andreas Prescod and his wife will meet with you."

"Where?"

"Here, actually."

"Fine. Send them a car."

"No need. They have their own transportation."

A tough-looking marine entered and whispered something to the ambassador whose face showed shock.

"What is it?" General Blount asked.

"Apparently, they're already here."

When Andreas and Eurydice entered the room, General Blount immediately saw the unity in their cadence. He extended his hand first to Andreas and then to Eurydice.

"That was quick."

There was a forced friendliness to his greeting, having not dealt with African Americans since the Expulsion. He was glad that Prescod and his wife had come without Ochukwu and Ernsky. Ernsky, in particular, would have been hard to deal with.

A real ball-buster when she was secretary of state, he thought.

"We don't have time for pleasantries, so I'll come straight to the point. We've sent four sorties against whatever this power source is in Antarctica. We can't get a bead on the damn thing from long range, and we lost two planes when we tried to get close. We have the smartest guys in the world working on a solution to the scientific problem and have gotten nowhere. You appear to have some notion of ... something. I can't say that I'm convinced, but life's gotten awfully strange in the last few weeks. We need a weapon, something to respond to this thing, and you seem to be our best shot."

"In what way?" Andreas asked.

"Well, you said you've seen one of these power plants in Antarctica. Maybe if you can give us an exact location, we could send something in to take care of it."

"It won't work," Eurydice said.

"How the hell do you know?"

"I know, General Blount."

"We can't keep sending boys in there to certain death. We have to do something else."

There was frustration in the general's voice.

"Is the something you are thinking of an ICBM, General? Didn't Branniff say no nuclear weapons?"

"Screw Branniff. Pardon my French, Mrs. Prescod. Branniff does not dictate to the United States."

"I will give you the exact location if you promise one thing," Andreas said.

"What's that?"

"Try to destroy the power source with a conventional weapon first. If it gets through, and you need a nuclear weapon, there's time enough for that."

"Why, Prescod?"

"Insurance. I don't think your weapon will succeed, and just in case it backfires, you limit the damage."

General Blount glared at Andreas, but it was Eurydice who said, "General Blount, if Branniff can scramble your electronics, how difficult would it be to reprogram your missile, targeting say ... New York?"

The general's eyes narrowed.

"Not even Branniff would be that crazy."

Just then, there was a discreet knock on the door, and the ambassador came in.

"What is it?" General Blount asked.

"It's your scientists, General. They're asking to speak with you. They say it's urgent."

"Tell them this is a private meeting. I'll see them later."

The ambassador was turning to go when Andreas said, "No, Mr. Ambassador. Let them come."

The general nodded, and the two scientists were ushered into the room.

"What is it, Metzer?"

Metzer did not answer. He was staring at Andreas' staff.

"Can I see that?" he asked.

"I'm sorry, Dr. Metzer. This is a very special gift."

"Is that why you came in here, Metzer? To see his blasted stick?"

"Actually, yes, sir. Tung and I tested the air in the lab back in Germany after Mr. and Mrs. Prescod disappeared. Tung speculated that the staff must be the means by which they were able to move through space instantaneously. He ran some calculations, plotting the energy source against the existing data and found the same energy signature as that identified in Antarctica. Actually, Tung's calculations are the most elegant variation of the equations of special—"

"I don't give a rat's ass about the equations, Metzer. Can we attack this thing? Does Prescod's staff give you any idea how?"

"Patience, General Blount," the Chinese scientist said in his careful English. "First, we find out what it is. Then, we make a weapon."

"I appreciate your optimism, Tung, but have you looked at the sky lately? I don't think we have much time."

"You have one day, General," Andreas said.

"How the hell do you know? My boys say that if the streaks in the sky—the suctors or whatever the hell they are—continue at the same speed, then we have several days."

"You do not. Would you explain, Dr. Metzer?" Andreas said, turning to the unkempt scientist.

"If I'm right, we're witnessing a brane world collision. The speeds will increase by many factors as the two brane worlds approach the collision point."

"You didn't think it necessary to tell us this before?"

General Blount glared at the scientist.

"It didn't seem to matter. We have no way to reverse it. But I'm curious about Mr. Prescod's staff. If he's using it to create a localized wormhole through which he travels, it opens up some really fascinating possibilities."

"Such as?"

"For one, we may not be witnessing the destruction of those missing planes and ships. They may simply be relocated."

"Relocated?"

"Yes. What I can't figure out is whether the relocation would be in space, time or dimension." Metzer turned to Andreas. "Obviously, you use the technology to relocate in space. Right?"

"Actually, Dr. Metzer, I never really thought about it. I simply use it."

"Sure, but in your hands you may have the technology to change what's going on. We haven't been able to analyze anything that makes use of dark energy. If your staff uses it, then the mechanism may be the same."

Andreas glanced at the golden staff. He never thought of it as anything but a gift from the goddess. What if Metzer was right? Shrugging his shoulders, he tossed the staff to the scientist. The strangest thing happened. The staff traveled half the distance and hovered in the air, a vibration evident. Andreas walked toward it and tried to hand it to Metzer. Again, it moved halfway and stopped. After several attempts, the staff always seemed to be getting closer but never quite reaching the scientist.

"Zeno's paradox, by God!" Metzer shouted.

General Blount, having lost all patience with the two, said, "I don't have time for this nonsense. Give him the damned stick, Prescod."

Andreas realized that, from the general's point of view, it must look like a trick to prevent analysis of the staff, but he did not understand what was going on either. Effectively, he could not get rid of the staff. As if to prove it, he tossed it toward the wall. It hovered halfway between him and the wall. Slowly, Andreas backed away, and immediately, the staff moved toward him.

In his mind sense, he said, "*Come.*"

The staff jumped across the distance into his open hand. Eurydice touched his arm.

"You can no longer part with her gift, Andreas."

"Whose gift?" the general asked.

Andreas smiled.

"It's a long story, and you wouldn't believe it, General. Dr. Metzer, I have no idea if your hypothesis is valid, but evidently, you won't be able to test it. If what you say is correct, you might profitably spend your time trying to see if the objects that disappeared left an energy trail. If they did, you might be able to track them."

"Actually, Prescod, that's not a half bad idea. Unfortunately, I need a pretty sophisticated lab to do the testing."

"I'm sure Branniff Enterprises has one on this continent."

"They do, but an American would never gain access."

"Not even if Natas himself arranged access for you?"

"Why would he do that?"

"Why wouldn't he?"

Metzer's mouth dropped open as Andreas changed, taking on Natas' features. A few hours later, the two scientists and Andreas stood inside the Center for Advanced Astro-Physical Phenomena at the southernmost tip of the African continent. Entrance had been simple. The guards looked frightened, and it occurred to Andreas that they were the first to see Natas, as they thought Andreas to be, after his "crucifixion." Andreas demanded their silence for one day. They would obey. Soon, Metzer was rubbing his hands gleefully, his eyes running over the particle accelerator that dominated the space. Andreas said, "Good luck," and then was gone, leaving, in embryo, a thousand stories behind him.

Chapter 61

"Will it help?"

Eurydice was staring at the sky. In front of her and Andreas was a sharp drop, with the thick, pine-green jungle below. Bumba, with its sparkling spires, was behind them.

"No, but while the research goes on, the military officers will be hopeful. While they are, perhaps the violence will not rise," Andreas answered.

"You said it was one day before the suctors make landfall. Then, the Repulsion begins. Natas 'rises' tomorrow, my love."

Her voice was uncertain.

How strange it is to have access to knowledge that Eurydice does not. I have come so far, changed so much, only to die now.

Andreas knew that "die" did not begin to describe his travail.

"The pain is greater now, isn't it?" Eurydice asked, her eyes searching his face.

"Sometimes I almost can't bear it. Were it not for what you taught me, I would be mad by now."

She smiled at the compliment.

"You would have learned in any case, Andreas. The goddess would have provided a teacher. Does the future frighten you, my love?"

"Not as much as before. I still have a difficult time with the uselessness of it all. I don't understand these beings who seem friendly and yet feel no compunction about eliminating us. It's not even personal, just some experiment that didn't quite work out."

"It is personal, Andreas. Don't you see that their need to perfect us reflects their love for us?"

"No."

"Don't be angry, my love."

Andreas reclined on the grass, feeling its life against his arms. In spite of the garish light in the sky that one moment appeared to be boiling and the next to be flaming, this was still a beautiful land. In the distance, low mountains reared up, futile watchers for the unknown. Staring at the mountains, their flanks covered by dark forest, brought to mind an old nightmare. He let go of a woman's hand in that dream, and she had plummeted from a helicopter to the ground far below. His eyes were warm with love as he gazed upon the woman who lay next to him. Andreas felt afraid, not of his death, but of failing her.

"You will never disappoint me, Andreas. Put it from your mind."

He held her, feeling the tenderness of her flesh and the pliancy of her mind sense. For a long time, they clung to each another, allowing the moment to come to life. There, beneath the frightening sky, she loved him. It was different, this love they made, having the quality of both hope and desperation. It was familiar, but with an edge of freshness as they sought to live within each other. They kissed throughout, feeling in the deepest recesses of their souls something that was themselves and yet was not. When he cried out, making of her name an invocation to the death-promising sky, she held him, feeling the slow, arduous progress of his life into her. She knew that Tiamat and Chango watched, for she felt the quickening of her womb when Andreas gasped. Under the lurid sky, Eurydice quietly cried in thanksgiving and with a feeling of utter loss because, with this act, Andreas had passed into her and from her. Later, as he slept, his soft breath disturbing the grass, Eurydice uttered a prayer. It was not for herself, but for the man who would, the next day, confront a god. Even as she prayed, Natas' power was rising.

Chapter 62

*N*ight over the continents bordering the Atlantic was brought to a sudden end with a thump. The world awakened to find that while it slept, the suctors had sped up. They were now connected to the earth, a low-pitched whine accompanying them. Eurydice was startled awake by that whine. She rose, noting, as she expected, that Andreas was gone. Her eyes turned to the funnel of energy that writhed and glowed in the near distance. It was dark, with a golden shimmer. She extended her mind sense cautiously, but the energy was impenetrable. In the city, she heard frightened voices and the trample of uncertain feet running this way and that. She sighed.

"Fear. The fuel of the gods."

There was nothing to be done. In the distance, the mountains changed from green to flaxen.

"I should feel joy," she said, ascending the low hill that had been her and Andreas' bed. "Tiamat is free at last and seeks reunion with her brothers. In this way, she becomes the three-in-one, again giving birth to Time and its children. I have known this day would come. I have taught that the end is but a beginning. I have bathed in the hallowed waters of the goddess. I should feel joy."

The last word, almost a hiss, merged with the whine of the suctor. She observed the sky.

"It looks like a stationery tornado. How many know its purpose?"

Without Andreas' staff, it would be a long walk back to the city, and she set out. The suctor had always been present in Andreas' haunting visions—Natas atop a mountain, with the lightning snaking down.

"My husband, you go to your fate asking 'Why me?' But the gods choose. They do not seek our permission."

Above, the sky was again changing, becoming purple with low-hanging thunderclouds. She found herself desiring the goddess' voice. For days, she had been without that solace.

"Where are you, mother? Why, in my most troubling hour, is your voice silent? You have already taken my husband, shaping him into your instrument Maatemnu. Now, he goes to do battle with your brother. You have shown me so much, but to his fate, you have closed my eyes. I know our purpose is to serve, but may it be your will, if you take Andreas, to take me with him. I—"

The air changed. Mother Mutasii appeared.

"Have you followed for so long, Empheme, only to question now at the moment of our glory?"

Eurydice fell to her knees, her thoughts unsettled.

"The world has accepted my brother. His image is the new idolatry. It must end as has been told in your stories from the beginning of the First People."

"But, mother, I had hoped that the rightness of the First People's actions would be enough to gain your favor. Do not the stories speak of one pure human saving the race?"

Mother Mutasii's voice was sad when she responded.

"Always, the people misread the text, Empheme. Yes, one pure human saves the race, as Ghalib gave his life for the survival of the First People so long ago in the depths of the Ilegu Forest. In that place, my brother Chango, whom you call Father of the Ilegu Forest, remained to guard and preserve the bloodline. For thirty of your millennia, he has done so. In isolation, away from my brother Baal, you have lived in the way of the goddess."

Eurydice, emboldened by the compliment, asked, *"Why must we die, mother? Is our imperfection so threatening?"*

"Threatening, my daughter?" Mother Mutasii asked, smiling. *"Not at all. It simply offends us. You can be better."*

"But why?"

"Because we will it. You fall too easily. Think upon your existence, Empheme. The First People have walked in the way of the goddess, but my brother Baal sent the one you call Natas, and immediately confusion reigned. In that confusion, dissension was once again fostered

between my brother Baal and me, although the ever-faithful Chango
stands at my side. In Natas, one impure man, you have brought about
this struggle. Now, I ask, if for one pure human we would save the race,
why should we not, for one impure human, destroy it?"

Eurydice had no answer.

"Do not despair, for as it has been, so will it be."

"You will forsake us?"

"We have never forsaken you, my daughter."

The image started to dissipate, and Eurydice shouted, *"My husband, mother, will he survive?"*

The presence was almost gone, but Eurydice heard the words.

"He whom you call Andreas will live in light and glory."

Eurydice was alone on the road. The darkening sky looked down
on the shimmering suctor that writhed in the air. It was toward a
towering shape that she hurried, knowing the suctor had landed on
the mandala that was the new cathedral.

Chapter 63

*A*nne Ernsky threw down the phone in disgust. Everything electronic died when the thing from the sky landed. This was particularly frustrating because she was trying to get in touch with Notah and Rene to find out what was going on in North America.

Could what Rene and Notah saw out west have been the contact point for the thing from the sky? she wondered.

Three years earlier, they found a mysterious object in Montana. None of their scientists were ever able to identify its purpose.

Did the Americans find it? Were they able to do anything with it?

Clearly, no one in Bumba had any intention of interfering with the suctor. There seemed to be little that anyone could do. No one saw it land, but the thump had brought the city to life. For a few hours, there was panic, and the faithful had rushed to the cathedral where it was believed Natas was "rising." The not-so-faithful, fearful of the heavenly object, tried to get as far away as possible. The bedlam of the first hours of wakefulness eventually gave way to a deep, resonant buzz—the sound of thousands praying.

In the far corner of the tent, Etienne knelt. She wondered to whom his prayers were directed. He had visibly aged, and her heart went out to him. Etienne now had no place where he could be comfortable. Having relinquished the faith of his genes, he was now rejected by the faith of his heart. Twice in the last hour, she saw the saurian skull, as if his will had faltered, exposing, for a moment, the self that hid beneath. The second time, seeing her horrified face, he apologized. They had searched for Teme and Marcus but had not found them. After a while, Etienne lost interest. Kneeling before the plain tent wall, his back was bowed, but even in his plain priest's robe, Anne Ernsky fancied she could see the outlines of an alien body.

She stared at the brilliant light, marveling at how the absence of so simple a thing as shadow could completely destroy one's perspective. The shimmering suctor attached to the cathedral seemed both brighter and closer. Anne Ernsky was about to enter the tent when the buzz of prayer changed, and a clear voice shouted, "The river! The river is going down!" She glanced at the suctor, noting the change. Something was being sucked at a high rate of speed through it. Etienne came to her side.

"They are saying the river's going down ...." Her voice trailed off as she saw his haggard face. "What is it, Etienne?"

He did not immediately respond, staring at the silver globules that were flying through the shimmering tube and disappearing into the sky.

"It is the beginning of the end, Anne. It will not stop until all the water is gone. Then, the planet will die."

"What do you mean all the water will be gone?"

"It is the basic material they use to create. I don't know where it goes, but it will be taken."

Anne Ernsky's body became rigid. A thousand questions were in her mind. She could not create a mental picture for what Etienne meant, except the improbable one of the Atlantic Ocean being gone. Only the wide, rocky basin that now contained the giant body of water would be left. Once, she had stood in the Olduvai Gorge, mesmerized by the dry, fossilized valley. This image filled her mind. As Etienne rested his hand gently on her shoulder, he changed. The crocodile face was there, as well as the huge body whose blackness seemed to suck in the light.

"Natas?"

Etienne nodded. Anne Ernsky shivered as the fierce, red eyes looked upon her. Seeking to find friendship there, she saw only a dark fury that blazed like the sky.

"Goodbye, Anne," he said and was gone.

Chapter 64

*A*ndreas felt the change in Etienne Ochukwu and knew that Natas had felt it as well. Since the descent of the suctors, they were aware of each other, feeling the animosity that was between them from that day, in a luxurious cabin in the Pocono Mountains, when Natas had first seen him with Eurydice. That animosity was now controlled, though each knew conflict was inevitable. Andreas stood on a hill, watching the water disappear into the sky and wondered when it would end.

He no longer wanted to fight, but Natas had to be defeated. He was the spirit of enmity and confusion and had to be reunited with his brother and sister. The Reunion offered a new beginning for humankind, another period of hope and possibility, another chance to please those whom humans called gods. If he, Maatemnu, who was set apart as the pure human, should fail, then all life, including the remnant Chango and Tiamat promised to preserve should he win, would exist in a hell created by Baal.

A Hobson's choice, Andreas thought bitterly.

He tempered his anger as the distance between him and Natas contracted. On top of the cathedral, invisible to those below, Natas, a huge saurian figure, towered over the city. Below him, in every available space, the faithful bowed and prayed, fear and faith contending in their breasts. Seeing the lack of concern in Natas' cold eyes, Andreas retracted his mind sense. The distance returned.

The crowd became agitated, rushing away from a path that was being cleared. Andreas had no need to look. Natas glanced first at him and then turned to face the man who had once been pope. Etienne was walking, head held high, staring at the cathedral's battlements. Natas' energy surged. Etienne was picked up as if by some invisible hand and pulled to the broad *chemin de ronde* atop the cathedral. As soon as he landed, Etienne charged Natas, claw-like hands held before him. For a moment, it seemed as if Natas would not react, but at the last possible moment, his left arm snaked out, slamming into and through Etienne's chest. The arm inside the body glowed briefly. Etienne slumped, shock in his eyes as life drained from him.

Natas contemptuously threw the body from the wall-walk. Andreas, recognizing the challenge, shot forth his mind sense, cushioning the fall. The huge body of the dying pope descended slowly, and when, finally, it landed, Andreas was there. The faithful backed away from him. He was now golden, his body reflecting the color of the suctor. In his hand, the golden staff glowed. This he touched to Etienne Ochukwu's chest. The hole closed. Etienne looked helplessly at him.

"I am sorry," he said.

Andreas shook his head, gently touching the saurian face and watching the rise and fall of the giant chest.

Perplexed, he asked, "How could it be you?"

Etienne's eyes closed, and no answer came. Andreas saw Natas move, and he jumped. When he landed, they were no longer outside the cathedral but stood on the southern Plain of Sotami, beside the Hall of the Onyes. Andreas surveyed the barren land, knowing that in the building was the power Natas had to protect.

"So, Maatemnu, we meet once more," Natas said in a voice that shifted the sands.

"As the sacred texts have told, as the goddess has willed, Baal," Andreas replied.

The figure chuckled.

"My sister, the goddess as you say, has always overestimated your capacity. How many times must your race lose? Would it not be better to end it for all time? You cannot win. If you defeat me, a remnant is saved to begin this whole miserable process all over again. If you lose, you worship only me. Forever. What a choice we have given you."

Andreas gripped his staff more tightly as Natas' face changed. He was aware of the startling brightness, the golden shimmer of the suctor that had landed on the power generator in Antarctica, the barrenness of the land and the pulsating center high above from which the three suctors emanated. Even with this hyper-awareness, he did not see Natas move. It was only when his mind sense screamed of danger that he flipped away, avoiding the kick that Natas launched. He rolled to his feet, knowing he was too slow. Natas' foot sliced the air in a low arc toward his stomach. The impact knocked him back, and Andreas twisted barely in time to avoid the second leg connecting with his ribs. He wiggled his feet, trying to find a solid place to stand. Natas smiled, and from his body ripped off a white staff that shimmered with a peculiar energy.

"You have learned much since Lusani, Tama, but you're no match for me," Natas said.

The staff glowed in Natas' hand, and he attacked with a fury that Andreas found all but incomprehensible. The white, glowing staff seemed to be creating many versions of itself. Even as Andreas parried, it was not where it was supposed to be but moving always. Andreas realized something else. His staff had a will of its own, so that while his mind told him he was too slow, the staff was defending against Natas' attacks. On the other hand, it had not struck a single offensive blow. Andreas loosened his grip, remembering what had happened in the Hall of the Onyes when he stopped thinking and allowed his mind sense to lead him. *Na isi.* Action in itself, Eurydice had explained. He relaxed, and immediately, the staff came to life, its golden skin crawling under his hand. He moved, becoming *na isi,* thought in motion.

The swiftness caught Natas unawares, but he parried, leaping high into the sky as Andreas flew at him. The staff glanced off Natas, and a streak of energy sliced through the air, colliding with the Hall of the Onyes. A section of the broad portico fell. Natas' eyes flashed to the building. Anxiety showed. That was why Andreas had come to the southern Plain of Sotami. Natas would probably have preferred to battle before the faithful, but Andreas felt certain that in this barren desert, in a land that was hidden for so long, was the key. The Hall of the Onyes. The two antagonists stood, assessing each other, searching for weaknesses.

Andreas pointed the golden staff at the building and deliberately propelled a burst of energy in its direction. Natas' staff glowed, and the energy was intercepted. Without delay, he attacked again, his body apparently weightless, his feet flying in brutal arcs as he came through the air. Andreas blocked the feet with difficulty, and at the last moment, as his body flashed by, Natas' hand snaked out, catching Andreas on the head. There was a deep burning in Andreas' mind sense, and he became disoriented. In that moment, Natas' staff flashed. Andreas was knocked down. He felt the sand part and fly upwards. Above him, Natas' staff, converted into a white spear, was aimed at his heart. In desperation, he pointed his staff at the Hall of the Onyes, propelling a golden blast. Again, Natas was distracted, and as he redirected his energy toward saving the building, Andreas flew away from him, giving his mind time to clear. He kept the staff pointed at the building. That was slowing Natas down as he sought to protect the beautifully preserved Onyes and the computers.

That's what he's protecting, but why is he monitoring the temperature of the continent? What does it matter, if everything is going to be destroyed anyway?

He flew toward the Hall of the Onyes. Natas moved equally swiftly, intercepting him at the portico on which marble blocks from the fallen roof lay.

"No."

Natas' face, for a moment, lost its beauty and showed something horrifying beneath.

"What frightens you, Natas?"

"He whom you know as Natas is gone, fool. I am Baal. My fire destroys."

"Yes, but you said we've met before. Then, a remnant survived. We're here again, so I must have defeated you. Is that your fear, Baal, that I will defeat you again, and you will become part of the Reunion?"

"Your understanding is as limited as your life, fool. Do you think my brother, my sister and I are different? Do you think they want a universe that is different from mine? We want the same thing. Order. They call it perfection. Does the word deceive you, fool?"

"And what do you seek, Natas?"

"Your worship."

The voice was blunt and harsh, but Andreas was not frightened by it.

"We will not be slaves."

Natas' laughter was the sound of crackling sulphur.

"You have a choice between different slaveries."

With those words, he attacked. The air became superheated, and the desert disappeared. Natas moved like lightning. Andreas felt a sharp pain as energy burned its way past him, but he stood firm, his staff deflecting the white energy of the god. A second charge had the same effect. Andreas turned away, striding into the Hall of the Onyes. His mind sense linked with the computers. Natas followed him inside, his face alive with malice. Andreas saw the naked bodies in the glass tubes and was again struck by the perfection of their forms. They were .... His eyes swiveled to Natas. *The bodies were naked! The wrappings had been removed!* Andreas thought of the image the god Chango had shown him—Natas and his scientists pouring over the cloth scrolls, creating the weapons of war.

Before he could say anything, Natas said, "Join me. You have their power within you. Together, we could win, turn them back. If you don't, they will destroy your world."

"The wrappings! It was not the mummies you wanted but the wrappings."

Andreas extended his mind sense and saw the codes, the divine mathematics, being translated by the computers. Instantly, it was clear.

"The calculations are not temperature changes of the continent. The wrappings contain the knowledge of the gods' power to create. Before now, none of you could use it separately. The Reunion is not simply the three of you coming together but the knowledge of the past coalescing. It is what powers the three-in-one, the god to whom the people give no name."

Natas breathed heavily, and Andreas felt the fire in him.

"But you would have it for yourself. Because of this computing power, you have the capacity to decipher and store the information without Chango and Tiamat's aid."

Before Natas could respond, there was a sharp change in the tone of the suctor. The ground shook.

"You are too late, human. They have come. Let us have done with this."

Natas leapt, his feet furiously thrashing. His power shook the hall so that pieces of marble fell. The air cracked as it was pushed apart and then snapped back together. Andreas stood, his mind sense trying to follow the lightning-fast movements of the god. Still, the feet cracked against his head, knocking him outside. He sensed Natas attacking again and again and covered up as best he could. It did not work. There was a new fury in Natas. Andreas was weakening as the powerful blows connected, and he felt gritty sand filling his mouth. Confident, Natas stood on the portico, a smile on his face. Andreas was aware of many things—the furious whining of the suctor, the odd stillness beyond that, the sand shifting ever so slightly. Most of all, he was aware of his imminent death. Natas was too strong.

Below him, the computers hummed. He understood what they were doing. Natas was gaining access to power that had never belonged to any one of the gods—the knowledge of how to bring dimensions together. If he possessed that, Chango and Tiamat would be powerless, and Baal of the fiery mountain would rule forever. It could not be allowed to happen. Finally, he could make sense of Mother Mutasii's words. Are you a good man? she had asked. In the last conflict between him and Baal, Maatemnu chose death rather than life because the life offered was always that of Baal's making, a life of fury, hatred and deceit. Perdition. Andreas could not allow that. Better that all life end than they should exist in the hell Baal would create.

Slowly, he pushed himself to his feet. Maybe it was something in the cast of Andreas' body, but the smirk slid from Natas' face. He stepped from the portico on to the sand.

"Last chance, mortal. We could rule together," he said, moving his staff into attack position.

"No, Natas. Death would be preferable."

"Then you shall have your wish, mortal."

Natas attacked as he spoke. Andreas parried and countered, his staff flashing toward Natas' head. The god was incredibly fast, and Andreas missed. He tried to react as Natas' foot slashed upward but was too slow. Once again, he was down and had to roll swiftly as Natas' foot pounded the sand, causing it to fly upwards. It appeared as if he had escaped, but Natas' other leg flicked backwards, bending at an improbable angle. Andreas was once again rolling in the sand, a burning in his side. It felt as if something was broken. Again, he stood, this time swaying, watching the shift in the god's foot as it slid to the right. Andreas was aware of a deep tiredness in his soul. Not good enough, he would die there. He had failed.

Then, something ... someone stood beside him. It was neither Chango nor Tiamat. Its spirit was gentle, but when Andreas thrust forward, it guided the golden staff into Natas' body.

"You!" Natas screamed.

His body shook, changing shape so rapidly that Andreas simply stared. Some shapes were recognizable; others were not. finally, he saw a crocodile change into a dragon. Andreas leapt, his body twirling in a series of furious turns. Seven. Eight. Nine. The art of *tusiata* did not have a name for his fifteen turns, but the dragon god matched him, the gigantic body lithe. At the sixteenth turn, Natas' momentum slowed. Impossibly, Andreas' body turned around its axis a seventeenth time. Then, his feet slashed across Natas' face with a sharp crack as the golden staff penetrated Natas' chest in a blaze of energy. The god's body was instantly petrified. Andreas watched as it drifted past the Hall of the Onyes, rising into the flaming sky until it hovered among a series of fourteen shining stars that appeared low on the horizon.

"The constellation Draco. He can't go home," Andreas whispered.

Mother Mutasii had once told him that Baal's journey began in Orion's Belt. He stared at the hole from which the three suctors emanated, aware of the darkness, composed of motes, behind it. Behind that was the impartial presence of Tiamat and Chango. The two divinities stared at the new star in the constellation Draco, Baal's essence, and with a nod to Andreas, they streaked in that direction. Soon, the brightest star in the constellation flared and then settled to a steady luminescence.

Andreas looked affectionately at the small, weak figure that lay on the sand, and, kneeling, cradled the dying god in his arms. Its face was that of Etienne Ochukwu. The all-knowing eyes blinked slowly.

The boy god who contained Etienne's spirit said, "Few men know their purpose, Maatemnu. I needed the strength of the one you call

Etienne Ochukwu. Now call to her. You need her strength for your sacrifice. I can help no more."

The head fell backwards, and Andreas gently laid the boy god on the sand. He looked to the sky, noting the threatening hole above. About to pray to the goddess, he remembered her words: "When your strength is not your strength, then you must call on Empheme." The ground shook beneath his feet, and Andreas linked his mind sense to the computers. It did not take long to understand the dying god's comment. He was not to make a sacrifice; he was the sacrifice. The hole in the ozone layer through which the black motes would soon be pouring had to be filled, and he was the means! The energy of the dying god within him would give his mind sense the power to close the gap, but he would be no more. Andreas saw the world as it was. The water was almost gone. Even if he stopped the black motes, Earth was dying. He looked around the barrenness of the southern Plain of Sotami, and his mind was filled with the image of the woman who possessed his soul.

"Goodbye, my love," he whispered.

Knowing that the knowledge Natas had accumulated was dangerous, he pointed his staff at the Hall of the Onyes, and with one blast, destroyed it. Then, his energy exploded upwards, spreading across the width of the brightly-lit sky, his essence changing from golden to black as he sought to fill the hole. The suctors lost contact with the earth, their energy crackling into his, but even as he absorbed their energy, he was aware of his failure. He was not strong enough. The celestial energy was stretching him beyond his will's ability to resist. Consciousness sliding away, his life was slipping into the limitless expanse of the cosmos.

"Eurydice!" he called.

She came on an instant, face serene, the placidity of the goddess upon her. Andreas felt joy. Around him, a furious energy flamed the sky. He thought it was shaped like the Marble Mountains. He and Eurydice joined, blocking the dangerous black motes. There was a monstrous jarring, as two universes bounced off each other, flying in opposite directions on their multi-billion-year journey, first away from, and then toward, each other. Still, it did not matter, as Eurydice and Andreas gave up consciousness, becoming one.

Epilogue

Three women sat on an open porch, smiling at two children who reclined on the uneven grass, preoccupied with each other. The boy handed the girl a lotus, and she brushed the petals, as if both cleaning and caressing them.

"They are almost here, Aduame. Maybe we should move the children indoors," the eldest of the women said, though she did not move.

She was gray-haired, and her body, while still slim, had lost its suppleness. She sat in apparent discomfort on a crude, wooden chair. It was not the one called Aduame who answered but another who was younger.

"Let them stay a while longer, mother. They so love the light."

Anne Ernsky pursed her lips, her eyes seeking the sky.

The light. What brilliance!

Her eyes had a filmy, white appearance. Though she could see things that were near, things in the distance were becoming difficult to distinguish. In the sky, the light was bright, and she stared at the luminescence that now extended the day. The sun had already set, but this brightness would remain for another hour.

"No, Teme. They must not learn inconsistency."

Teme, the youngest of the women, sighed. She did not see the point of the discipline Anne Ernsky imposed on the children.

"Are they not beautiful?" Aduame said.

There was pride in her voice, but neither Anne Ernsky nor Teme answered. Their smiles were enough.

Yes. They are beautiful. The boy is the last gift of the goddess to Empheme, for he was born without sign, Teme thought.

Observing the sky, Teme wondered whether the things being said were true. She had not seen the high priestess taken up as so many now claimed they had. Empheme had come to her, administering the kiss of love and giving her the boy. The high priestess had named him Lona Amitabha. Teme felt joy in her heart at the naming, which signified the infinite light.

Let me be worthy of her trust, Teme thought, kissing her fingers and raising them to the sky.

"Do you think she is really there? I don't," Aduame whispered, her voice hesitant.

"She's there. How else do you explain the change in the night sky?"

When the sky lost its fury, and darkness returned, many fewer stars were visible. Low on the northern horizon was what many called the Nose of the Dragon, the brightest star in the constellation Draco. There was, too, this light that shone with a planet's brightness and, for a while, kept the day from departing. This was Empheme and Maatemnu, those from the Land of Tiamat said. Others called them Eurydice and Andreas. Sometimes, late at night, Anne Ernsky believed this because it was as if she could hear their voices. Their presence gave life to the shrine that she, Teme and Aduame guarded.

We guard the children, she thought.

Watching the two children sit quietly near the Edge, a grim look came to her face. To the right, the Edge was a reminder of the horror the earth had endured. She and the others moved west from Bumba immediately after the destruction of the world and had built a small hut on the edge of the continent. What drew them there, so near the edge, she did not know, but Bumba had felt empty. It did not take long for the pilgrimages to begin, and after a few years, a much more substantial edifice was erected. The gardens were recently constructed, and the blaze of color was the glory of the place. Though she could not see it, somewhere in the nearby valley a town was emerging to serve the increasing number of pilgrims who came to get a glimpse of the boy and girl who were believed to be the descendants of Natas.

Anne Ernsky glanced at Aduame, the young girl's mother and the widow of Natas. The young girl had herself been briefly bethrothed to the deceased Lona, the natural son of Eurydice and Andreas. In the emerging mythology of the people, the new Lona was the god Chango's gift to Empheme and the Son of Ghalib. The girl child, Lakshmi, was the daughter of Natas, born fully of the First People. The two children were inseparable, and though having the run of the place, they always ended up sitting on the Edge. Anne Ernsky could almost not bear to look at the scar in the earth, the place from which the water of the Atlantic Ocean had been taken.

"Do you think they live?"

"No one knows, Aduame," Anne Ernsky said. "We know that three suctors touched down. Maybe each area where they touched was protected as we were, but the truth is, no one knows."

Her own heart was heavy. Having lost Notah when the Reunion occurred, she secretly hoped that, to the west beyond the dry basin that was the remnant of the Atlantic Ocean, her friends were alive.

Rene, too, went west with Notah to check out the mysterious object.

The face of the man who had loved her was clear in her mind. Once the suctors appeared, travel became impossible. Before that, she was too busy. Anne Ernsky stared at the fractured ridges beyond the slight shimmer of whatever enclosed the continent, protecting it from the violent air and the heat outside. Far to the south, somewhere near Cape Town, Dr. Metzer, the mad scientist, was talking about testing the strength of the shield. They would have confined him were it not for his work during the period of the Reunion. Many said that it was not only Prescod and his wife, or as these people called them, Maatemnu and Empheme, who saved them, but this man Metzer, whose mind seemed at one with nature.

Anne Ernsky stood. The children noticed and looked questioningly. She did not respond but stepped down from the porch, going to the left of the newly-built shrine. She stopped before a tomb with a huge stone cross. It was the only cross on the premises, but its sheer size drew many to it.

"Etienne, old friend," she said quietly, pushing a stray strand of hair back into place. "How strange that you should be here. I'm still not sure what you were, but I miss you."

The stories told about Etienne, the Roman pope who, as the people believed, came home to the old religion, sustained the beliefs of the remnant. Anne Ernsky sighed at the irony. Natas and Etienne emerged as the names of reverence after the destruction of the earth. None of the religion's adherents identified the saurian figure, whom Natas killed, with the Roman pope, and the three women at the shrine cultivated the story of his role as an aide to Natas. This was easy enough to believe since the faithful had last seen the pope apparently worshiping at the cathedral. In this way, Etienne was integrated into the remnant's belief system.

She bent with difficulty and pulled a single weed growing beside the tomb. Straightening, aware of the two children behind her, she smiled.

Without turning, she said, "Are the two of you sneaking up on me again? I'm not so old that I can't hear you, you know."

There were muffled giggles, and something warm went through her. Anne Ernsky turned, looking into the children's shining faces.

"Lona was saying, mother, that some day he will cross the Atlantean Gorge," Lakshmi said.

"I will, too," the boy responded.

"I don't doubt you will, Lona. And you, Lakshmi, will you go with him?"

The girl gazed at the sky where the luminescence was on the verge of disappearing, bringing dusk.

"I will go there, mother."

The three of them turned to the disappearing light.

"Maybe we will all go. Come. You must make ready for the night," Anne Ernsky said.

On the path up from the valley, she noted the three pilgrims—men, it seemed—who were walking toward the shrine, and she thought how unusual it was for men to come there where women reigned. She put that thought from her mind, and taking the children's hands, made her way in the growing dusk back to the porch. High above, the luminescence winked briefly and then was gone.

End of Book Three

Made in the USA
Middletown, DE
25 November 2022

16020140R00220